1

The mosquito circled its target and attacked.

Ida slapped a block of text onto the insect perched on her knee and raised the tome. Keen eyes dissected the splattered insect stuck to the homemade cover.

"What time is it?"

Ida herded lunch remnants into her woven bag.

"Past two o'clock." The woman sat at the end of the bench loosened the strap of her wrist watch. "Don't worry about it."

"I will be in such trouble!" wailed Ida.

"Fretting won't help." The young woman glanced across at the lazy tide. "Relax. You're already late."

"Easy for you to say, you don't have my boss. I'll see you same time tomorrow." Ida raced off, the rainbow bag flying in her slipstream.

The trio watched the slim figure dart across the flagstones towards the town square. Each woman sat with arms crossed on the sand-blasted bench at the end of the jetty.

"She'll be docked again."

Ida sped across the street as the Billy can jostled her legs. She flew past the dust-sealed windows of the island's only department store and careered around the corner as a figure stepped out of the ornate doors of the Windward Bank.

Ida found herself entangled in the dirt with an additional set of limbs.

"What the hell do you think you're doing?"

Ida tugged at the strap of her handbag, which lay sandwiched under the felled businessman. A flutter of scratched notes sailed across the pavement like unseasonable leaves on a puff of wind.

"I'm sorry. I didn't mean to bump into you, I just, I don't know." Ida sawed at her top lip with her teeth as she sought something sensible to say.

"You speak English! Thank Christ for that. You are just what, an idiot?"

The man smoothed the club tie into place and slapped the dung-coloured soil from precision-pressed trousers, his lips compressed into a paper-thin line. Across the road, townspeople stopped to watch the debacle, a commonplace thing to do in a town with no entertainment.

"I said I was sorry." Ida shoved the man's pigskin briefcase at him to focus on gathering her notes.

Daring a sidelong glance, she watched as the man clambered to his feet and brush at himself. He spared her a final, disapproving glance, to stomp away, brow furrowed with indignation.

A few moments later, he turned back, no doubt expecting to see her walking away with the crowd.

Ida perched on the kerb to nurse her battered knees. All thoughts of returning to work fled as she scowled at the holes in her thick hosiery. They were supposed to last until Friday.

The man's determined steps slowed and, after a few moments of indecision, halted across the street. He retraced his steps.

"Are you okay?"

He shuffled from foot to foot and rubbed at his neck. His suit looked more expensive than her parents' house. Maybe he would be a gentleman and help her up. The man shoved her belongings aside, placed his case on top of the sheaf of notes, and sat down.

"Did you hear me?"

Ida twitched her head away; chin poked out with shoulders high. She didn't want him to see her tears. She was nothing but an ignorant native to him.

"Go away."

Ida wrapped her arms around her knees and turned a shoulder away too, to watch him from the curtain of her eyelashes. The man raked at his hair till his locks quaffed higher than an outraged cockerel.

He whipped out a handkerchief from his top pocket with the panache of a magician and thrust the delicate silken square at her.

"Stop snivelling!"

After a moment's hesitation, Ida snatched the hanky from the well-manicured hand and gave a mighty trumpeting blast.

"That wasn't dainty."

Ida fixed him with an unwavering stare. "I don't DO dainty."

The corners of his lips twitched upward. "So it would appear."

"Hankies are for using aren't they?"

Ida crossed her arms and leaned back expectantly. With loose curled ebony locks and tanned skin, it was hard to tell his origins.

Maybe Argentina.

Maybe Italy.

Who knew?

His suit jacket threatened to burst where it was stretched tight across his muscular frame. He had the strangest accent. Ida unpeeled her tongue from the roof of her mouth and licked at her moisture-barren lips.

English?

American?

Young men arriving from distant shores meant the promise of her Sunday frock turning into a party dress. He was handsome, unlike the local uneducated buffoons. She squirmed as a tickle of perspiration meandered between her shoulder blades on its journey to the small of her back. His eyes were expressive and sensual. They were reminiscent of the natural jet she found on the beach last month. Ida grabbed at a bundle of study notes and fanned herself.

"I said, did you know it was rude to stare?"

God, he was handsome.

"I wasn't. I was thinking."

"About what?"

"Never mind. I must go. I'm late for work."

Rising, she remembered her knees. Holes at the knees of her stockings had laddered along each leg and in its place were two raw areas.

"Why must you women wear those stupid things? It's so hot here."

She snorted her disgust. "Then why are you wearing a suit jacket? Besides, only fast women wear no stockings."

He let out a whoop of laughter and elbowed her off the kerb into the road.

"You're alright."

Arm in arm they made the slow journey to the library where she worked. Stallholders plied their trade to fools cajoled into purchasing their fragrant tropical fruit when above them trees sagged with their unpicked jewels.

The crowd wandered along the vegetable strewn street, a pungent reminder of the last market day. They gossiped as calloused hands clutched baskets perched atop fabric-swaddled heads. Fishermen, exhausted from the heave of early nets languished in the shade of palm trees beside moored striped canoes. Hagglers warred over mounds of exotic marine creatures as the days catch warmed in the heat of the sun. Townsfolk stepped with eagerness from bargain to bargain slowed by the drag of leaden-footed children. Their naked toes twitched to play by the roadside as women greeted each other in a lilt of colonial French patois as they scrutinised their shopping lists. Outfits clashed in a variety of patterns. Wizened men looked on as they played infinite games of dominoes.

Everyone found time to stare.

Together they made a striking pair. He, tall and elegant, strolled along the main thoroughfare like royalty. His sculpted physique complemented by his sharkskin suit.

Ida stood to his shoulder, her slender body in a plain cotton blouse and full circular skirt that accentuated her long legs. They had many admirers as they strolled through the town. Ida felt comfortable and secure with her handsome companion. Sometimes, when he clasped her gloved hand, she struggled to breathe. When they arrived at the large oak doors of Castries main library, they had exchanged names, and Marcel secured a sacred promise they would meet again.

Ida was in love.

2

A blanket of moonlight covered the land by the time Ida returned to the dilapidated cabin overlooking Castries town. Every nub of cartilage in her body protested as her books slid onto the veranda swing.

The head librarian was predictably mean, but Ida kept her job thanks to Marcel. It took a file full of character references and a lifetime of good grades to obtain such a job. He sweet-talked the old crow till the squat librarian beamed like a lighthouse. Unpaid overtime struck as Marcel disappeared through the main exit.

"Good evening mother."

'Pale' patois ti famme!'

'We manman.'

'Ou oblije' fe sa mwen di ou.'

'We manman.'

The words sounded guttural and uncultured to her ears. She preferred the language she had learnt at school, but mothers' house. Mothers' rules. Their native language was the only one permitted over the threshold, however as a colonial island, French Creole may have been on the tongue but England was at its heart.

She stooped to kiss the diminutive woman who presided at the head of the table. Every family member present followed her around the dining room as her mother plucked at the elevated collar of her starched ivory blouse. Every inhabited buttonhole checked and accounted for with twig-thin fingers.

"Where's papa?"

Her brother stretched across the unvarnished dinner table and swiped a piece of cornbread from its platter.

"Cutting down some green bananas to sell in town tomorrow. Up a tree somewhere."

Beneath heavy brows, birdlike eyes bored into Ida with the intensity of a diamond cutter.

"You're two hours late. I had to fix dinner myself. Honour your father and your mother, as the Lord your God commanded you, that your days may be long and that it may go well with you in the land that the Lord your God is giving you. Deuteronomy Chapter Five, Verse Sixteen."

Ida twitched her nose with distaste. Her brows huddled together as she slipped behind her mother's chair. By the time she circumnavigated the table to her accustomed place, ignoring several questioning glances from her siblings, they had drifted back into place. Another passage from the Bible. Mother knew every word of the most popular book in the house and endeavoured to ensure everyone else within earshot knew it too.

"I'm sorry; I had an accident this afternoon and Miss Claron had me make up the time."

Mother scrutinised her with reed-thin lips puckered in concentration. "What kind of accident? I don't see blood. I don't have money for hospital bills."

"It wasn't that kind of accident. I collided with someone leaving the bank at lunchtime."

"Anyone we know?" Joseph pursued the last of his dinner around the plate with a fork.

"I don't think so. He said his name was Marcel. I don't know anything else about him." Ida spooned aromatic drumsticks and multicoloured salad leaves onto her plate.

"Listen to me." Ma Solomon jabbed the bowl of her spoon toward Ida. "You stay away from that man, you hear! Those people are evil." She stared at each child, challenging them to defy her.

"That goes for all of you. Stay away."

"Why?"

"He is a no good lazy piece of boy, that's why, so don't let me catch anybody talking or even standing near him. Don't think I won't find out. I know plenty of people around here. His father is a wicked man. He is the Devils' servant. Do I make myself clear?" Ma Solomon slammed her spoon onto the table as her mutton-chop sleeves billowed and settled, giving temporary size to an emaciated frame. Eyebrows hitched in surprise at her vehemence; they mumbled a reply.

"I can't hear you."

"Yes, mother."

She settled back in satisfaction. "When your father drags himself home, tell him I'm at my prayer meeting."

Ma Solomon rose from the dinner table. "Ida, clear away the dishes when you're done eating."

Retrieving her weathered straw hat from the warped sideboard, she perched it atop her corkscrew-curled silvered hair, skewering it in place with an 'I love Jesus' hatpin at a no-nonsense angle.

"Men like them use girls like you for fun, don't be a fool. He won't marry you."

They sat in silence as she stepped into the night. As the door closed behind her trailing ebony skirts, a cool breeze tugged at the threadbare curtains, bringing fresh relief to its inhabitants in the stifling room.

'Marry?'

'You're not supposed to be speaking English at home.'

'Shut up, Joseph.'

Joseph took his cue to disappear into his bedroom with a pot of home-brew hair straightening cream under one arm, to play the latest tunes from America. Soon the walls were vibrating to Little Richard, the new kid on the musical block.

Vera settled back in her chair and unfastened a button, releasing the pressure on the waistband of her pencil skirt. "So what's he like then?"

"What are you talking about?"

"Oh, come on! Calisticka Theresa Solomon, you've been floating about and grinning like a fool since you arrived, and you have managed to get mama vexed in two minutes. What's he like?"

Ida rested her elbows on the tabletop and gazed beyond her sister and the dark mantelpiece complete with its yellowed wedding photograph of her grim-faced parents standing to attention.

"He's an average type of guy."

Eyebrows hitched high in ignorance; Ida glanced at her sister. Vera had the same look on her face she reserved for Joseph when he arrived home late and tried to convince them he had extra music lessons at the church. On the same night, the local rum shop ran their all night Blues sessions. Vera did not believe a single syllable of his story then, and she didn't believe Ida's now. Vera tucked her romantic novel under her elbow.

"I hope you know what you're doing."

Ida, a small smile playing about her lips and her head in Wonderland, watched as Vera walked down the hall to her bedroom and closed the door.

3

Marcel staggered into the tomb-like mansion as lubricated hinges swung the ornate door to slingshot him into the hallway. A cacophony of insects chirruped in full song among the rain-sodden rainforest as a car disappeared into the steaming landscape, the occasional firefly the only illumination.

He closed the tall panel of wood with a resounding click. Set to autopilot, his body slid along the wall in search of a light switch, to no avail. He slipped off a shoe, four hundred U.S. dollars' worth followed by its partner, to shove them into the pockets of his rum-saturated custom-made business suit. His alcohol saturated brain refused to calculate the size of his pockets in comparison to the breadth of his shoes. They fell to the floor.

Marcel began his epic journey across the marble expanse with the aid of gossamer silk socks and arms outstretched, to pause and let the marble settle.

His hot date wasn't quite so hot for him when he tracked her down at a beach party in Gros Isle, but Marcel was a persuasive man. He ignored the gaggle of male admirers to whisper a few pretty words in her ear. In seconds, she had melted like ice cream beside steaming apple pie. The party for two moved to her house soon after. He left the woman sleeping the sleep of the fulfilled as he departed without a thought. It was the memory of eyes the shade of troubled skies, which surfaced in his consciousness.

He hadn't wanted to attend the bank meeting, and Ida had ruined his favourite suit, but he wasn't sorry.

An intimate tingle in his trousers stabbed at the fringes of his senses.

Shit.

If his father found him drunk with the fug of sex about him, he would be subjected to a lecture that would last eons.

The old man had forgotten what it was to be twenty-six and full of the excitement of life.

Holding onto the crotch of his trousers with one hand, Marcel began the ascent of the grand staircase. Using the bronze handrail as a climbing rope, he swiped at his brow with the edge of his jacket.

As he neared the summit, his vision aligned with a pair of evergreen slippers bearing the initials V. A. emblazoned in gold. Marcel's stomach somersaulted as Jerk chicken, rum, whiskey, and pineapple chasers fought for dominance as he stumbled on the penultimate stair.

"Good evening or shall I say good morning?" The slipper ceased its tapping. "Might I enquire as to the whereabouts of my car?"

The voice was friendly and courteous. Marcel clenched his jaw against the icy puddle of resentment coagulating in his chest. Mr. Victor Aubertine II was Lucifer in a smoking jacket.

"At Andre's house, he drove me home from the bar." Marcel caught himself in possession of an inane grin. He sat by his father's slippers and addressed them instead of risking all to look his father in the eye.

"I want it in the garage this morning at eight o'clock. I'm glad your mother isn't here to see this. You should have died at your birth instead."

Marcel's teeth clacked together in annoyance at the well-used insult as the slippers rocked back and forth.

"I want you in the office at eight-thirty after you have replaced the car."

"But tomorrow is Saturday!" Marcel ran a hand over his face. His face burned as if sandblasted, and his epiglottis rinsed with acid.

"I don't care what day it is. I wasted my time sending you to public-school. Other boys would have welcomed the opportunity to learn something. Not you. Not everyone gets a chance to see the world as you have."

"England was tedious. All they do is sip cold tea and talk about the weather. I thought it would be a nice change from New York and Los Angeles."

"So you livened things up with the housemasters' wives."

"It's not my fault they followed me everywhere; I couldn't help that."

"There were plenty of women in the village. Educating you in the arts and sciences was the idea, not fornication with every female out of pigtails associated with the school! "

"The local girls were ugly and agricultural." Marcel's lips pursed with distaste as his stomach flipped over in rebellion against its undigested contents.

"I received another bill from a company you owe money to."

"I said I would pay them."

"You are not dragging my name into court again. You will pay me as agreed from your wages until everything is paid. Until then, you go nowhere. I birthed every thought you ever believed was yours. Do what I say or make your way in life as I did. At your age, I built my business after leaving the Marines."

"So you forever tell me." Bile surged and ebbed in his stomach as he fought to loosen the neck of his shirt.

"Things could be worse. I started work in a meat market straight from leaving school, then in a Detroit car factory."

Marcel wished his father hadn't mentioned meat.

"You will never endure a fraction of my trials. My father left me not even his family name, mother never knew it. 'Auber' was all she deciphered on a scrap of paper he left behind, that and the ring you wear. She professed to be a widow to survive the scandal."

Marcel gazed down at the ornate band wrapped about his smallest digit; the familiar initials etched into the precious metal. Same story, different day. He knew every nuance of the tale.

"You said I would be meeting important people."

"I said nothing of the kind."

"What am I supposed to do on this rock?"

"As I said, you learn about the business and then we will see. You work in the morning."

"I was booked to play tennis with the boys tomorrow."

A moment passed in tense silence as he felt the bore of eyes identical to his drill a tunnel into the top of his head. Marcel nodded. He was out of options. Either he conducted himself by his father's wishes or leave home with nothing but the clothes he wore. The contents of his wardrobe cost more than the contents vaulted in the Bank of St Lucia, even with his limited-edition Swiss watches excluded from the equation.

"Get out of my sight, you make me sick."

On cue, fetid bile erupted from Marcel's slack mouth, to land on the slippers. He fought to clear his throat. The expected blow to his head never arrived.

"Get this off my stairs, you whoring fool!"

Marcel's mouth twitched upward at the words. His father's words still rang in his ears when moments later, he realized his father had departed leaving his slippers abandoned in the lemon-scented vomit.

Marcel descended the stairs on his backside, step by step.

Marcel Aubertine III cursed as he attempted to squeeze yet another report the filing cabinet's bulging top drawer.

Eventually, the unwelcome document squeezed in. Marcel flopped back on the nearest office chair, brushing at his hair with the crook of his arm. Catching a glimpse of his sweat-saturated armpit, he sniffed at it.

To hell with the filing.

A shower and change of clothes was a priority. He located a couple of dusty painkillers in the back of his drawer and swallowed them dry. He cast a glance at the clock on the far side of the room. The regulation magnolia walls and aerial photographs of featureless landscapes only served to magnify the blandness of the day.

2.30pm.

Each tick of the clock resonated like a sonar blip. His eyes trekked down the wall until it came to rest on a colossal mahogany table devoid of everything except a silver Rolls Royce paper-weight, an ivory telephone and a fountain pen. He glanced sidelong at his own which overran with paper cups, jagged stacks of documents and other assorted oddities, which had migrated to his desk. The telephone trilled in the silent room, as it had several times earlier that day. Each ring bounced off the walls to stab Marcel in the temples. He glared at the ugly Bakelite object. His fingers twitched to tweak the cord from the wall and hurl the device into a drawer.

Ring, ring.

Whoever was at the other end of the line could sit and sweat. For the umpteenth time that day he wondered why the hell he put up with his father and came up with the same word every time.

Money.

Ring, ring.

His lack of funds had made him a pawn in his father's plans. Now he was tied to his father like a simpleton, a beggar for every coin. His brow corrugated with the injustice of it all. He abhorred being treated like a fool.

The village idiot.

Ring ring.

Stuck on a thimbleful of land, surrounded by farmhands and parish priests.

The telephone fell silent.

Wonderful.

It was just as well he could hop across to Martinique, the next island over in the chain of Windward Islands, to visit the local women. Sometimes he flew to the Miami casinos with his fellow trust fund pals. It felt good spending time with fellow Americans, talking loud and spending as much of his father's money he could find, when he got fed up looking at irate landless farmers and building sites.

That morning, Marcel had considered breakfast for a single moment before his stomach roiled in disgust. A full American pancake and syrup breakfast with his father looking on were more than he could stand. He had beaten the alarm clock into submission and furrowed a deeper trench in the bedclothes. How he had managed to wake up in his bed when the last thing he remembered was lassoing the banister rail with his club tie was an enigma. When he had left for the office later that morning, the habitually taciturn gardener tending the hibiscus plants in the landscaped gardens had bared his toothless maw at him in mirth, leaving him feeling stupid and perplexed.

He was only just beginning to feel human, with his head clearing of its low-lying fog and questionable equilibrium.

As he gazed out of the open window, he was oblivious to the gentle sway of palm fronds, fragrant with a tinge of brine carried on the breeze from the tepid sea. Across the plain the Aubertine oil refinery hummed, men laboured with dried coconut or copra as it was known locally. It was turned into oil, bottled, and exported to countries worldwide. His father had grown rich on its export after stopping off at the St Lucian base as a U.S. Marine. Another chapter in his father's life, he could not stand to hear.

When was he going to stop hearing about his father falling in love with the island when he realised a small time man could nurture big-shot ideas?

Nobody had asked him if he wanted to leave boarding school to accompany his father, fresh from demobilisation to that hell hole. Why couldn't he have had regular parents with a mom who baked casseroles and a pop who had a boss? They could have had trips to the supermarket in their station wagon when he wasn't playing with the neighbourhood kids. Instead, Victor Aubertine started on the island working in a small company until he had enough money to start out on his own and undercut everyone in the business.

In time, he had all the vital contracts and a plethora of enemies. As a boy, he, too, had spent many lonely hours lifting his spirits by conjuring up innovative ways to murder his father, to find the entire island clamoured for the honour. Victor Aubertine II kept his son's wallet as dry as a sponge left out in the sun. His father proclaimed his son would never leave, as finding employment was hard work when there were skirts to pursue and parties to attend.

He was right.

The sound of metal being scraped against metal cut through the quiet room. A pair of dusty mocha-coloured fingers crept onto the windowsill. Marcel strode over to the window, grabbed the hands and yanked upwards. Dusty close-cropped hair appeared, under which sat a long, sombre face. A pair of feline eyes blinked mournfully back at him.

"So that's where you hiding. You had lunch yet?" Marcel watched the man scrutinise the rubbish strewn desktop for an edible treat. Grime-encrusted elbows peeped through rents in the faded work shirt as he hugged the windowsill.

"Not yet. You hungry?"

"No, I was just making complication." The man's gaze slid across the room to the silver pen bathed in a glaze of sunlight on his fathers' desk.

"You mean conversation. Clem, the pen stays put."

The man glanced over; head cocked in confusion.

"I was just looking around; that's all, boss."

"Never mind. I'm too tired to give you another English lesson today." He stole another look at the wall clock and smiled with satisfaction.

2.50 pm.

It was all the work his father would get from him today.

"I'll see you at the main doors." Reaching for the door handle, he glanced at the window.

It was empty.

The squeak of unoiled hinges sang out as he entered scoured the austere entrance hall. Clement was scouring the drawers for anything of interest again. As he passed the mahogany expanse, Marcel wondered, as he often caught himself doing, how a man so thin had such large, gnarled toes. A pair of plastic, girly pink flip-flops chewed to near extinction by canine jaws adorned the monster feet. He was sure Clement could walk on molten lava and not feel a thing.

"Come on." Marcel pulled the main doors open. The labourer cocked his head to one side.

"Where to?"

"Town."

"Then what?" Hopping off the desk Clem pocketed his acquisitions and followed his friend out into the heat of the day.

Marcel decided to ignore the items disappearance, as he had so many times before. "I don't know. We'll make it up as we go along."

"You the boss."

"How did you get up to my window?"

Clem smiled his famous megawatt smile as they turned the corner.

Marcel clutched the wall for support as his legs buckled under him.

His father's imported limited-edition Aston Martin was parked under the window. Two oil drums balanced on the roof of the car.

"How the hell did you get those up there?"

"I went to see if you at your house. I used the car to get down here."

Marcel had discovered Clem sitting behind a timber shed drinking a bottle of something illegal in his patched shirt and borrowed work pants several years ago. The other labourers struggled with a tree stump at his father's new office building site. Marcel knew he had found a kindred spirit.

He kept him close as one would a pet, as long as he was entertaining, dismissing him when bored or in the company of people of his class. Clem was different from his trust fund friends.

"You're crazy. We have to return it before someone finds out it's missing. You're lucky my father is in Soufriere village on business otherwise he would use your balls as a metronome."

Marcel, impeccably dressed in slacks and open-neck shirt, drove the racing green sports car toward Castries. Clement, dressed in threadbare, tattered garments, dusted the passenger seat with a layer of cement powder as he folded himself into the car.

Marcel shut off the engine and stepped out of the car as a thick-waisted woman hurried down the mansion stairs. Silver tendrils of flyaway hair from her ballerina tight bun created a halo around her plump cheeks.

"What a relief!" The lacy handkerchief usually pressed to perfection, was as mangled as an old washcloth between her doughy hands. She leaned against a stone lion, her dove grey regulation dress straining to contain a figure it was not cut to accommodate.

"What's the matter?"

"I thought someone had stolen the car."

"Who would be stupid enough to do that?" He glanced across at Clem languishing in the car. He bared his teeth in a jaw-cracking grin in return. The housekeeper, preoccupied with resuming a regular breathing pattern, failed to notice.

"When did you realise the car had gone?"

"Two hours ago. I tried to contact you to see if you had it before I called the police. I have been trying for hours."

"You called the police?"

"Yes. They said they would be right over. I don't know what is taking them so long."

Marcel's eyebrows shot upward at the news. It was a fair bet the car wasn't a high priority since Victor Aubertine ran the brother of the Chief of Police out of his business last year. The island was 34 miles long and 17 miles wide. The police should have arrived already, even if they were travelling from South Carolina.

Another unsatisfied customer.

If any of his father's property disappeared, it was an unwritten rule on the island it would stay 'missing.'

"I decided to take it for a drive to give the engine a run. Cars like these need it."

Mrs. James' broad features puckered in confusion.

"Mr. Aubertine gave specific instructions for the car to be dealt with by him alone."

Marcel opened his mouth, ready to launch into his tailored excuse when a telephone rang inside the house.

"There's no harm done. It's safe now. I must get that." Mrs. James traipsed inside leaving a lasting impression of her pumpkin-shaped backside disappearing through the wide doorway as laughter snapped at her heels.

Within an hour, they were back in the car. Marcel, showered and Alpine fresh in laundered shirt and trousers, sat behind the wheel of his beloved vehicle. The ex-army jeep had seen better days. He believed the holes in the bodywork were due to heavy artillery fire in active duty.

After the war, the U.S. Army chiefs struggled to organise transport home for troops stationed on the island while the soldiers played Blind Man's Bluff with live ammo and bigger targets. Rusting army jeeps still littered the countryside long years after the last G.I. had stepped off the island.

As the wind whipped through his hair, Marcel glanced at his passenger.

Clem had changed, too.

He wore his khaki work pants, and a scarlet Hawaiian shirt Marcel's eccentric aunt had given him for a Christmas long past, which he pushed to the back of the closet in disgust. For shoes, there wasn't a lot a person could do for dry, soil encrusted feet. Clem, ever resourceful, managed to squeeze an old pair of Marcel's Penny Loafers on after much cursing and olive oil.

Marcel did not offer the use of his shower-room with its array of colognes, scented soaps and unique custom-blend aftershave. Clem tried his best with his hair and remaining drops of olive oil.

He was too cautious a man to bite the hand that clothed him, so there he sat.

Looking clean.

Smelling decidedly funky.

It was a small matter.

They were going to town.

4

The car meandered through the main thoroughfare as Marcel drove slower than a preacher leaving church.

It worked.

It always did.

Women clamoured to admire the Adonis on Pirelli tyres. Wide-eyed girls elbowed each other as the petrol-powered chariot passed, while veterans of bygone love reminisced on escapades of a sepia era. Marcel chattered nonstop about yet another woman, not that Clem gave a damn for any of them.

"I'm hungry."

"Where do you want to eat?"

"Somewhere you can sit for a while." Wearing Marcel's dainty shoes were a colossal mistake.

"Big Jim's."

"The Spice Pagoda."

"It's too far. The Pink Elephant."

Clem had big plans for one of the waitresses working there before her dog-faced man began to make plans about him. He made it a top priority to frequent the premises at all hours to ensure his girlfriend stayed just that. His.

"I don't like it there."

They drew up outside The Pink Elephant and piled out, past the quartet of police officers who loitered beside the No-Parking sign. Peaked hats pushed back on close-cropped hair, polyester 'Stay-Pressed' trousers riding high on regulation boots.

"Bonjour Monsieur Marcel." The officers touched their caps as one as they glared at Clem, who stood a little taller and tilted his head a little higher. With Marcel beside him, the police could do nothing about his little problem without invoking the wrath of the country's biggest non-religious employer upon them. Not that Victor Aubertine had ever met him, but the police didn't know that.

The owner scuttled out of his cubbyhole by the main doors as they approached.

"Welcome, Monsieur Marcel. It's such a pleasure to see you." The aggrieved party of six tutted and clucked with displeasure as they were corralled to a less desirable location. The owner spared Clem a brief nod which told him all he needed to know. The restaurateur had not forgotten the theft of a trio of whiskey bottles the previous month.

He gave his best megawatt smile in return. Marcel waved off the proffered menu.

"Get me a large gin."

"Yes, sir."

"I'll have the chicken and avocado with pine nuts."

Clem leisurely calculated the black-market price of the Oriental wall hangings suspended from the candyfloss walls and elegant ebony lacquered furniture, for future reference.

"A particularly good choice, sir." Mr. Simmons kept his eyes fixed on Marcel. "What now, Clem?"

"Let's see." He flicked open the menu with a flourish. "What smells good?"

Clem savoured the intense aroma of delicately spiced flying fish and fragrant herbs that tickled his nostrils and fired his taste buds.

"I'll have your deep-fried lobster tails with rum sauce. No, I'll take the tuna steak."

A snatch of the menu brought it to rest under the crook of the restaurant owner's elbow.

Clem tore the fold of plastic from under the man's' pudgy joint.

"I've changed my mind. I'll take the smoked salmon club sandwich with a side order of scallops. No avocado, extra -" The owner scuttled off to the kitchen to declare war on the chef leaving a cobweb of annoyance lingering in the air.

"You should watch what you say to that man. I don't know what you did to him, but he looks as though he would like to squash you rather than…"

"Than what?"

Clem glanced up to find Marcel staring at his left ear. "What?"

"Not you."

Marcel listed to one side for a better view. Laughter emanated from the main doors, siphoning all conversation in the overcrowded room. Clem followed the trail of admiring glances to a group of women awaiting attention. A petite woman in the group, with skin the hue of creamy Blue Mountain coffee, negotiated the seating arrangements with her heavyset companion while another lady chatted with her companion. Brushing the six-foot mark with cascading chestnut hair, she reminded Clem of a willow tree, but it was the girl hovering in the doorway that captured his interest. Ida was a beacon among the mediocre. It wasn't just her exquisite looks, but her poise and style that made the others seem clumsy in comparison. In her silky, midnight-coloured dress with a buttermilk cardigan draped over her shoulders, she looked sophisticated in her kitten heels among the bobbysoxers and two-tone shoes scattered about the plush restaurant. Clem cast a quick glance back at Marcel as he sat transfixed. Ida peeled her white gloves off and popped them into her ornate bag. Her hands self-consciously stroked the base of her neck, curving up to push back escaped strands of thick ebony tresses, fastening them under her minuscule stylish hat.

Clem gaped at Marcel and the ladies in turn.

It wasn't long before the women were seated in a corner by the window, sipping lemonade and exchanging juicy snippets of conversation as they waited to order.

Marcel grinned, exposing perfect teeth.

"Isn't she fantastic?"

"She's okay, I suppose." Clem squinted back in puzzlement. "Which one?" He had his eye on one of the girls, but sure as hell was not going to tell Marcel. Too many times he had done so only to be outmanoeuvred by his friend in his stupid game of one-upmanship.

Marcel hooked the arm of a passing waitress.

"Are those ladies' regulars?"

The bony young girl stared wide-eyed at Marcel as if she had never seen such a handsome man whose face wasn't in a Hollywood film.

"No, Monsieur.

Marcel looked so crushed; Clem almost felt sorry for him.

"I know it's the smallest lady's birthday though, her name is Ruth Germaine. They booked the table ages ago." She blushed as Marcel furnished her with a hopeful smile.

"Send a bottle of your best champagne to their table with our compliments."

A shy nod of her head and the girl disappeared. Moments later the bottle arrived at the table to the delight of the women. A quick comment in Ruth's ear passed on to the other girls soon had all eyes focused on Marcel. Ida fluttered her fingers at them from across the restaurant.

Marcel had risen before her hand reached her lap. He strutted across the floor skirting tables with the easy grace of someone used to being the epicentre of all attention, leaving Clem behind at their table, and greeted Ida. Pushing into the booth between Ida and Willow, Marcel made himself comfortable. She eagerly introduced him to little Ruth, Helen the willow tree, and bubbly Celine, who were all soon under his influence and were getting on just dandy. Seeing Marcel wasn't returning anytime soon, Clem sauntered over, introduced himself and squeezed into the corner of the booth.

Nobody noticed.

Willow seemed to be a woman who knew what she wanted and wasn't afraid to take it. She batted her eyelids furiously, which looked like she had a nervous twitch as the other refused to cooperate, much to Clem's entertainment.

The eye in question also appeared to be looking over Marcel's shoulder, with nobody quite knowing what to make of it as a whole, seeing it was casting a gaze independent of its counterpart.

The evening was a success or a failure depending on the point of view. Marcel and Ida drank far too much champagne and chattered endless nonsense. Marcel twirled and twiddled with a lock of Ida's hair until Clem was ready to stab him with his fish fork. Ida was clinging so tightly to Marcel's chest; she might as well have been another rib.

The evening drew to a close, so the two lovebirds decided to take a trip up to Pigeon Point.

To gaze at the sunset over the placid glass of the Caribbean Sea, compared to the angry turquoise of the Atlantic waters on the other side of the sandbank, they claimed.

It was bullshit.

They were going to have sex.

Things were not so good for Clem.

Left with the other women to deal with, he had plenty to occupy him. Thank God Willow had taken her leave early on, but not without making sure her friends knew she was upset about not getting a chance to flirt with the best-looking man on the island.

Clem did his best with the intellectually superior Tiny and Bubbles, but by the end of the night, he felt like an old shoe between two mischievous puppies.

Clem slammed the misshapen door shut. He hurled the bag of dinner scraps across the tiny one room shack, startling a teacup sized spider from its home on the makeshift table. Inside, humidity clung to the stale air making breathing difficult despite the sun's rays having crept from the sky hours ago.

He didn't give a damn Ida was the girl Marcel mentioned in the car earlier in the day.

Marcel did nothing but jabber. He didn't see the old woman sat by the side of the street selling her produce. She abandoned her yams and green bananas in the gutter to walk toward them as the men waited at the junction of the town's main street, waiting for emaciated cows to cross the dirt road.

Clem had never gotten around to telling his family with whom he spent his free time with as he knew his father would open his cavernous maw and make a mess of everything. He hoped his mama would do a better job and keep hers shut.

Being Marcel's new sidekick suited him. It was clean; he got fed, and it was an exciting time in an otherwise dreary life. Besides, he had big plans.

Once the cattle had ambled across to the ravine bubbling along the side of the road, he swivelled his head toward the prematurely ashen-haired woman as they passed. He felt strangely numb as she swiped tears from her battered face with the corner of her soil flecked apron.

He wasn't like them.

Clem remembered seeing Ida months ago at the market with her mother. One glance at her serene face and he began to compile a list of suitable wedding venues.

You couldn't live on an island that small and not know everyone sooner or later.

She was something unique. Remarkable.

He dreamt of nuzzling close to her neck to inhale her honey-scented warmth as it enveloped his senses.

Tearing off his shirt, he flung it into the lone easy chair, spurring the slumbering tabby cat into bolting for the door, its flight hastened by the toe of Clem's boot.

Why didn't he make his move sooner? Why didn't he stop to talk to her that day long ago at the market?

He knew she worked at the library. Clem had followed Ida one afternoon while mooching around for something to do. As per usual, Marcel had gone to Martinique with his loud-mouthed friends. The invitation was not extended to him, not that he could compete with the vast yachts moored in the bay and even bigger egos. Maybe it was just as well. The last time he had accompanied Marcel and his high-ranking friends to the island; he was full of anticipation and joy at leaving St Lucia for the first time. He had ended up carrying luggage and chaperoning the men home when they lost the ability to propel themselves after visiting the local rum distillary.

Placing his work boots in a corner, he pulled off his pants and dropped them on the bed. He carefully unbuttoned his shirt before storing it in a crate posing as a drawer. Clad in threadbare boxers, he sauntered over to an ancient icebox and fished out a bottle of beer. Gulping half in one swallow, he tried to figure things out.

His younger sisters often spoke of their classmate, when they used to attend school, but he never listened to their juvenile bullshit. Like all women, much of their talk was far too loud with no content. The few times he saw Ida back then; she didn't look like much to him, nothing but bulgy eyes and scabby knees. If only he had paid attention, they could have been married already.

Cursing to himself, he hurled the beer at a wall where it exploded on impact, leaving a fermented amber trail advancing toward the rusty iron bed. In contemplation, he licked at the speckled liquid splattered on his arm and considered his next move.

Now Marcel and Ida had met, and it was obvious they were well on the way to becoming a courting couple. The only thing he could do now was sit and wait for things to develop, good or bad.

He had to stay close and make himself as useful as possible. It was imperative he knew their whereabouts and monitor them. There had to be a way to turn the situation in his favour.

He had to watch them carefully. There would be no hiding from him and no exclusion. If they were the slices of bread of a sandwich, he was going to be the filling right in the middle.

Clem's mouth twitched into a tight smile. He sauntered across the room and picked up the remnants of the bottle piece by piece.

He should have taken his chance sooner.

Memories of his former junior school headmaster being in utter despair of him came to mind. His school days were over, but he could still hear the wheezy voice as if it were yesterday.

"You idle stupid boy. You wait for other people to do the work and jump on for the ride. If you came to school more often, you might learn something."

So let them do all the work, he would reap the harvest. His hands rubbed together in rhythm crushing the glass clasped within, oblivious to the ruby beads dripping from his calloused fingers.

5

"How many times did you say?"

"A hundred times."

"How many was that?"

"Okay, okay, two hundred times." Grinning broadly, Marcel half-heartedly tried to bat Ida's hands away.

"Not good enough."

"Alright, five hundred times."

"Try again" Ida slurped the end of his nose.

"Stop it! Okay, I love you a thousand times." He tried twisting his head again, but wherever he went, she found his nose, having the added benefit of sitting on his chest. With his arms pinned under her knees, he was going nowhere, not that he was complaining as he gazed up at the twin globes of perfection.

"You might as well give up. I'm the boss, and I suggest you stay right there."

"I've had it. I give up. Happy now?"

She grinned in triumph.

"YES! Now where was I? Oh yes, do you love me a million times?"

He felt her thighs loosened their iron grip fractionally. He mustered his strength and arched his back sent Ida flying with a yelp of surprise. They tussled, ducking under flying pillows until neither had the energy to raise their arms, laughing in uncontrolled silliness they collapsed on the bed.

"Do you love me, Marcel?" Ida snuggled up to his lean body as they curled together, her bottom tucked into his pelvis. There was nowhere else in the world more attractive to her than where she was just now. Safe in the arms of the first man ever to have touched her intimately. She had given everything to him.

Her body. Her heart.

She drowsed on a bed the size of a small island listening to the tide below lapping at the cliff-edge under the open window.

Ida would never have to worry about anything as long as he was by her side. Life was perfect.

Today.

Tomorrow.

Forever.

"You know you don't ever have to ask me that question." He twirled the silky tresses which poured across his shoulders.

"I know that, but I like hearing it."

He paused mid-stroke, gently touched his lips to her ear tucking her ever closer to him.

"I think you know what I think."

Ida woke to the sound of flesh pounding wood.

"Marcel, there's someone at the door."

"Whassamatter?"

"Somebody's knocking on the door."

"It's most likely Clem, don't worry about it." He closed his eyes. The door handle rattled loudly.

"Hurry up your father's coming up the drive," yelled Clem.

The couple stared at each other for a millisecond before galvanising into action. Ida flew to the muddle of fabric strewn across the floor as Marcel fought to detangle himself from the bed sheet. He fell to the floor in a heap.

"He can't find me like this." Ida tugged at the zip of her Capri pants. There was no sign of her bra.

"Don't worry, we have a servant's staircase at the back of the house, we just have to get down the hallway." Marcel scooped up his clothes and cast one last glimpse at her pert breasts before they disappeared under a layer of lace, sheer enough to tantalise his senses. Marcel rewarded her with a cheeky wink.

"Get the door."

Ida raced across the room and turned the door handle. Clem lounged in the doorway.

"I thought you were supposed to be looking out for Aubertine Senior!"

Clem stepped into the room and closed the door behind him.

"I did. I saw his car turn into the drive."

"The drive is almost a mile long! What the hell have you been doing all this time? Why do I smell barbeque sauce?" Marcel fumbled with the buckle of his trousers.

"Cook just take out drumsticks, so I had a little taste."

"For goodness sake!"

"Let me sort this out. I'll talk to my father."

"What are we going to do? Your father doesn't like me. He'll have me lock' up."

Ida scowled at him; Clem was never one to put himself last. Another thing she couldn't stand about him.

"Just shut up."

"Don't worry, I'll sort things out." Marcel straightened his clothing, slipped on his shoes and sprinted across the room to nudge Ida and Clem to one side. He opened the door a crack and peered out. They listened keenly as the driver placed Victor's cases inside the main doors and returned the car to the garage.

"His car is here, so check his room. I want to see him." Mrs. James mumbled a muted reply.

Victor's steps echoed throughout the house as he stalked down the hallway toward his study as Marcel closed the door.

"Mrs. James is coming." He glanced searchingly for a hiding place around the sumptuously furnished room with its pale duck-egg walls and vanilla floorboards.

"Go in the bathroom. When I leave, wait a few minutes then make your way out through the back door."

Ida folded her arms and jutted her chin in defiance. "I'm staying put. I'd like to speak to your father. Why are we hiding? We're doing nothing wrong and we are over the age of consent."

"I've no time for this now. We'll talk later."

"No, we won't."

Marcel dragged her by one arm to the en-suite bathroom.

"Now is not the time to confront him. Just let me handle it my way."

"I want to talk to him!" Ida's fingernails dug into the doorframe as Clem tried to conceal his giggles as coughs.

"Clem?"

Clem hopped forward and saluted. "Boss."

"Get Ida back to your place and I'll meet you there as soon as I can."

Marcel kissed Ida's brow and turned toward the bedroom door.

"Sure boss." Clem bundled Ida into the bathroom as Mrs. James tapped on the bedroom door.

On the other side of the bathroom door, Ida and Clem pressed their ears against the varnished surface. After a moment's hesitation, Ida opened the door a crack and peered through the gap.

"Mr. Marcel?" Across the room, the housekeeper knocked again without waiting for an answer.

"Coming."

Mrs. James' stubby fingers, was curled into a loose fist, hovering in midair when Marcel flung open the door.

"What is it? I hope it's good. You just woke me from a nap."

The plump woman glanced at her watch and cast him a puzzled glare as she swayed from side to side as she tried to see into the room.

"Sorry to disturb you, sir. Your father requested to see you." She looked pointedly at his feet.

"I'll be there in a moment." The woman continued to stare at the floor.

"Mr. Aubertine said NOW, sir, in the study."

Ida wondered what the housekeeper found so fascinating about Marcel's shoes that she couldn't tear her eyes away.

Marcel glanced down. Ida gasped in surprise. Hooked around his right shoe heel was a bra strap.

"How did that get up there?" He kicked the scrap of lace under the bed.

"I wouldn't know, sir."

In the bathroom, Clem pressed his hand over Ida's mouth. She squirmed as he leaned into the curve of her bottom, his long arms holding tight around her slender waist. In the bedroom, Marcel ploughed a row of furrows through his hair in frustration.

"Okay, I'll come now."

"Yes sir," she turned her back to him "I'll fix your room when you've gone downstairs."

"That won't be necessary. I intend to return to finish my nap."

Marcel followed Mrs. James down the corridor.

Clem and Ida heard the door close. Those five extra minutes of waiting felt like forever to Ida, with Clem breathing whisky fumes down her neck. Her stomach was seconds away from rejecting her last meal. When he eventually released his iron grip, she delivered a swift kick to his groin. It landed on his upper thigh. Sucking in his breath, he rubbed at the tender muscle.

"What's the matter with you?"

"You touch me again, and next time I'll make sure I don't miss" Grabbing the door handle she flung it open, and marched out, leaving the door to fly back onto Clem. Nursing a bruised thigh and throbbing shoulder, he hobbled meekly behind her, as she pressed an ear to the door. Ida turned the handle, and crept across the landing and down the stairs, following the sound of raised voices.

"If you're not going to come into work, don't expect to get paid. I tolerate no slackers in my business."

"I was going to come in this weekend."

"That may be so, but you still have to inform Ms. Andrews of your plans. The woman was swamped with *your* paperwork. If you had done it there would have been no need to discipline her for not completing *her* work. Now I have to find a replacement. Don't even think about any of your idiotic friends."

The clink of exquisite crystal punctured the tension like a syringe. Ida watched Clem lick his thick lips from the other side of the telephone desk in the stairwell. No doubt he was still savouring the taste of Victor's finest whiskey on his tongue. He smelt as though he had used the alcohol as a face pack. She wondered if he had topped up Victor's decanter with water again. Marcel mentioned his father measured his alcohol to ward against over-familiar servants. Clem, as always, had found a way to get the best out of the bottle without Victor getting the best of his hide.

"They don't make whiskey as they used to" murmured Victor wistfully.

Clem giggled like the idiot he was.

"To other business. The secretary of the country club says you have been seen consorting with undesirables."

Beyond the open door, Ida bristled at the comment. Her feet involuntarily found themselves on a journey to Victor's library. A moment passed before she realised she hadn't covered any ground between her and the room. Calloused hands had clamped themselves to her shoulders, before she showed Victor what an 'undesirable' could do. Clem steered her toward the rear of the house as she slapped at him with teeth bared. As the warring pair turned the corner, the library door slammed shut.

They moved in the direction of Clem's house, with only the sound of their shoes and the chirrups of crickets to break the silence. Ida was not in the habit of being manhandled by smelly labourers. She was not going to let him forget the incident. Her family was well respected in the community, unlike his who were nothing but thieves and vagabonds.

Squat banana trees loomed out of the darkness, tropical spectres of the night, broad leaves motionless in the suffocating humidity.

Before long, the couple was damp with grime and sweat. Around them, fireflies playing tag.

"Are you alright?" Her swift sidelong look gave him no clues. "Are you alright?"

"I said are you...?"

"Yes. Leave me alone." She continued her march down the narrow track.

Clem tried lengthening his step to keep up. "No need to carry on like that, I was just trying to be friendly."

"Don't give me your sad dog look. It won't work."

"I'm sorry."

Ida slowed her pace. Clem, off-kilter, staggered after her.

"I could kill Marcel. I have to hide in bathrooms and prowl about the back stairs so he can keep in with his father." Ida's pace slowed a little more. "Why can't he face up to him and tell him that we have been together for months. Is that so hard?"

Clem shrugged his shoulders in reply.

"I know he's rich, and I'm not, but I don't want his money. It just makes things harder. I just want him."

Ida halted in the middle of the dusty path. Clem shuffled uncertainly in the gloom, perturbed at being caught out in the countryside without any artificial form of illumination.

"I don't know what to do anymore. My mother is after his blood for some reason. Almost every sentence out of her mouth is a verse out of the Bible aimed at me. I can barely get out of the house these days unless I say I'm visiting Willow or Bubbles."

Clem held out a hand. She unfolded the pristine square of lightweight cotton. The initials "V.A" was painstakingly embroidered in a corner. Ida hitched an eyebrow upward at Clem. He, in turn, gave another shrug.

Refolding the hanky, she dabbed at each eye, fully intending to have a good cry. Her voice bubbled out in a cascade of laughter. Clem's voice rumbled in unison though he no clue where the humour lay. As the episode subsided, she regained her composure enough to gasp a few words.

"Can't you leave anything alone?"

He gazed down at her; his brow pleated in consternation.

"What?" Clem kicked at a few loose stones with the toe of his work boot. He slouched with his oversized hands plunged in his long khaki shorts. "I haven't done anything."

"I bet you've got half the contents of the man's house at your place."

A sly smile tweaked his mouth upward.

"Could be."

Somehow Clem always seemed to find a way to make her giggle. He could be a bit fresh, though.

"You don't always have to make yourself available whenever he feels like it. Good-looking woman like you,"

Ida turned away, a slight smile played about her lips.

"…I reckon you would have plenty of admirers, don't you think?" He nudged her with an elbow. Linking arms with Clem, she swung him round till they were facing away from their intended path by ninety degrees. "You're taking me home."

"And Marcel?"

"It will be good for him to do a little good old-fashioned chasing. It might help him work out his priorities." They swerved off the dirt path, through the lush vegetation toward the main road and Ida's house.

6

Marcel bored an index finger through delicate lace as he sat on the edge of his bed. The matching parchment-coloured cushions lay scattered across the polished floor like browned marshmallows. He watched a slender lizard, hidden amongst the breadfruit tree leaves that skimmed the windowsill. It skittered up the wall to rest in a corner by the ceiling. Its pale skin blended perfectly with the buttermilk ceiling.

He was too old for dismissal like an errant child. He kicked the bedside table with a sandaled toe.

Good fortune was with him when he heard Clem and Ida's soft tread approaching in the hallway earlier as they made their escape. He shut the library door.

The club secretary was a curious bitch. He would talk to one of his friends with influence, to persuade her to relocate to another island. Maybe Guadeloupe or Haiti. His father had no business there. That way, everything would be clear for them to continue meeting without gossip reaching his father, not that he was ashamed of his Ida.

When he looked into her smoky eyes, all logic fled.

She invaded his every waking thought and sabotaged his dreams.

Every time he found someone, he felt like spending more thana few days with, his father would find a way to put an end to it, which infuriated Marcel. He would either remove the woman by frightening her away, paying her to stay away, or transferring himelsewhere. Victor often stated if Marcel didn't do as he instructed;he would inherit nothing. This time, Marcel would not care as long as they were together.

Money wasn't everything.

It wouldn't come to that.

His grandfather had been negligent. His father was different. He was cold and unyielding, but he was not vindictive. He would explain the situation, and his father would see sense. After so many years of there just being the two of them waited on by a regiment of staff, his father might like a little femininity about the house. Marcel smiled to himself at the thought of Ida sitting down to breakfast with them as the new mistress of the house. The housekeeper and Ida could go through the daily menus and arrangements for dinner guests while he did a little work with his father or went sailing with his friends.

She could keep his father company when he went to the casino in Barbados with his friends. Ida would be waiting for him in their bedroom wearing something short and transparent.

He stepped across the room to the vast oak wardrobe and peered inside. They needed to be careful. He needed to find somewhere discreet for their trysts. Marcel tugged his favourite shirt from its hanger and slipped it on. He popped each button through its bound opening.

Somewhere cosy and out of the way. Somewhere isolated and inconspicuous. Somewhere deep in the lush rainforest where only confident feet trod.

Deep in thought, he wandered down the hallway. Passing the study, he glanced meaningfully at the closed door before stepping out of the house in search of Ida.

Victor watched his son wander down the drive to the garage.

"You start tonight. He is leaving the house now but will be at the office tomorrow at 8.00am. Each week I want a report on his whereabouts and with whom he spends his time. Something is going on. I want to know what it is. Understood?"

Replacing the bulky receiver, Victor settled into the custom-made leather armchair as the gilt fan whirred away softly above him in the dimly lit room. Examining the amber liquid glinting in his crystal goblet against the twilight, he contemplated his days' work on his vested interest and was satisfied. He prided himself on being a shrewd man who trusted his instinct. His American dollars would find out exactly what was going on. He was going to make sure every dime was put to good use when it came to his son.

The boy needed watching. He had a head-start on the situation, thanks to the club secretary. No doubt she thought he owed her dinner and more.

Not a chance.

He downed the rest of his whisky and grimaced against the burn as it seared a passage to his stomach as his tongue savoured the aroma on his palate.

"Mrs. James!" His bellow reverberated in every corner of the mansion. The nervy woman popped her head around the library door as if permanently stationed there.

"Yes, sir?"

Victor held his glass to the light and scrutinised the liquid.

"Take this shit away and get me another bottle."

7

Ida and the boy arrived at the Solomon household in high spirits. Through the gap in the snowy curtain, Ma Solomon watched Ida push the skinny boy off the first stair into a nearby bush.

"Don't cheat, I beat you!"

They stepped up onto the veranda as the door opened. Ma Solomon brandished her faithful cutlass in one hand.

"Child where is you been?"

Ma Solomon surveyed the tall young man with deep suspicion. Ida flopped onto a chair and stretched her slender legs out; her toes arched to the last solar rays of the day.

"I went to see Celine but forgot the time. Sorry. Bumped into Clem though, Clement Rochard. You know his family. I went to school with his sisters. He took me home as it was on his way."

Ma Solomon gave the boy a good long hard look as the pair waited with bated breath. They were obviously waiting for something to happen, but what, she knew not.

She was not a fool.

Something was going on, maybe or maybe not with this skinny boy; he didn't seem to be a bad one, but he was stringy and shabby. The fool didn't look smart enough to tie his shoelaces.

He had a slow mouth, but fast eyes.

Ida had left the house earlier that day wearing her Jezebel brassiere. Ma Solomon had seen it through her blouse. She opened her mouth to speak to Ida about her heathen ways, but her husband had chosen that moment to drop the bag of ashes from the oven in the middle of the back yard. The fool needed supervision for every task he undertook. By the time she had finished berating him, Ida had disappeared down the lane.

Now the red brassiere was gone, and she could see things no self-respecting young woman should be showing.

All that jumping and bouncing around.

It wasn't Godly.

Ida was too old to manage effectively with a slap now; otherwise she would have beaten her daughter with the length of sugarcane she had just chopped down.

She heard talk the skinny boy's mother was a beggar and his father a hard liquor drinker. Their daughters spent much time by the docks with few clothes on. They were not her kind of God-fearing folk. She was going to make it her business to find out what was going on. She had been hearing half whispered gossip for weeks around town, and Ida's name peppered the chatter.

If such talk continued, she was going to take her daughter to see the Deacon in Soufriere village and get her to bathe in the spiritual waters from the Sulphur Springs. Ida needed some hard talk and an extra prayer meeting invoking a special visitation from the Holy Ghost. As an upstanding member of the biggest church in St Lucia, it was her moral obligation to make sure her family upheld standards.

Ma Solomon stood ruler-straight, ignoring the oppressive pull of thick humidity sucking at her bones. She cast a disapproving eye over the dirty-looking boy with a suspiciously pure white handkerchief sticking out of his ragged pocket and turned to stare at Ida, who smirked in the chair. She stepped closer to lean toward her daughter; her thin lips almost touching Ida's ear.

"I don't know what you are up to child, but be careful of what you do. Don't forget, if you don't respect yourself who will respect you? 'And the carcass of Jezebel shall be as dung upon the face of the field in the portion of Jezreel; so that they shall not say, this is Jezebel.' Kings Two, Chapter Nine, Verse thirty-seven."

Bold with embarrassment, Ida shot to her feet. Clem's face twisted in confusion, stepped back onto the path in sprint mode.

"Nothing is going to happen, and I am not a Jezebel. I just want to be like any other nineteen-year-old on the island. Why can't I go out with my friends and just have fun? What I don't need is a quote from the bible in every conversation or when I invite a guest home for supper. Is that too much to ask?"

The boy kept his fleshy lips closed. Ma Solomon had plenty to tell him if he forgot his place.

She considered her next move before answering as Ida and Clem batted at the occasional mosquito in search of succulent skin. She was head of this household, and nobody was going to make a fool of her and Jesus, especially not a big-mouthed teenager. However, it was always prudent to be patient, so she decided it best to temper her words to appease the heathen pair. She had time.

A storm was coming, and she had the only boat.

The boat of Salvation.

"The Lord's words find a vehicle when needed. I am but a vessel of his work. I will not apologise for that, but I will consider my words in company. However," Ma Solomon faced the teenagers, "if I find anything that is not to my taste, my retribution will be mighty."

After a moment's hesitation, Ma Solomon placed the weapon inside the door within easy reach as a sign of peace and let them enter. For the duration of Clem's visit, the honed steel was never far from Ma Solomon's hand.

8

Electric blue streaks of the new day had begun to bleed across the sky by the time Clem arrived home.

His slender fingers had barely touched the makeshift handle when his ears detected strange noises inside. He backed up and crept into nearby foliage behind the shack, cursing to himself for neglecting to the door. There were always thieves about, ready to steal innocent folk's hard earned possessions. From his vantage point on the incline by the outhouse, he watched through the window as Marcel crossed, and re-crossed his legs as his fingers beat imaginary time on worn armrests. His many cigarette butts sculpted a pyramid of twisted ends on the scarred floor.

He was the last person Clem wanted to see. The faint crescent scars on his palms tingled as he squatted in the bushes. The leaves were slick with moisture. He rubbed his hands on his work pants as he calculated a wait of maybe half an hour. His friend was not a patient man. Clem hoped Marcel would get the hell out of his house a lot sooner. Marcel scratched at the exposed wadding of the chair seat. He rolled a ball of fluff between his thumb and finger and fired it at the cat who deftly batted it aside with an ebony paw.

The big hand on Clem's new watch made one revolution of the ornate face. Marcel still showed no signs of departing. He had taken up residence on the rickety iron bed. Clem sucked his teeth in annoyance as he watched muddy shoes leave stains on the threadbare sheets as Marcel fought for a more comfortable position. He hissed with anger as the soles of Italian footwear were cleansed on the iron footrest.

His knees creaked in protest as he settled into a more comfortable position. A clink of metal, as his backside touched the ground, ignited his consciousness. Pulling the hip flask from a back pocket, he poured a shot of amber fluid down his throat as the seat of his pants soaked up the early-morning dew.

It was a good night's work. Grinning inanely, he watched as the inky night sky lightened to a purplish haze on the horizon while he ticked off his mental checklist.

1. He had helped himself to more items from the Aubertine household.

2. He had gotten a handful of round, tight ass courtesy of Ida. Clem absentmindedly rubbed his throbbing thigh.

3. He had managed to convince Ida to forget Marcel for a while and had sold himself as a likeable guy.

4. He had met Ida's parents, and her mother hadn't used the cutlass on him.

Ma Solomon was an old crow. He knew the type, all bible bashing and brimstone. How did a thing so mean begat such a delicate, beautiful creature such as his Ida from her loins? Thank God she took after her daddy because her mother's face looked like the work of a sloppy carpenter. All irregular angles and ugly as hell. He didn't believe the local gossip she had been the prettiest girl on the island when at the same age Ida was now. Involuntary shudders wracked his emaciated body. Ma Solomon was the boss, no doubt about it. She needed to know her place like his daddy showed his mama.

That was a man who knew everything when it came to women.

Through the gap in the foliage, he glimpsed Marcel still sprawled on his bed. Above his shack, two gigantic shadows loomed in the distance. He knew them to be the twin peaks of the only volcano in the world where a person could stroll around its perimeter at their leisure as sulphuric fumes seeped into their lungs. Named 'The Helen of the West,' situated between Martinique and St Vincent, St Lucia was hot and green and lush.

He despised every square centimetre of it.

Repositioning himself, he downed another swig.

Clem respected his daddy. He didn't always like him, though. Nobody messed with him, whoever did regret it.

'Boxer' was king of the ring from way back when, until a bigger, meaner man took all the punch out of him in the eighth round. He always proclaimed he still had a mean right hook.

His mama could testify to that.

His father Jerome was nothing more than a general labourer who worked cutting cane on another of Victor Aubertine's businesses, a sugar cane plantation when his back allowed him. He despised when lack of funds forced him to work alongside his father. Labouring on Victor's new office building digging the foundations was even worse.

His daddy was head of the household, without an ounce of tolerance. He remembered when he was a little boy; his mama had tried getting fancy with Boxer Rochard, but his daddy always got around her. Soon, he wore the fancy right out of her, especially after all the baby mishaps. After Margaret and Sylvia had been born, she stopped that nonsense altogether. Daddy regularly imagined Mama was getting high-minded and set about putting her straight.

It took a little time these days as his sisters were like her, too, but they didn't count. They would get pregnant and leave to be with their men like his mother did.

They didn't matter. They never would.

You take a man like Ida's daddy. He was tongue-whipped for sure and gave Clem the creeps, always silently skulking and lurking in dark corners like a ghoul.

The birds had started their early morning uproar when Clem remembered to look in on Marcel. The rusty bed was empty. Scrambling to his feet, he staggered to his cabin clutching the antique whisky. There was no way he was going to work today. His boss could kiss his ass. He banged the door shut with his heel as a hand grabbed the base of his neck and pushed him face first into the centre of the room.

"What took you so long?"

Dazed, Clem stared back. An inebriated grin plastered on his face.

"I will be using your place as a hideaway."

Clem knew better than to think it was a request. Sprawled on the ground, he struggled to his feet. They would not obey his commands, so he settled for looking as dignified as possible with dockers' breath and a wet backside.

"Hi there! What are you doing here at this time of the night?"

"Cut the crap, I know you were out there watching me by the shit house. Don't play innocent with me. Gimme."

"Whassamatter boss?" Yanking Clem to his feet, nimble fingers quickly found the container. Clem crumbled onto the end of the bed.

"Full moon, shiny object, dumb move." Marcel tucked the flask into his pocket. "Where's Ida?"

Clem felt a sudden urge overtake him. "I'd love a cup of tea."

The sting of the slap arrived a second after his neck snapped to one side.

"Where is Ida?"

He considered throwing a punch, but Marcel looked in much better shape than himself.

"She went home to her mother, but I'm here." His white teeth gleamed in the semi-darkness.

"Did she say anything?"

"Dunno." Sleep had begun its stealthy onslaught on his brain cells.

"What did she say, dammit!" Grabbing Clem's poly-cotton shirt in one hand, he shook him till his eyes refocused.

"Said you were a fun duck."

After a moment to work out the strange sentence, Marcel was no less satisfied. "A dumb fuck, eh? Wake up."

"Mmnn?"

"Did she say anything else?" Marcel pushed Clem back onto the single bed using the toe of his shoe.

"Said you were a baby, and she got no time for those. Got no spunk, no balls. Gonna find her a real man?" Giggling like a five-year-old, he rolled his eyes toward Marcel to find he was talking to an empty room.

"Dumb pluck." His last thought was of his stolen flask as he drifted into unconsciousness.

9

Miniature legs swung from an elegantly sculpted chair as the man opened his tatty notebook. Across the room, Victor flared his nostrils with distaste against the waft of historical perspiration and tried not to breathe.

Waving his lavender-laden kerchief across his face, he waited for the report to begin.

"Sunday 12ᵗʰ October.

The subject was seen at a Clement Alfred Rochard's house. Said person observed to be hiding behind an outside toilet. Fifty-eight minutes later, an altercation in shed. Subject leaves.

Monday 13ᵗʰ October.

"Marcel followed to Castries main library where he waits until…" the man peered closely at his notes "…Calisticka Theresa Solomon leaves for lunch. They argue for seven minutes."

"Who are these people?"

The man raised the little book back to eye level.

"Clement Rochard is a labourer on one of your cane plantations with his father Jerome, who is also a labourer. He has also been working on your new office block. His mother sells junk and some fruit that grows by their house. There are two sisters. One is a prostitute on the waterfront, has a couple of kids that she gave to a cousin, and the other is a washerwoman."

Victor digested the news as he readjusted the desk fan. Warm air ruffled iron strands splayed at his temples.

"What does his father look like?"

"Big and mean as a rhino. Big hands, huge feet."

Victor recalled hiring someone like that. At the time he didn't like the look of him, but as he was short-handed that season and behind schedule, he employed anyone vaguely healthy.

"What about this 'sticker' girl?"

The detective consulted his notes again.

"Calisticka comes from a respectable family. Her father is a shipping clerk. People I've questioned at his workplace barely recall Mr. Rochard despite him working for the company for years. I spoke to Mr. Rochard myself. Very tall, got a hunchback, hangdog face."

There was a snort of disdain from across the room.

"People reckon the wife rules the roost. The family are Bible folk; they go to church every day, all day Sunday. Two daughters, Calisticka is a librarian, the other, Vera, a schoolteacher. One son, he's a book-keeper. Mrs. Rochard is a lay-preacher.

"That is most interesting." A light of recognition gleamed in Victor's eyes.

"People say Mrs. Solomon is gifted. Some new-fangled American thing, having women preachers. It won't catch on."

Victor was beginning to lose the little patience he possessed. "I don't pay you for your opinions, what about the girl?"

"Very pretty, well brought up. No, history." He closed the notebook firmly, deposited it in his weathered safari jacket and awaited his next orders.

There were none.

Minutes ticked by as the little man perspired under his clients intense stare, despite a fresh breeze wafting through the study. His eyes darted with longing to the wide strip of azure water beyond the window. Under Victor's scrutiny, he grew more alarmed with each tick of the grandfather clock in the corner.

"Has the family money or connections?"

"A little, enough to eat regularly, and a bit over. The mother is popular in the community for conducting blessings."

Victor snorted in disgust. "Real money, not scrapings. Anything else about my son?"

"Er, yes" he stated morosely as he slowly opened the notebook again.

"Spit it out, man."

"Yes, sir."

"Monday 13th.

A row ensues between said subjects…"

Victor was beginning to regret hiring the tiresome jackass. He was just another idiot from town. The detective reminded him of a petulant child dressed in his fathers' suit.

"Yes, yes, get on with it."

"Marcel and Ms. Solomon argue in the street for seven minutes before subject departs in the direction of the office.

Monday through to Saturday 1st, he is also seen in the Blue Star Bar, Big Jim's Harbour Bar, and Henrietta's Jive Joint -"

"Enough names. Skip over that."

"Sorry, sir. He is seen in various bars and houses of ill repute-" He smiled to himself at his use of vocabulary, further irritating Victor, "- alone, then with Mr. Rochard."

He shut the book with lightning speed and popped it back in his pocket.

"If that's all, I have another pressing engagement, sir."

"I haven't dismissed you yet." Victor's voice slithered down the man's back like an ice-cold penny. He resumed his seat with reluctance, his eyes tracking back to the enticing view.

"Where is my son now?" Victor watched the man squirm with satisfaction.

"I think ..."

"YOU ARE NOT PAID TO THINK!" Spittle flew, spattering the polished surface as Victor rose to his full towering height.

The detective's sphincter muscle fought to retain control of his urinary reservoir, failing somewhat, enough for a few renegade spots to make an appearance on the fly of his wrinkled pants.

"Either you know where my son is or you don't. Which is it?" Victor watched as the small face contorted with indecision, weighing up the consequences of the answers he could give against what the potential outcome might be.

"He's about twenty minutes from here."

"It's time to let him know I'm onto him. Let's go." Victor strode across the cavernous room.

"Sir, my prior engagement?"

His voice sounded ridiculously high for what reason, Victor had no idea, but he was going to find out why.

As Victor flew past his chair, his hand hooked itself onto the back of the man's gaping collar, forcing him along in his slipstream.

It was dark by the time the Volkswagen Beetle came to a stop on a ridge overlooking the valley. The detective pointed to the shack partially obscured by banana leaves.

"He's down there."

Victor eased his solid frame out the rubbish-strewn car. He had contemplated rousing his driver from slumber above the garage, but now was not the time for grand appearances. Stealth was what would give him answers.

"Let's go."

The man remained in his seat with eyes fixed on the windscreen.

"What are you waiting for?"

"I'm staying here."

"We're not on a picnic. We're taking my son home, if necessary by force." Victor wondered if he hadn't been too hasty in charging up here with an underfed runt instead of some of his capable foremen for effect.

The man refused to budge.

"I'm staying here."

"GET UP!"

The detective looked away, his face burning. "I'll drive you back when you're ready."

Victor had bought many men. He also knew when it would do no good. Something bigger than him had frightened the ass. Leaving the car door open, he headed for the shack.

There was no light showing under the door as Victor touched the handle. Inside, he heard a familiar sound he couldn't quite place. Pushing the door open a notch, he stepped inside.

The detective watched Victor enter the house from his car. He scanned the scene before him as his trembling fingers sought for his pack of Marlboros. Before he had the time to light up, Victor came charging out of the door, sagged against the corner of the building and retched in the tall grass, his face slack with bewilderment. He made a slow return to the car. He seated himself, devoid of the energy he had possessed when they arrived, smearing bile across the faux leather seat. Pulling the door shut, he rounded on the driver.

"You knew didn't you? That's why you wouldn't leave the car."

There was no response. None was required.

The detective revved the engine into life.

"You-" Victor stared straight ahead as did the detective, neither wanting to face each other.

"Yes, sir."

"-You will keep your mouth shut."

"Yes, sir."

Victor spoke quietly, as they sat in the dark staring at the building.

"You will be well paid. If I hear this mentioned anywhere, I will kill you, your wife, and your bastards. Do I make myself clear?"

The detective cursed his grasping wife for talking him into seeing Victor. Lighting up his forgotten cigarette, he inhaled the blue-grey smoke, before slipping the car into gear.

"Yes, sir." As he turned the nose of the vehicle toward the main road, a hand stopped him.

"We're not finished yet." Confused, he followed the jerk of Victors's thumb to the back seat.

In the shack, wiping his mouth with the back of a shaky hand, the spirit glasses and empty liquor bottle along with the tiny box of under the bed was pushed under the bed. He drew the sheet up over their nakedness and made himself comfortable. Volkswagons were not the ideal car with which to spy on a person. Smiling to himself, he cuddled up to his bed-mate who lay unconscious, oblivious to the evening's drama.

10

The site foreman whistled an inventive melody as he scrutinised his equipment. He gave each one a swipe with the tail of his shirt and placed them in the battered workbox with the practised air of a musician attending to their beloved instrument. Beside him, his workmates mirrored his preparations for the day ahead. He paused as a figure sauntered down the muddy path toward the site. Clem's boat-sized feet pounded the rain-drenched ground while tied about his neck swung half-laced boots.

"Nice of you to stop by. I have some good news."

"What news?"

"You had your walking papers as from Monday gone."

The foreman turned his back in search of his Billy-Can.

"What's going on?" Panic simmered in Clem's chest. "Where are you all headed?"

There was no reply.

"I'm talking to you." He prodded the foreman's work boot with a dirt-caked toe.

"I've had my orders to let you go from them upstairs so get out of here. Don't come round here no more, you're out."

"There's been a mistake."

The foreman, back fresh from an ass-chewing from the boss over someone else's screw up was not for playing games.

"Look," launching himself to his feet with surprising dexterity, he grabbed a handful of Clem's shirt and shook him like a wet flannel. "You've had your fun. The boys have put up with your shit for too long. You think you can come and go like you royalty and do squat because you the Aubertine family dog? Let Marcel find you a job. You are done here and at the cane plantations, too, so don't even bother heading over there. Don't let me see your skinny ass around here no more."

One last push sent him sprawling to the ground as the work crew filed by, each one sporting a broad grin. They had traipsed several yards up the track before he realised nobody was going to turn around and tell him they were fooling around. There would be no courting Ida without coins in his pocket. He got to his feet and slapped at the soil clinging to his pants.

"I thought you said you had good news!"

"It is-," the foreman paused long enough to remove the cigarette dangling from his mouth. He arranged his moisture barren lips into a grimace of a smile fixed around teeth the colour of dead leaves, "-for us!"

Helpless in their hysterics the men staggered down the track and disappeared over the hill, their laughter echoing across the field. Enraged, he went in search of a champion.

He found Marcel in Big Jim's bar, nursing a hangover of epic proportions. Clem clambered onto a nearby stool as his friend cranked open a sleep encrusted eye, to peer at himself in the smoky veneer of the aged mirror hanging above the bar.

"I need my job back!"

Clem's roar reverberated around the sweaty interior of the fleapit. The alcohol preserved man behind the counter shuffled along the groove in the floor as he lined up cloudy whiskey glasses on the scarred counter. The few decrepit souls desperate enough to be in need of a drink before noon turned their attention to the men at the bar. The slow-motion domino game forgotten in favour of the free in-house show.

Shoving Marcel's elbow aside, Clem grabbed the nearest glass, drained the contents and flung it at the pitted mirror. It shattered, leaving the old bartender clucking and shaking his head at the unnecessary work.

"I need money!"

"Why don't you just fuck off? I don't want to see your face right now.

"What am I going to do?" twitched Clem. "You gotta help me get my job back. I need that money. It's all right for you - you got lots of it, I need hard cash to get out of this dump."

Marcel swatted him away like an angry wasp.

"You don't have problems."

He gestured to the old men across the dingy room.

"None of you have any problems."

He swayed unsteadily to his feet, his eyes whirling wildly across the room.

"You people got shit to worry about. You wake up. You eat. If you're lucky, you'll get laid. You die. You'll be gone before you've even known you lived."

"Did you get yours last night?" Domino man squinted at his playing partner who in turn cast a glance over at Clem.

"Hell yeah, I got me some from his mama."

Cackling with merriment, the men cleared the rickety table in preparation for a new game.

"I got some from your daughter," retorted Clem.

The drunks, too broken by misdeeds to beat anyone in a fight did the next best thing. The laughter came to an abrupt halt.

Sinking onto his broken barstool oblivious to the hurled insults, Marcel muttered under his breath. "Now me-" He studied the pitted counter top carefully. "-I got problems."

He counted them off on his fingers as Clem beckoned to the barman and charged the two shots of whiskey to Marcel's account. He pushed a shot over to his colleague.

"First, Ida doesn't want to see me. She's going around town with some bank jackass. My head hurts as if someone squeezed it in a vice all week. I've been on worse benders than this and not felt half as shit."

He paused to take a sip from the caramel liquid.

"My father wants to see me this afternoon, and I don't know what the hell all that's about."

Clem finished his drink in one gulp. He clapped his friend on the back.

"That's too bad. My mother always says that, after the rain, the sun always shines."

Marcel stared at him in such a way it would have made a wiser man head for the nearest exit.

"Last but not least, you're not funny anymore. In fact, you're a royal pain in my butt so do me a tremendous kindness and please just give me some peace."

He motioned to the bartender to pour him another shot. Clem decided his time to convince Marcel to do anything was later.

Much later.

Sighing, Clem placed a hand on his friends' shoulder. It was shrugged off.

"I'm sorry. I was only thinking of myself. Look me up on your way home tonight, and we'll talk."

"No. I'm not going near that shack."

He quickly tried another tack. "What if I drop by later on this evening and we'll talk?"

Marcel, barren of words, dipped his head in acknowledgement. He slowly rose to his feet.

"Where are you going?" There was no way Clem was letting his money box out of his sight.

"I'm going to see Ida. I'm going to try to make her see sense."

"Why don't you leave it alone? I'm sure she won't even look at you dressed like that. Marcel peered at himself in the mirror. Clem's paint spattered shirt looked back at him. His usually impeccably styled hair stood on end in clumps. He slumped back onto his chair and gazed down at extra-long battered jeans and oversized flip-flops. He gaped across at the finely woven Egyptian linen shirt that billowed over trousers with hems five inches short of their destination on the other man.

"Typical. When did you take them?"

"We swapped clothes to play a joke on your country club friends, don't you remember? They fell for it too, the idiots."

"Yeah, of course, so much happened last night."

"Which night?"

"You know, last night" blustered Marcel.

"We saw them on Thursday."

"Thursday?"

"Yep."

Marcel skin prickled at the thought of four unaccounted days. "We had a good time though?"

"Yeah, the best." Clem gave him a reassuring pat on the back. "I've got to find work. I'll see you later, okay?" Motioning for another drink, he finished it one swallow. Smacking his lips together, headed for the exit, leaving Marcel to examine the contents of his glass.

"Yeah."

As Clem passed the old men on the way to the door, he winked theatrically, to their annoyance.

Marcel's voice stopped him at the door. "Wait a minute." For a single moment, Clem's heart pounded hard enough for moisture to creep onto his brow.

"Yeah?"

"I'll talk to my father; see if I can't get you reinstated." Clem grinned with gratitude.

"Appreciate it. See you later."

11

Marcel ordered a shot of rum.

Four glasses later, he felt well enough to brace the midday heat. Shuffling past the magistrates' court, the only three-story building in town, he wondered how and when he and Clem managed to switch clothing. He settled himself on the steps of the town square fountain beside all the other dropouts and drunks alongside him, to watch the world go by. They, like he, had little else to do, but doze till the next shot.

He was too scared to face his father and too drunk to go to work.

If he still had a job himself.

As the sun stroked his skin, he absentmindedly rubbed away at it in mild revulsion, unaware of the raised raw patches of skin on his forearms and neck. He watched the lunchtime crowd swarm about the marketplace in their quest to find the perfect dining spot.

Marcel wandered light as a bubble drifting around his imaginary sky. His ears tuned into the sounds of laughter, playful chatter, and the occasional whisper of a melodic voice calling his name.

Searching it out, he drifted down to earth, the voice getting stronger and more insistent during his descent.

Ida stood over him gently slapping him about the face, her pert nose wrinkled in distaste. Hoisting her dainty bag up her forearm, she waved her gloved hand across her face in disgust.

"Wake up!"

Marcel groaned as every muscle screamed in protest.

"Look at you, you're disgusting."

He spat out a thick wad of phlegm before answering.

"Nice to see you, too."

He cleared his throat and repeatedly coughed, each one sending his body into painful spasms. Ida glanced at her watch, before plonking herself on the bench, waiting for the episode to pass. It eventually subsided, leaving Marcel weak and bleary-eyed. In silence, they sat watching the crowd heading back to the daily grind each person had to endure.

"Aren't you going back to work?"

She smoothed her full pleated skirt over her knees.

"I took the day off. Sitting here by the side of the road does seem extremely familiar."

Marcel briefly considered mugging someone for a cigarette as he patted all his pockets in vain. No doubt Clem had taken them, too.

"Aren't you going to ask me why?"

"No," he was not in the mood for games "I don't give a damn what you do. You take off, and now weeks later you waltz by. Where's your bank flunky? Leave me the hell alone, Ida."

Ida gaped in awe at his outburst.

"Don't look at me like that. Do you know I've been trying to talk you for ages? Your mother threatened to cut off my dick and give it to the Juju woman for her potions if I came by your house again, and your brother and cousins trashed my car."

"How do you know it was them?"

Marcel sighed with weariness. "I saw them when I came out of the bar, but they took off before I could whoop their asses. I've been over to the library, but that stuck up bitch said-"

Raising his voice an octave, he stuck his nose high in the air "-my girls don't fraternise with vagrants like you."

"Clem didn't tell me."

He spun to face her. The little gnome hacking away inside the recesses of his head with a hammer had turned unto an ugly troll with a pickaxe and an attitude problem.

"He comes by the house all the time. I saw him yesterday. He stayed for dinner."

"What has he been saying?"

"He said you were dealing with some 'hot piece.'"

"And you believed him."

Ida reluctantly dipped her head in agreement.

Marcel shrugged his shoulders in defeat.

"He also said that you often said women were like pebbles on a beach, and although I was a good lay, I was too much like hard work."

"You believed all that crap?"

"I don't know." Ida bit her lip self-consciously. Seeing the confusion plainly on her face, he took her gloved hand.

"Look, I don't know what Clem's playing at, but I didn't say any of that."

"You do realise I love you, don't you?"

"Why didn't you ever say it before without making a joke out of it?"

"I thought you knew that. It's not my way to say that kind of thing."

She smiled briefly. "Too macho for you."

"If you like." He lightly ran his fingers across her wrist. "All that mushy stuff sounds stupid. I don't know what he has been saying, but it's not from me."

Out the corner of his eye, he caught a glimpse of a familiar shirt in the crowd across the street. Marcel's face flushed with anger.

"Love is not stupid."

"You bastard!" As he rose to follow in hot pursuit, Ida's hand stalled him.

"Stop it."

He hollered across the square at the receding figure, drowning out Ida's pleas, glaring at the indignant lunch diners and sleep-deprived vagrants who were unlucky enough to be in his field of vision.

"You lying bastard! After what I've done for you, I thought you were a friend."

People paused to view the spectacle of a vagrant shouting to nobody in particular and the elegantly dressed woman who struggled to keep hold of him.

"Will you sit down?"

"I got thrown out of the Rodney Bay Country Club because of you. They think I stole that bracelet!"

"Marcel!"

"Now my real friends think I'm a thief like you!"

"Marcel!"

Incensed, he ignored Ida.

"I took you everywhere, introduced you to all my people. Now you come after me for a job AND my lady. Is that it? Is that why you have been filling her ears with filth? You didn't say any of that earlier in the bar, did you?"

"Marcel!"

He continued to bellow, spittle flying in all directions, regardless of his shirt having slipped away.

"Think you can do better than me, is that it? Want to get into her panties, huh?!"

"MARCEL, that's enough!!" Ida latched onto his arms, stepped in front of him and stared into his eyes blocking his view.

"What dammit?!"

"I'm pregnant."

12

They approached the door to his father's study door hand in hand.

His lips touched the tip of her nose inhaling her incredible scent; all the sweeter knowing that within in her body nestled a part of him. He straightened his tie and knocked on the door.

"Come."

Marcel ran a hand over his damp hair and pushed open the door. Even though he had hibernated for a few days to let the alcohol work its way through his system and had groomed himself fastidiously, still, he quailed at the idea of confronting his father.

With spectacles at half-mast and manicured hands steepled on his desk, sat Victor. The mahogany surface of the desk was barren but for a large manila envelope that fluttered slightly in the breeze floating in from the wide French doors.

"Sit down." Marcel stepped inside as Victor caught sight of his companion hovering in the doorway.

"You must be Miss Solomon. This meeting will be entertaining." He motioned for her to enter. Clutching her handbag to her breast as a shield, she entered the room.

Mouth agape at his father's knowledgeable disclosure, Marcel approached the chairs opposite his father's desk. Three were set out instead of the customary pair. His quizzical gaze produced chuckles from Victor.

"All in good time."

Marcel chose to speak before his courage fled as he and Ida took their seats.

"You wanted to see me sir, but I have something to say first." As he opened his mouth to continue, there was a soft knock at the door, and Mrs. James entered.

"Your visitor has arrived sir, shall I send him through?"

"Do that."

Marcel resumed his monologue, but his father's raised hand stopped him.

"I said, all in good time. First, I want you to meet someone."
They all turned as the door swung open. A man stepped through
the doorway, preceded by the housekeeper and waddled across the
immense room. His enormous torso rippled in its ill-fitting sand
coloured double-breasted suit, the lapels pushed into curved
pockets, cupped sagging breasts to which a sweat saturated oyster
silk shirt was plastered. The moon face above the tightly knotted
tie was flushed crimson with exertion. Fat beads of moisture
dripped onto the front of his jacket.

"How lovely to see you, sit down. Can I get you a drink"?

"Please. Island taxi drivers are horrid." He produced a damp
handkerchief and mopped his fleshy neck. In his hand, was a
similar large manila envelope.

"They are too lazy to make a living. Can't find a suitable one
on the whole island. Do you know, I had to walk from halfway
down the drive? The goat got fed up. Said the driveway was too
long. Too long!"

The armchair creaked under the weight of the excess flesh.
Victor stepped across to the drinks cabinet, mixed two drinks and
passed a glass to his guest. The offer was not extended to Ida nor
Marcel.

"Martini?"

A surprisingly slender hand gripped the drink against the lake
of stomach.

"Just what I need." The man exchanged his envelope for the
martini.

Victor placed it alongside its twin on the desk.

"This is my son." Marcel noted his father did not bother to
mention Ida despite the obvious interest from the visitor, so he
took it upon himself to take the initiative. Ida wrinkled her nose in
distaste. She cast a questioning glance at Marcel. He opened his
eyes wide in puzzlement in return.

"At your service madam." Ignoring the exchange, the man
doffed his Panama hat to reveal long, pale wisps of hair carefully
positioned across an expanse of heat reddened pate. As he nodded,
his chins gathered under his neck. A creeping uneasiness settled
about Marcel's chest in an unfamiliar, restricting band.

"And your name is?" The man held out his hand as a friendly gesture. Marcel shook it. It felt akin to holding warm and sticky mashed potato.

"Gordon, Edward Gordon." His ratty eyes raked over him.

"Now we're all one happy family, shall we get down to business?" Victor resumed his seat.

"But I need to speak to you first."

"Whatever it is can wait."

Marcel rose to his feet.

"No, it can't. Ida's pregnant and we want to get married." Too late to take it back now. If he thought his father would be outraged and shocked to the core, he was mistaken. Victor merely raised an eyebrow, his face blank.

"I never thought you had it in you."

"What?"

"I must say, how nice for you dear." Ida flinched in response. Marcel collapsed back into the armchair nonplussed.

"Now, Mr. Gordon, the stake you plan to invest sounds very nice but as you can see the commodity is tried and tested."

"Indeed, indeed." The obese man giggled conspiratorially sending ripples across the lake of his belly.

"It seems rather paltry in light of the new developments. Shall we add an extra 10% on each addition per year over the next ten years?" The proposal lingered in the air for long moments in the silence of the room. The only noises were Edwards's loud slurps of martini and the occasional ladylike sniff from Ida. Marcel cast a sidelong glance at her. Shame prevented her from looking anywhere but at her knees. His eyes prickled with unshed tears when he thought of the heartache he had gifted Ida. If her mother knew where she was just now, her skin would be peeled from her back with a strip of cured leather. Lost in a world of confusion, Marcel looked from his father to Charles and tried to decipher the conversation. The turn of events could not have been more different to what he had envisioned.

Charles cleared his throat.

"That sounds a reasonable proposal."

"What proposal? I'm going to marry Ida. We've already set the date and time with the local pastor, and we don't want your money or your approval. I'm telling you because it's what Ida wanted. We can just walk away from each other, and you don't ever have to be bothered with me again. Ida is all I want. We will find a way to get by."

In an impromptu gesture of good-will, he reached across to shake his father's hand. Victor's chair shot back against the wall faster than a cannonball blast.

"Get away from me, you subnormal ingrate."

Beads of perspiration broke upon his greying temples. Marcel had never seen his father simultaneously frightened and disgusted. He would never have thought it possible.

"You," Victor fought to compose himself "are for once in your life going to do as I tell you." He cast a hasty glance toward Ida. "I didn't know where you found this 'piece', but you're not marrying it.

"We love each other and want to get married. I don't see what the problem is. Our child needs a father."

"How do you know it's yours?"

Ida shot to her feet at the accusation.

"Marcel has been the only man I've ever been with."

Victor and Charles exchanged glances and smiled.

"So you say."

Marcel propelled her toward the front of the house.

"Let's go, we have said what we had come to say."

They had almost made it to the door before Edward spoke, his face grey, banana fingers twitching in agitation.

"Victor, I'm putting good money your way, do something."

"One more thing, Marcel."

Marcel glanced back. The room stank of greed and hate and he wanted no part of it. Victor held up one of the envelopes.

"Would you care to check this, my eyes aren't quite what they used to be."

His father's eyesight was magpie-sharp. His one glance had relayed a thousand messages of suspicion to Ida before he walked back to the desk beside Edward. Without looking at his son, Victor handed it over and turned his face towards the French doors to gaze out at the panoramic view, but not before Marcel caught his smile of immense satisfaction.

He opened the envelope.

Marcel felt a spike of fear drive deep into his chest, coupled with the burn of shame. The events of that night so many weeks ago still lost in the mists of inebriation. Unable to contest the photographic evidence along with the knowledge things would never be how he had dreamed of for the two of them, he staggered with the weight of the revelation.

Ida stepped forward. "Are you alright?"

He shook his head motioning her to retreat.

Uncertain what to do she stepped a little closer.

"What's wrong?"

"I'm fine. I'm okay." His voice shook as he tried to reassure her. Ida took another step as he moved away clutching the tan envelope. He folded himself into a corner; his body seemingly diminished in the high-ceilinged room and buried his head in his arms.

"Look at me Marcel." As she reached the point where he had once stood, she confronted Victor, who had turned to watch the spectacle.

"What's wrong with him?"

"Let's say, my dear, some people should take care when partaking in certain activities."

"What is that supposed to mean?"

Victor was not about to explain anything. He was thoroughly enjoying himself to Marcel's disgust, as was Edward, who tittered into his tiny square of cotton.

"This is for him, too, but as he's a little preoccupied. You can do the honours."

Pushing the second envelope to the edge of the desk, he sat back and waited. The clock slowly chimed the half hour as Ida cautiously reached for the envelope and stepped back. Glancing first at Victor then Marcel, she broke the seal with a fingernail and peered inside.

"Don't look at it." Marcel's voice was tiny in its wretchedness. "Put it down and walk away."

"I don't understand."

He lifted his head to reveal a tear streaked face, nose streaming. He drew his sleeve across his bleary eyes bringing her into focus.

"Don't. Please, Ida."

"Aren't you curious?" rasped Victor. "Don't you want to know what's going on? Why not show some guts and find out?" He leaned in closer as whisky fumes tickled her nostrils. "Or are you going to be a sheep and run away?"

"Don't listen to him." The pain conveyed in those few words brought Ida rushing to Marcel. Wrapping her arms around him, she rested her chin on his head.

"I don't understand what's going on."

He held onto her body as if she were a life-raft and he a drowning man.

"Do you love me, Ida?"

She kissed the top of his head. "You know the answer to that."

"Do you love me whatever the cost?"

"Don't be silly, you know I do. Now you are beginning to sound like one of those characters out of Vera's silly romance books."

Victor strolled over, picked up the fallen envelope and pulled out the contents.

"Evidently you're a sheep, my dear." He thrust the records under their noses. "Do you know who this is?"

In his hand lay a picture of a woman. Her long dark auburn tresses piled high in a chignon. The beauty portrayed made Ida catch her breath in awe.

"Should I?"

"I should say so, my dear. She is Marcel's fiancée." The look on her face made both Victor and Edward laugh aloud. "Don't you know anything?"

Slowly she drew away from her lover, her voice a cobweb of sound.

"Marcel, is it true?" He raised his head until his eyes rested on the picture. She watched every move, every nuance in those few moments as she watched him carefully for signs of familiarity. His eyes registered no recognition.

"I don't know her."

Victor's voice cut across the room.

"True enough, but you are going to marry her shortly."

"What have you done to Marcel? Why do you always torment him over everything? Can you not just leave us alone? I am just an island girl, but I can make him happy. We're getting married. I'm sorry you're not happy, but there's nothing you can do about it."

Victor took his time pouring himself and Edward another drink while Ida stood and gaped at his nonchalance. At her feet, Marcel continued to sob.

"You know…" he paused theatrically for maximum effect before continuing. "Marcel has always been a lazy wastrel. Partying all night, and sleeping all day. He is my only son. All I have will be in his control one day, or would be if he made a decent account of himself. He needs to stop playing around with the local whores."

Ida's mouth dropped open in disbelief.

"It has come to my attention my son has been enjoying your company these days, and until recently, I must say that it did bother me somewhat. You will be pleased to know that I consider it a small matter that no longer concerns me." Marcel dared to glance up to find his father glaring at him, no doubt fighting the urge to kick him or beat him to a pulp with his fists.

"What does bother me is what he was doing one particular Sunday night." He turned his attention to his son. "Are you going to show her or shall I?"

Indecision played across Ida's face. She was reluctant to stay and listen, yet was unable to make herself leave.

"It's not necessary." Marcel clutched the envelope tighter. "What do you want?"

"NOW you're beginning to see the light. How wonderful. Where shall we start? You are going to marry your fiancé in a few weeks."

Ida looked on, a pawn in a game where the rules were a mystery to her.

Marcel's heart skittered in his chest. The air grew heavy with unspoken words. Victor advanced toward the couple. He was almost close enough to seize the envelope from his son's hand when Marcel finally spoke.

"Alright, whatever you want, just leave Ida out of whatever you do."

A strange high-pitched keening sound cut through the quiet room.

"I will find a way to make things right, Ida. Please don't cry."

"You don't mean it."

"Yes, he does." Victor made himself comfortable once again behind his desk and opened a desk drawer.

"I DON'T WANT TO HEAR IT FROM YOU!"

Edward spluttered into his drink at the unexpected outburst, wincing at the desperation in Ida's voice.

"Marcel?"

There was no response.

"Marcel, I'm not going anywhere; we're the ones getting married."

She brushed tears from her eyes as she forced the words out.

"TELL HIM! TELL HIM, MARCEL, DON'T JUST SIT THERE YOU BASTARD, GET UP AND TELL HIM!"

Victor looked pointedly at his watch, stepped toward her, and dropped a tiny slip of paper down the front of her blouse before she could protest.

"This is cosy, but we have legal matters to attend to, you must excuse us."

Marcel rose from the floor, approaching her on unsteady feet. In his pocket, protruded the offending envelope. As she looked deep into his eyes, the reality of the situation dawned on her. Kissing her softly, he pushed something into her hand and closed her fingers around it.

"Take care of our baby."

As he left the library, he allowed himself one last glance at her.

A look long enough to last a lifetime.

Eyes closed against tears and pain, perspiration slipping down her, face Ida slumped to the floor.

13

Clem was in a quandary.

He swung his floral scythe as he wandered along the dirt road. Occasionally his hand pressed against the breast pocket of his jacket. Each time he was rewarded with the soft crinkle of paper.

He still hadn't decided what to do with the letter.

One evening months past, he had padded bare-footed to the bottom of the Aubertine's grand staircase, his pockets bulged with trinkets. Intent on leaving via the library patio doors like a man, the oak panels opened as his hands slipped around the ornate handles.

Creeping to a corner of the hallway like a spider, he stole a glance at the emerging figures. In the gloom of dusk, he saw an astoundingly large pale, alien head above a light-coloured suit, giving the impression of an eerie apparition.

"Damn those taxi drivers!"

He slinked down the hallway till he found a window left ajar. He gently eased the wood upward and slid out feet first till he hung by his fingernails from the ledge. His body fell to the sun-bleached gravel with a soft crunch.

"It was the only one I could find at this time of the evening. He refused to drive up here. He's waiting for you at the gatehouse. I can accompany you, or you can stay here tonight, Edward. I apologise for, not being able to provide you with the services of my driver. It is his half day off."

He had just seen the chauffeur examining the contents of the cleaners blouse in the kitchen while she wore it.

The man waved a plump hand in dismissal. There didn't seem to be any affection or friendship between them. Clem wondered what business brought the two together.

"What about the girl? What are you going to do about her?"

Clem's ears perked up with interest. What girl? He scoured his mind for a reason two old men would be interested in a girl.

He didn't like the result his brain calculated. He wondered who she was.

"My staff will attend to her. There is nothing for you to worry about. Everything is in hand. Go home and set things in motion."

The apparition named Edward appeared unperturbed by the 'taking care of the girl.' He appeared more bothered by the trauma of trekking to the taxi seen idling beyond the wrought iron gates at the end of the drive. His mind raced with murder-mystery possibilities.

Would Victor kill the girl?

Would he put her in a car and push it off a cliff?

Maybe she was to be fed to sharks at dawn. He wouldn't mind seeing that.

"Scum of the world, these people. You would never get such treatment in New York." The man puffed and wheezed as he negotiated his way down the concrete stairs.

"Telephone to ensure the wedding date is suitable."

Clem smacked his lips in anticipation. He loved a good wedding. Lots of free liquor and the rare occasion a man could kiss a married woman, and her freshly hitched husband didn't slice your throat.

"Not to worry, I will prepare Arianne on her nuptials," he chuckled. The hairs on Clem's neck rose at the sound. "I'm certainly looking forward to this partnership I can tell you. Profitable, very profitable, indeed."

"If that is all, good night." He watched as Victor raised his hand briefly, to disappear inside the house and close the door.

"Cursed taxi drivers, it's enough to give a man a heart attack," muttered the big head named Edward as he lumbered down the drive.

Eager for more information, Clem clambered onto the terrace using the rosebush trellis as a ladder. He let himself into the silent house and up the stairs to Marcel's room, scurrying past the study where Victor had entrenched himself, judging by the clink of crystalware. He illuminated Marcel's room but found it empty. He scanned the pristine dimensions before checking the contents of the drawers and bedside table for clues. The scent of aftershave saturated the air, seeping into his clothes and leaving a sour taste in his mouth. Marcel needed to cut back on the perfume.

Otherwise, folk would start thinking he was a Nancy-Boy. He helped himself to a few more items of interest before heading to the bathroom for a bottle, or two of something sweet-smelling before Marcel showed up.

Pushing open the door, the overpowering stench of aftershave hit him like a tsunami.

Inside lay utter carnage.

Scent bottles lay scattered across the chequerboard floor. Jars were strewn everywhere including in the sunken bath, their contents seasoned with glittering shrapnel. Every surface was thick with shaving cream marbled with rivulets of blood rendering the scene macabre. Amongst the chaos sat Marcel, his glassy black eyes fixed on Clem. He held an empty bottle of whisky in one hand, in the other his razor and a letter. Clem wished he could read it.

From Marcel's numbed lips, only one word bubbled out. "Ida."

Against his better judgement, Clem roused the housekeeper. The old woman never stopped moaning as she put her teeth in and took her curlers out. She insisted on being presentable at all times in the presence of her employer. Only then did she check on Marcel at the insistence of Clem and alerted Victor. By the time the clock in the hallway had struck the half hour, the whole house was in an uproar. Not that Clem cared.

He was long gone by then.

Clem attempted to visit Marcel in the hospital, but the nuns refused his entry. Not that it bothered him. He was a busy man over the following days. Not having gotten anywhere with Marcel, he looked for the next information source. The girl in question had to be Ida, judging by the state of Marcel. Whatever was going on, she was the crux of it. There was talk in town that she was found late one night wandering in a ravine clutching a scrap of paper in one hand and something in her fist even the strongest labourer failed to prise open.

When Clem visited her over the weeks, Ida was in a permanent daze. He always took fancy trinkets when he visited or accompanied her to the library on the few days she attended work. All the while her waist got thicker, not that anyone but him noticed. She hid it well, but Clem was no dummy.

He had sisters. He knew the midwife would soon be knocking on their front window.

At times, they would share milkshakes at lunch. His new workmates down at the waterfront barely saw him, but Clem didn't care.

Sometimes, he and Ida talked, sometimes not.

Sometimes she read the local paper, and he scowled at the black scratches on the folded paper as they sat together, sometimes not.

Try as he might, she would not talk about anything to do with Marcel.

Clem told only one person of the existence of the letter. It wasn't Ida.

One lunchtime a few weeks later, he was gazing at the sports pictures while Ida read the front pages of the same paper. She abruptly collected her handbag, mumbled something about returning to work and disappeared.

He sat alone with a mouthful of banana shake and a frown.

It was only twenty minutes into her lunch hour.

Nonplussed at her strange behaviour, he idly flicked to the front page to be confronted with a picture of an emaciated Marcel with a beautiful woman with vacant eyes wrapped around him.

The way forward was pretty clear to him after that.

"I'm taking flowers to some girl whose kid isn't mine. I must be all kinds of fool." He looked upon the flowers expectantly. He resumed his leisurely pace as he continued to chatter.

"Of course I feel real bad for her, so I've got to do my bit to help, you understand." His comrades wilted a little further in the suffocating humidity of the day.

Unthwarted, he continued.

"I'm a concerned friend who cares that's all." He struck a sympathetic pose with his companions drawn up under his nose. He held them close for a few seconds before dissolving into laughter spiked with shards of hysteria. He spun them around his body with arms outstretched to the sun. Clem stopped in a tiny scorched bald patch in the middle of the tropical greenery and stood to regimental attention.

"I'll deliver that letter to Ida, yes sir, you can be sure of that. You can go to Brazil safe in the knowledge she will get the envelope first thing in the morning. You write a letter in the middle of the night to my girlfriend before you try to kill yourself, like some kind of Hollywood star." Step by step, he picked through the dense foliage towards his destination.

"I was busy that morning, so I left it for the next day. Do you know what? I was busy again. In fact, I've been real busy for a long time now, so she'll have to get your mail when I'm good and ready. If I feel like it."

Having dealt with the matter at hand, he navigated through the foliage toward the symphony of many metal instruments pounding soil. As he passed, each labourer respectfully greeted him, the elderly and young alike. He nodded, superior in his dandified finery. He brushed past weary field hands in their soiled rags and dust choked lace-less shoes as he followed the pungent smell of cigar smoke hung in the air like a beacon until he reached his final destination.

Arranging his face suitably, he addressed the back of the bullhead.

"I've just arrived, sir."

The burly man flexed its enormous back muscles for a few seconds before turning to him.

"Where you been, boy?" The few remaining tobacco-tinged teeth clamped themselves around a large cigar nub.

Tendrils of fear meandered down his spine, but he respectfully kept his head angled toward to the gigantic hob-nailed remnants of leather that had once been work boots.

Eyeballing Pa Rochard was an expensive affair if you had no health insurance.

Out the corner of his eye, he saw the closest workers fall back to a safer observation distance in amongst the sugar cane.

"My boss made me run an errand for him, sir. I had to pick up supplies."

Pa Rochard digested the news as the cigar swivelled across his wide mouth. Clem waited patiently as he watched a long-haired spider creep into the open toe of his father's boot.

Mental agility was not one of his Pa's strengths.

"So, you gittin' presidential treatment."

"Yes, sir."

Pa raised his voice for the benefit of the many ears supposedly hacking away at the tough cane stalks.

"Looks like yous'e gittin' plans boy."

His reward was a pat on the back with a hairy paw leaving him momentarily stunned. Pa crossed his thick forearms and rocked back on his heels to contemplate his eldest child from his slicked back hair to his winkle-picker shoes.

"So where you headin' fixed up like some prize hog?" Grabbing both jacket lapels in one gigantic grime encrusted fist, he yanked him close. They stood toe to toe and eyeball to eyeball. Pa Rochard swept his hand over Clem's oily head.

"Dat my pomade boy?" Cuffing him about his head, he sniffed the air. Clem tried not to peer into the twin caverns and what may have lain within, but as always, succumbed to his curious nature.

"Who you eyeballin' boy! I said dat ma pomade?"

"No, sir!" He waited for the next blow, but his pa satisfied at present, snorted his agreement.

"So, where is you goin'?" Clem brushed at himself, trying not to think of how much he still owed on the suit.

"To Ida Solomon's house, sir. I came as soon as you sent word."

"Dat' so?" Pa stepped back to have a quiet word with the terrorised supervisor before pushing Clem to a small clearing away from the main work crew.

"She's had dat' baby then'?"

Pa's conspiratorial voice sounded harsh in the quiet surroundings.

"Yes sir, she had it four days ago."

"Well, what it be den?"

"A boy, I don't know what the baby called."

Pa mulled over the information.

"Dat's good, the boy's always best as a first-born. Aint dat right, boy?" His father winked conspiratorially.

His face flared with heat at the rare compliment.

"Yes, sir."

"So" his father snorted, spitting a thick glob of mucus millimetres from Clem's foot. How you know about everything?"

He tried not to baulk at the string of spittle spattered across his gleaming shoes.

"I know one of her girlfriends, from that birthday dinner, the one I told you about. Her nickname is Bubbles."

"Oh, dat' fat one I see'd you with. You giving her sugar, son?"

He squirmed uncomfortably. "No, sir."

His father clapped him on the shoulder with the force of a rhino.

"A man needs a little loving where he can get it, son."

"She's been seeing Ida though her daddy is vexed and told Bubbles not to be seen out with Ida, in case people think she's loose too." Pa Rochard's eyes lit up with mischief. "So," he hurried on, "Ida was sacked from her job. The sow who runs it said she was setting a bad example. Her parents sent her off to some crazy aunt out in the country to have it on account of people talking real bad about them. They had to hide her somewhere. Ma Solomon is well-respected in the church."

"I know. Damn bitch tried to convert me only coupla' years back. Said I had to stop beating on your mother. Can you believe it! I treat her good."

Clem clamped his tongue fast with his teeth.

"I hope you going to reach there like I tole you."

"Yes, sir."

"Don't fuck this up, boy. You know your brain can't hold shit. You'se gotta hol' onto that woman. She down now but she a good woman, she smart. Shit, her whole family smart. You mess up, and you be cutting cane jest like me. I had big plans before I got way-hayed by that bitch with a fat ass called your mother and look what happened to me. You hear me, boy!"

"Yes, sir." Standing to attention, he tried to ignore the landing strip hair on the head the colour of dung directly in his line of vision.

Too late.

"What you looking at boy?"

"Nothing sir."

Having been struck by his father countless times over the years, he still was ill-prepared when it arrived. He was sure a cow had hit him.

"Don't mess with me boy or you's going down!" Staggering on his feet, Clem found the sweet-smelling hibiscus rolled in the brightly-coloured paper strangely soothing.

"Yes, sir."

Pa Rochard flexed his muscles and preened self-righteously. "Get over to Ma Solomon's house and go court dat girl. Keep making a good friend outta her ma, and when dat' time is right ask her if she want to see dat her daughter married to a fine man like youse."

"Yes, sir." Uncertain of whether to wait up for more orders or leave, he hovered from one foot to the other.

"Well, what you waiting for, Christmas?"

Yes sir, I mean no sir." He had taken a few steps before his father hailed him.

"Clem?"

"Sir?"

"What did you do wid' dat' letter Marcel gave you for her?"

"I burnt it up."

"Good boy, it ain't nothing but trouble."

300lbs of muscle gone to fat lumbered back to the work detail crew. The men had cut sugarcane in record time toward the clearing and the most fascinating conversation they had heard in a long time. Faster in the last half hour than of the whole day, to get a ringside view.

"You folks trying to git in my business?"

"No, sah'!"

"Too busy cutting cane."

"Hear what?"

Clem quickened his steps. He did not want to see his taking on an unwilling sparring partner again, so he left him warming up his rhetoric brandishing a stout piece of cane at his co-workers.

"Don't get all fresh, I still got me some moves for y'all. Sonny Liston, a Girl Guide, compared to me."

"Is that why you are still cutting cane bundles on the dollar with spiders up your ass?" muttered Clem as he followed the track leading up the hill.

The sun had begun its slow decline when he arrived at the Solomon household. The flowers were well past liquid resuscitation. As Clem rapped on the front door, butterflies darted about his stomach as he waited on the front porch of the single story dwelling.

Vera appeared at the window. Her tense, pinched face relaxed into a welcoming smile. She unlocked the door and let him in, accepting the crispy offering as he stepped past her into the narrow hallway. He began his second best performance of the day. Setting his voice to just the right pitch for a concerned friend, he enquired after Ida and her mother. He followed Vera's curvaceous body into the parlour where all manner of religious paraphernalia adorned every surface of the oxygen deprived room.

Settling into a lumpy armchair complete with starched crocheted armrests, he did his best not to fidget as he was subjected to endless of drivel concerning the birth of the child. Sweat crept from his pores and trickled through his close-cropped hair to gather at his temples. He interjected as soon as Veronica paused for breath. It took several minutes.

"So what's the baby called?"

"I didn't tell you, did I? It's Ivan." She took one look at the surprise on his face and burst into an infectious snigger he caught in seconds. At that moment, the similarity between her and her younger sister was illuminated, to die just as suddenly as Vera's humour evaporated.

"I know, it's terrible. We watched Ivanhoe at the church hall a while back. The pastor has a brother that gets them on the cheap if you catch my drift. Don't tell ma, though. That child one day is going to thank me for persuading her to drop the "Hoe" bit.

"Well," he rubbed his hands over his face to quell the grin that refused to budge, "it's different."

"It's that, alright."

"At least he," he leaned forward "it is a he isn't it?"

Vera nodded her assent, delicate hands covering her mouth, eyes dancing with merriment.

"He is healthy I suppose. Any chance of saying hello?"

Vera jumped to her feet, smoothing out her many net petticoats.

"I'm sorry. Of course. You should have stopped me earlier."

"If it's no trouble."

"Oh, it's no trouble at all."

Following her lead, he furtively glanced about him.

"Is your mother okay with me being here?"

"Fine," glancing back, she threw him a reassuring smile, "don't worry. She made my father take her to a church revival in Martinique."

"I wasn't trying to avoid her."

A corner of Veras's mouth curled upward in response.

Following her lead, he admired the sway of her shapely hips as she sashayed along the hallway. All the doors were ajar except one, behind which a male off-key voice practised Little Richard's hit song "Long Tall Sally".

Don't mind that, Joe is listening to his devil music again." She rolled her eyes heavenward.

"I'll see you later." Never one to pass up the benefit of an audience, Vera swung her hips with her hands hitched to her waist for maximum effect as she stepped further down the hall before disappearing into her room. He pushed open the door and stepped inside.

Late afternoon shadows splayed across the spartan room, to caress the crude homemade cross on the furthermost wall. A figure lay on a wooden bed in the corner. He tiptoed across the whitewashed floorboards and peeped into the frayed Moses basket.

It was empty.

He stared with undisguised longing at Ida in repose. Her skin gleamed like honey in the weak light as her silky raven hair spilled across the crisp ivory sheets, her full lips parted in contentment. Clasped to her chest, a small bundle of fabric moved.

He found an unadorned breast forgotten in slumber after suckling, a smooth, generous mound topped by a delicious aureole. Fighting the urge to trace his finger over the dark nub, he drank his fill for long minutes. His fingers twitched in anticipation of tracing a line down the valley between her breasts, under the bedclothes and beyond. Before his imagination caused him to perform misdeeds in view of the Blessed Cross, he coughed.

She did not stir.

Placing himself near the head of the bed, he touched an arm resting above the sheets.

"Ida."

Beautiful, sleepy eyes opened to rest on him.

"Hi, how are you?"

"Fine. A little tired." She moved the baby closer to her bosom. Her eyes flew open with the realisation her nightdress gaped. Clutching at the neck of the flowery cloth with one hand, she struggled to sit up.

Desperate to find something for his fingers to do before mischief found them first, he held out his hand.

"Let me take the baby."

Holding the small bundle at arms length, he wondered how he got in this predicament. As Ida fussed over her night dress, he took a moment to look at the unremarkable arrival.

Clem scowled at the scrunched up face the colour of Courvoisier swirled in cream and Marcel's black eyes which glared back in anger and resentment. The scrap of humanity stank of talcum powder, petroleum jelly and shit. The baby's thick ebony hair stood to attention in one giant cowlick. Clem took an instant dislike to the new man in Ida's life but wasn't going to let the child derail his plans. He would deal with the boy if he gave him any trouble.

"You're the only visitor I've had apart from Bubbles."

Clem cooed at the miniature troll with mock affection.

"I'm sure you'll have plenty tomorrow."

She cast him a strange look.

"I was talking about AT ALL since I've had Ivan. After all I've done, it's a wonder my mother didn't throw me onto the street, never mind entertain visitors. I humiliated her in the eyes of the church. She beat me for days."

"Oh."

"Don't worry it's okay. She has calmed down a bit now." Ida gestured for him to return the baby.

"He's a cute boy." Her mouth slipped into a shy smile as she took Ivan back. Clem thought maybe it was sheer coincidence, but then, oblivious to Ida, the baby stuck its tongue out at him.

"I think so, but I would of course." Attempting to smooth the cowlick down, she hummed softly to the baby.

"I can see you're going to be a devoted mother" he simpered for good measure and strategically seated himself on the snowy bedspread for the best cleavage view on offer. He put his battle plan into action.

"What are you going to do now?"

Ida took her time answering as Clem struggled to keep his knees from jiggling with impatience.

"I'm not sure. I want to go back to the library, but I don't think the old cow will have me back. My mother saw an advertisement in the paper, and she wants me to do that. I saw it before, but I wasn't keen on it."

"What's that?" He didn't see any pictures of interest in any paper. Rubbing the baby's back, she rested her head against the fluffy pillows.

"The British Government is looking for people from the colonies to work in the mother country. They have a workforce shortage."

A cold, distant land where one had to toil endlessly to pay for warmth. Why do all that when you could stay put and stay warm for free? He had heard the streets were paved with gold, but when his uncle wrote his mother after leaving in 1948 from Jamaica on the SS. Windrush, he said it was a living nightmare.

"It could be a good start for me."

He detected an element of excitement in her voice.

"And at least people won't know what happened and criticise me for it."

"What about Marcel?"

There. He had said it.

Silence invaded the confines of the room.

"Are you going to contact him?"

"Ivan doesn't have a father."

He struggled to contain the relief that bubbled inside him, threatening to spill into uncontained joy. Gazing out the window, Ida continued.

"I wasn't keen on the idea of going to England because I would have to leave Ivan with my mother." Snuggling closer to the baby, she whispered in his minute ear. "Mummy doesn't want to do that does she? Mummy loves her babies." Ivan stretched a tiny hand in slumber towards his mother and curled around her index finger. Ida smiled in contentment.

Ignoring the baby crap, Clem pressed for more information.

"When are you planning on leaving?" There had to be a way of making the disclosure work to his advantage.

"When Ivan's about six months old. My father has relatives in London, so all my mother has to do is make a few arrangements. I have little saved for any paid lodgings, which means my family has to borrow money to afford a passage. It is nearly sixty English pounds!"

"But it's too cold. You'll freeze over there."

"Well, I should feel fine, seeing as it's just as chilly around here." Ida jiggled Ivan from one arm to the other.

"But I've heard those English people are strange."

She cast him a sideways glance as she raised Ivan to sniff his nappy.

"Strange how?"

He played with the soft folds of the blanket, avoiding her inquiring gaze.

"My uncle lives there and says they eat their food out of newspapers!"

"Really?"

"Yep."

"Wow."

"And they wash themselves only once a month but wash their hair three times a day." Her eyes flew open in disbelief.

"Lies!"

Clem threw up his hands in defeat. "That's what my uncle says, and he should know, he's lived there for years." She digested the news for long minutes as he watched. Squaring her shoulders she came to a decision.

"I can't stay here, and it's far enough for me to be anonymous. We thought about St Croix, but a friend of my mothers is going to live there, and her mouth is as wide as the Ganges River."

"Why don't you fight it out here?" He drew closer to her and ventured a squeeze of her knee through the bedclothes. "You know I'm on your side."

Laughing, she patted his hand then firmly removed it.

"For a man I hated not too long ago, you're not annoying these days." Her icy stare pierced through to his white blood cells, "But don't get fresh."

Flashing a toothy smile, he stood to his feet. "I'd best be going as I'm sure you could do with the rest."

Ida made no move to detain him.

"I am still quite tired."

He bent down to kiss her, but she tilted her head a fraction at the last second in the guise of attending to Ivan. He placed a chaste kiss on her forehead and retreated.

 "Can I visit again?"

"Of course, it would be great." Smiling in pleasure, he departed.

He fancied if he had opened the door again, he would have most probably found Ida poking her tongue out at him in a most unladylike fashion.

1958

14

It had been difficult, but it was over. The day had finally arrived. As Ma Solomon watched the SS. San Marini depart, long held tension slipped away. The further the ship got from shore; the better Ma Solomon felt. She could still see Ida waving her kerchief from the railings. Ma elbowed her husband in the hip. It should have been the ribs, but the man would insist on being so damn long.

"Let's go."

"But Ida's still waving, we can't go yet."

"Now!" Grabbing hold of the piece of rope that doubled as a belt she gave a yank and drew him forward. Back ramrod straight, Ma conducted herself as royalty at all times and today was no exception. The crowd turned as one as she negotiated her way through the milling crowd of abandoned loved ones. They in turn shuffled aside for the mean-mouthed midget and her Frankenstein husband.

Everyone knew about her daughter and the rich man's son, but where many relished the idea of making Ida a social outcast, only a fool would make an enemy out of Ma Solomon. She had the ear of every religious dignitary on the island. Her husband had not a hope in hell of controlling her.

With eyes downcast, Pa Solomon followed as always, several paces behind his wife. Sniggers behind them only succeeded in making Ma Solomon all the more superior, and him feel all the more stupid. He never understood the turn of events that changed a once happy couple into master and servant, and Ma Solomon never enlightened him.

"I'm going to the bakery to order our bread for next week."

Ma spun around. A bony finger prodded him in the chest. "Man cannot live by bread alone but by the blood of Jesus."

"I'll leave it till tomorrow then."

Confusion marred his broad forehead. He couldn't see what God had to do with their breakfast, but he kept his thoughts to himself. It was better that way.

He followed in silence.

When they were courting, they were happy and in love. She was beautiful, exquisite, charming. Very much like Ida was now. In a matter of months, she had turned from an engaging woman with a sunny disposition to a religious harpy. Maybe he should have fled, but she was pregnant, and he would not shirk his responsibility.

The early days when Ma and Pa Solomon were a loving couple were but a memory.

As they retraced their steps home, Ma made her calculations.

With Ida away for five years, Ma Solomon would have plenty of time with her new grandson.

Things didn't seem too disagreeable. Whatever people thought of Ida, they knew better than to treat her or any of her family with disdain. Soon Ivan would be calling her mother, which was just, seeing as she had banished one child, she received another in return. Ma Solomon muttered a quiet 'Thank you, Jesus.'

Pa cast his wife a dubious look.

Ma powered up the hill, her husband wheezing in tow as she recounted the events of the previous day. Heat seeped into her fusty clothing as jewels of sweat gathered at her brow; Pa struggled to keep up, his tattered shirt flapping in the salty breeze.

Ever mindful of the day Jesus took on the moneylenders in the souk, Ma had gone to The Windward Co-Operative Bank in town reciting Proverbs Three. Clutching a bag full of Eastern Caribbean currency to change into English Sterling, she bumped into Victor and his son in the overcrowded office.

Marcel had seen her first. Otherwise, she would have slipped away into the crowd and out the office.

Marcel's voice was friendly and cordial.

"Good morning, Mrs. Solomon."

Victor's eyes gleamed in recognition. "Well, if it isn't Jezebel's mother."

Marcel visibly winced at his father's condescending tone as he walked past into the manager's artificially alpine-fresh office.

Her back stiffened at the insult.

"Good morning unbelievers of the healing blood of Jesus."

She turned her back to them and headed for the dumpy cashier. Ma Solomon hadn't bargained on Marcel's tenacity. He followed her into the bank; his intended business with his father but a memory.

"How is Ida?"

"Fine."

Digging deep into the sackcloth bag, Ma Solomon counted out her cash.

Marcel moved closer. Her nose twitched at the spiciness of his fancy aftershave.

"Is she well?"

"Fine."

All well and good to be thinking of Ida now thought Ma Solomon, but if he had done that in the first place, she wouldn't be spending the family's savings on fixing the problem. She wished he and his demon father would leave her alone.

"Any news about the baby?"

He pressed closer, ignoring the growing interest of the inquisitive bank teller. "Has she had it yet?"

"None of your business."

"It's my baby, too!" The noise inside the busy bank dissipated. Ma Solomon's back snapped ramrod straight and resolute.

"Do you know if she received my letter?" hissed Marcel.

Drawing back as if stung, she made the sign of the cross inches from his face. "Get behind me Satan, your wickedness will not work on me, for I am a child of God."

Satan or no Satan, Marcel seemed determined to find out about Ida and his child. He pressed closer.

"Is this man bothering you, madam?"

A slight inclination of her head was all that was required to set off the security guard's finest cowboy impression. Drawing himself up to his full height of five feet and a scattering of inches, he stuck his thumbs into his front belt loops with feet apart. He pursed his lips, all set to draw his imaginary gun. A chew of tobacco was all he needed to complete the re-enactment.

"We don't take to folks harassing our women 'round these parts."

"I'm not doing anything. I just want to know about my woman and our baby." Marcel looked uncertain as if he didn't know what to do first. He seemed uncertain whether to prise the information out of her or punch the security man. He cast a glance at the manager's glass partitioned office. Maybe he was going to storm in there and strike the mocking grin off his father's face. He settled on glaring at the teller, who, having completed the transaction for Ma was generously spreading gossip. Not only was the public looking at them, the bank staff were also. Ma Solomon retrieved her new money and headed for the door.

Marcel trailed after her, followed by the security cowhand.

"I'm afraid you'se gonna hafta wait here till the little lady's gone, suh."

"I need to speak to her!"

"If you wanna git fresh ah kin accommodate you." From his pocket, the security guard produced his unused pride and joy.

"Okay, okay." Marcel didn't seem to like the look of the shiny solid-looking handcuffs. He retreated to the sanctity of the manager's office, much to the security cowhands' disappointment who returned to his corner by the potted palm mumbling to himself about batons.

Ma Solomon fled the bank. She hoped Marcel hadn't noticed what bills she had exchanged the Eastern Caribean Dollars for.

Outside, a tiny smirk brightened her sour demeanour. She had returned from the lion's den triumphant. The Aubertine family would not deceive her again. She had become too powerful for that.

Once home, she distributed the cash to Ida. She did not mention Marcel.

The ship had sailed.

Ivan was hers.

According to the newspapers, Marcel was due to marry another woman, and would soon be gone, knowing nothing of his son.

Ma stopped in the middle of the dirt track. Pa Solomon, distracted by thoughts of lunch, ran into her.

"Fool!"

She pushed him off. Where was she? Oh yes, Clem. She hadn't seen him for a few days.

He was such a lovely boy. Real manners, and so polite and considerate. It was a shame things didn't work out differently. She would have liked him as a son-in-law. Ida was lucky he had visited often. When he heard of the date of departure for Ida, he seemed unusually jubilant for a man who was about to lose a good friend.

At that moment, two men were travelling in opposite directions with one thing on their mind. Ma Solomon hadn't bargained on Marcel's tenacity. Despite his hatred toward his father, he was still an Aubertine, and failure wasn't something they excelled in.

After Marcel had departed from the bank with his father, he returned an hour before the close of business. His suspicions were confirmed by the bank teller.

Ida was on her way to England.

Sitting back in his seat on his father's private plane, he ran through all possibilities to avoid the impending nuptials and abandon his father to find Ida.

As for Clem -

He reclined in his cabin across from Ida's in the bowels of the ship. He had waited patiently for the beginning of Plan B, courtesy of his father's money and somewhat dubious connections with the Port Authority. He smiled to himself and hummed in time with the vibration of the engines, oblivious to his cabin mate's glances from the top bunk, where the worried man lay.

Life was sweet.

He had a new life awaiting him in England, money in his pocket, a beautiful girl across the corridor and two weeks crossing time in which to woo her.

15

Ida's long, artfully curled tresses crept upward into a transformed halo of fizzy puff.

She was past caring. Most women on board soon found it was impossible to maintain a decent coiffure, with the ever-present mist of icy sea spray. As she stood on the deck of the SS. San Marini in the early morning light, the Channel winds buffeted her on all sides, stripping moisture from exposed skin.

She knew things would be tough, but never had imagined the true horror of a transatlantic crossing.

Clad in a thin cotton dress and cardigan, she hopped from one sandaled foot to the other. Clamping her elegant ivory and bronze clutch bag to her chest, she battled against the freezing Atlantic elements for supremacy of her minuscule hat. Even her hands, encased in white crochet, were raw. Beside her, fellow travellers all equally ill-equipped for the final leg of their journey muttered amongst themselves. In Zoot suits and Panama hats, the men were handsome in warmer weather, and calmer seas, boasting to all with idle ears. They went head-to-head with big talk of anticipated success in England. The women, with their pointed bosoms and dainty legs, lingered on every word, oblivious to the rabble of children in their Sunday best weaving among the throng. The crewmen chuckled at such talk, having heard it before on the same journey countless times. That was when the ship bobbed in the calm Caribbean Sea.

Before they were in rough Atlantic waters.

Ominous cliffs loomed on the horizon. With the end in sight, hundreds of seasick passengers voiced misgivings about the mother country. Ida, as usual, kept to herself and said little to her shipmates. She knew they thought her snobbish, preferring Clem, the friendlier of the two, but she didn't care. Even now, she could feel their stares burn into her back as she clung to the railing on the listing deck while the wind bruised her lips. Clem was below deck, warm and comfortable, as everyone froze on the deck for the first glance of their new home.

Ida didn't know what to make of him sometimes.

The last person she expected to see and get attached to was Clem. She was glad to see him, once she had gotten over the shock of finding him aboard fleecing passengers of bed sheets in a poker game. They had become good friends. A familiar face from back home among a mass of confused passengers from a dozen islands. With disembarkation imminent, her stomach lurched at the prospect of being without him.

As always, her thoughts strayed to Ivan. She had no idea when she would see her son, but she hoped it would be soon.

Disembarkation and immigration were a long, tedious exercises executed in near silence by the officials. The exception of occasional backhanded comments in the nature of 'them darkies', 'it's not proper', and 'those strange people.' Sometimes it was hard to determine whether it was the officials or the immigrants which muttered the latter.

It was 11.03pm by the time the British Rail train pulled into London's Victoria Station and spewed its frozen, exhausted, and bewildered passengers from its damp interior. They searched for welcomes, most of which were early morning cleaners, grudgingly waiting for family and friends. Refreshed from his nap on the train in his newly acquired seaman's coat, Clem carried one of Ida's suitcases onto the main concourse.

The Salvation Army assisted their new friends from the sun into adequate outerwear and shepherded forgotten immigrants to temporary accommodation in Clapham. Ida found herself in possession of a moss coloured wool coat. Eventually, she stood in front of her angular cousin Bernice and slimy husband Clifford with their brood of unruly children, before being whisked away as soon as bare pleasantries allowed. There was no opportunity to find a pen or paper to jot down her cousins address for Clem.

With no Uncle Felix in sight, as the old man having stopped at the pub en-route to the station forgot the reason he left home, Clem ended up a hostel in Westbourne Park for the night. In time, he decided to forgo his relative to share a bed-sit with a Barbadian porter, two Senegalese students, and a Jamaican bus-conductor.

It snowed all of February and brought London to a standstill. Ida had never seen snow, nor a country so dirty. She soon developed a phlegmy cough from the ever-present smog that hung in the air like mucus. Each morning at first light, she rose from the cot she shared with her cousins' youngest child. Her first chore was to light the paraffin heater and make cornmeal porridge for the family, under strict guidelines from her cousin. Ida often wondered as she queued with other families on the third floor to use the solitary filthy bathroom, why the woman didn't make breakfast herself and let her be.

Ida always hoped there would be enough hot water for her to wash. More more often than not she was forced to wash with chill murky water in the bathroom tundra after a quick visit to the outside privy. Dressing behind the modesty curtain she erected to deter Clifford's wandering gaze completed her toilette, and she was late for another day at work. Ida always ended up racing out of the front door of the dilapidated house. Such was her haste, on more than one occasion she was nearly run over by her landlord's gleaming Rolls Royce. The obese man devoured his pretty young passenger with his piggy Polish eyes; moist lips clamped around a nub of thick Cuban tobacco. Every time Ida saw him he had a different girl stapled to his side.

It was a long bus ride from their one-bedroom flat in Notting Hill to the Charing Cross Hospital. She rode in silence the entire journey in the overcrowded vehicle every day. Bernice did enough talking for both of them. There were always references regarding Ida's 'mistakes' back home, but she had learned to tune them out long ago.

Ida hated her job.

She didn't tell her family back in St Lucia what she did for a living. She was too ashamed to let them know she was a hospital cleaner when her sister and brother were doing so well at the high school and bank. They assumed she had gotten a job in a library. She did nothing to alter their opinion. That's what she had tried for when she first presented herself at the Labour Exchange. The crabby woman who ran the agency had other ideas.

Ida had sat in the shabby office trying ignore the hum of conversation and chair scraping in the overheated room. Ida hadn't liked the look of the woman who sat behind one of the desks in an ill-fitting suit. She wanted to speak to the young lady with lovely yellow hair sitting near the door. She seemed to have an awful lot of people clamouring to see her, and the older woman had no queue. Ida mulled over the significance of the long line and had concluded it must be because she was popular when the older woman beckoned her over with a gnarled finger. Reluctantly, she picked her way across the room. After listening to Ida for a second or two, the woman set about excavating the interior of a card filled shoe box.

"We don't have jobs like that for your people." She peered over her half glasses as she shuffled papers.

"But I'm a qualified librarian," replied Ida softly as she played nervously with the pleats in her second-hand skirt.

"I'm sorry duck; the only things we have on out books right now are Charing Cross Hospital for staff nurses, cleaners, and porters, London Transport, British Rail, and the British Museum. The woman's badly fitting dentures clacked loudly as her lips struggled to retain her teeth.

Ida perked up.

"What are they looking for at the Museum?"

"Junior Archivist."

"Junior Archivist?" her eyes widened at the thought of owning the job of her dreams.

"Yes, it's a person who catalogues…"

"Yes, I know what an Archivist is."

Having had to look up it up in a dictionary, the woman was not best pleased a mere chit of a girl knew what it was. She had the audacity to think she might be suitable for the job, too.

"As far as I know, it's taken."

Ida leaned closer. She pointed to a sheet of paper lying on the table.

"It says the job is still open." The woman snatched it off the table and stuffed it into a drawer.

"We sent a girl last night, and she rang to say she got the job."

Ida squinted across the desk; her head cocked to one side.

"When did she ring?"

"Like I said, last night." The woman had quite enough of the impudent girl and rose to her feet.

"But at what time, maybe I could…"

"Look" She fixed her with a steely glare. "The job is taken. Now, we either fix you up with something else, or you can bugger off back to your country, alright duckie?"

Ida ducked her head in embarrassment.

"Yes, ma'am."

"Now, let's see what we can do for you, dear."

Taking a few cards out of the crumbling box, she glanced over them before placing one the table. We've got a charming little job in Charing Cross Hospital as a ward cleaner at 8 shillings and 6 pence. There is also a tea lady position on the London to Bedford line at 12 shillings."

Ida's mind raced with possibilities. If she worked on the Bedford line, it was more money but sounded like she would never get a chance to find a decent job in her field. She would be up and down the line all day. On the other hand, if she took the hospital job, she could use her lunchtimes to job search. It was less money, but she wouldn't be able to get away from the awful bed-sit, nor the letch her cousin had married to, either. An emaciated man in a cavernous suit came forward from the end of the blonde woman's queue.

"Look lady," his voice escaped in a sing-song Barbadian lilt. "I need to find something today; can you make up your mind?"

Unsure, she lingered a second longer.

"Lady, please!"

"I'll take the cleaning job." The old lady beamed in approval.

"Lovely, I'll get that all sorted for you. How soon can you start?"

Months later, Ida was still scrubbing floors at all hours, too exhausted to look for a new job, too poor to move out. Sometimes on bad days, she often wondered what would have happened, if she had chosen the London to Bedford line instead. Still, Ida supposed, she was left alone. In the beginning, she had tried nipping out to look for another job. However, on her return she had so much work to catch up on, the exhaustion of trying to clean the twelve wards assigned to her before her formidable supervisor checked them, had nearly killed her.

As long as she did her work, her thoughts were her own as she cleaned the days away. It was in those moments her thoughts drifted to her son.

What did he look like now?

Was he crawling?

What kind of baby noises did he make?

Ida supposed Ivan wouldn't remember her now. Her mother wasn't the letter writing type, so it was left to Vera to bridge the gap. Her utility shoes clumped down the eerie hallway toward the next ward, the squeaking wheels of the mop bucket keeping time with her footsteps as she reached her destination. Holding tightly to the handle, she inhaled deeply before opening the doors and stepping inside. The previously lacklustre ward became a hive of activity.

Some of the reclining men hoisted themselves into a sitting position to better their view. Other patients who were too sick to move ogled her horizontally.

"It's our island beauty, come to visit us again."

Ida kept her eyes on the floor as she began the daily routine in her least favourite ward.

"Hello, darling."

"Good morning to you, Mr. Jonas."

"Who's that, Bill?"

Mr. Jonas took it upon himself as pack leader, to make the introductions, being the longest serving inmate.

"Say hello to Ida, boys."

Greetings echoed around the room. Ida in return muttered an appropriate greeting as she mopped furiously down the centre of the long room. She wanted to get away not only from the men who could be overly familiar, but to avoid the scrutiny of the nurses who were of the belief she was flirting with their charges.

Ida mopped around and under the beds, as the men all tried checking their recovery by whether they were strong enough to grab her bottom before she went to the next bed. It was a horrifying nightmare. When she tried to report it, the ward sister asked how many had touched her. On hearing the amount and who were responsible, laughed and commented she could expect those men to be strong enough to leave by the end of the week.

"Come 'ere, let's see your coconuts."

Ida slipped aside, avoiding a hairy paw.

"Never mind him, Luv, I've got a banana under these blankets for you if you're nice to me." Raucous laughter erupted around the room. Face burning, Ida scuttled past the last curtained bed at the end of the ward to the utility room as she tried to block out the noise.

"Didn't mean no 'arm Luv, just having my fun. Come out darlin' I've got something lovely here for you, how about some chocolate?"

She didn't believe old Joe for a minute. It was common knowledge his wife was less than half his age and barely out of school when he married her. He was always boasting that he liked his girls 'fresh.'

"I wouldn't mind licking some of that chocolate off her, mind." Laughter rang out yet again. Turning off the cold water tap, she made her way out of the utility room and into a conversation, with her as a topic in question.

"My Beryl says they're always at it, like rabbits." The wizened man collapsed onto his mattress, spent of energy to say his piece. The agreement came from every bed.

"I've heard that."

"Me too, fancy a few rounds, darling?"

"You a go'er then, Ida?"

"No sir, not me." She struggled to maintain her dignity while trying to steer the mop bucket in the right direction. Catching the drawn curtain with the handle, it drew aside revealing the occupant.

"Clem!"

He lay curled in a foetal position; the regulation blanket rucked up around him. Gently she gently touched his hand. There was no response. His hand was warm to the touch, but still she felt the threads of anxiety pulling at her. She leant close and checked for breathing. She smiled to herself. Up this close, she scrutinized his face and long eyelashes, high cheekbones and button nose before stopping on those sexy lips. Finding herself drawn to them, she stepped closer until there were only millimetres between them.

A voice whipped across the length of the ward. "Ida, I want you down here now." Brought to her senses, she jerked her head away.

"Yes matron, coming matron."

Wiping her sweaty hands down her uniform, she went in search of the head nurse. She was sharing coffee at the nurse's station with Laurel and Hardy. One staff nurse was as long and skinny as the other was short and wide. Matron glared at her with distrustfully.

"What took you so long?"

"I was tidying the supply cupboard."

Matron took a few sips of the tepid brew, leaving Ida to loiter uncertainly.

"There's a spillage in Nelson Ward, go clear it up. When you've finished, you can continue here."

"Yes, matron."

With twenty minutes from the end of visiting time, Ida returned. The early shift had departed, and she wasn't familiar with the night shift. She slipped down the room, noting the men were on their best behaviour when their relatives were about.

She took a seat at the head of Clem's bed and for the first time, saw the grimy "NIL BY MOUTH" sign tied to the bed railings above his head.

He seemed the same as when she left him earlier.

"Can you hear me?" Ida tapped his hand and was rewarded with fluttering eyelids before they opened and focused on her.

"I've gone to heaven."

She grinned like a fool.

"Oh, shut up."

A tremulous smile appeared on his lips.

"That's no way to talk to the dying."

"Oh, Clem." Her voice dropped to a whisper as she squeezed his hand. "Is it cancer, tuberculosis? How long do you have? God, just as I've found you." Ida's eyes clouded with tears. "Tell me everything."

He muttered something unintelligible under his breath.

"Sorry?" She moved a little closer catching his words as he muttered it again. Jumping to her feet, she wagged a finger at him in disgust.

"How dare you!"

Indignant shushes reverberated around the room. Grapes lay forgotten as everyone listened to slivers of gossip. Clem shrugged his shoulders in apology. Ida stood in defiance with her fists squarely placed on her hips ready to vent her anger.

"How can you just lie there taking up space when genuinely sick people need that bed?"

Before he could answer, the surrounding curtain was abruptly pushed aside by the matron. The woman did not tolerate any form of noise on her shift.

"What's going on?" Ida turned to face the dragon. The battle commenced with Clem as referee.

"He's not sick. He shouldn't be here."

"Don't talk rot. Of course he's sick."

"It's okay; she's just a bit nervy."

Ida jerked her head his way.

"Look at him, he looks healthy to me. He says it's a personal problem." Ida jiggled her handbag at him vehemently. "There are names for people like him, and there's me coming up here thinking he's at death's door when all the while he's been sticking his wick in everything."

Ida cringed at her choice of words. She had only been living in England for five minutes, and she was already picking up the offensive lingo.

"You listen to me young lady; he's not in for that. We don't deal with THAT kind of thing on this ward.

Ida arched a plucked brow. "So what is it then?"

The matron tilted her chin arrogantly.

"Are you his wife?"

Ida wilted slightly. "Well, no."

Sister put on her best hospital voice. "According to hospital rules, it is not policy to disclose particulars on patients in our care unless the person is next of kin.

"But-"

"The rules are the rules. Now, I must ask you to leave the ward."

The matron stepped forward, ready to steer her out. She halted as a voice drifted across from the next bed.

"I know what's up with him, Luv." All eyes swivelled to Honest Albert, small in size, big in mouth.

The ward sister was not pleased.

"Mind your own business, and that goes for the rest of you." The roomful of gawkers immediately resumed their inane chatter with their eyes firmly fixed on Albert. Ida, determined to find out about his illness despite Clem's protests, gave her sweetest smile. Albert grinned in return, revealing smooth, baby pink gums before remembering he was minus his dentures and quickly popped them in.

"Well, I see it all Luv, he's..."

Clem made a final effort to keep his personal problems private.

"Albert, give me a break" he begged, rising onto his elbows.

"Wot mate?"

Albert, having done his soldiering part in the First World War and blackout Warden Duty in the second always lived up to his nickname. Honest by name and honest by nature.

"Ain't nuffing to be ashamed of." He gave Clem friendly thumbs up before continuing to a captivated audience.

"E's gone and slipped a disk ain't he and he's got jumbo piles. Seems he's been doing a bit too much lifting and carrying over at Spitalfields Market. He's not bin' eating too well, neither. I know cos I 'erd the doctor talking when e' first came in. Anyhow I 'erd him in the khasi, yesterday. Flaming 'ell what a rip up, talk about bunged up mate, no wonder they had to operate on you."

The room erupted into sniggers of muffled laughter. Clem found shelter under his blanket. When it came to certain things, they were better left unsaid. Especially when it came to his bodily functions.

"Reminds me of when I was at the Somme, the cook's food didn't 'arf give you gyp."

"Albert, that's enough!"

Having spotted the student nurses giggling in the far corner, Matron was desperate to keep order.

"Visiting time is up, ladies and gentlemen." Nobody paid the slightest notice.

"Martha, ring the bell."

The bells pealed, but there was no response. Honest Albert wasn't done yet.

"From what the doctor said, they were the size of cannon balls." The ward erupted into another fit of hysterics. Matron's face twitched into a semblance of a smirk. Ida dabbed at her eyes with the sleeve of her blouse.

"That's the reason I came back to see you? I shouldn't have bothered." Forcing herself to stop giggling, she walked the length of the ward and disappeared through the double doors, the sound of laughter still reverberating through the air.

She returned the next day and the next and continued to see him until he made a full recovery.

By the then, they were inseparable.

She supposed she had old Albert to thank for it, else she would have continued to think he had been up to no good as always. Not that it was any of her business. Ida wanted to thank him, but he was discharged the day after what she thought of as the "night of the piles."

By the time Clem left the hospital, having been thoroughly worn down by his whining persistence, Ida had agreed to marry him. She wasn't in love with him, but she was fed up with her life. She was tired of waking up in cold urine, after spending her nights ferrying the youngest child to the outside privy, while Bernice and Clifford lay like sloths on the other side of the threadbare curtain. She would not spend a second more in that hovel.

Be he a scoundrel, cheat, or liar, there was never a dull moment with Clem.

When they married at Southwark Registry Office, though she tried so hard not to do it; all Ida could think of was Marcel.

16

For the second time that week, the lights went out.

"Not now!"

Ida huffed to herself as she tossed her work to one side. She stomped to the mantelpiece. Grabbing the purse, she clicked it open to find an ancient shopping list. Raiding the next best place, she delved into the Kennedy's cut-price broken biscuit box, in search of her hidden stash.

A shilling and a crown left.

Seizing the shilling, she stepped into the cluttered room and out onto the landing. A melody packed with pipes and drums emanating from Number 4b hammered at her ears. It was better than the conflict that was wont to happen far too often.

She shuffled along the arctic landing to the kitchen area or to be more precise, the ancient cooker complete with burnt on Paupers Stew. Squatting at the gap between the stove and the grease spattered wall, Ida located her meter, punched her money in and hurried back along the dingy landing to the illuminated safety of her room. Turning the paraffin heater down two notches, she resumed her sewing and cast a glance at the garish wall clock above the mantle. Ida huffed again loudly in the silent room.

1.47am and still no Clem.

Earlier when he had said that he would be stopping for a few drinks after work, she assumed the pub would be local, not apparently halfway around the world. It was no wonder they never had any money.

His friends seemed to see more of his earnings than she did. He bought round after round and generously handed out fistfuls of pocket money instead of penny sweets to their children. She had seen it often enough. He always had so many 'friends' sponging off him. Ida had given up trying to tell him about it a long time ago. It always ended up in the same way.

A blazing row.

These days it was safer and easier to keep things to herself.

Settling back onto the lumpy armchair, she re-threaded her needle before resuming work on the seat of Mr. Curtis' pants. Thank God their mother had insisted she and Vera learnt to sew.

No time to waste.

She needed the money from the alteration to feed the meter. The bed-sit was a damp disgusting hole, but that was all they could afford. They were lucky to have found it.

It had taken weeks of demoralising rejections, from self-righteous pinched-faced housewives in spattered tabards, lolling in filthy doorways of shell-shocked homes. Their dirt-streaked windows sported homemade signs daubed with tar.

"No Irish, no dogs, no coloureds."

People like herself could never buy a house.

No bank would give them a mortgage. They had no permanent proof of address, and nobody would give them a reference, even if they could secure an interview with terrifying bank managers.

The one person who seemed to be able to find them housing without too many questions being asked was the same piggy eyed Polish landlord, Peter Rachman from Notting Hill. The only other way any of the Caribbean islanders could buy even the cheapest ramshackle house was to band together in a "Partner" system. A group of them would put a little money away each week to a trusted individual for some months, pooling their finances for each of them to buy in turn. It was a laborious and painstaking process, but it worked. However, it still didn't solve the problem of where to live in the meantime.

In the end, they found refuge in a dilapidated house owned by a jovial, rotund woman from County Sligo.

As Ida's hands stitched, she could hear murmurings out on the landing. It rose in pitch till it was a full blown slanging match.

The Murphy couple was quarrelling again.

Snipping off the last thread, Ida shook the trousers out and folded them neatly. She popped them in a brown paper bag and deposited them on the makeshift table.

2.05am.

Ida sucked her teeth in annoyance; she knew how this was going to end. Clem would roll in drunk and barely make it to bed, never mind working the next day, and lose his job.

Again.

It would take him at least a week to get off his backside to go down to the Labour Exchange to find a new one. She wondered what it would be this time as she paced the cramped room. Some days Ida wondered why they married. Ida stopped abruptly.

She knew why.

Fear of being in a strange place on her own. Of having to explain the existence of a son who was older than their marriage. Of competing with a hundred fresh-faced girls with good looks and no children. Of being found out. Now she was married and respectable and stuck. She would make the best of it.

England may be enormous in comparison to St Lucia, but West Indians tended to stick together regardless from which island they originated. People always knew your business.

Involuntarily, her feet stepped away from the well-worn path from the door to the window, to the solitary wardrobe with its pile of suitcases and hung clothes nestled within. With practised accuracy, she selected the appropriate container and eased it out onto the floor. She listened keenly before untying the string. Searching amongst the bric-a-brac, her fingers came upon her most prized possession. Ida placed the solid gold signet ring on her finger over her copper wedding ring. Her fingers danced over the intricately etched initials. The slam of the front door three floors down interrupted her reverie. Frozen in anticipation, her ears strained for new sounds. Hearing the laborious footsteps begin their ascent on the bare staircase, Ida galvanised into action. Throwing everything into the box, she pushed it back into the wardrobe, yanked off her dressing gown, turned off the light, and dived into bed.

Seconds later Clem burst through the door and switched on the light.

"Hi honey, I'm home!"

Under the bedclothes, Ida cringed at the All-American phrase.

Humming "Knees up Mother Brown to himself, he almost sat on top of Ida and yanked his shoes off. The bedsprings groaned in protest.

"Get off me."

"Whassamatter, you are not pleased to see me, baby?" He lunged for a kiss, treating Ida to a waft of stale alcohol and cigarettes.

"Yuk, getaway, you smell awful. Leave me alone." Wriggling to the furthest reaches of the sagging bed, she cocooned herself in the blankets.

"I thought you were coming home earlier. I wasted a good dinner on you."

"Where is it? I'm starving." Stripped down to his vest and boxer shorts, Clem scratched his taut stomach and peeped into the paper bag.

"That's not it. I had to throw it away. It ended up as hard as a rock I heated it up that many times."

"Ah, sod it, where's the bread?" Delving into the enamel bread bin, he retrieved the crusty loaf and cut a chunk off, slathering it in margarine. Ida hated when he spoke like a common Londoner. She couldn't believe he had already lost his accent. She tried another tack.

"How was work?"

"What can I say? Sweeping factory floors is sweeping factory floors." He poured out a fingerful of concentrated orange squash into a chipped mug. Leaving the front door wide open, he sauntered down the hallway, his drink in one hand, to the bathroom, singing all the way. In his absence, Ida thought how best to broach the subject that had been uppermost her mind for some time. From the other side of the landing, she heard yells of complaint from an unappreciative audience.

Long minutes later, he returned, slamming the door shut. He settled onto a rickety kitchen chair.

Clem spoke first.

"A mate of mine down the pub was saying you could earn good money from working in the theatre."

"Theatre?" She wasn't even sure he knew what one was.

"Yep." He took a swig of orange, burped and continued. "You know, acting stuff."

"Yes, I do know."

"I might look into that, who knows; it could lead to more money. I think I might sign up for some reading and writing classes, too. It would help with all the script reading."

Just like him, she mused. Some idiot in a pub tells him a bucket of nonsense. Now he wants to be a thespian. She wasn't going to support all that foolishness, and she sure as hell wasn't going to spend the housekeeping money on classes for him either.

"I need you to sign those papers."

"Tomorrow."

"You've been saying that for months now."

"I said I'll do it tomorrow."

"I hope so because my mother is too sick to keep him any longer, those papers need to make things legal. Her treatment is not working, and my father is too old to raise a child."

"I SAID TOMORROW."

His roar was still reverberating in her ears when the neighbours banged on the wall yelling something about decent people and getting up early to make a living. In the silence that followed, the only sound was the slurping of orange and mastication of bread.

"I'm pregnant."

Ida had blurted the words out before her courage left her entirely.

The beaker froze halfway to Clem's mouth.

Twisting the edge of the blanket between her fingers she hurried on, hoping her words would stem the tide of anger she knew was to come.

"I know we said children later but…" Ida hastened to find the right words; she knew her best chance was to hit him where he was most vulnerable.

"You are so irresistible. You give me the shivers when you touch me."

The corners of his mouth twitched upwards as he resumed his early morning snack. She pushed that fateful night of drunken fumbling to the back of her mind, though the alcoholic fug permeating the tiny bed-sit made it difficult. Climbing out of her warm nest, she padded over and sat opposite him.

"Tell me that you are happy, it's your child, our baby. I know it will look like you." Grasping his free oversized hand, Ida gazed into his eyes. Still he said nothing. He continued to chew thoughtfully to the point where Ida could have happily hit him on the head with the mug.

"Maybe we could get a slightly bigger room, make it home. I could still work at the hospital. Mrs. Thompson down the road takes in children for working people, and I've heard she's extremely reasonable. I could do a little sewing for the new boutique that has opened up around the corner. It could be so good." Leaning forward, she kissed him lightly on the lips. She came away with a smattering of the margarine and crumbs. He scowled at the remnants of crust splayed across the table as he spoke.

"I get to name my baby."

Ida's hands grabbed for the edge of the table for support. She could keep the baby. There would be no need to see that awful woman on Grifton Street she had heard whispered about by women with young faces and tormented eyes.

With his breakfast consumed, Ida brazenly led him to the understuffed bed. They climbed under the mismatched blankets as the blue-black sky hinted salmon on the horizon. She smiled to herself in the darkness. Her thoughts were only of the growing baby and her beloved son Ivan. All the love and companionship she craved. Tucking the borrowed trashy romance novel further under her pillow as Clem flopped onto his back on top of the floral bedspread, she made a mental note to return it to the library in the morning.

It was astounding where a person could get their inspiration.

Clem was already warming up for one of his trademark post-drink snoring sessions.

Turning away from him, she made a decision. He was not leaving the house until he had signed those papers. They had been lying around for months now, and she wanted her boy. Ida twitched a bit more blanket from under him before settling down, a knowing smile on her lips.

17

Another late night.

Ida repositioned the rack of damp clothes closer to the squat paraffin heater before checking on the children. As per usual, Ivan was immobile in the same position as when he first drifted off to sleep several hours before. In her crib, Ingrid had already gone through several revolutions, twisting blankets into a jumbled mess. Ida still thought it was a stupid name for a child, but Clem was adamant.

"It's all the rage now," he had said that night for the umpteenth time as he brushed down his only suit in preparation for the night's outing.

These days, everything was "all the rage". Ida was beginning to feel like his mother. He would insist on reciting every new phrase he heard, just like a teenager.

What kind of idiot would call their child Ingrid?

It was an old argument, one which she had clearly lost, but still she couldn't help commenting on that stupid name.

Ida couldn't care less whether it was in fashion or not, come to think of it, he was one to talk. When she met him, he thought 'style' was combing your hair and owning a clean shirt. Ida had always been the stylish one. She remembered once upon a time when girls in her community back home used to wait for her to step outside to observe her attire, so they could run indoors and try to recreate it. They never could.

She ruled.

Now she spent her days in green work wear and her nights in cheap market caftans. Decent dressing gowns were a luxury.

Marcel always loved her dress sense.

Ida suppressed a giggle as she recalled when Clem decided to give her a lesson in cinematography.

"Ingrid is a person, you know Ingrid Bergman. She was in Casablanca." He picked imaginary lint off his jacket as he went on. "She's a huge film star in Hollywood."

So he wasn't just drinking when he was out of the house.

"Isn't that a Swedish name?"

She could see from his face that he didn't like the interruption, or that having been a librarian by profession also meant you were well read or ought to be.

She still thought it was a damn stupid name for a black child.

"I'll be back later, don't wait up." The next thing she knew, he had gone without answering her question. Ida snorted loudly in the quiet room as if she would do such a thing as wait up. She stopped all that waiting up nonsense a long time ago.

It was another night with the children in the same old cramped, damp bed-sit with a table full of sewing and a rack of washing with a pile she had yet to tackle. At least he was consistent in his ways, and she found it relatively easy to work around his irregular working pattern.

Since he had started evening acting classes and worked as an extra with a back-street agency, he had been like a dog with two cats to chase. Nothing deterred his passion, despite having to keep the factory job to supplement his income. He loved to be around "his kind of people." A happy Clem created less stress. She hadn't the heart to tell him black actors in England were non-existent unless you wanted to be a gangster, slave, or thief. The latter probably suited him better. He still had his "acquiring ways" about him, she noticed.

He would roll home at all hours with his brain on a cloud. Life had to go on. Ida had to work in the morning.

"Ida, go to Haematology and clear up a spillage." All crispness and efficiency, the younger woman's voice was loud in the echoing corridor.

"Yes, nurse." The woman marched off. "Yes sergeant major," muttered Ida. Shaking with weariness, she traipsed upstairs to the department, passing Agnes and Doreen on her travels.

"Y'all right Ida?" Agnes paused buffing the floor to scan her gaunt face. "You tole him yet?"

Ida took the opportunity to set down her bucket and rest awhile.

"Not yet."

Doreen as always had to tell her piece.

"Well, hurry. Otherwise you will have it, and he will still be messing about."

"If I tell him, it won't make any difference. He is still going to do whatever he wants."

Doreen snorted in derision.

"Huh, I can't take all that la-de-da foolishness. Who him 'tink he is anyway, Harry Belafonte or something?"

"Like I said-" Agnes dropped her voice conspiratorially, "- I know a woman…"

Ida touched her arm. "I'm too far gone for that now I think, but thanks. I'll see you at break?"

Agnes smiled sympathetically.

"You bet."

She watched Ida slowly make her way down the corridor.

Doreen spoke first.

"She's such a nice girl and pretty like a film star."

"Me know. Not ugly like we."

"She smart, too, you know." Doreen pushed her horn-rimmed glasses back up her nose and adjusted her headscarf. "What Ida is doing with that worthless piece of nothing I don't know. Him cute but what a lazy waste of a man, eh? You know my niece Edna she saw him coming out of "The Calabash Club" with some white girl?"

"Lie!" Agnes's jaw dropped revealing several gaps in her tobacco-stained teeth.

"Truth!"

"Well, what a ting.' Don't tell Ida though, I don't want her to lose the baby over that idiot boy."

"No way, girl. It's such a shame. You can see one day she's going to be somebody, not like me," mused Agnes. "If she doesn't let that man and children run her down."

Clucking to themselves, they resumed work.

It had been another long hard day, and sergeant major had been hounding her for three days now. Ever since she made the mistake of telling the newly qualified nurse, she heard the doctor say Mr. Jamison needed 50cc of morphine, not 500cc, seconds before the needle surged into the old man's arm. She should have

saved herself the trouble because ever since then the nurse made
her life a misery with snide remarks, about jumped up jungle
bunnies thinking they knew everything. Now Ida was called to
every spillage and area that needed cleaning if she was stupid
enough to be seen idle. It was a never ending battle dragged down
by eternal morning sickness and abdominal discomfort. Glancing
at the ward clock, Ida surreptitiously made her way to the cleaning
closet and tidied her things away before sneaking away to the
changing rooms. She felt bad, but it was her clocking off time. She
was only supposed to work 8 am to 6 pm with two 10-minute
breaks and half an hour for lunch six days out of seven. Somehow,
she always ended up leaving later, so by the time she got to Mrs.
Thompson, the children were always half asleep. Many a time Ida
thanked God for the woman. Having no children of her own, she
was ready to indulge the children in their every desire.

Freeing her hair from its headscarf, she ran her fingers
through the lacklustre tresses before pulling on her threadbare
coat.She grabbed her bag and ran out the double doors, ignoring
the persistent pain in her lower abdomen which had been coming
and going all day. By the time she arrived at Mrs. Thompson's
terraced house, the pain had magnified by several degrees.

Ruby pushed her horn-rimmed glasses further up her nose and
squinted up at her.

"Child, you don't look so good. You eat something nasty?"

"Probably."

"Wait right there, I've got something that will do you the
power of good. Try some of my bay leaves." The elderly woman
disappeared into the back of the house for a few minutes, chatting
all the time. "Jest boil some in a pan with water, pour and add a
little honey, it'll fix you up real good."

When she returned, clutching the herbs with Ivan and Ingrid
in her arms, Ida was doubled up over the garden gate

"Come and lie down, child you need someone to take care of
you."

Ida grimaced in pain.

"I can't, I've got to get dinner on, Clem will be coming home
to get ready to go to the theatre again tonight, and I haven't laid
out his clothes yet." The little woman held Ida fast in a
surprisingly strong grip.

"Why don't you stay here tonight, the children don't need no dinner. They packed full, and Clem is an adult. He can fix himself something to eat. As for his clothes, well humph!" Ruby pursed her lips in distaste. "To hell with his clothes, you hear me?"

Ida flushed with guilt but wasn't strong enough to stop the woman railroading her. When that lady said you were doing something, by God it had to be done just right.

"Okay." She was rewarded with a satisfied nod of a braided head dusted with greyed hairs.

"Well now, that was easy, wasn't it? Jest let ol' Ruby take care of you. I'll send my Rupert with a note for Clem. Don't you fret. Fix his clothes? Girl, you must be crazy." She clucked her disapproval. "Neighbours here have to watch out for one another you know, we don't got any family to watch out for us now. We have to live loving no matter who comes from what country. We are family now."

Ida made no comment as she followed the woman inside the neat little house. She was just glad to have a friend.

The bleeding started during the night. By the early hours, Ida was admitted to the same hospital she worked at.

It was too late.

As Ida awoke later in the crease of the night as nurses brewed leaves during their tea break, her hands slid over her vacant stomach. She caught a whiff of a familiar scent. For a moment, her pulse quickened, but the smell was gone as fast as it arrived.

Along with her hope.

The only visitors were Ruby, Agnes, and Doreen.

Even Nurse Sergeant Major made a shamefaced appearance.

There was no Clem.

18

Clem tipped his trilby over his eyebrows as he watched the leaden-footed night shift depart. His ears cocked at the sound of brisk sure steps heralding the day shift as they prepared the medicine cabinets for the daily round from his vantage point, across from the Ward.

He tightened the belt of his trench coat a little tighter about himself as he retreated to his original position against the serene interior wall. He stared across at the pristine granite altar, its surface adorned with a cranberry cloth, edged with gold.

In the centre, a heavy cross balanced on an oak plinth, its golden radiance a beacon in the gloom.

Clem had contemplated for some time whether he should have grabbed the cross and smashed it against the head of the person he least wanted to see leaving Ida's bedside. Whether he should have gone in immediately after they had trudged out the double doors and battered hers instead, he did not know.

Either way, it would have eased the wrenching pain in his chest which would have made him feel immeasurably better.

In the end, he had backtracked as the person exited, cowering in the mop cupboard like a beaten dog till they had left, then slunk into the chapel to brood and seethe.

It was his right to be at his wife's bedside, not them.

Clem's sleep deprived eyes squinted in the gloom of the new day. Its solar fingers had yet to penetrate the grime of the arched stained glass window as he fought to comprehend all he had witnessed.

The stillborn baby had been prised from Ida's fingers and bundled against prying eyes. Earlier, Clem had discreetly followed the nurse, keeping several paces behind, down into the impersonal bowels of the building to the morgue. He stood at attention by the door, to return to sneak into the sluice room near the nurses' station.

His whereabouts, Ida's husband and father of the child, had not been raised.

He had not been mentioned.

No authority had been sought for his son to leave the warmth of the maternity unit, to lie unloved in a drawer.

He had hurried to the hospital to be with Ida, blazing across busy London junctions to her because she needed him. He needed her to know that he was responsible and strong.

Loving.

He wanted to be the first person Ida saw when she opened her eyes.

He'd been working hard to perfect his craft to be respected and admired by her. He had done the best with his hands and mind, to provide a decent home for her and the children. She had an attentive and dependable partner in him.

Clems face burned with the injustice of it.

What more could a woman want?

He had thought she loved him.

Everything he had fought for was tainted.

His glance fell upon the bruised sugar-candy roses he had vaulted a garden fence to liberate. Thorns plucked at him as they lay across his light wool navy thighs.

He had burst through the doors in a maelstrom of anxiety, barging latecomers, to find someone else at the far end of the room stroking her limp hand as she slumbered.

Gazing with longing at her beautiful face.

It was his place to do that.

His hand to stroke, his forehead to kiss.

Her soft lips to press to his.

He hadn't worked so hard for someone else to touch his wife.

From which hole had they sprung?

As the person rose to leave, he fled from the chapel.

His nostrils twitched at the faint, sickly sweet odour weaving across disinfected oxygen molecules as he cowered behind a steel rimmed door.

A seed of doubt germinated in his subconscious. His imagination watered it.

Soon Ida would return home to fawn over that bastard child he adopted. Perhaps that was the plan. That way, everything he worked for would go to the first male child.

An hour later, a newly resolved Clem opened the chapel doors and stepped out into the stark light of a newborn day.

Hearing the slam of a door, Ida opened her eyes as the double doors swung back and forth, closing the gap where a few seconds earlier Clem had passed.

Behind him in the chapel, sugar candy petals lay crushed under the last pew, the evergreen stalks stripped bare.

19

Ida arrived home a few days later. She left the children with Ruby against her better judgement, but the old lady refused to hear otherwise.

She opened the bedsit door to carnage. Mouldering half-eaten food, discarded clothes, odd shoes, and assorted rubbish choked the tiny bed-sit. The pervading stench of discounted perfume even saturated the moisture curled paintwork.

Sitting on the unmade bed, she surveyed the mess, likening it somewhat to her life thus far. One minute everything was in order, the next moment, chaos reigned. Living a miserable existence was not what she imagined when she came to England, a fresh start was what she wanted, not a continuation of the steady decline she had endured thus far.

Feeling a hundred years old at twenty-four, Ida hated everything.

Her job.

Her home.

Her husband.

Clem let money slip through his fingers like pollen from a flower. Every penny ended up either on his back or in his stomach, without a thought for the children. Small wonder he was filling out nicely from the stick insect he used to be, unlike her and the children.

Unchecked thoughts wandered to the miscarried child. Her hands gripped the edge of the mattress against the wave of emotion.

Where WAS he? Judging by the state of the bed-sit, she had a vague idea. There was no point trying to talk to him. Whatever time he arrived, she knew Clem would either plead ignorance or say he was hoping to see her in the hospital but was too busy. At an acting class or something.

It didn't matter. She was tired of his chatter.

There was nothing he could say which would interest her in the slightest. She didn't want to hear it. What mattered was the baby. He hadn't been there for her. She had to rely on the kindness of neighbours, something she would never do.

She would never feel the same about him.

When they married, the vows never said anything about forgiveness. It was just as well. She had no intention of doing that, but for the sake of the children she would find a way to hold on. Her carefree days were gone, with two children by two different fathers; she had no choice but to prepare for the long haul journey of marriage to Clem. Fuelled by second-hand love.

Before, it was shameful. Now she would be an outcast. Ida wished she could unravel the wool of her life like a sweater, and knit the last few years into something worthwhile.

Ida set about clearing up the bed-sit, her pert nose wrinkling in disgust. The first thing on the list was to get rid of the stench of cloying perfume. She propped open the dirt-encrusted window with a spotted plastic beaker to freshen up the place. As the metallic London air began its invasion of the cramped space, she rolled up her sleeves and got to work. As she disposed of the bags of half-eaten food, sorting the limited crockery and cutlery, the mental fog was an unwelcome companion. She clung eternally to her senses as she toiled buffing endless floors day after day, accompanying her and the children home to the rancid bed-sit. The barrier began to dissipate. Seeds of change crept in, taking up residence in a minuscule part of her mind.

Maybe something a bit different for dinner from the traditional West Indian food of yam, banana, and plantain with meat or fish – maybe something like the English people ate would be agreeable.

Fish and chips?

No, far too strange. She didn't like foreign food. Maybe she would try something more recognisable such as a thing called 'meat and two veg.'

That's what she heard the old men in the ward moaning about what they missed from home. Then again, maybe not.

Ida had seen what passed for food when the meals were being handed out in the hospital. The vegetables were always watery, and the meat always looked as it would take less time to eat a tyre.

The kids wouldn't mind as it might only be the once or twice. They would love the change.

She wondered if it would be possible to take five minutes between dropping the children off and starting work to call in at the Labour Exchange. She could find another place of work, like a department store or a library. If she were sweeping floors in that type of establishment, at least she would be where she ought to be. In her rightful place. If she worked exceptionally hard, she might be able to apply for another position in the building.

Even a slightly different route to work could be a positive step. She could make something of herself. After all, she was in England now. She could find another area of London in which to start over, just her and the children. She had a distant cousin in Tottenham who swore it was possible to find cheap accommodation in Finsbury Park, though it was a Jewish area. She didn't understand Saturday church Jehovah Witnesses nor the Jewish religion. If she minded her business and were polite to all, surely people would probably mind their own business, too and everyone would get on just fine. Everybody knew cleaning and shopping was for Saturdays with church on Sundays. For heaven's sake, others moved all the time. Folk only needed to know the essentials of her life. She could even move out of the capital. She had heard of large communities of St Lucian's in Basingstoke, Reading and Luton.

Ida stopped short.

No.

No, St Lucian's.

She would end up bumping into someone from back home, and then she would be back to square one. Best stay in London; it was a good place to hide.

Maybe farther afield.

She had heard of black people in places as far as Manchester, Birmingham, and Sheffield. Maybe that would be better.

Ida paused to lean out the window careful, not to get too close to the mould invading the wall that was beginning its assault on the windowpane.

Looking out over the slate rooftops, she surveyed the stormy skies. Ida would have given anything to have one week of continuously warm, sunny weather. It was June, and she was still in her faithful green winter coat. All the fabulous new clothes she had brought with her from back home were still hanging up in the cupboard. Preserved, outdated, and moth-eaten. Ida had bought them primarily for the trip, to make a good impression, but from what she saw, the people here didn't seem to give a damn about appearances. It was quite a regular occurrence to see women queuing outside shops with hair twirled in newspaper strips or spiked curlers; their pale faces tinged grey in the murky smog clutching thin coats around bony shoulders. The only people she ever saw wearing gloves were those who rode in fancy cars. These people had the audacity to say "coloured" people were dirty, hostile creatures. No self-respecting West Indian woman was seen on the street without her hat and gloves, never mind wearing curlers.

If she had known she was going to be permanently in uniform, she would have saved her money and spent it on a suitable winter wardrobe instead of having to rely on handouts from the Salvation Army. Who knew where the clothes came from?

Maybe the dead.

Ida shivered at the thought.

If it kept her warm in this god-forsaken place, she would not abandon hers. The cost of heating in England was unbelievable. One would have thought as England was such a cold country; heating would be cheaper as it was a necessity. Clem had warned her so long ago of the perils of living in the United Kingdom, and she hadn't believed him.

It no longer surprised her so many pensioners perished in the winter. Trudging home with bags of shopping, she often caught the quiver of a faded curtain and the glimpse of a single gnarled hand. She dared not look too closely for fear of reprisals from those too busy to care.

In St Lucia, all a person had to worry about was the water supply being cut off for repairs by the government; even then there were wells, stand-pipes, and ravines. Every household had its water tank for emergencies. There was always more than enough water for all during the rainy season, not to worry about reservoirs.

She watched the local kids playing with marbles on the drain in the gutter across the street, nothing but bowed legs and skinned elbows. Ida knew their diet was atrocious. She had heard from friends the English ate nothing but toast and something called dripping for breakfast. What dripping was, she had no idea. Jam sandwiches for lunch and an egg and a chipped potato for dinner or tea, or was it supper?

Were they the same thing?

Where was the fruit?

Ida knew rationing was no longer such an issue, but they ate strange vegetables occasionally which they grew in their little gardens away from the house. Some types of food were expensive in the shops. All she could afford was West Indian food from specialist stalls in the market run by her fellow countrymen. Even the smallest items on their stalls led to bitter haggling over the exorbitant cost.

Back home in St Lucia when the fruits and vegetables ripened in season, after harvesting for their needs and putting aside that which would find its way to market, people would gorge themselves. They finally resorted to kicking discarded food about like pebbles on the beach as children played with them and let them rot where they fell unless a neighbour in a fit of pique cast them into the nearest bush.

She would give up a years wage for a mango the size of a cannonball. To feel the warmth of the sun on her back as she walked along in the shade of the swaying palm trees. To turn her face into the caress of the breeze as it brushed against her skin and bleached everything bright and white and clean by the sun as she bit into lush, ripe fruit.

She recalled once being taken to an artist's studio with her class on a school trip as a child and had watched as the artist painted mugs for intrepid new tourists from American cruise ships in Castries. It had made her laugh at the time, but now the image crept into her mind.

Years later she could still remember the mugs in brilliant clarity.

Each one held a picture of a cruise ship. On one side, the passengers ascended the gangplank in winter clothes, each sporting a down-turned mouth, and everything painted grey. At the other end of the ship, passengers descended the gangplank in summer clothes sporting smiles, with the mug painted in bright colours.

She knew now what the artist had strived to portray.

Neatly folding the tea towel, her gaze flicked across to the kitchen clock.

"Oh my goodness. Ms Thompson's prayer meeting night!"

Ida donned her faithful coat and hurried to collect the children for their dinner.

The following day, Ida awoke full of vitality. The children, who were mostly quiet and wary of their parents' moods first thing in the morning, picked up on her good humoured excitement and chattered as they readied themselves for the day ahead.

Eager to please their happy mother, Ivan skipped around the bed-sit fixing the table for breakfast as Ingrid babbled and looked on and Ida fussed over her long hair, getting it just right.

At work, her workmates admired her new hairdo, comparing it to Lena Horne. The jealous ones quickly changed the subject, ashamed of their scraggly strands coaxed with pomades and heated curling irons each morning trying to make it do the impossible.

It was too much she had "good" hair too.

Ida waived them off saying they were making fun of her, but she knew she looked good. At lunchtime, Ida raced to the Labour Exchange intent on finding the perfect job, but not necessarily the highest paid. The 8 shillings she got paid she was sure would be easy to match, but she wanted to find one with prospects for someone like her.

One thing for sure, she wasn't going to let another old lady talk her into anything she wasn't comfortable doing.

She left the Labour Exchange, running 10 minutes late for work. Ida had details for a cleaning supervisor at Jones and Higgins in Peckham, a warehouse clerk for Goldman Fashions in Great Titchfield Street in the West End, and a bus conductor at Camberwell bus garage. Ida decided on Goldman Fashions, mulling over what she would wear for the rest of the afternoon much to the chagrin of her friends. She decided not to tell them, knowing full well what they would say. Things like she was 'getting high and mighty' and "don't forget who you meet on the way up because you may need them on the way down" was recited. "What a way she gets big for her boots" would all pop up in the conversation.

She had heard it all before when someone else had left last month. Agnes moaned for ages, so she thought she might as well keep it to herself.

The interview for Goldman Fashions was arranged for midmorning on the coming Monday, perfect for dropping the children off at Mrs. Thompson's house.

All through her Saturday shift, she mulled over what to wear. Would the blue dress with the Peter Pan collar be best? Or the green that complemented her skin tone and accentuated her smoky eyes? Her favourite scarlet frock clearly showed off her slim waist, but she would not wear it to an interview – Ida would not tolerate the idea of being seen as a loose woman. As a woman in the Labour Exchange had said, "Goldman's are Jewish, and Jews don't hold for such things as loose talk or loose morals."

Ida didn't understand what the woman implied but kept the facts in mind. After all, she was brought up respectably.

The Sunday before the interview, during church, she fretted over her hair. Around her, babies wailed, and children fidgeted during the ridiculously long service. Men pretended to be reading The Word from The Good Book while cat-napping. The women conducted their affairs behind reminders of back home with gaily-decorated fans made from palm leaves. Folded slips of paper and Chinese whispers passed along the rows of mismatched seats in the condemned building, ensuring they shouted "Hallelujah " and "Amen" in the right places. Everyone prayed not to attract the attention of the lay preacher from their wrongdoing. A few of the more "faithful" hopped about speaking in tongues in time to the ministry's prompting.

Should she go with a stern, no-nonsense bun at the back of her neck or wear her hair a little more relaxed with a few curls escaping?

The children took full opportunity of their mother's daydreaming by taking turns kicking the seats in front where the neighbour's children sat until Ms Thompson ended their fun by jolting a bony elbow into Ivan's rib.

By evening, Ida's carefully selected clothing was prepared and hung up behind the front door, her hair bedecked with curlers and pins.

Clem arrived home in the early hours of the morning, weaving with inebriation. With no explanation as to where he had been for the past few days, he was just in time to drag Ida out of bed by her hair, demanding breakfast. He terrified the children by hurling his hastily prepared coffee at her when she didn't move fast enough. Ida narrowly avoided being burnt by the scalding liquid that landed on her carefully prepared clothes. The battle ended in victory for Clem, who set off for the nearest cafe for a decent breakfast.

Typical, thought Ida as she went in search of the sliver of braised lamb she had set aside for supper.

She placed it carefully onto her face, took a seat at the rickety kitchen table, and gathered the sobbing children to her. Ida wondered how she was going to explain the bruises on her face at the interview.

It was then she realised she no longer cared.

When she desperately needed Clem, he could never be found.

When she wished him to disappear permanently, he wouldn't bloody stay away.

20

"For Christ's sake, hurry up. The guests are arriving in fifteen minutes."

Marcel burst open the shutters to disperse the stench of expensive scent. Crossing the expanse of claret carpet to the ornate four-poster bed, he grasped the silk sheets and pulled them off to reveal a slender figure draped in lavender chiffon lying diagonally across the bed. Grabbing the spray of ruffles about the woman's neck, Marcel shook his wife like a rag doll. She rewarded him with a lopsided grin as he pushed her back onto the sheets in disgust. Drawing in his breath, he let out a bellow.

"Angela!" The door swung open, and a waiflike figure appeared in the doorway. He suspected she was hovering there since his arrival on the first floor.

"Sir?"

"I thought you were keeping an eye on my wife." Agitated fingers raked through his unruly hair until it stood on end as he paced. The sour-faced maid inclined her head apologetically.

"Sorry, sir. I was making sure Roberto was ready."

"Where's his nanny?" The woman's gaze dropped to the floor before sliding across to the open window.

Marcel knew what that look meant. That damned stablehand was at it again with his female employees. He had meant to get rid of him.

"Alright, carry on."

"Sir." She made good her escape.

Marcel stared helplessly at the semi-naked woman draped across the bed. Surely a person couldn't get drunk that fast.

No doubt she had taken something else, not recommended by a pharmacist.

Straightening his bow tie, he raked his hands through his hair again as he tried to work out what to do first.

Once, his breath would quicken at the prospect of entwining himself around his wife's lush curves on the ornate bed. Now, his very marrow ached with the weight of people sucking him dry, financially and emotionally.

Especially Arianne.

No wonder she appeared so happy at lunchtime.

Leaving her in a stupor, he locked the door and pocketed the key before seeking the catering manager.

On reflection, Marcel would have thought the evening was going quite well.

Until Arianne appeared at the top of the stairs.

The Minister for Agriculture and Victor Aubertine Senior were in a heated debate on property rights for tenant farmers as he entertained the other guests. He explained away his wife's absence with a "migraine," aware his father-in-law knew what was going on.

He always did.

Marcel felt the brunt of his father's gaze burning a hole in his spine.

No doubt blaming him for everything as per usual.

The ambassador for Guyana elbowed him in the back.

"It looks as if your wife is feeling much, eh?"

The words bubbled out around the minister's misplaced teeth which appeared to have been thrown to stand wherever they landed in his mouth. Marcel averted his face to avoid the oral stench in time to see his wife languidly descending the grand staircase. Perspiration bloomed on his brow. She was going to embarrass him in front of a room full of dignitaries. The orchestra came to a halt as one by one the musicians ceased playing to view the spectacle.

Victor appeared at his shoulder. "I thought you locked her in the bedroom."

"I did," hissed Marcel.

"I expect you to deal with the situation." His father promptly strode out of the ballroom to distance himself from any scandal that might arise. He and Arianne were going to have a long talk before the night was over. Marcel watched as every nerve in his body vibrated as she sashayed around the packed room, a vision in a scrap of emerald. She flirted with every male within reach at the gathering, oblivious to their wives icy glares, knowing full well the three stooges, as she liked to call them, were furious. She never gave a damn. Party now pay later.

Marcel knew he shouldn't have gotten involved with Charles and his daughter but, thanks to his father he was in the shit right up to his hairline despite all trappings of wealth. He watched as Arianne wrapped herself around the British diplomat, his face the hue of a radish, much to his portly wife's chagrin. She stuck out her breasts, which threatened to spill from the sumptuous gown. Amazingly, the alcohol and drugs hadn't affected her gorgeous body.

His wife's vacant grin, as she recited her vows on their wedding day, was a clear indicator of things to come. Arianne was doped to the eyebrows then and had been most of the time since. The palatial house he acquired along with the disinterested servants when the previous owners had been "moved on" was paid for by his father. He often meddled yet Marcel was unable to dislodge him. He spent long, worrisome hours working for his father, he soon found was involved in money laundering. If brought it to the attention of the police, he was likely to be spending quality time with South America's finest undesirables. Marcel watched the prison governor from the corner of his eye. The man stood with his back military straight, at his self-appointed post by the orchestra. One wrong move and Marcel knew he would be wearing a different type of cufflink. Victor and Charles weren't going to do anything about the Arianne. He would have to do something. Anything.

He wove through gaping bystanders. He wrapped his fingers around his wife's forearm.

Marcel had hesitated for a millisecond before he opened his mouth, his brain rapidly calculating his pitch to the appropriate level. Not too sharp, not too loud.

"I think it's best you come with me."

Arianne pouted at the request and flung an arm around the Englishman's sagging neck.

"I've only just gotten here. There are so many people see. I need a drink. Do you want one darling?" The mortified minister shook his head. Wisped grey hair flew about his head like a halo.

"No, he doesn't, let me escort you to your room." The minister's wife looked ready to break a bone in her corset with rage. Her fists looked like they punched through concrete on a regular basis.

"Mr. Aubertine, will you please do something about you before I do!" Muffled sniggers sprinkled the ballroom to disappear as his head scanned the crowd.

He tried a different approach.

"I can send whatever drink you like to your room, but let go of this gentleman."

"Don't try getting around my husband."

Searching the crowd, he noted Victor and Charles were missing, as well as the Minister for Agriculture. He beckoned to a clutch of waiters.

"Escort Mrs. Aubertine to her room." Two grasped an arm and unwrapped her from the grateful man while the others fell in step behind.

"I want my drink now!" She grabbed a passing tray, missed and fell to the floor, losing a shoe and her modesty as an expanse of tanned thigh crept into view. Marcel hoisted his wife upright, as the waiters retrieved the stiletto. They frogmarched her screaming from the room, regulation heels clacking on the marble floor.

"I must apologise for my wife's conduct."

The woman pursed her wafer thin lips with distaste.

"Disgusting. I've heard stories, but I thought it rubbish, mind. It's outrageous." The woman, ready to release another tirade, was cut short by her husband.

"I'm sure Mr. Aubertine has other things to do, Henrietta." The man hovered between Marcel and his heavyset wife, pleased at being the focus of attention of any breathing woman, excluding his wife, never mind one as beautiful as Mrs. Aubertine.

"I'm sure he has." It seems you have your work cut out for you, Mr. Aubertine. Come, Gerald."

The mismatched pair departed, leaving him in a ballroom full of bemused guests. It was typical of Arianne to drape herself around the Ambassador just before he was expected to sign a contract with the Aubertine Corporation. It was doubtful whether it was going to happen if that fat sow had anything to do with it. Composing himself, Marcel announced dinner was served, diverting the audience's attention with the promise of exquisitely prepared dishes.

The rest of the evening went without a glitch, despite having to endure endlessly ambiguous comments. During the evening, Victor, Charles, and the Minister reappeared, looking remarkably pleased with themselves.

As he bade farewell to the last of the guests in the early hours, he spotted Victor heading for the stairs.

"Where did you disappear to?"

Victor chilled him with an icy stare. Marcel released his grip from his father's tailored silk sleeve.

"I thought you were doing so well on your own; you didn't need any help from me. Besides, Arianne is your spouse. If you can't handle her, there's not a lot I can do."

"You seemed to have plenty to do when you got me into this."

Victor paused on the bottom stair and smiled innocently at his son.

"Whatever trouble you're in, you did by yourself." Victor walked up the stairs without waiting for an answer.

Marcel paused at the foot of the stairs, as his thoughts ebbed and flowed with uncertainty. He turned toward the first step. Thoughts of Arianne were uppermost in his mind, as the clink of crockery heralded the start of the clean-up operation. As he stood deliberating, his ears picked up a strange, low-level noise. Long moments passed as Marcel orientated the direction of the sound above the clamour of cutlery collection. It led him through the wide doors past the gardens toward the pool house. His hand closed around an imaginary baseball bat as he crept on silent feet along its whitewashed wall as the sound intensified. He came to a halt outside the wooden door. He flung it open.

In a corner upon a nest of soiled towels, dress bunched around her waist and minus her panties, lay Arianne in the throes of ecstasy clutching a bottle of vintage champagne entwined with a pair of waiters. He shut the door and walked toward the main house. Everybody was having sex but him.

What a night. He was relieved Roberto was asleep in his room.

As he traced a route through the ballroom, his thoughts rested on the boy. Many a time in the tempestuous marriage, he thought to put an end to it, only for his father to remind him of his duty.

He cared nothing for Arianne, and she didn't give a damn about anyone but herself. Roberto was the deciding factor.

Only a small child, people were already claiming he would be a ladies' man. He recalled similar things said about him. A small grin that had begun at the corner of his mouth faltered. He recalled his eye for the girls' right from the beginning, not to mention being spoilt and selfish in ways that now made him cringe. He would ensure the boy would never be like him. He was already proving to be a handful; Roberto could be stubborn as hell sometimes, but he would never give up on him.

He secured the windows and indicated to the butler who turned off the hallway lights.

Marcel prayed he could make things work somehow for those he loved.

21

"Hurry up!"

They swapped places.

They moved with the agility of boxers in the cramped kitchen.

Ingrid in one corner, in charge of meats, gravy, and rice.

Evie was across the room from her sister, responsible for vegetables and serving dishes.

In the middle, stood their opponent, weighing in at fifty-five kilos – the washing machine.

They worked at a furious rate in the heat, keeping a sharp eye on the plastic butterfly clock over the back door. She was eight years old, but Evie was well practised and had honed her skills.

They swapped places.

Ingrid's ample posterior, adorned in green nylon, twitched from side to side as her yellow flowered forearms pumped in time.

"Are you done yet? The food needs to be on the table, and there are only two minutes left."

"It's coming, it's coming."

The washing machine hummed in preparation. The girls spun around, flinging themselves onto the appliance.

The spin cycle had begun.

It shuddered and bounced on the dark linoleum leaving fresh scars on the pitted flooring. The drainage pipe began to swirl murky water down the nearest vertical obstacle that happened to be Evie's thick mustard stocking. It ended its short journey pooled in her red wedge heeled shoe. She wrestled with the rubber tube and plonked its curved end into the sink.

"I'm hungry. When are we eating?" Inez loitered in the doorway separating the kitchen and dining room. The crumpled pink tutu stuck out rudely from under her black, white and red Bay City Rollers T-shirt. Her hair, one side plaited, the other half afro-ed having lost one of her barrettes earlier.

"Naff off or help us, then."

She duly naffed off to rehearse another plié.

Ian raced into the kitchen, skidded on the wet floor and came to a stop by Evie's other shoe. He peeped under her tartan skirt. She in return kicked him in the back.

"Piss off."

"Mums up," he scowled.

Within seconds, dinner was on the table with Ingrid, Inez, and the twins sitting in their accustomed places.

Evie tapped her right shoe on the carpet and was rewarded with a loud squelch as she glared at her brother in his stupid maroon dungarees and a stripy top. He stuck his tongue out in turn. Ingrid elbowed him sharply in the ribs.

"Did you fix the table leg like mum told you?"

"Yeah."

She eyed the offending furniture before her with some doubt. Since her older brother was now an Army man, it was up to her to see that things ran smoothly at home.

From upstairs, they could hear the sneezing and sniffing which heralded their mother's appearance.

"Where's dad?"

"Buggered if I know," retorted Evie. Ingrid elbowed her sharply in the ribs too for her outburst. Heavy footsteps echoed at the bottom of the stairs along with another sneezing bout of epic proportions. Ingrid wished their mother would find something for her allergies.

Ida gazed at the table with undisguised suspicion before taking her place between Inez and Ian around the circular table. Her African caftan billowed and settled.

Seconds later, the front door opened. Rapid steps sounded along the dark passageway to the dining room.

"Now that's what I call a feast!" Clem slapped the surface of the table in satisfaction.

A second later, an audible ping was echoed. The faulty table leg dropped to the floor, and the Sunday dinner dishes slid gracefully to the ground to land with a crash.

"Shit."

Oblivious to Ian's outburst, time froze as they glanced sidelong at their father, whose cheery attitude had morphed into one of surprise. They stared at the steaming mush and broken crockery concoction. Clem was first to break the silence.

"What else is there?" He seated himself, his long legs neatly sidestepped the mess. Silk socks peeped from between expensive Italian shoes and wide turn-ups.

"Pilchards and rice" muttered Ingrid.

"Pah! I've been rehearsing all day. I expect to come home to something a bit more appetising than that."

"As you can see, there was something more." Ida sneezed loudly once, wiping the residue on her caftan before continuing. "But, seeing as you still hadn't fixed the bloody table leg from when I last asked you, it's not Ian's fault. You want dinner ON the table you FIX the dinner table. It is as straightforward as that."

Ingrid watched her father squirm like an eel headed for an East End pie shop. As always, he attempted to bluster his way out.

"I did fix it. Somebody has messed about with it."

Sensing yet another row brewing, Ingrid interjected.

"I'll take everyone upstairs."

Ida nodded her assent, hands on her hips, ready for battle. All the children scuttled out of the room to their usual place at the top of the second staircase. It was the perfect place for prime viewing through mismatched spindles of the staircase. Ingrid pursed her lips in disapproval at her brother who promptly covered the crispy roast chicken quarters poking out from his top dungaree pocket with a greasy hand.

The tenants' radio in the loft bedroom rose in volume when voices rose, as was his custom on such days.

"You come here, and sit your fat arse down demanding everything, but you do nothing. You think this place is a hotel!"

"Why should I spend time here with a fat sow and her piglets? I'd rather spend time with friends of my class."

"So I'm not in your class now? Mind you, it was me who put you through school when I was sick. I wanted to be somebody too, but you found every reason to stop me doing what I was trained to do, or work anywhere but in that bloody hospital." Ida paraded around the room in a caricature of their father as he thumped the lopsided table in frustration.

"Who will cook my food when I get home? I can't do anything by myself. We can't afford a child-minder for the children, so there is no point you trying to find any decent work. You have shit for brains, anyway."

The children sniggered at the parody as they munched Ian's fought over chicken.

"You want to be the boss of me and look at you; you can't even begin to understand my skills as an actor. You know nothing about the arts, just making babies and eating, if you stopped feeding your face for a while, you might find there's a whole world out there where people respect me."

"More like your money. There is never enough money to buy food in this house."

"Not if you're going to eat it all!"

"It's not me. When you come home late at night, those fools you call friends pick the house clean, and for your information, it takes two to make babies." Ida moved nearer the pantry door, much to the children's consternation. It was a blind spot for prime viewing of the in-house floor show.

"Don't mention my friends; at least they're not all washerwomen and cleaners."

"True. They're bloodsuckers and thieves. They take all your money; you're too stupid to see that. You're their petty cash box!"

"What I do with my money is my business. I work hard for it. I spend it whenever and with whoever I want."

"It's our money. Family money. I do get a say, especially when we have to do without when you give it away. Get away from me!"

Ingrid imagined her mother's bosom jiggling as it was wont to do when she got worked up about something. She clutched her chest in surprise as the sound of ceramics breaking on economy carpeted concrete reached her ears and the thud of fabric covered flesh being slapped.

"Shut your mouth!"

"It all adds up, five pounds here, ten pounds there. You give money to their children on their birthdays, but I've yet to see you push your hand into your pocket and give your children a penny.

"I gave Evie those shoes for her birthday."

"They fell off the back of a lorry."

"How do you know that?"

"Use your one brain cell Clem; you got them from a man in a pub! They were the ugliest shoes I'd ever seen in my life."

"They *were* disgusting" whispered Evie, her eyes as enormous as plastic hula hoops.

"There was nothing wrong with them. They were lovely."

"You see! You're a skinflint. It's a wonder we even managed to buy this house. Mind you, if I remember rightly, it was me who did all the work."

There was a clatter of plates. Ingrid pushed her younger siblings aside and leapt to her feet. She charged downstairs to halt mid-flight by a loud bang that sounded from the dining room followed by the slam of the front door. Steeling herself, she crept down the last set of stairs with Ian following in her wake, the others hovered in safety on the stairs.

As Ingrid hovered on the last step, she noticed the adjacent parlour door sported a neat half-moon crescent in the middle. On the floor directly below it, lay an unopened salad cream bottle. Ingrid entered the dining room to find her mother sat on the floor amongst the dinner dishes. Her printed caftan enhanced to psychedelic proportions by the rice and gravy patterns, blending smoothly with the orange mustard patterned wallpaper, which also sported Sunday dinner.

Ingrid stood motionless as Ian sniggered, his cheeky face poking over the banister.

Ida appeared rather comfortable in the congealed mess as she made no move to rise.

"Ingrid." Her voice was friendly and gracious as if sitting in a mess of food was an everyday occurrence.

"Yes, mum?"

"Find my bag, take some money and buy some chips for the children but before you go, call them down to clean this up. You can give some to the dog."

Ingrid, not only worried about her mother's state of mind, being a dedicated animal lover was sceptical about giving her beloved pooch food like that. "But it's got glass and stuff in it."

"I DON'T GIVE TWO SHITS!"

Ida's voice carried through the house like a foghorn frightening the children.

"What, a single shit won't do; it has to be two?"

"Shut up, Ian," hissed Inez.

Ingrid decided right then she didn't ever want to be like her mother, and although she would buy the chips, she wouldn't feed the mess to the Alsatian crossbreed. It was one Caribbean meal her beloved Pugwash would not be getting. He was her only friend.

Clem had not returned by late evening by the time Ida was ready to leave for work. Strict instructions were left to ensure the chores were completed. The children were often unsure which parent was worse.

When in a good mood, their father was funny, bringing life into a house full of drudgery with his stories of the stage and all the characters. The family knew he received small parts, but when he spoke of his career, the reality was suspended. When he wasn't in a good mood, he was Beelzebub himself in, with all his tricks. On those days, he would explode at the slightest provocation and fly into rages, which made them run for cover in fright, except Ian, who thought it funny.

Mother was different.

She never smiled, nor cracked a joke. She never did anything just for the hell of it. Some days, having arrived home from work, she would be smiling or laughing to herself. She looked like a young girl with her face glowing under painstakingly applied makeup. Ingrid would catch the scent of the lavender perfume she only wore on special occasions. Her mother's mood never lasted. By the time she had travelled through the hallway into the dining room, all sweetness had fled, leaving nothing but a scowl and a sullen disposition.

Nobody quite knew what Ian was up to or where he was, just like his father. When called, he came eventually but never divulged where he'd been nor what he had been up to. There was always an air of mischief about him. On those Devil Days, as she liked to think of them, Ingrid would lock herself in her room and turn on her record player. She would listen to Bob Marley, Burning Spear, and other such "conscious" music as she tried to ride the storm.

Inez was never at home. Every afternoon saw her either at ballet classes, gymnastics, judo, chess club, anything that involved being absent.

Evie preferred being out of the house, too. Her favourite place was the Wendy house she had made out of the dilapidated shed at the bottom of the garden, complete with muddy 'swimming pool.' That left their parents to fight it out. The day's victor was the one left in the house yelling for a cleanup team.

Most days after school there were numerous chores. Once they had let themselves in with the key hanging on a piece of string attached to the inside of the letterbox, there were broken biscuits and orange squash that was never Robinson's. Ingrid made sure they ate properly, then did the housework work with Evie assisting her. Inez was at her classes, and Ian went missing, as per usual.

So the days passed in the Rochard household, surviving somehow as a family and would have continued for years if it hadn't been for Action Man.

22

"Did you see mum come in last night?" Ian churned his lumpy cornmeal porridge around in his mouth.

Ingrid was elbow deep in washing up. Evie shook her head. Pugwash skittered into the kitchen, his dark claws clattering over the worn lino, to rest in his preferred place under the table, amber eyes fixed and alert. Tongue primed and ready.

"She had fancy shopping bags with her." His mouth widened into a milky smile.

"Doesn't mean they were full of Christmas presents, though, smarty pants." Evie stretched her mouth wide, showing her brother a matching mouthful of porridge.

"Yes, they were."

"Weren't and don't kick me again or I'm going to spit in your eye!"

"Yes, they WERE."

"I'm telling Ingrid you're fighting." Inez primly laid her spoon on the table and crossed her arms in defiance.

"Piss off."

"Ohh, I'm telling Ingrid you swore, Ian."

"Kiss my arse."

Evie giggled.

"I'm telling."

"Shut your mouth."

"Ingrid!"

Ingrid set a soapy jug aside. "What?"

Before Inez could utter another word, Ian plonked a piece of toast in her porridge.

"What is it?"

Inez grinned in satisfaction as she rescued the drowning bread and took a bite.

"You look nice today."

The twins crammed more porridge into their mouths, but the giggles bubbled out in a splash of lactose and splattered across the table.

Everyone knew Ingrid and the word 'nice' didn't belong in the same sentence. Ingrid smoothed her hand over her hot pink jumpsuit which threatened to spill its fleshy contents. Ian thought she looked like a massive, burst sausage.

"Do you think so?" Her chubby face took on an angelic glow as she savoured the rare complement.

"Yeah, that's a nice colour; you should wear it more often."

Cereal erupted from Evie's mouth onto the table.

Ida appeared at the kitchen door, dressed for work as per usual in her slime green uniform, hair curled into cellular igloos and face stripped of cosmetics.

"Stop the noise right now! What's going on?"

"Nothing mum."

Ingrid made herself a cup of hot chocolate as Inez and Ian gulped their breakfast leaving Evie to mop up the mess with a rancid tea towel.

Ready to unleash a tirade of abuse, Ida stopped short at the sound of letters being pushed through the letterbox. She hastened to the front door, at a rate only seen on certain days of the month for some strange reason, and sure enough, it was that time.

Oblivious to the undisguised observation, Ida scanned the post, quickly dismissing the scarlet bills and circulars. She flung them onto the rickety hallway table, next to the avocado coloured phone with its industrial lock. Soon only two crumpled blue airmail rectangles and a crisp white rectangle remained. She savoured the pristine envelope for a few seconds before popping it into her battered handbag. Ida tore open the blue letters. They soon joined the pile on the hallway table. Ida dragged her moth-eaten coat off the banister and slipped it on.

"There's a letter from Ivan and one from Grandma Solomon next to the telephone if you want to read it."

A murmur of derision passed around the room.

"Ingrid will make dinner for all of you. Inez, the stairs need to be swept from top to bottom with the dustpan and brush."

"But I've got..."

"You've got sweeping to do."

Inez bottom lip drew out in irritation. Ian's fingers twitched to pull on her lips till they looked like inflatables. No judo training for her today, no point arguing with mum. Nobody ever won, except dad.

"Evie, wash the dishes when everyone has finished."

No surprises there.

Evie often declared when she was rich she would never touch a dirty plate again in her life.

"Ian, you put the rubbish out." He pushed his chair away and rose from the table.

"I'll start now."

Evie's eyebrows crept toward her hairline in surprise. Ian staggered to the dustbin, his face etched with agony.

"What's' wrong with your foot?"

"Nothing." Ian painstakingly dragged the pungent, overflowing container toward the back door. "I just hurt it a bit yesterday when I fell."

"Fell? How?"

Ian caught his bottom lip in his teeth as he pulled at the bin-liner. "I tripped, and a tyre went over my foot."

"A tyre?"

From the corner of his eye, he watched as Evie's eyes lit up with the realization she was about to be outwitted.

"It was a bicycle tyre, mum."

There was no way he was going to let his chatterbox sister scupper his plans.

"How do you know, you weren't there, Sherlock Holmes. It was-" he struggled to find something appropriate "a bus, sure the number 12 bus went over my foot, but I can still do the bins, don't worry mum."

"Well, not to worry, Evie can do it. Go rest your foot."

"It's not fair," bellowed Evie, "I always have to do his work. He does nothing!"

Ian smirked in triumph. He was just too good.

"I don't want to hear any more about it, Ingrid. If your father comes in later, tell him I'm working late."

Before Ingrid could answer, Ida was out the front door and gone.

"You shit-stirrer. I hate you." Evie lunged for her brother. He ducked, turned on his heel as she reached for him and slapped the back of her neck. Reaching out to steady herself, she ended up with her hand in the reeking dustbin. Ian cackled at her antics as Inez and Ingrid tried to fish her out.

"If any of you plonkers want me, I'll be resting in my room and don't forget to bring me a nice cold drink."

With a spring in his step and a song on his tongue, he left them to cleanse Evie's arm under the cold tap

"I'll get you," yelled Evie.

They started bickering before his foot touched the first stair so, as the good brother he was, he stopped to watch.

"You wait, I'm gonna fix you good and proper."

"Shut up. You're giving me a headache."

Inez rounded on her.

"Who are you telling to shut up? You fat bitch." He could tell Inez itched to be out of their crazy house.

"You can't tell me to shut up; I'm older than you, so you've got to respect me. Anyway, you said I was pretty."

"Yeah, pretty ugly. Sod off, do I? Don't kid yourself. I was only joking, you've got a face like a donkey's backside. With diarrhoea."

"Shut your face."

"Come and shut it for me, then."

A fleshy hand wrapped itself around Inez slender neck.

Evie squeezed between them. "Why don't you both shut up?"

"You can talk, Ms. Coconut, when mums away I'm the boss, so it's just tough. You HAVE to do what I tell you. You always want to skive off with your white friends."

"At least I'VE got friends."

"Please shut up."

"You're nothing but a tart."

It was Inez turn to be aghast.

"I'm not listening to some ugly big-foot roly-poly stink breath yeti." Inez folded her arms and pushed herself up against her elder sister.

In a rage, Ingrid grabbed the first thing to hand off the draining board. The chipped enamel teapot flew toward Inez's forehead, spout first. It stopped short of its mark as Evie grabbed Ingrid's arm.

"Get out before I kill you." Evie swung on Ingrid's fleshy bicep, preventing her from making a new hole in Inez' face.

Ever the coward, Inez fled to the sanctuary of her attic room and her best friend Suzie Quattro singing "Devil Gate Drive." On the way, she passed her parents' bedroom door. It stood ajar.

Behind the bedroom door, Ian gasped and wheezed from his race to beat Inez up the stairs.

There was nothing he liked more than a bit of family disruption to distract from whatever current mischief he was up to, and today was no different.

He closed the door and switched on a tarnished bedside lamp in the murky room before he began a thorough search for Action Man.

Served his mum right for forgetting to lock the door in the first place.

He reckoned it must have been the letter that distracted her. Every month at around the same time it happened, regular as clockwork. He hoped she had bought the action figure. Maybe it was the latest model with the eyes which moved from side to side. One thing he couldn't stand was a crap present.

Last year all he received were three reading books for school.

That was purely for Brain Boxes.

The Pirates, Roger the Red, Gregory the Green, and Brian the Bloody Blue, or was it Bazzer the Blue?

Who gave a damn?

He just wanted a decent present – no socks like the year before and no Y-fronts like the year before that.

Life was tough when you were a kid.

The forage under the bed garnered no result. He replaced the garish pink candlewick bedspread, skirting the islands of dirty garments and mismatched shoes, and headed for his mother's ancient mahogany wardrobe. If he didn't find anything in there, that would be that. He knew there was no point looking in his father's wardrobe. It was full of eye-watering flash clothes. All the trousers sported bell-bottoms and fancy shirts with nose picking length collars. He even had funny little packets of white balloons, but Ian never saw any of that particular type at birthday parties.

Turning the tiny ornate key, Ian dived into the sea of hanging clothes, hefty bin-liners and battered suitcases, grabbed everything and hurled them across the floor. With his parents out of the house and his pea-brained sisters at each other's throats, he had all the time in the world. They always ran to different corners of the house to recover before starting to argue again.

A bit like his pet hamster on its wheel.

Evie had more brains than Ingrid and Inez combined for sure. She was always soaking up information. Bus timetables, ketchup labels, his school reports, not that it had anything to do with her, only to regurgitate it at the most inopportune time. One day, he reckoned her head would reach maximum capacity, and her head would explode. That would be pretty spectacular to watch. She had to be smart if they were twins, but he hated her for being such a goody two shoes egg-head. They could have made a fantastic team. He methodically sifted through each bag, which was boring apart from a pair of lacy red suspenders like the ones he saw in his friend's magazine. After testing the elastic for its sling-shot capability, he duly deposited it in his back pocket for further investigation. As he dumped the last bin-liner back into the wardrobe, he pondered briefly on the suspenders, wondering when his mother wore things like that.

Surely not under her uniform?

He shuddered with distaste and reached for the nearest suitcase.

Fifteen minutes later, Action Man was still missing. Muttering every obscenity he could muster, he threw the last box into the back of the wardrobe and slammed the door shut, not caring if it came clean off its hinges. The wardrobe lurched forward, dislodging all the paraphernalia on the top.

Ian righted the polished wood, as items rained upon him, leaving his head and shoulders burning with the impact of many sharp corners. He kicked at the multi-coloured bags and boxes strewn across the faded carpet, past caring if he got a beating when his mother found out he had been snooping.

He wanted what he wanted. It was as straightforward as that.

His mother could go to hell. He never asked for anything, well, not this week so far. Stomping on another box, he paused as a white envelope popped out; identical to the one delivered earlier that day. Squatting amongst the rubbish, he peered inside the battered container. Turning it upside-down, he tipped the contents onto the floor.

Stacks of matching white envelopes tied with scarlet ribbon thudded onto the ground till they resembled miniature icebergs in a sea of junk. The sweet smell of something unidentifiable tickled his nostrils.

His skin prickled with anticipation. Something strange was going on. He could feel it, and inevitably, his brain went into overdrive. Sitting amongst the letters, Ian untied the ribbon of one stack and began to read.

23

Ingrid prepared the traditional Saturday meal of oxtail stew. Chopping the onions at a furious rate, she was glad she had the excuse to cry. She hated her family.

Inez made her sick with envy.

She wanted to study drama and go to gymnastics and stuff too, not work as the family maid. Sniffing loudly, she grabbed another onion and slowly stripped its outer membrane.

Ever since she was small, when something needed to be done, she was called. She liked to be of help, but a girl liked to have fun too. It seemed everyone had an excuse not to help around the house. Ivan joined the army to do his thing at the first opportunity, and Inez was in every tin-pot show, exhibition, or jamboree being little Miss 'Look at Me.' Brushing aside the rivulets of perspiration on her forehead with the back of her hand, she inadvertently stuck a piece of onion to her broad forehead. She deposited the diced vegetable in the cavernous cooking pot and started on the oxtail.

She hated red meat.

The trouble was, if you didn't eat meat in their house, you didn't eat. Unless you liked boiled fish, cabbage, and potatoes every day.

She wondered where her pain in the arse baby sister had disappeared to. Wrestling with the large end of the piece of meat, Ingrid reached for the cutlass and proceeded to chop it into rough chunks.

She supposed Evie could be useful at times, but she was far too lippy for her own good. That's what happened when you read too many books. All those words ended up falling out of your mouth. She used to slap her on a regular basis when her mother went out. Lately, she noticed her clothes were often minus their buttons when she pulled them from the wardrobe. She knew who the culprit was and wanted to put a lock on her door, but her mother wouldn't hear of it.

Rinsing the meat under the cold tap, she set a portion aside and threw the rest into the pot. She filled it with water, turned on the hob and paused.

Silence reigned throughout the house.

She didn't know where Ian was. He often went out without permission. Where to, nobody knew. Nothing seemed to faze him. She dreaded some days how he would turn out. There was never a dull moment with him.

Ian was her favourite, but she would never tell him, his head was large enough already. Linval thought he was brilliant, giving him all sorts of expensive things he shouldn't. Her mother didn't like her boyfriend. Her father had never even seen him, but Ingrid didn't care. Her boyfriend thought her fabulous. He even called her his African Princess and that was good enough for her. They were going to get married when he was on parole again, but she hadn't told anyone yet. It was their secret. Wherever they ended up living, she was going to make sure it would be far from this house.

Several loud barks sounded in the back garden. No doubt Pugwash was getting impatient. Opening the back door, she called to him. The dog bounded toward her as she opened her arms to catch his sturdy body.

"Hello boy, where have you been?" The canine tail thudded on the dusty ground in rapture.

"I've got a present for you."

Pugwash delicately clamped the oxtail morsel in its mouth and trotted off around the corner toward the patio doors leaving Ingrid to examine the overgrown garden complete with ravaged apple tree and multicoloured shed.

Somebody needed to sort it out. She would not be volunteering.

"Lovely day isn't it dear?"

"Yes, not too bad. How are you today, Miss McDonald?"

The wizened face smiled, exhibiting all three of her teeth.

"Oh, I'm OK, couldn't be better, the excellent weather is good for my arthritis. Mind you, the weatherman said there could be blustery showers tomorrow. It could be tricky."

Ingrid wondered if all Scottish people scrutinised the climate. On a bad day, you could be stuck out there with her for hours talking about weather systems. Still, they had to keep on good terms with her. Who knew when the next family member would get locked out and would need to knock on her front door to jump the fence, which they all seemed to do on a regular basis.

"Well, at least it's fine now."

"I'm sorry?"

Ingrid raised her voice a notch. "We have to be grateful for that."

"What did you say, dear? You mustn't whisper."

The old woman cocked her head to one side. Ingrid raised her voice considerably.

"I SAID WE HAVE TO BE GRATEFUL FOR THAT!"

Miss McDonald nodded vigorously "Oh yes, I am - every single day."

She wasn't going to stay out there all day talking to Ms McDonald, sweet as she was. "I must go; I've not finished cooking dinner." Mentally she cursed herself. Why did she always think she had to justify everything?"

"Do say hello to your mother for me, such a fine lady."

Ingrid retreated a few paces. "I will. Bye."

Ingrid checked the outside toilet before stepping back into the kitchen and locking the back door.

She would take Pugwash for a walk after dinner.

Two hours later, eyes burning with unshed tears, Ian re-tied the ribbon around a pack of letters. Pugwash pushed open the door and silently padded into the room, his bone tucked into the hinge of his mouth. He circled several times before taking up residence behind his master.

Turning to one side, Ian pulled a battered metal wastepaper basket to him and put all the letters in with shaking hands. He fished around in his pockets until his fingers wrapped around the rectangular object nestled at the bottom.

Ian stared thoughtfully at the bin.

He took the letters out again and laid them back on the floor.

After a moment's hesitation, he put them back in and snapped the on lighter.

As he lowered the flame into the bin, he thought better of it and took all the letters out once again.

Pursing his lips, he switched off the lighter and tore up the cardboard box.

Metal on metal resounded as an object hit the bottom of the bin.

He peered inside and retrieved the object. After much scrutiny, he popped it in his front trouser pocket, put the pieces of cardboard in the container and set it alight.

24

Under the eaves of the house, Inez, having worked out all her frustrations with Suzie Quattro, was limbering up. Raising her right leg, she positioned her heel on the door handle and turned her body at a ninety-degree angle. With her upper body and legs straight, she gently stretched to her right with arms raised above her head until her muscles burned. Inez loved testing her body. Klaus had said she could be the next Olga Korbut and promised to concentrate on her and the other lucky girls he had singled out for extra lessons. A tiny grin slid across her lips. Peter was in the group. With his gorgeous blonde hair and defined biceps, he stood out amongst other boys like a diamond in a coal mine. Sometimes, when she could conjure up a reason to talk to him, his friends would snigger, but she didn't care.

He was a prince amongst vagabonds.

Moving on to the next exercise in the cramped space, she rifled through the pitted cupboard sagging against the wall. Maybe he would like to see her in her emerald outfit instead of the cobalt blue she had already chosen. Her friends thought she didn't have a chance as he was considerably older, but when she was eighteen, he would be twenty-one. They could elope to Golders Green. She had read about it in her Jackie magazine. Anybody

could do it. Parental consent not required. Five years was a long time to wait.

As the red-gold flames teased age softened cardboard, Ian stepped back to admire his handiwork. Pugwash yelped and hobbled to the door as Ian whirled about, kicking over the waste paper basket.

The ravenous flames picked up momentum in its race to consume everything in its path. It was soon a healthy fire in the centre of the bedroom carpet.

"Oh shit, shit!" Grabbing an ancient fur wrap, he beat at the flames, fanning them to a sizeable bonfire. It outpaced him as the open door created a wind tunnel with slivers of charred paper wafting across the room, setting light to the billowing curtains.

"Shit!" He flung the charred moth-eaten garment to the floor to pick his way to the door before a thought struck him.

Siphoning sips of contaminated oxygen, he returned to the fire, gathering the letters to him as he fought to breathe in the blackened room, his nostril hairs crisped with heat. His heart beat an irregular rhythm at the prospect of being caught. It was past time to leave.

Before he killed himself.

Grabbing an oversized jumper from a corner, he stuffed the letters into its wide hem and trapped the arms around its bulk to secure it. He caught sight of a rogue bundle rapidly turning a dark mahogany as the fire cut a path around the bed, capturing its secrets within.

Ian's mind raced with possibilities.

Seizing the neck of a perfume bottle, he broke it open on the edge of the bedside table and sprinkled a few drops around his mothers' squat Lourdes candle. The rest was flung about the room before he picked up his load. He dipped his hand into his front pocket.

Empty.

Gagging on the acrid fumes, his blurry eyes scanned the sweltering room for the square of metal, determined not to leave till he found it. He found it twinkling at the edge of the fire, taunting him with its gleaming sheen. Lurching forward with his woolly parcel, he kicked at it with a plimsolled toe. He popped it into his other hole-free pocket and made a run for the door before the whole room went up in flames.

He locked the door on his way out.

Mid-stretch, Inez caught the first scent of acrid smoke but still in the land of Peter, she dismissed them as Ingrid's occasional burnt offerings. When the smell refused to subside, in a fit of pique she flung open the door, lips peeled back and primed to hurl abuse down two flights of stairs. The sound died in her throat. Thick smoke billowed from beneath their parent's bedroom door.

All words fled.

Fear took up residence as she pounded on her neighbour's door.

"Mr. Cecil, we're on fire!" She burst into the empty room. She took the stairs two at a time, stopping to squeeze through the gap left by a missing spindle and jumped down to the next landing, avoiding the rising heat.

"Ian, Evie!" Sidling up to the door adjacent to her parent's room, the heat emanating from the blistered door painted her cheeks red as she opened the twins' room.

"Fire!" Inez frantically kicked at the broken toys and clothing strewn across the floor. There was no telling where those two could be.

"Ian!" Inez's foot stumbled on the strap of a pair of stinking maroon dungarees. She found herself face to face with Tribble. Leaving the hamster to find its means of escape, she rose to her feet, launched herself out the door and charged down the stairs taking the last flight three at a time. She made the trip to the living room in record time as Ingrid emerged from the kitchen, curiosity etched upon her face, her hands covered in dough.

"What's wrong with her?" Ingrid jerked a thumb toward her sister.

"Fuck knows. Mind out the way. I can't see the telly."

Ignoring her brother, Ingrid scrutinised the hysterical girl.

"Shut her up, I can't hear anything." He moved closer to the television as Ingrid, having rapidly exhausted her knowledge of soothing tactics, stood helpless as Inez continued to scream.

"She won't stop!"

Sighing deeply, Ian stood, walked over to his distraught sister and struck her squarely in the middle of her forehead with the flat of his hand.

Silence reigned.

"Now," Ingrid, with hands on hips took charge, "what's all the fuss about?"

The single word came out in a wail.

"FIRE!"

"What do you mean fire?"

"Upstairs, mum and dad's room. Fire!"

"Show me."

Ian made himself more comfortable on the couch and drew his rucksack closer to him.

Inez, ever the coward squirmed. "Don't wanna."

"You come, too."

"But I'll miss Star Trek, and this is my favourite bit."

Ingrid seized an ear and yanked him from his seat.

"Bugger Star Trek, if you have seen it already, you don't need to see it again, do you?" His eyes widened at her use of language. It wasn't every day you heard Ingrid swear.

He followed them back through the hallway, his bag in tow, and up the first flight of stairs.

Inez pointed a shaky finger at the flames licking at the base of the door. "See, I told you, fire!"

"Oh, my Jesus." Ingrid stumbled on the top step, her eyes wide with shock. Ian, it appeared, was the only one unmoved.

"Oh, my Jesus."

"He ain't helping, luv." He picked at his teeth with a fingernail.

His words had the desired effect. Ingrid pursed her puffy lips in determination.

"Where's Evie?" Wide eyes flickered from face to face. All three charged onto the landing.

"Hang on a minute," Ingrid brought them to an untidy halt, "did you check Mr. Cecil's room?"

"Yes," replied Inez between gasps "his hat and coat are gone."

"Good."

"I checked the twin's room as well."

"Thank Jesus."

"I told you…"

"I know." Ingrid continued. "What about the toilet and bathroom?"

Inez opened her mouth. Nothing came out. The landing swirled with toxic smoke.

"We've got to hurry. Inez, fetch the Fire Brigade. You check downstairs."

"I'm faster. I'll go." A streak of blue denim and Ian was gone.

"Leave your bag!" The front door banged shut in reply.

"I'll check the garden, too."

"Leave the garden. Pugwash will be fine, but make sure you switch the cooker and oven off." Ingrid yanked her polo neck up to maximum stretch, covering her mouth, exposing her fleshy midriff to the soot laden air.

By the time the distraught sisters had regrouped in the front garden, Ms McDonald was doing an agitated jig at their front gate. Several firemen had already jogged up the road in full fire-breathing apparatus and had begun their assault on the inferno licking at the upstairs windows.

"Oh, dearie me," chanted the old lady as she wrung the blood supply from her hands.

Ingrid glanced toward the new red-brick fire station at the bottom of their road as a fire truck emerged and headed their way. Ian lolled out the cabin window reminding Inez of Pugwash lolling in the back of their dad's car.

"I'm so glad we live near the station" gasped Inez.

The nosiest of Peckham's finest watched at their front gates while providing a running commentary. The more discreet twitched at pristine net curtains.

Ms. McDonald plied the girls with cups of hot sweet tea and blankets as they sat at a safe distance from the road in dread, as the search for Evie commenced. Thick black smoke taunted them from every first-floor window and popped and crackled with ominous intensity, which contaminated the sweltering air with particles of soot the size of hailstones.

Ian sauntered up to them as two police cars arrived. A pair of plainclothes officers with a matching pair of uniformed constables stepped out. Inez reckoned an overzealous neighbour busy minding someone else's business called them.

Ian perched himself beside her.

"I rang mum's workplace, but she wasn't on the rota today."

Ingrid's lips puckered with annoyance. "They must have made a mistake. Mum told me this morning she was doing a late shift."

Ian shrugged his shoulders. "They were pretty sure. They even put a call out on the tannoy system."

Ingrid shook her head in disbelief. "What about dad?"

Ian adjusted the strap of his rucksack. "Same."

"Same what, he isn't working, or they put a call out?"

"Same both."

Inez watched as Ingrid chewed the last of the bubble-gum coloured lipstick from her lower lip while the plainclothes officers made their way toward them. Leaning his lanky frame against the wall, the man began in lacklustre fashion.

"Right, first things first, I'm Inspector Smith and that is Police Constable Jackson." He gestured to the plain-looking woman sporting a dodgy crew-cut and ill-fitting culottes' suit.

"Now," the middle-aged man tugged at the collar of his ill-fitting sports jacket before producing a battered notebook and pen. "What's going on here?"

"Tea, officer?" inquired Ms McDonald, teapot poised.

"No thanks, luv."

Inspector Smith licked the tip of the ballpoint before remembering it wasn't a pencil.

Ian sniggered loudly.

"Think something funny, sunshine?" Smith handed the pad to PC Jackson. "You do it."

"Yes, sir." The woman's lips thinned to infinity as she began to scribble.

"A lovely cup of tea, dear?"

"No, ma'am."

Inez watched as Ian squirmed under the inspectors' intense scrutiny. Everyone knew people like them and the police were not on the friendliest of terms. She instinctively knew he would say as little as possible.

"I can see you're a real comedian, I'll start with you."

Ian gave his name, and the others followed suit.

The wiry man hoisted his shiny trousers up a notch before continuing.

"How did that start?" He pointed his chin toward the house swarming with black and yellow figures in various stages of dishevelment. For once, Inez was the first to respond.

"I don't know sir."

"Me neither."

"I'll start again. Where are your parents?"

"I dunno, sir."

"Me neither,"

Ingrid shook her head making her Boney-M style beads bounce.

Smith sighed and settled his bony posterior against the low wall more comfortably. His body language spoke in the universal ways of the police when they were dealing with folk like them.

Typical blackies.

Every cell in his body projected what his mouth wasn't allowed to say. Black people never knew anything, especially when it came to crime.

Even when they weren't the criminals. Which wasn't often.

Regret at his decision to take the call when it came into the station was written all over him like a manuscript.

"Alright, let's try again. Was there anyone else in the house at any time?"

All three siblings began to speak at once. Smith held up a hand.

"One at a time, you first."

"Tea?"

"No."

Ingrid took a deep breath, puffing out her ample bosom, hypnotizing the inspector with their fullness.

"Evie, she was in the house, at least I think she was."

"Do the firemen know that?"

Inez nodded in confirmation.

"We had a massive argument, and she walked off. I don't know where and now I can't find her."

Inez put a comforting arm around her sister's burly shoulders.

"It's okay. There's no need to cry."

She threw Inez's hand from her.

"It's not okay. She is probably injured or lying dead somewhere in the house, and it's my fault. I'm the one in charge. I should have been looking out for her instead of fighting with you, and now it's too late!" Inez tried to hug her while Ian opted for the 'I don't know them' approach.

Having held his tongue through the melodramatic episode, Smith turned his attention elsewhere deliberately catching Ian off guard.

"What do you know?"

"Come again, mate?"

"Tea now?"

"I said no. You heard me." The inspector fixed him with his well-practised stare. It had its usual effect of reducing its victims to gibberish.

"We... um... I uh... was in my room, sir."

Inez interrupted, "No you weren't."

"Yes, I was."

Inez pointed an accusing finger at Ian.

"When I had the argument with Ingrid, I went straight to my room. I didn't hear anything coming from your room. You weren't there when I came down looking for you."

Smith looked pointedly at Jackson.

"I was. I was playing with Tibbles then went downstairs to watch TV."

"What's a Tibbles?"

"Our pet."

Ingrid sniffed loudly. "He was doing just that when you came down screaming your guts out."

"Tea for you?"

"No thanks, Ms. McDonald. So what?" Inez sensed a cover-up, but of what, she knew not.

"This is rubbish," interrupted Smith. "I am trying to ascertain the whereabouts of your sister, not trying to find out what was on television."

"Too right, sir."

"That's enough, Jackson."

"Sir." Suitably cowed, the woman resumed her note taking.

"I'm going to have a word with the firemen. You lot stay put." He pointed at his own eyes with his index and forefinger, then pointed to the trio.

"Watch them, Jackson."

"Tea now?"

"Sir. Yes, please."

It was late evening before the blaze was vanquished, and the firemen were able to clear away their apparatus. The inspector returned, picking his way around the group of die-hard nosey neighbours in the dusky light. Smith hooked a finger into his shrunken collar to give himself some breathing room.

The tension in the crowd was tangible.

"You'll be pleased to hear…" he paused for full effect.

"Look!" All eyes slid toward the front door of the soot engulfed building.

Emerging from the doorway was Evie, relaxed, clean, and cheerful with Pugwash trotting in her wake, his bone still wedged in his mouth. Loud cheers erupted as Ingrid lumbered across the road followed by her siblings and lifted Evie off her feet in a bear hug that threatened to suffocate her.

"Get off me! I thought you were going to call me for dinner. Why is everyone hanging about outside our house?" She wrinkled her nose in distaste. "You smell disgusting."

Oblivious to the remarks, Ingrid wrapped her arms about herself.

"Oh, thank Jesus." Flesh jiggled as she fought to contain her joy.

"Stop it, you're making me seasick." Evie crossed the street. Catching a glimpse of the Inspector and his assistant having a chat with the chief fireman, Evie's brow puckered with indecision.

"Are the police here to take Ian away?"

There was a ripple of laughter. She turned her attention to Inez.

"Why is everyone dirty?"

"We were looking for you, stupid."

"Why?"

" 'Cause there was a bloody fire! Why do you think the firemen are here for, dumbo?"

"All right, keep your hair on. I was outside with Pugwash. He smells like crispy bacon. God, I'm thirsty."

Ingrid intervened.

"No, you weren't, I locked the back door after I fed him."

"Yeah, well I was on the patio by the side door." The others stopped to consider the viability of the explanation.

"Did someone say they were thirsty?" Ms. McDonald enquired, cup in hand.

Evie took it gratefully. "Thanks."

Inez continued. "I suppose it makes sense, but didn't you smell anything?"

"I did smell smoke. I saw it coming out of my bedroom window, but I thought it was Ingrid burning food again."

Ian watched the Inspector pick his way across the water saturated street on his way over to where they huddled under the canopy of chestnut trees. Grabbing Evie by the arm, he spun her round.

"You know you're a dope, even for a girl."

"Piss off!"

"Let's get out of here."

"Not so fast, matey boy." Smith laid a hand on Ian's shoulder as he addressed the crowd.

"I smell trouble." Smith's mouth cracked into a thin smile. "I'm done here, although I'll be keeping an eye on you." He cast a sidelong glance Ian's way.

"I also think you'll be getting a visit from Social Services."

"Why?" inquired Ingrid. "I'm old enough to look after them."

"It doesn't look like you're doing a good job, does it?"

Inez pointed down the long road. "Mum's coming."

"Just whom I want to see. Jackson, come along."

"Sir." The duo made a beeline for Mrs. Rochard.

All four looked on as the police intercepted their mother and watched her go through a myriad of emotions in mime.

Inez's eyes held a faraway look. "I'd love to know where mum's been all day."

"Dad, too."

"By the way, these almost knocked me out!" Evie dumped a blackened tee-shirt and plimsolls into Ian's hands.

"Anyone for more tea?" chirped Ms. McDonald.

25

The neon lights lent a lurid tint to the night sky as the men meandered along the marketplace of humanity. Occasionally, they paused to inspect the goods on sale. From every doorway, male and female chameleons lounged, as signs above advertised indulgences fulfilling the most depraved of appetites.

Tourists in loud shirts and outsized sunglasses gaped as experienced punters haggled over dazed juveniles while poseurs strutted in strips of leather from first-floor windows. Sporting whips and chains behind sheets of glass, feigning ecstasy against the backdrop of pulsating music, they undulated in the thick humidity of twilight.

Drunks grabbed unsuspecting females and flashed hairy buttocks, duty forgotten as they revelled in a few nights of shore-leave madness.

Among the throng, the gang staggered up the dusty street with legs kicking. Singing an out of tune rendition of the Can-Can was Tanker, Boo-Boo, Spider, Wing-nut, Jacko, and Donut. They crashed into several stalls, spilling freshly cast antiquities.

Wing-nut hugged Jacko closer to yell in his ear.

"I love Vanilla!"

Ivan winced against the alcohol fuelled blast, but he grinned. They all expected him to.

"It's not Vanilla, its Manila!" He slapped the broad back, causing his comrade to crash into the old woman crouched by a crate of mangoes at the side of the road. The crone unleashed a string of Filipino words, of which he was convinced were not in any translation book or dictionary.

"Fuck me, she's out to chop me balls off."

Wing-Nut staggered down the road followed by the crone brandishing a length of bamboo. It reminded Ivan of a crazy kind of Tom and Jerry cartoon. He yelled after the cockney as he disappeared into the crowd.

"Does that mean I'll catch you back at base?" Ivan, having quit his dance, felt rather foolish by himself. Across the road, his friends loitered at the entrance to Honey Buns nightclub, fondling a few of the "working girls" as they paraded their wares. All vyed for the rustle of lilac pound notes as the doorman ushered them inside the the sweat-drenched interior.

Spider waved a gangly arm in his direction as the others piled into the entrance.

"You coming mate?"

"I'll catch you later."

Spider disappeared inside, leaving him marooned among the crowd, an odd fish in a school of identical fish. There was no sign of Wing-Nut nor the madwoman. She reminded him of Grandma Solomon.

Tiny, but mean as a rattlesnake. Being the first grandchild, he only got her sweetness. Plenty of people experienced her venom.

Ivan cast the receptacle lodged under his elbow into a nearby bush, leaving the clear, odourless liquid to seep into the undergrowth. He pulled his sweat saturated shirt away from the taut ridges of his stomach, as he skittered past open doorways exposing bowed treads leading to havens of iniquity.

The first night at barracks, after refusing the offer of a magazine filled with enough images of the female anatomy to satisfy even a veteran gynaecologist, he found himself with a decision to make. Either spend possibly the rest of his career with his head down a latrine or find a way to distract his disgruntled fellow squaddies. Hence, the Michael Jackson gags. So began the start of a sound friendship with his team, as long as he played the clown.

The shops and bars slowly morphed, along with the clientcle who frequented that part of town desiring something a little different from the average punter. Ivan picked his way through the throng, his eyes shuttered against the glare of fluorescent tubing.

Conducting a life based on deception was madness. Every comment and jibe were sifted for content and hidden meaning in itssubtext before he responded. Portraying drunkenness was just another facet to the camouflage.

Nobody knew him. Not in the Army and certainly not at home.

"You looking for honey, sweetheart?"

Ivan sifted through the crowd toward the melodic voice. A lean-limbed body poured into a figure-hugging shimmering gown waved at him from across the dusty road. The woman's luminous green eyes flicked over the crowd as she perched delicately on a stool, the high split affording him a splendid view of her offerings. She filed her immaculate nails as she sheltered in the flaking doorway of a once magnificent hotel, complete with ornamental balconies with cascading window boxes and marble pillars pockmarked with age. Perfect teeth peeped between full, rosebud lips.

"If you like, honey, I can show you a good time."

Her voice carried across the dull roar of a myriad of languages like a shaft of lightning. He pivoted, in search of the object of the woman's desire. The chattering street traders continued to stir battered pans of unidentifiable meats.

"I don't think so, maybe another time."

He swiped at the rogue beads of salt as they sprang from his hairline. The dusky beauty paused, sizing him in one long cool look. With a flick of her raven tresses, she slipped off the stool and sashayed through the throng to stop inches away. Placing a surprisingly strong hand on his wrist. Ivan stiffened against the pull of her personal gravity.

"Hey, Koko knows what you want. Trust me."

Small hard breasts push against his chest as she drew a finger softly across his face, her knowing eyes never leaving his.

A flicker of recognition passed between them. Ivan placed a hand into her open palm and followed her into the hotel.

26

"Ben, the two of us need look no more,
We've both found what we were looking for,"
Inez flung open her bedroom door and leaned over the banister. "Hey, fatso, turn it down. I can't practice with that crap on!"

Evie closed her eyes as she mentally acted out the usual scenario.

Inez would pause in search of a reply, of which there would be none. She would step back into her sanctuary, and crank up her record player a notch. Clearing her throat as she selected a record and hummed a few notes, she would find the right track and set the needle.

Packing her audition bag, Inez would start singing along with the record player.

On cue, a new song filtered through the house.
"We had dreams, some really rough dreams,
We hit the road to feel life; we made a good start,
Then it all fell apart,
Welcome to the real life."
Downstairs on the ground floor, in her makeshift bedroom, Evie screamed in frustration. The open textbook sailed across the room to flutter out of sight behind the foldaway desk.

"Will you two pack it in? Bloody Michael Jackson, frigging Rock Follies!"

She surveyed her bed littered with an assortment of educational volumes.

So much for O Level revision.

Thank god Ivan and Ian weren't home; otherwise she would have to contend with Desmond Decker and The Maytals, with Ska and Reggae battling for supremacy, too.

She was a huge Madness fan, herself.

Pushing the tower of books to one side, Evie lay on the bed with her arms wrapped around her head. She closed her eyes against the cacophony of sound as above her, the puff-headed crooner and the female rockers went head-to-head.

She wondered if living in a lunatic asylum was quieter, what with the inmates on medication and everything. If it wasn't Ingrid and her Motown Crew, it was Inez and her rock rubbish.

No wonder her head was always aching. Too much bloody noise. It was no good talking to her parents, either. Her mother always came out with the same thing when anyone complained, especially her father;

"If you don't like it, you can always piss off. Just leave the front door key on the table on your way out, I'll even make you a packet of sandwiches for the journey."

Her mother had a way of getting right to the crux of the matter whether it was settling disputes, telling you whether the dress you bought suited you, or explaining the facts of life. Evie shuddered at the latter. The day her mother decided to tell her the last one, she swore she would never even talk to a member of the opposite sex again unless she were related to them.

As for her father, the less said about him, the better.

Nobody in the house made sense. Evie long convinced herself she spoke a foreign language unknown to anyone else. She could not wait till she could bugger off. Trying to find a little peace at home was impossible. When the noise didn't drive her crazy, the constant fighting and bickering did. Why should a high-performance mind have to deal with the single cell amoebas that cohabited the house? To add to her problems, she kept having a reoccurring nightmare that caused her to nap during her lessons and left her wide awake at night. If the problem continued, she would need extra incentives to induce slumber.

The rasp of fingernails on painted wood echoed across the room.

"What now?"

Swinging her feet onto the cool faux oak Lino, Evie took a step toward the Magnolia coated door. She stopped short at the sound of a voice speaking through the crack between the door and its frame.

"It is me."

She backed away till her shoulder blades jarred against unpainted plaster. She raised her open chemistry book to her chest, not that the periodic table would have been much use in a fix as she surely was.

"Evie, open the door, I need to talk to you." Diana Ross with her Supremes wove dulcet harmonies through the rhythmic crash of punk rock.

There was no way she was going to talk to him about anything, and she was damn sure he wouldn't dare try opening the door. Her eyebrows rose toward her hairline as the door handle jiggled.

Cheeky bugger! Good thing she always locked it.

"I know you're in there, open up."

Frustration sieved the man's voice, till each word glazed with tension. What was a girl to do to get peace? Held captive in her bedroom.

Several minutes passed without the skitter of untrimmed nails scraping chipped paintwork before she dared lower her shield to creep to the door on painted toes. It was impossible to hear anything other than the musical cacophony. Her fingers wrapped around the shaft of worked metal protruding from the keyhole, but instead, found herself looking at a triangle of white cartridge paper protruding from under the door. Taking it to the safety of her bed, she prised the envelope open with a jagged fingernail.

"My beautiful African queen."

A lurch in the pit of her stomach roiled the bile up to the back of her throat.

"Today I tried your door, but you were not in, so I have left a note to tell you how much I am in love with you."

Shit, this was not what she needed right now, a lovesick lodger.

"When you pass me on the staircase, I feel I could hold you in my arms forever, but I know I cannot until I make you mine. I have seen the way you look at me, and I know you feel the same way, too. I cannot wait until we are together."

Why was it things like this only ever seemed to happen to her? The only time she ever looked at him was to wonder why his trouser hems were always miles away from the top of his shoes.

"I am going to meet my uncle visiting from Lagos, and we are going to spend some time at my cousin's house. When I come back on Sunday, you will meet him when he will bless our marriage, and start the arrangements with your father to send you back to Nigeria to start making plans for the wedding. My family will take good care of you.

Until then, I will think and dream of nothing but you."
All my love,
Bola"

Marriage? She was only fifteen. What did he mean "make arrangements with her father?" She hoped dad hadn't been pissing about with Bola and telling him bollocks.

Mum was going to hear about it. She was sure it was going to start another huge fight between them, but there was no way she was going to be some African Queen never mind going to Nigeria. For one, everything she saw Bola cooking had tinned tomatoes in it. She was sure if he made apple crumble; it would have some in it. Since he arrived six weeks ago, nobody could get anywhere near her mother's blender without there being red goo churning away in it all day, every day.

Revision forgotten, she raced out into the hallway. Through the wood trimmed opaque glass door separating the hall from the lounge, she could see a figure sat in front of the television.

Mum had never been known to sit and watch anything unless it had some churchified moral to it, so it wasn't her.

"What are you doing?"

Inez, dressed in her best clothes, draped herself over the banister rail swinging her workout bag. Evie hadn't noticed Diana and her friends were singing by themselves for once.

"Is mum up there?"

Inez strolled down the remaining stairs.

"She went back out to church. Said she would be back about ten o'clock."

Evies lower jaw flapped open. "Why does she always have to be at church ALL day Sunday?"

Inez shrugged with disinterest.

"No wonder I stopped going. What's wrong with a couple of hours like normal people? She's getting more like Grandma Solomon every day, and I couldn't wait for her only visit to be over I can tell you," fumed Evie. "Flipping hell, did you swim in that perfume or what?"

"Shut up. Just cos' you can't afford it."

"If you're looking for a bloke, you will kill him before he gets within 20 paces with that stink."

Inez arched an eyebrow in response.

"I don't know anything else. That's all mum said. You know what these Pentecostal Churches are like. Why don't you ask Ian? He goes to the same church, doesn't he?" Inez hoisted her bag onto her shoulder. "I've got an audition in Covent Garden. I'll be back later." With a flounce of her paisley skirt, she unlocked the front door and slammed the door shut behind her, leaving her sister alone in the dust speckled hallway. Evie went in search of her brother. She found him swinging a gangly leg over the arm of the battered sofa, with one arm resting on his rucksack beside him.

"How come you're here, and mum has gone back to church?" Evie watched in surprise as he leaped to his feet and ran for the door.

"Chuck that in my room, will you? And mind your own beeswax. Keep your nose out of it."

Before she could think of a reply, he was gone.

"Was it something I said?" Evie plonked herself in her brother's seat.

Did her brother ever use or wear any other colour?

Pushing his burgundy bag aside, Evie wondered why he needed to carry what felt like toilet paper around with him. She giggled to herself for the first time that day. Maybe he had the squirts. She drew open the mouth of the bag. Her smile disappeared as she peered in.

Inside nestled bundles of pound notes.

"Bloody hell, he's got about a million grand."

"What's a grand?" Startled, she looked up to see Shirley the One-Pot man standing at the kitchen door, dressed as usual in his floral pinney over his clothes, holding that day's concoction in his pristine saucepan.

She scrunched the top of the bag shut and buried the bag under her backside.

"I'm not sure. I heard someone say it at school."

"Well-" he smoothed his immaculately straightened hair with his free hand and ran a finger down the centre parting. There could be a nuclear strike, and it would still be there. Such was the precision of his dated hairstyle- "Let me know if you find out, it is such a strange word. A bit like "pleurisy."

Evie wondered where the hell her mother got her lodgers. Two were more than enough. Give her back Mr. Cecil any day. They really ought to pop in to see how he was at the respite home. His family never did.

"Cheerio."

She found herself staring at the back of his pristine white shirt and tailored trousers.

She didn't like his sherbet-coloured mules.

He gave her the shivers, always creeping up on people, listening to all sorts of things.

Home was like a hotel with the lounge the makeshift check-in area.

Her hands were still on the money bag.

She hoped One-Pot hadn't had a chance to see what was inside. Though she could have done with some money herself, she wouldn't touch a penny. Wherever it came from, no doubt if Ian had anything to do with the cash it was dirty, and she wanted no part of it. Besides, she knew her brother. He would know if as much as fifty pence was missing.

Despite them being the same age, he often seemed older than his years, ever since the fire. She noticed he watched their mum at every opportunity. If she went out, two minutes later, he went out. Evie was sure he was following her, though for what reason, she didn't know, but it was weird.

She had even caught him watching Inez and Ingrid.

Whatever he was doing, Inspector Smith was bound to catch up with him. He had been tracking her brother ever since the house fire. Every so often she would catch sight of the policeman in the Chomert Road Market or outside the Houndsditch Store in Rye Lane. Still, it wasn't going to be her problem if she left the money alone. She smiled as a thought entered her head. There was a way of making the money work for her though without touching it. She fancied her marriage situation was about to be resolved.

The slam of the front door caught her attention.

Her father was back, just when everyone was beginning to breathe a little easier. She pushed the bag under the settee and focused on the television.

"Hello, I've just arrived!"

"You don't say," muttered Evie.

She didn't like when he did that. Someone would see him enter the house then he would say, "I've just arrived" like everybody in the house was deaf and blind. Besides, nobody could miss him in those disgustingly tight trousers, which had way too many zips and that stupid frilly shirt. Thank god mum finally wore him down with all her nagging for him to cut down his seventies afro to something a tad less ridiculous.

"Hello, dad."

He set his bags in the hallway and stepped into the lounge.

She groaned in derision.

Why did he have to bring his skanky friend?

Had her dad already known mum was out when he brought his female friend, or did he have a death wish? If her mother ever saw the skinny cow, she would be minus more teeth.

That was something she would pay to see.

Evie wondered if her father was turning into some middle-aged punk rocker, like Johnny Rotten.

No chance was he going to her school parents evening.

"Where's everybody?"

Evie took a deep breath before answering.

"Mums at church, Ingrid's upstairs, Inez is at an audition, and Ian is, I don't know."

Her father didn't seem the least bit bothered at the last part. None of them ever were.

"Where's my food?"

She felt like answering, "Where's your manners?" But Ian wasn't the only one with a nasty temper. So, she settled for "I don't know, dad."

Unfortunately, it wasn't good enough. She trembled with apprehension as his face contorted with fury.

"A man expects food to be ready for him when he gets home from touring."

"No one knew what day you were coming." Evie pushed herself further back into the battered settee. Some tour. It was only summer season in Brighton. He made it sound like a world tour.

"That's beside the point, hot food should always be in the house unless your mother ate it all again."

She knew she should have kept her mouth shut, but somehow the words popped out.

"But mum said you didn't leave us any money, and she had no wages left after paying the bills."

Evie sailed through the air before crashing into the television.

"Didn't I tell you not to talk back to me girl?"

Her father had shaken them about but had never pushed or hit either she or her sisters. He had always saved that for Ivan.

"Yes sir, I mean no sir," Evie fought to still her trembling legs.

Cowering in the corner, she waited for the next blow that never came.

Venturing a peep, she found her father staring back at her in that odd way of his.

The woman quickly linked arms with her father, tossing her white blonde hair coquettishly aside.

"Don't worry about food, darling. Let's go to the King's Arms for a pub lunch, we can read the script there."

Evie wanted to punch the ugly cow and smear the cheap scarlet lipstick all over her pale face. The womans' cheeks were so red maybe someone had slapped her already. Her dad was such an arse.

"I'm going to be famous, aren't I?"

"Oh yes, you are darling. This script is perfect for you, it's only rough, mind." The woman kept talking as she slowly steered him to the front door. "The Professionals are the hottest programme on the telly just now."

Evie watched as the woman winked at her before pushing her father out of the house. Once the door had closed, she checked the back of her head for blood but found none. Her afro had absorbed much of the blow.

Hopefully, once Ivan was home on leave, their dad would have another punching bag and leave her alone. Evie pushed the Ferguson television further back onto the chipboard television stand. Silly arse dad. He was probably going to be a mugger or something on telly this time, and she was going to get trouble at school over it again.

Maybe the stick insect wasn't so horrible.

A movement on the stairs caught her eye.

"Thanks for the help."

Ingrid shuffled back up the stairs to her music. Sticking two fingers up at the broad back, Evie stomped to her room, stopping to hurl the door into its frame with every molecule of energy she possessed. She dived onto the bed, burying her tearstained face into the musty sheets.

27

Sunday afternoon, Evie and Ingrid were in charge as per usual, with Inez riding shotgun. The washing machine was tucked safely away in the corner waiting for the repairman on payday.

"What time does mum's church end?" Evie spooned the rice into a large oval serving dish. Ingrid paused to ponder the question.

"Three thirty, I think. Maybe that was Blessed Be TempleChurch." She resumed stirring the black-eyed peas.

"I thought it was half past one."

"No." Inez squeezed past the wide Black Watch Tartan back to get at the cutlery drawer.

"That was Build my Rock Tabernacle. The one with the funny pastor."

Ingrid smiled despite herself. "Pastor Adu Shankagi."

Evie spun on her heel, and using the serving spoon as a microphone mimicked the minister to perfection. Moving her knees from side to side, her legs gave the illusion of being made from jelly. She flapped her elbows like a chicken as her sisters fell in step behind her parodying backing singers.

"Jesus!" Evie doubled over as she executed a perfect James Brown screech, joining her sisters in the chorus.

"You got, you got, you got, what I need."

She sang another solo and joined by her backing group.

"Give him your lurve,
You got, you got, you got what I need!"

Delicately, Ingrid placed a tea towel around her little sister's bony shoulders and tried to lead her from the kitchen, but she was having none of it.

Staggering a few steps, Evie threw off the towel and returned to do her thing, shuffling her feet from side to side as if trying to extinguish a cigarette, James Brown style.

Ian sauntered into the kitchen. "What are you doing?"

The trio dissolved into hysterics as his lips quirked upward.

"Don't tell me, Pastor Agu, am I right?"

The acknowledgement was a slow-motion wave from a jiggling Ingrid as Evie fought to control herself. Inez had no such trouble.

"Why does she keep changing churches anyway?" She held on to the drawer handle for added stability.

"Probably 'cos she's looking for one which preaches what she wants to hear," retorted Ian dryly, which set his sisters off into hysterics again.

Evie watched him inspect the new dining table. It was a shame there wasn't enough money to change the dated chairs.

He scanned the room for the familiar burgundy bag.

"If you're looking for your bag, don't worry, it's safe."

"Don't piss about."

Her eyes were wide open in mock innocence.

"Who's pissing about?" Evie's eyes hardened noticeably. "I need a favour. You need your money, what more can I say?" Her grin would have been more at home on a shark. She thought of the thousand odd pounds stashed behind the old Wendy house. Behind her in the kitchen, she could hear animated conversation as Ingrid and Inez resumed their food preparation.

Ian pulled her aside.

"Look, I'm not getting into any trouble for you, get that straight, yeah?"

"That so?" Evie prodded him in the chest. "Looks like from where I'm standing you did that all by yourself, unless…" she squared up to him. "…the tenner I saw mum give you this morning can multiply itself or we've got a money tree in the back garden."

Ian shuffled his feet uncertainly. "I found it."

"Sure, you did, if you're telling the truth, you won't mindhanding it to your mate the inspector then, will you?"

He stared at his sister in, eyes wide.

"What do you want?"

Having won a hearing, she relaxed fractionally. Blackmailing people was not as easy as it seemed on TV. "Don't laugh. Bola wants to marry me."

Ian let out a bark of laughter.

Ingrid poked her head round the door. "What's the joke?"

"Mind your own business." Evie promptly stomped on his foot bringing his humour to an abrupt halt.

"People never let me in on their secrets," muttered Ingrid. Evie shut the door as her sister returned to the kitchen to supervise Inez. The girl could burn water.

"I said don't laugh."

"Sorry, my Nubian Princess."

"Keep it up, and I burn the money."

He raised his long arms defeat. "Okay, I'll sort it. Where is he?"

"His uncle's house, but he'll be back next Sunday."

Ian ran a hand through his cropped hair.

"Yeah, no worries, got no choice, have I?""Nope."

"Gimme the money, then." Having made the deal, he looked keen to attend to his business.

"I'll get it for you, wait here." Evie stopped abruptly. "Don't hurt him, just scare him a bit."

She was robbed of his reply as they heard a key inserted into the front door lock. Expecting one of their parents, they were thrilled to see Ivan. Entering the hallway laden down with his kit bag and various packages he struggled to shut the front door.

"What, no hug for your big brother?"

All thought of the money was forgotten as she sprinted the length of the lounge, down the hallway and jumped squarely in Ivans' arms. His bags scattered across the gaudy carpet. Wrapping her arms around his neck, Evie squeezed happily.

"Whoa, are you saying hello, or are you trying to strangle me?"

"Sorry, I'm just so glad to see you."

"Me too."

Carrying his new bundle, Ivan walked into the lounge where the others had congregated in wait for their greeting. Throwing a giggling Evie onto the settee, he greeted them as they all spoke at once asking a hundred questions each. Ivan did his best to answer the main ones as well as asking a few of his own.

"Where's mum? No, don't tell me, church."

"Yep."

He smiled ruefully. "She's getting more like Grandma Solomon every day."

They often heard how he attended church twice a day, every day for the first few years of his life till he was rescued by their mother after much wrangling.

His mother had failed to get him near any church since, but she had more success with the others. Once on a Sunday seemed to be their limit, though. If she pressed for them to attend a Bible study class or young people's choir, they went AWOL, apart from Ian, who liked to spend his time chatting to the deacons and pastor. Grandma had spent most of her free time informing them of the heathen ways of the world by way of fiery correspondence every week. The only person who seemed worthy of her praise was her wonderful son-in-law. Keeper of the family morals. No wonder nobody had been in a hurry to go to St Lucia for a holiday. Grandma and Grandpa Solomon may be long dead, but Clem's father, Grandpa Rochard was still around finding things for people to do. He hated to see an idle person lounging. Himself not included.

"That's what I said," exclaimed Evie. "Didn't I say that to you yesterday?"

"All right, keep your hair on," scowled Inez.

"How come you lot are here then?"

Ingrid answered for them. "We've been."

"What, you too?"

Ian feigned nonchalance. "So what?"

"He's an altar boy at St Theresa's," volunteered Ingrid.

"Thanks, big arse, I can speak for myself."

"He goes to mum's church, too," she added for good measure.

Ivan's bottom lip jutted out in admiration. "Well, good on you."

"Thanks."

"St Theresa's is Catholic, isn't it?"

"Yeah, so?"

"Isn't mum's church Pentecostal?"

"Yeah." Evie knew where Ivan was going with his train of thought. Her sisters and herself had numerous discussions on it themselves but had failed to come up with any conclusions.

Ivan rubbed his chin, seemingly deep in thought.

"Well, they are pretty different to each other, so how can you attend both churches at the same time and believe both doctrines?"

"Well, I, uh, I'm just comparing the doctorings and um, I'm going to make my decision on which I will follow soon." He smiled self-righteously at them, obviously pleased at his quick thinking.

"Oh, of course. Good idea."

Ivan cast a glance over at his little sister. She, in turn, raised her eyebrows in silent agreement. They were in accordance. Neither could even begin to contemplate what their brother was up to in the churches. Whatever it was, it didn't bode well. Ivan's eyebrows drew together in alarm. Evie reckoned he would put it to the back of his mind. Whatever it was, he was on leave for a few days. It was none of his business. It wasn't wise to get involved.

"Where's your father?"

"I don't know," piped Inez. "He came in yesterday with some old trout, then buggered off sharpish. Haven't seen him since. That's his stuff at the door." Evie pointed to the heap of luggage in the hallway.

"What? You just left it there?" exclaimed Ingrid. "Your father's going to have a monkey when he sees that, you know he expects it to be washed and put away."

"You saw it too and stepped around it like everybody else. Why do I always have to do it? You're the eldest and," Evie folded her arms over her budding chest self-righteously, "I'm not allowed to use the washing machine since that white shirt-red dress thing even if it was working."

Keen to avoid the row, Ivan took his kit to the spare room with Inez hot on his heels and on the scrounge as ever for anything of interest he may have to offer. Evie would bide her time. Ivan always saved the best for his favourite sister.

"If I were you, I would get cracking; your father might come in at any second."

Evie s face grew hot with irritation. "He's your father, too, you know so don't make out like he isn't. He's father to all of us, even Ivan, so I don't see why I've always got to do stuff for him. Besides, I can't crack; I'm not an egg, you know."

"Look, stupid, I do enough around here. I'll be damned if I'm going to pick up after YOUR father as well."

"Oh, for God's sake, I'll do it."

Both sisters turned to their gangly sibling in surprise.

Evie spoke first.

"You're going to wash dad's clothes?"

"Yep"

Evie and Ingrid looked at each other. Ian never did anything for anyone unless there was some sort of advantage in it for him, and they sure as hell couldn't see what that gain was.

"Anything so I don't have to hear you two screaming at each other again. Evie?" Her head spun round to face him.

"Don't forget, I want my stuff when I get back from the laundry."

"Yeah, sure no problem, and thanks a lot."

Ian had offered to do two things for her that day. Well, one and needed a little encouragement with the other.

Strange.

He dipped his head in acknowledgement and headed for the front door.

"You're lucky; I've never seen him do anything like that for anyone before. He must be turning over a new leaf."

Evie didn't believe that. She reckoned her father's cases were going to be a lot lighter and not due to the dirt being washed out. She knew her brother well. He would probably pay a visit to his old friend at the Pawn Brokers in Rye Lane before coming home.

Ida returned from church a short while later with Ms. Ruby, and Ms. Doreen in tow, resplendent in enormous hats bedecked with artificial flowers, paste jewels, and sequins. The only thing missing was a stuffed pigeon.

"Ingrid!" bellowed Ida as stepped through her front door. Her voice, as always, carried right through the house.

"Coming mum," sang Ingrid.

Upstairs, One Pot Shirley paused in buffing his nails to increase the volume on the television.

Next door, a man lounging on his overstuffed sofa buried his head even further behind the News of the World, as his wife tutted to herself in the kitchen.

"That woman is at it again. I'll get one of my migraines no doubt before the night is out." The woman ceased stirring the gravy to wave the wooden spoon in her husband's direction.

"I thought you said you were going to have a word."

"Don't' worry luv, it's in hand."

The man raised the paper a tad higher, a flimsy shield against the shrill edge of his wife's displeasure.

He liked the Rochards. They brought a bit of life to an otherwise staid and stuffy road. The children were well behaved, apart from the lanky one. He often thought their only child could learn from them. They only ever saw her when the bank was after her.

Sometimes when the Rochards' eldest daughter cooked, she even saved him some of that spicy chicken he loved when his missus was visiting her Medusa mother. As much as he loved his wife, she was not an adventurous cook. Black pepper was a tad too exotic for her.

He watched from the corner of his eye as his wife opened her mouth, then to his immense satisfaction, promptly closed it again. She aimed her spoon at him, redesigning the carpet with a line of gravy.

"Oi, mind out!"

All interest for the soccer round-up and wrestling with Big Daddy was forgotten as he checked himself for stains.

"You've been saying that for years. I'll have a word myself, thanks very much."

She touched her fiercely curled locks with a delicate hand.

"It shouldn't be allowed. That sort lowers the tone of the neighbourhood."

"What tone?"

"What was that?"

"I'm off out." He knew from past experience what she was like when she got riled up, and he wasn't going to hang around to hear about the neighbours all night as she was wont to do.

"But I've just finished the roast." She followed him down the narrow hallway.

"It'll keep." He had his jacket on before she could stop him.

"Where are you going?"

"Down to the pub."

It's early yet. If you wait, we can go after dinner."

That was the last thing he wanted, her nagging all the way to the boozer. Besides, it would spoil his pint.

"The guv'nor will open up for me, he's alright. Don't worry; I'm only having the one." He stepped out into the warm afternoon sunshine.

"But the roast will dry out."

"You have it then."

A peck on the cheek and he was gone, leaving her staring down the road, spoon still in hand. She shut the door when she spied Mr. Rochard approaching. It wouldn't do to have the other neighbours thinking she fraternised with that class of person.

Ida gave another yell for good measure while she unfastened her thick overcoat and handed it to Evie to hang up.

Doreen was, as always, the first to speak.

"Ida, its June. Why are you still wearing that big coat? You not hot girl?" She removed her lightweight jacket, tossing it aside where it landed on the telephone. Ms Ruby removed her lace shawl and carefully placed the folded item on a dining chair.

"After all these years, I still feel the cold. Besides, you never know what this weather is going to do," added Ida.

Ingrid lumbered into the room. "Yes, mum?"

"Is dinner ready?"

"Yes mum, we've just finished making the carrot juice. Ivan is here."

A broad smile crept onto Ida's face. "You haven't met my eldest, have you, Ms. Ruby?"

"Every time I'm here, he's away. After all these years, I'm sure he's doing it on purpose."

Ida laughed while Doreen twisted her lips in derision and clutched her oversized Bible to her mountainous bosom.

"I've heard plenty about him."

"Leave your bibles on the dresser, let me introduce you."

They followed her into the crowded room. After greeting her older son with a bear hug and leaving him crumpled, she introduced him to her friends, proceeding to talk about his comings and goings despite his many attempts to interrupt. His failure to provide a grandchild was the hot topic, much to Ivan's chagrin and Evie's delight. Evie would have throttled her mother if she spoke about her like that. Ms. Ruby appeared to have politely tuned Ida out whilst looking completely enthralled. Doreen foraged in her wheelbarrow sized handbag. She produced a small toothed comb which she scraped across her sparse oily fringe. Evie was convinced her mother only liked to listen to her own voice. There was never any interest in anyone else's children or their activities, as if her children alone could do no wrong. Many times she had witnessed when her mother met strangers or friends, she would tell them about her precious children, regardless of those people being the greengrocer or Prudential man who came for the hire purchase payments every Friday. Even the soft drinks man who popped by every week selling fizzy pop from the back of his truck was enveloped with their day to day activities. People were always complaining in front of Evie about it when her mother was out of earshot. As though she was invisible or was someone else's child.

Eventually, Ida ran out of steam and came to an end much to everyone's relief; with the realisation she hadn't introduced the rest of the family.

"You know my girls?"

Ida jutted her chin toward the open door where Ingrid was putting the last few drops of vanilla essence into the carrot juice. She waved back in acknowledgement.

"Ingrid."

She pointed to her middle daughter perched on the window ledge.

"Inez."

"Yes, me know them long time."

Evie was seated in her usual spot on the floor beside the sofa, trying to stay awake by flicking through a sports car magazine as The Walton's said goodnight to each other on the television.

"This is one of the twins. Don't ask me where Ian is, nobody ever knows," she added for good measure.

"So, what did you think of our church? Didn't it make you want to be saved?"

Evie knew her mother's friend well enough to know Doreen was happy enough to go to church for a day out, but didn't want to be sucked into any religious business. That kind of thing was fine if you were ancient like Ms. Ruby. They didn't even have cars when she was young.

"It was alright." Evie was willing to bet it was way too long for Doreen's liking.

"But what a way Ingrid fat, eh?"

"Yes, and she's strong. You know she can carry all the weekly food shopping on her own," Ida added with pride.

Ms Ruby was aghast. "You send her on her own?"

"Why not? She doesn't mind."

"But can't Ian help?"

Ida shrugged her shoulders. "You can't count on him. He's always off somewhere."

Doreen parked her ample backside on the settee. Ankles together, knees open wide under the flowery skirt as she eased her feet out of her ivory shoes and massaged her wide charcoal stockinged toes.

"She looks like she could do with the exercise."

Ms. Ruby rallied to her goddaughter's defence.

"Let the girl be."

Doreen carried on regardless, her Barbadian accent seeping in. "You need to put that girl on a diet, Ida, she's not going to find a man looking like that. Someone needs to get a hol' of dat hair and do something wid' it, da 'ting look like some kind of bush." On a roll, she continued. "It's a shame she's not pretty like Inez, she's got long good hair, too. Dat all yours?"

Inez nodded, her plaits bouncing in time.

"Yep, it's hers, she bought it," piped up Evie.

Ivan slapped her playfully on the head. They grinned at each other conspiratorially.

"You really think I should put her on a diet?" Ida gazed thoughtfully at her eldest daughter.

"Of course."

"Stop your foolishness. Doreen, she can hear you," warned Ms. Ruby as she ambled across to the kitchen to rescue Ingrid. "We just came from the house of the Lord, remember?"

"Sorry honey, but it's only de' truth me a' tell"

Ingrid sniffed back a tear as Ms Ruby gently patted her back.

"Don't pay her no mind she's ignorant. I don't know what her fool husband saw in her in the first place that's for sure, especially with those man-feet of hers."

Ingrid gave a tremulous smile that Ms Ruby returned with her own newly purchased regimental teeth.

"That's much better, come dry your eyes. Don't give the old fool the satisfaction of seeing you upset. You're beautiful and don't you forget it."

"Hello, I've just arrived!"

Clem shrugged off his sports jacket and threw it at Inez.

"No shit, Sherlock," muttered Evie.

"Be a darling and put that away for me, hmmm?"

"You just passed the coat rack. You could have done it yourself."

"Shut up, Evie."

"Yes, dad."

Still muttering under her breath, she squeezed past her father who stood in the doorway. A diva making an entrance. She hated when he did that.

"Hello, my dear."

Ignoring everyone in the room, he took Doreen by the hand and kissed it like they did in the movies. She in return gave a girly simper. Evie watched her mother curl her lip in disgust. He always came over all Clark Gable when they had visitors and, like idiots, people bought the whole production like pre-schoolers in Disneyland.

"Where have you been?"

He winked at his captive audience before releasing her hand.

"Hello, Ms. Ruby." The old lady flicked her hand at him dismissively.

"I had a script reading last night, so a friend put me up on his sofa."

Ida snorted in reply.

Evie caught the odour of cheap perfume emanating from her father. Her mother wouldn't row with her friends in the house. Ms Ruby was alright, but everyone had heard of Doreen's mouth, reckoned to be wider than the Grand Canyon.

"Can't you say hello to your son?"

Clem wafted his hand in a vague fashion towards Ivan, "I've only got one son, and I don't see him here right now."

"Don't start that nonsense again. You signed the adoption papers years ago."

Evie elbowed Ivan to stop the conversation before it got nasty.

Clem had always complained about him having only one son to all who would listen, not that it was a big secret. Once upon a time, it would hurt Ivan deeply. Nowadays he seemed way past caring. Everyone at home knew he was a peace loving man.

Why he joined the army, nobody knew.

Taking the initiative, Ivan reached for his bag.

"I got you a present." Fishing about inside he pulled out a handful of individually wrapped cigars.

"Look, he's so thoughtful."

Ivan's shoulder blades bunched together under his regulation shirt with embarrassment. Their father snatched them from him, brushing past him to the kitchen.

"Where's my food?"

Ingrid covered steaming dishes from invading fingers. Ignoring Ms Ruby, he slipped between the women and helped himself to a couple of exposed drumsticks. He was rewarded with a pair of murderous stares.

"Come on chop chop. I've got to be back at the studio tonight."

Turning her back on her father, Ingrid yelled for her sisters to lend a hand as Ida excused herself to her newly painted bedroom, courtesy of the sluggish insurance company, desperate to get out of her pinching panty girdle into something a bit more comfortable.

By the time she returned wearing her beloved caftan, the food was steaming on the table. Clem had already loaded his plate with chicken, pork, rice, and anything else that could find space on his plate. He could eat enough to feed a family of ten and remain a bean pole apart from a barely discernible paunch while all mother had to do was think about food and she gained a stone.

"It's rude to eat before people are seated, Clement." Ms. Ruby rearranged her bony limbs on a threadbare dining chair.

"Find me something to drink."

Evie returned with a bottle of iron fortified wine. Her mother snatched it out of her hands before it touched the table, placing it beside her on the floor.

"Not that one, you know it's for my nerves. Look in the cupboard, you'll find two bottles of Zinkano Blanco, take one."

"Bring both," corrected Clem.

Doreen slid him a sidelong look. "I love a good drink."

Ms. Ruby clucked with disapproval.

"No," interrupted Ida, "get only one. The other is for the prayer meeting here on Wednesday." Evie went back to the kitchen.

"Amen," agreed Ms Ruby.

"I thought church people didn't drink," scoffed Clem between mouthfuls of seasoned rice.

"Pastor Adu pours a drop on the carpet to bless the house."

"You should know that, living in a God fearing house." Ms Ruby helped herself to a generous portion of coleslaw.

"No wonder the carpet stinks."

Evie sniggered, but came to an abrupt halt when her mother cast a filthy look toward her as she placed the cut-price bottle of imitation Martini on the table. She returned to her seat much subdued, reaching for a chicken breast.

"Not that piece, Evie. You have wings."

"But I always have chicken wings. I want a thigh or breast bit."

"She can have my thigh," offered Ivan.

"No. You know how it goes. Ivan and your father get the breast or thigh, and I like drumsticks, Ingrid or Inez the neck."

"I don't like the…" started Ingrid. Inez picked at the neck on her plate with distaste. Their mother carried on regardless.

"We have two chickens today, so our guests get whatever they like. The youngest in the house get wings. That's how it is. I buy the shopping."

"You said I -"

"That is how it IS!"

The table fell silent as all eyes watched Evie replace the chicken piece with reluctance, picking a wing in its stead.

"One of these days, I'm going to be able to fly away with all these wings I'm eating."

She cast a look at her big brother who sat motionless in his seat, a vein at his temple throbbing. She knew what that meant. He was pissed off again.

Ms. Ruby recited the blessing over the meal. Her father had almost finished eating.

"Bounteous isn't a proper word."

Evie received a swift kick in the shin from Ingrid.

The rest of the meal passed without further incident, culminating with Clem's favourite dessert, despite Evie's many complaints to her mother for a change. Tinned fruit cocktail without the syrup and vanilla ice cream much to their father's delight. As per usual, she had to resort to make-do measures. She retreated to the kitchen to add granulated sugar and Milo drinking chocolate to the ice cream to make her favourite chocolate ice cream after trading in most of her fruit cocktail for her father's syrup. Ida only ever bought what he wanted, heaven alone knew why.

It wasn't as if he contributed to the cost.

Everyone was trying to breathe without popping a button when Clem jumped into his Ford Cortina and headed to the studio, to rehearse his audition piece for the new sitcom. Doreen made her excuses and left soon after him. She had gotten what she was after. A free meal.

Ms. Ruby lent a hand in the kitchen, dragging Evie into service. Ivan went in search of his mates. Inez did what she always did on a Sunday afternoon. Soon the house was vibrating with the sounds of the Top 40 hits from the Binatone hi-fi system in the front parlour.

"She's just like your Uncle Joseph. He's always playing music, too." Ida stomped up the sagging staircase to her bedroom. Her mother could be incredibly modern at times. She could shake a few moves, too, on occasion. Evie smiled as she dried the dinner plates, she had never seen anyone move like Uncle Joseph. He was in a class of his own.

There was never a dull moment in their house. Other times she wished she could divorce her family and join a saner, quieter one. A normal set of parents and siblings who did loving things for each other was all she craved.

Their house was a war zone with each person representing a country. She envied Ivan. He was able to enter and exit with no trouble. He was gone so often, he was almost classified as a visitor. Evie itched to flee, but had two more winters before she became eighteen. How Ingrid could still be living at home was completely beyond her. Inez should have moved out, too, instead of using the house as a hotel. It was left to Ingrid and Evie to complete all chores, not that Ingrid had to do it. Evie was grateful for that small mercy.

28

Ms. Ruby had boarded the number 36 bus home an hour earlier. Ingrid and Evie snoozed on the battered settee in front of the telly as Hawaii-Five-O began its theme tune when Ian rolled in. He dumped the suitcases in the hallway, where they had originally stood. He came to a halt in the doorway. A tatty C&A carrier bag swung in one hand.

"Here comes the prodigal son. We ate your dinner."

"Don't piss about, I'm starving."

"It's in the oven. I'll heat it up." Ingrid struggled to her feet.

"Where is everyone?"

Evie gave him a quick rundown of everyone's whereabouts as her sister lumbered off to the kitchen.

"So," Evie cast a wary glance at her brother, "what did you steal?"

"What makes you think I stole anything?"

"Come on. You never offer to do something for anyone unless there is something in it for you. It's a fact of life, like breathing."

"I'm sorting out your African Prince for you or have you forgotten already?"

Ian smiled at the flickering screen. Steve Mc Garrett had gotten a tip-off and was in hot pursuit around the lush island.

His sister would have been surprised to find the carrier bag held: £73.64, a tin of Pepsi, a pair of ladies knickers and half a pack of Mints. He decided to throw the half empty bottle of vegetable oil into the rock salt container at the end of the road. That he could do without. Sometimes she was too brainy for her own good.

"Where's mum?" As always, he had to know their mother's every move.

"She's upstairs resting."

"No, I'm not."

Ian stepped aside to let his mother pass, Evie watching him scrutinise her from head to toe. Evie had to admit she looked bloody good for her age. Even Ingrid came out of the kitchen to admire her. Dressed in a beautifully fitted navy jacket and matching pencil skirt, she looked amazing. Even her long unkempt hair was clean and swept up into a neat chignon with not a strand out of place.

Her makeup was perfect, and she smelled divine.

Although she had lost her petite figure years ago, she was by no means as big as their father liked to make out, she was a tad matronly but still had all her curves courtesy of Playtex.

"You look fantastic, mum."

Ida ran her hand over the silky fabric of her skirt self-consciously. "Thank you."

"I didn't know there was a special preacher at church tonight."

"Every first Sunday night of the month is guest preacher night."

"Anyone I know?" Ian leant against the door frame with his arm effectively barring the exit.

"If you spent more time at church listening to the service instead of talking to the deacons of worldly things, you would know, wouldn't you? Ingrid, tell your father if he decides to come home tonight I'm at church."

"Yes, mum."

Having checked her bag, Ida strode toward the hallway.

As his mother approached, Ian held his ground.

He caressed his mother's sleeve. "I've never seen that outfit before mum, is it new?"

"No, it isn't." Ida snatched her arm back. "Mind my clothes." Ida glanced at her watch impatiently. "Get out of the way I've got to leave now if I'm going to catch the bus."

Ian made no move to step out of her way. He seemed quite happy to loiter all evening.

Evie held her breath in trepidation. Although Ian was a bit insolent, he had never been so forward as to ask their mother about her business in such a fashion. None of them would have dared.

Evie and Ingrid exchanged glances.

"It looks new to me – expensive, too. Maybe I should become a cleaner, too. They seem to get paid a lot of money these days."

Ida stepped toward her son, her eyes aflame with undisclosed anger.

"Whom the HELL do you think you're talking to? I'm not one of your stupid friends. I'm your mother, so show some respect. Since when have you been an expert on women's clothes? You can't even piss straight never mind anything else, unless you have something to tell me about yourself." She crossed her arms, her face twisted in disgust. "Is it because you like wearing women's clothes you have such a fascination with mine, or you just like admiring me?"

Ian was by no means cowed by her outburst. He seemed quite happy to challenge her, which infuriated Ida all the more.

"I was admiring you," he spat contemptuously. "I was admiring the perfume you wear and the fact you always go to church every Sunday all day. You dress particularly well every first Sunday evening of the month," he sneered. "Is there something you want to tell us?"

Ingrid gasped. Evie wasn't surprised. It was one thing to be insolent to their mum, but something entirely different to accuse her of - of what Evie wasn't sure. Dressing too well? Something was up to make her brother challenge their mum.

"I see that we have a regular Sherlock Holmes here."

Drawing back, she pierced him with a stare. "You can't read properly. You can barely wipe your backside without my bloody help, but you think you can stand there and tell me my business?"

Evie groaned. When her mother started to swear, there was going to be big trouble. She wished they would go somewhere else so she could catch the end of their TV programme.

"You think I'm going to stand here and let some good for nothing waste of space like you talk to me like that? Well, let me tell you something, mister."

Evie heard the thump of flesh upon flesh. She looked up to find Ian rubbing his chest, but looking no less cowed.

"You need to keep your nose out of things that don't concern you. I don't know why you think you can stand there and ask me stupid questions in my house when you seem to have a problem handling your own business." Ian opened his mouth to protest, but

Ida continued. "I know all about you. Inspector Smith keeps me nicely up to date with everything, thank you very much. If you don't straighten yourself out at this rate, you will be lucky if you end up packing tampons in a factory for a living. I'm not going to waste my time finding you yet another school, so you had better sort yourself out, or you will end up at the school for bad kids. Your headmaster can't wait to send you there."

"Don't worry, I know what I'm doing, but do you? Everything that happens in this house is my concern. It's not only your house, but dad also bought it. We all live here. Whatever you do, we all suffer the consequences."

Ida drew in a deep breath. Uh oh, thought Evie, here it comes. She tensed against the coming backlash as she noticed Ingrid had. The last time something like this happened, Ingrid ended up thrown against a wardrobe, how, no one was sure.

"For your information, Mr. Big Shot, it was my money that bought this house." Her voice came out in a barely audible whisper laden with raw emotion. Ian himself seemed surprised at the change in tack.

Your father drinks his money away with his so-called friends, while I work my fingers till they bleed so all of you can be together. I don't have to do it. I could have pissed off and had a bloody good time, thank you very much. I could have been a college professor by now if it weren't for you lot. When your father was out with his women, it's me who put food on the table. I made sure you were clean and went to school every day. I tried to make something out of nothing for you, and this is the thanks I get. If it was up to your father, you would all be in foster homes, strangers to each other and spread across the country. So the next time you start to wonder about my business, you think about that. You think it's fun being a cleaner? Do you think when I came to Britain my burning ambition in life was to mop up peoples' sick without even so much as a thank you because they didn't even notice me?"

"Don't you think I wanted something better in life for myself, to achieve everything I wanted? Life isn't a fairy tale where the princess always gets her Prince Charming. It has a way of turning out the way you least expect it to, and you just have to get on with it. I had a chance, but it was taken away from me. I want all of you to have one, too, so I do what I have to. If that means I have to put up with your father who has never given a damn about anybody but himself, then fine."

Ian, recognising the truth of her words, took his arm away from the doorway and crossed them over his chest, which was about as much as he was going to concede in front of his sisters.

Ida, however, wasn't done saying her piece and, coming closer, continued where she left off.

"I work bloody hard. If I want to dress up like a dogs dinner and piss off out to church or anywhere else I fancy, that's between me and Jesus, I'm sure we'll settle up later. If you don't like it, leave. If you think I'm too hard on you and you feel you can do better on your own, be my guest. Just leave my front door key on the dining room table, I'll even make you a packet of sandwiches to help you along.

I don't know what happened to you since the fire, but every time I turn around, you're there. If I go to church, you're there. You were never interested before. If I go shopping, I see you in the high street.

I didn't raise you to be my keeper; I raised you to be responsible members of society who have nothing to be ashamed of to anyone. Keep the hell out of my business!"

Slamming Ian into the wall, Ida stormed out the front door, slamming it shut behind her rocking the very foundations and leaving the girls stunned at the outburst.

Ian glanced toward the door, his face unreadable.

Ingrid was the first to break the silence.

"Mum forgot her hat."

She nodded toward the woven headpiece, bedecked with sequins and ribbons perched atop the sideboard.

Ian snatched it and ran into the street in pursuit of his mother, the wide brimmed hat flapping in the wind.

Standing on the corner, Ian scanned the road left and right, his ears listening keenly for footsteps in the eerie silence. The street was devoid of life except someone in the telephone box a hundred yards away and a fancy black car parked directly across from it. In the dusk of the evening, he could faintly see two figures in the back and one in front.

The first real opportunity to catch her red-handed and he had lost her. Cursing softly to himself he slapped the hat against his thigh, punishing his mother's hat in place of her for disappearing. He retraced his footsteps back up the road toward the house oblivious to the car that pulled away from the kerb and disappeared down a side road. It was as he approached the front gate he noticed the slip of paper dancing across the road on a stiff gust of wind. Money. Trotting across, he trapped it eventually with the toe of his Dunlop trainer before walking to the nearest illuminated lamp post.

It was a used airline boarding ticket.
Miami Florida to London Heathrow.

As the footsteps receded, the door to the telephone booth opened, and a head poked out. Ivan leant against the door in relief. He was looking a bit of privacy to call his lady, and the next thing he knew, his mother was kissing the face off some man he had never seen in his life.

Shaking his head in wonder, he caught himself smiling.

He never thought she had it in her. She looked bloody good, too.

The man looked vaguely familiar to him in a way he failed to fathom. Good on her. As far as he was concerned, his mother was far too good a woman for the idiot she married.

It was no secret Clem had affairs. It seemed only right and fitting that she should get a chance to do the same.

It looked like she was doing it in style, too.

The man must be mega rich with a fancy car like that. The only other one he recalled seeing like it was when the Queen came arrived at RAF Northolt on her way to Africa while his regiment were waiting to board the plane bound for the Falklands.

Ivan stepped out onto the street and meandered back up to the house making sure he gave his brother plenty of time to arrive well before him. He would have loved to wear clothes like the man in the car. They were not 'off the peg.'

Koko was rubbing off on him in more ways than he cared to admit. Her sense of style was second to none when it came to clothes. She could spot a cheap suit at a hundred paces. Ivan wondered what she would have made of his mother's sophisticated outfit. Any fool could see it was not church gear.

A slight wrinkle marred his smooth forehead.

Why was Ian waving her hat about?

If she were going to church, she would have still been sitting at the bus stop at the bottom of their road. Why didn't he just walk up to the car and give it to her?

Unless, he didn't know she was in the car.

The slight wrinkle became a deep furrow.

That must mean he was the only one who knew what his mother was up to.

Ian must be losing his touch.

It was common knowledge in Peckham that what his brother didn't know wasn't worth knowing.

Less than twenty-four hours back and he had uncovered plenty.

Ivan released a deep sigh. He always ended up getting embroiled in the rest of the families' issues when home on leave. There was always some disagreement or row. Well, he wasn't getting mixed up in anything in the few days he was around this time. As if to seal the decision, he slammed the gate, pursing his lips in satisfaction as it clanged shut behind him.

It was time he got his own stress-free place where he could come and go free of scrutiny and comment. The further away, the better.

Fishing for his keys, he located the correct one and inserted it. As far as he was concerned, he was going to continue to adopt the three monkey's attitude to life.

Hear nothing,

See nothing,

Say nothing.

From the other side of the door, he could hear yet more uproar. Taking a second deep breath, Ivan turned the key and pushed open the door.

Before he had taken a step inside the house, his nostrils were assailed by the smell of noxious fumes.

"Ingrid! Where is everyone?" He reached for the hallway light switch, turned it off and raced toward the kitchen, the source of the all the noise. He paused to switch off the dining room light too and open the windows for good measure.

"Inez!" Panic rose in his chest as the sickly sweet stench found its way to the back of his throat. His thoughts raced with the possibility of evacuating everyone before the gas found its way upstairs to the bathroom boiler. He wondered if the house was insured since the last fire had probably sent the premiums through the roof.

Would he be able to get his gear in time?

He placed his hand on the handle as the kitchen door flung open. He stumbled backward in surprise. Inez popped her head round the door.

"What are you doing?"

He couldn't believe his ears,

"Me? Can't you smell gas? Open the doors and windows in there! Someone call the gas board."

Inez placed a steadying hand on his shoulder. "Alright, don't get your knickers in a twist."

"I can't leave you people alone for two seconds without something happening."

"We seem to do alright when you're on manuvoures."

"Can't you smell that gas?"

"Yeah, yeah, don't worry about it, we had a little mishap." Inez jerked her head toward the kitchen where he muffled laughter could be heard from inside.

"Where's the rest of you lot?"

"In the kitchen, come on I'll show you - you won't believe it." Grabbing his arm, she yanked her confused brother into the next room where he most definitely not believe it.

The source of the gas appeared to be the oven. It stood wide open, in its belly sat Ian's cold dinner in its floral ovenproof dish. Next to the ancient appliance, stood Evie convulsed in laughter, one hand covering her mouth, blinking back tears.

In voluminous red culottes and tight green blouse, Ingrid cut quite a figure especially since he was used to his sister's conservative dress sense. It was her new, eye-catching hairdo that took his breath away.

Instead of her usual curly ebony afro, Ingrid now sported one tinged bronze at the ends.

"What the hell happened to you?"

Ingrid, still muttering to herself, ignored him, so Inez filled in the gaps while Evie, still fighting to get herself under control, lost control again and collapsed over the sink.

"I was listening to music when I heard a kind of boom. I ran in thinking, I don't know, the ceiling had fallen or something and I found Ingrid holding onto the oven door staring into it with this new hairdo and Evie laughing her head off.

"She put the fire out?"

Inez smiled broadly.

"Well, that's the funny thing." She swiped a hand over Ingrid's crispy hair, receiving a frosty look for her trouble.

"There wasn't any fire. She forgot to light it." Inez glanced over at her little sister who could only wave a hand in slow motion, having covered her face with a tea towel from behind which, she gasped for air.

Ivan could only gape and wonder.

"Gas did that?"

"Yep."

"Hello, I've just arrived." Clem shouldered past Ivan toward the fridge.

"Move."

Ingrid did as she was told.

"Hiya, dad," chirped Inez.

He grunted in reply while he scoured the appliance for something to eat.

"Where's your mother?"

"Church."

Ivan kept his mouth shut. Evie took a few deep breaths, dabbed her eyes with the tea towel but was unable to talk.

"What about Ian?"

"Don't know," Inez replied. Suddenly her face lit up. "What do you think of Ingrid's new hairstyle?"

"Since when did she have style?"

Ingrid was not amused.

"It's not easy finding stuff in my size, what's your excuse?"

Shutting the door abruptly, he looked directly at his eldest daughter, folding his West Indian bread in half.

"Don't get fresh with me, madam."

Ingrid glared back, ready to do battle as he took in her appearance from head to toe and back again before answering.

"What's different?"

"Can't you see?"

"See what?"

"My hair."

"What about it?"

Inez was beginning to tire of the game.

Ivan had tired long ago.

"It's browny yellow!"

"So?"

"So forget it," Inez growled in frustration and stalked off to the sanctuary of the dining room, plonking herself onto the settee, leaving her sisters to deal with her father and his snack.

"Well," remarked Ingrid emphatically, "I think it looks pretty, right on."

Evie rolled her eyes. Ingrid was always at least ten years behind when it came to saying cool things.

"Stop your foolishness and go tell your mother I'm hungry."

"What, again?"

Ivan could hardly believe his ears. He was still stuffed full from dinner only a couple of hours earlier.

"Shut your mouth" growled Clem.

"I said mum's gone to church." His eyebrows arched upward.

"What, again?"

Ivan wondered if there was an echo in the house.

"Yep," piped Ingrid. "She always goes twice on Sundays."

"Humph, just like her mother." Flinging the crusts on the draining board, he left the kitchen.

Ingrid called after him.

"What shall I tell her when she comes in?"

"Tell her what you like," came the reply. Crossing the lounge to the telephone perched in the hatchway separating the room from Evie's bedroom that used to be the sewing room when Ida was more ambitious.

He snatched the receiver and immediately sent it crashing down onto its cradle.

"Why is everything around here always locked?"

He whirled to face his audience who had already anticipated another tirade. Ever the showman, he never failed to please.

"EVERYTHING HAS A LOCK ON IT." Clem flapped his hands in frustration.

"The phones locked, the doors are locked. Even the fridge needs a fucking key. I'm living in Fort Knox!" Evie tittered behind her Ivan whose face as usual was blank. "Where the hell is the key?"

Ingrid stepped forward to put her father out of his misery.

"I've got it." Pulling a bunch of keys out of her pocket, she singled out the correct one and unlocked the offending metal rectangle for her father who elbowed her out of the way for her trouble.

"Bloody Belmarsh prison, that's what this place is," muttered Clem. "Move that backside, girl."

He began to dial, paying extra attention to the broken numbers on the dial. "Who the hell keeps breaking the bloody thing, can't you uncivilised fools use the phone properly?"

"It was you," replied Inez flatly. "The time your last agent dropped you from their books."

Ivan happened to be around for that night's particular antics. He hoped his father would wisely change the subject.

"You can all piss off."

Having been given their orders, the siblings filed out.

Inez stared at her sister's crispy copper strands as she followed her upstairs. "I'll sort out your hair if you like."

31

Evie found Ian on the landing mulling over their mothers hat, which swung back and forth from hand to hand. Pausing to let his sisters pass in their quest for scissors, Evie sat beside him.

A minute passed in silence before she spoke, her voice soft in the silent hallway.

"What's the matter with you?"

"Plenty."

Her brow wrinkled at the reply. He had always been a bit weird, but recently he was taking it to a new level with the fascination concerning their mother, scrapes with the police, and talking in riddles. They used to be close when they were younger, but these days, they were strangers living under the same roof.

Ian's voice broke through her thoughts.

"What would you say if I told you there was something wrong with this family?" Evie's smile on seeing the seriousness in his eyes soon melted away.

"Well isn't there something wrong with everyone's?"

Ian's lip jutted out in contemplation.

"Maybe."

"Well okay, so we are not the stereotypical rice and peas' eating West Indian family, but someone has to be different."

Ian shook his head vehemently.

"That's not what I mean. None of my friends' families have sisters who are gymnastics mad, or brothers in the Armed Forces, but that's not what I'm talking about."

Evie was nonplussed.

"What ARE you talking about then?"

His voice came out in the barest of whispers. "There's more to it."

"Like what?"

"Ivan is our half-brother."

"Tell me something I don't know," she hissed.

"We all know the story about his dad being a criminal chased away by Grandma Solomon."

"Yeah, so what?"

Evie eager for answers dug her elbow into his ribs.

"Well?"

"What I tell you, you have to keep to yourself, okay?"

"You know me," she replied, theatrically making the sign of the cross against her chest.

"Well," Ian's voice dropped another notch. "What if I told you Ivan isn't the only…"

"Isn't the only what?" Evie's voice was loud in his ear. Keeping an eye on the door, Ian continued.

"Ivan isn't the only pain in the arse around here. There's you as well."

Evie was not amused.

"Flip off." Shoving him to one side, she ran off to her bedroom fuming. Sometimes Ian could be such an arse, he had her worried. He seemed serious for once. That was the last time she was going to listen to anything he said.

Their father uttered his last sweet farewell to his girlfriend before replacing the earpiece. It rang immediately.

"What the hell?" He picked up the receiver.

"WHAT?"

Ivan rubbed his forehead as he leant against the doorframe, deep in thought as his father yelled into the telephone.

What was Ian up to and what did he mean when he said he wasn't the only - only what? Everyone agreed the boy was strangeness itself. Maybe it was everybody else that was crazy, and Ian was the only sane one in the family. God knew he felt he was going mad.

His thoughts were interrupted by Clem yelling into the receiver.

"Don't ring here again!" The receiver slammed back onto its cradle, then picked it up a second time to crash it down harder for good measure.

Ivan was glad he hadn't unpacked all his gear. It was time to stop at a mates place before heading back to barracks early for a bit of rest and recuperation. One thing was for sure, he wasn't going to get it hanging around this house.

Less than 36 hours had passed, and he had witnessed adultery by both parents, potential dementia, and an accidental gassing.

32

Clem was not a happy man.

He cursed with vigour as he drove his Ford Cortina out of the film studio and onto the high road. It had not been a good day.

First, Annabel had dumped him for that Rudolph guy.

"You're just not my kind of man," he mimicked to himself in the rear view mirror. "I need to be with someone who suits my lifestyle."

She had conveniently forgotten the lifestyle she enjoyed was mainly funded by his money - a bit of jewellery here, a new outfit there. Not to mention that bloody car of hers which cost him more than the wages he got for playing a drug dealer in the Sweeny last year. He still hadn't forgiven his agent for talking him into doing that. Even now, he caught people in the street giving him strange looks when they thought he wasn't paying attention and hurried to the far side of the street.

He gripped the steering wheel till he felt he could bend it into a pretzel. Annabel was high maintenance. He knew it, but the woman was addictive. She had style, looks, and connections.

A whole lot of woman.

He felt he could go anywhere, do anything, with her on his arm.

She had everything, but her own money.

Daddy held the purse strings, being a big man in the city, so he had helped a little here, and a little there. Before he knew it, he had used up his 'rainy day' money and had resorted to picking up one or two items on his travels.

Nothing of significance anyone would miss.

Fat droplets spattered onto the windscreen obscuring his view momentarily before he engaged the wipers. It soon became a deluge, turning the South London streets into a miniature monsoon in the descending gloom.

He had often thought of finding a nice bachelor pad in the middle of town. Peckham was not exactly the hotspot of London;

it was too full of ignorant, backward thinking cockneys and illiterate immigrants.

He never told anyone where he lived. It was too embarrassing. He preferred to cite Camberwell as his current manor. Being en-route for many South London buses, it was close enough to be feasible and dull enough to be forgettable. All his mail was sent to his girlfriend's flat, so even his agent hadn't a clue he lived in that madhouse with a pack of wild pigs and chief sow.

He tried his best to avoid them as much as possible these days. For convenience, he kept a set of clothes at Annabel's house. That way he only had to go to the Peckham house a couple of times a week which was more than enough, especially when the army idiot was on leave. Every time he looked at that string bean fool, he saw Marcel looking back at him. He had his eyes, his colouring, even his mannerisms that eternally grated on his nerves.

Clem wound down his rain spattered window and breathed in the dank air as he negotiated the perplexing Vauxhall one-way system.

He wondered if the sow was at prayer meeting. Maybe he could grab some fresh clothes and dump the dirty ones for Ingrid to clean, and leave before his wife returned.

He could only hope.

With all the church-going he reckoned she could give the Pope competition. What could anyone expect, having a mother like hers?

These days, she was looking very sharp for 'Service.' Sharp suits, and pretty dresses were not quite de rigueur from what he had seen. Skin-tight fancy clothes and teetering ugly shoes bedecked the typical brethren on their way to a service of hollering and gesticulating. A religious workout for the saved.

Maybe she wasn't going to church.

It was a ridiculous notion; Ida was too stupid to exercise independent thought.

He laughed at his foolishness as he waited for the traffic light to change.

33

Clem was keeping a low profile at home. He was in a foul mood, which made everyone edgy.

Having spent most of the day complaining of an upset stomach, he seemed confident he had convinced Ida, but as per usual, she was one step ahead and had already been informed by Inspector Smith of her husband's activities. Clem had been forced to visit Queens Road Police Station with regard to certain stolen items from Shepperton Studios. Ida was grateful for the information but wasn't about to get sucked into another row with Clem. She had other things on her mind.

The headmaster from Consort Street School had already rung, informing her he would not tolerate Ian's continued behaviour. Ian had gone AWOL from school. Her son was becoming quite an adversary these days. She would have to be quick and cunning to fathom what he was up to, but in order to do that, she would first have wait for him to return home. Five o'clock had come and gone with no sign of her errant son. She continued to bustle about the kitchen, making the usual dinner she always made when her head was bursting with untold thoughts. Her fingers automatically went through the motions of preparing boiled cabbage, a whole one cut into four quarters. Boiled potatoes and steamed red Snapper fish, with each one cut into three bits, followed the cabbage into the pot. It was the same one her mother had made her cook since she was a little girl.

During the food preparation, Clem cut his toenails in the lounge, with a pair of tiny scissors. With one eye on the television, his clippings flew to all corners of the room. Dressed in a string vest and boxer shorts, his bony joints were at odds with his bulbous torso.

He yelled through the open doorway from which the latest gospel tunes were blaring. "What's for dinner then?"

"Fish, cabbage, and potatoes" was the reply. He rolled his eyes heavenward and continued to clip away.

"Don't you know anything about roast, grill, or fry, woman?"

"If you don't like my cooking, you get off your backside, do it yourself, and keep your big flapping mouth shut."

Clem sat pondering on the advantages of bursting through the door and slapping her for the hell of it, against letting the altercation pass to create hell at his leisure later, when Ivan came traipsing in to the lounge in full army uniform with his overstuffed kit bag slung over one shoulder.

"It's time for me to go." As per usual, Clem ignored him.

Hefting his bag onto the settee, narrowly missing his father, he continued into the kitchen careful to avoid his father's immense pungent feet, closing the door behind him. His nose wrinkled with distaste against the odorous simmering mulch, but as always, his face settled into impassivity.

He called over the powerful tones of Mahalia Jackson. "Mum, I've got to go." Ida, lost in the music was oblivious to her companion, so he eased the volume down a notch, which had the desired effect. Wiping her hands on the lap of her favourite caftan, she gave her son a bear hug.

"I'm off mum, I said."

"So soon? I thought you said you were going back on Friday." She turned to check the pot bubbling on the cooker. Ivan flicked migrant fish scales off his pristine fatigues.

"I'm picking up a mate, so I was going to stop over for a couple of days before heading back." He was doing nothing of the sort, but there was no way he was going to spend any more time in the house even if it meant spending the night on a park bench. It was way past due to find his own place.

"We haven't spent any time together, and I was hoping you would be coming to a prayer meeting with me." Ida gazed up longingly up at her eldest son.

"I'll be on leave again soon, and we can go then, can't we?"

"But I was looking forward to it. There was someone in particular I wanted you to meet. She's such a lovely girl. She cooks a nice curried goat and rice dinner, too."

"Don't start mum, I'm not interested. You know I don't even like curried goat. I won't be gone long," he put an arm around his mother and pulled her close. "Then we can do whatever you want."

Blinking away her tears, Ida reached for an onion and began to chop it furiously into small pieces.

"Mind how you go. Have you got fresh underwear?"

"Yes, mum."

"You know what I always say..." together they recited the age old phrase. "...you never know when you might be hit by a bus!"

Once the laughter died down, Ivan placed a hand on her calloused fingers and squeezed gently.

"Seriously mum, I'm not a baby anymore; you don't have to worry about me."

Ida patted his arm in return. "I know, you're all grown up now, but you will always be my baby boy."

He smiled down at her. She was loud. She was blunt, but she always cared.

"I think you had better take care of yourself rather than worry about me."

Ida gave him a puzzled look.

"Of course I'll take care of myself, I always do, son."

"I mean it, mum. Just mind out, and for goodness sake be careful."

"Of course I will." Uncertain what exactly her son was implying, Ida gave the pot another stir for good measure.

"So where will you be going on movements next?"

"It's MANoeuvres, and we will be doing a tour of duty in Northern Ireland at the end of the month."

Ida's eyebrows shot up in surprise.

"Ireland! You tell me to watch out for myself then you calmly tell me you are going to that godforsaken place. You can't trust those people. I've heard all about their kind. Remember the Murphys who used to live next door to us?"

"You can't think like that, mum. You shouldn't believe everything you read in the newspapers – it's not always accurate."

"I don't care, you just mind those people, they don't like people like us."

"Actually it's the opposite, one of my mates was posted there last year, and the girls wouldn't leave him alone, they don't get their hands on too many West Indian blokes over there."

"Maybe if that is the case, you might find yourself a woman. You never bring anybody home for me to meet and I'm not getting any younger. I want grandchildren."

Time to leave.

Ivan gave his mother a peck on the cheek and headed for the door.

"Remember what I said, mum."

"Humph," was her only reply.

34

In the lounge, Clem had progressed with his personal hygiene and was engrossed in picking his teeth.

"I don't think those scissors are supposed to be used on teeth" advised Ivan. If he thought his father was going to thank him, he was much mistaken. There wasn't so much as a flicker as he sat languishing. One side of his face was scrunched up to reveal half of his unusually large teeth. The results of his foraging he had thoughtfully slathered onto his step-son's army kit bag.

It is high time I get right out of here, thought Ivan. Before I kill the old fool. Grabbing the bag, he wiped the food residue off with an old tissue and headed for the door. Clem always had a way of making him feel like an outsider within his own family. In some ways it was very convenient being in the army. He visited once every few months. He had leave far more often, but long years past, he had decided what they didn't know wouldn't hurt them.

He turned to find Inez at the top of the stairs, dressed as always in high fashion warm-up gear along with Evie newly arrived from school in her self-customised uniform.

"I'm heading back to barracks."

"Already? But you said we could go to the cinema. I went to find out what was on at Peckham cinema and everything."

"I'm sorry; we'll go the next time."

"But that's what you said the last time!"

Ivan felt mean. There was nothing he would have liked more than an evening out with his sisters but there was no way he was sticking around.

"Come here."

Setting down his bag he beckoned to his sisters. With reluctance, Evie sauntered to the stairs whilst Inez chose to linger on the top step. Placing each hand on a bony shoulder, he stared into her eyes.

"We can go next time; in fact as soon as I get home just get the tickets, okay?"

"I suppose."

"Look here." Sticking his hand into a pocket, he drew out a five pound note. "Take this to pay for it."

Evie took the money, her eyes wide with wonder. "Next time you come?"

"Next time. But no alien films, I hate those."

"They're the best ones!"

"No aliens. You watch out when it comes to him," he cocked his head toward the lounge where Clem languished.

"Okay."

He kissed the top of her head and called up to Inez. "Where's the other two?"

"Ingrid's at work, and Ian I don't know."

"Never mind. See you later." Without another word, he was gone, leaving Evie standing there clutching his five pound note.

35

"Were there any calls for me today, dad?"

"How should I know, I've been at school? Duh."

Inez pushed past and asked her father instead. Evie loitered in the hallway, out of arms reach.

"It's none of your business, move out of the way, I can't see the telly."

Inez stood firm in her resolve to receive a decent answer.

"Well, have you?"

"Have what?"

"Taken any phone calls"

"For who?"

"ME"

"Why?"

"You have, haven't you?"

"Maybe."

Inez rolled her eyes heavenward. "So were there any phone calls for me?"

"No."

Inez was halfway out the door when Clem spoke next.

"Not today."

"What do you mean?"

He tutted to himself. "Exactly what I said, NOT TODAY!"

She took a step closer.

"When then, yesterday?"

"No, I think it was last Monday."

"Monday! Why didn't you tell me before?"

"You didn't ask me before!"

Inez flapped wildly. At a momentary loss for words, she was so angry, she itched to fly at her fool of a father and slap him.

"I saw you on Thursday, on and off the whole weekend and yesterday, and you never said a word about any phone call."

He shrugged his shoulders in dismissal. For a few moments he sat watching the television leaning to one side in order to view his program around Inez before realizing she was still staring at him.

"What?"

"So who was it?"

"A Malcolm something or other."

"I don't know a Malcolm."

"Well that's what he said."

"How about Marian?"

"Maybe," replied Clem vaguely.

"Was it a man or woman?"

"Man. Get out of my way, I want to watch Star Trek."

Evie rolled her eyes heavenward. "What is it with Star Trek all the time in this house?"

Inez pondered on the dilemma whilst her father sat transfixed to the television screen.

"Michael?"

"Something like that."

A little thought popped into Inez' head. "Please don't tell me it was Martin." To her horror, his face lit up.

"That's the one, Martin."

"Nooo!"

"Uh-oh," muttered Evie

Ida came rushing out the kitchen wielding a serving spoon in her hand.

"What's going on?"

"Dad has done it again," wailed Inez.

Leaping to his feet, Clem rounded on his daughter.

"Will you shut your noise? You're spoiling my programme. This one is special, Kirk kisses the green woman."

"But Martin Kinyon called"

"So what? He'll call you back some other time."

"NO, HE WON'T!!"

Ida stepped in before their father got really mad. Evie could see his anger mounting already. A dead giveaway was always the flexing of his wide nostrils as they were now.

"Don't worry, whatever he wanted will keep….."

"IT WON'T KEEP" wailed Inez. "It's too late now, that was THE Martin Kinyon of the West End shows"

"We're doing a bit of one of his shows at school next term," added Evie as she perched on the far end of the settee.

"Oh shut up!"

"Well sod you, then."

Ida was intrigued. "What's going on?"

"I went for an audition to be in one of his shows and I got through to the last ten. I was supposed to find out this week if I got the part."

"Did you get his telephone number?"

"No."

"He NEVER takes messages properly, mum. Why can't we get an answering machine?"

"I don't have money for that kind of thing."

"You should get a mobile phone," exclaimed Evie. "I saw one on telly."

"Don't be stupid, they're too big and heavy. Anyway only rich people have those."

"What about your agent? He might know something."

"What do you need an agent for; you can't act, sing, or dance."

"You can't either and you have one."

"You need to shut that mouth of yours right now."

"I know you are a waste of space and, and…."

"A crap dad?"

"Yeah Evie, a crap dad. Nobody's even seen you in anything on telly, anyway."

"I was in "Love Thy Neighbour.""

"That was in the olden days and you were an extra."

Her father puffed out his chest in pride, the string of his boil-wash vest strained to accommodate the liquid paunch. "I'm in the Sweeny which is on telly this autumn."

"You mean you WERE in the Sweeny," Ida corrected.

"Yes, well let's not talk about that. I'm up for Empire Rd."

"I'm not going to hold my breath waiting to see you on the box. I need to ring MY agent."

"Here." Ida took the key hanging from a thin emerald ribbon from around her neck. "Don't spend too long on the phone, it costs, you know."

Inez went in search of the phone. "My one big break which I've dreamed of for years and my dad buggers it up."

"I don't know what all the fuss is about," declared Clem. "What's the worst that can happen? You don't get it, no big deal. It's not like you have any talent."

"How would you know who has talent? Having none hasn't stopped you."

"I do have talent. Inez is wasting her time."

"You don't know anything; you're never here most of the time, never mind knowing what anyone is doing!"

"I know you are a loudmouth fat arse who likes to tell everyone what to do, think, and say."

"I do not!"

"Hah! Everyone I come across who knows you moans about you and your mouth." He cocked his head to one side, copying her stance. "My son runs the whole army and my eldest girl ate a franchise McDonalds store, oh, did I say ate I mean *owns* a franchise McDonalds store."

"At least I care about my children, which is more than I can say for you."

"I might care if I knew for sure they were…"

"They got someone else." Inez replaced the receiver slowly.

"Oh well." Her father gave her a hearty slap on the back. "No harm done. You can get a proper job now. Ida, there must be something going at the hospital."

"Well, there are a few vacant auxiliary jobs, and if you play your cards right, they do a very nice government pension package."

"I'm not going to work in some stinking hospital!"

"Well, it's good enough for me."

"I'M TOO YOUNG TO START THINKING ABOUT RETIRING. I HAVEN'T EVEN STARTED WORKING YET!"

Ida flinched as the lounge door nearly came off its hinges with the force of Inez's haste to fly upstairs.

"I hope you are pleased with yourself."

Clem flapped his hand in annoyance. "It's not my problem."

"Who's retiring?" Ian sauntered into the room in search of a snack, the strap of his battered satchel flung over his dishevelled blazer causing it to puff out at strange angles.

"What time do you call this?" Ida was in no mood for nonsense. Clem made a timely exit. Evie, having fought the dragon, thought it time for someone else to have a turn.

"Just look at the state of you!"

Ian looked down at himself. His tie hung halfway down the chest of his grubby shirt, with its knot pulled too tightly to be undone. The bottom half had been unravelled to a fringed finish. The rest of his clothes were covered in a fine layer of typical London clay dust as were his shoelace deprived shoes.

"Alright, don't have a monkey," he muttered. "It will wash off."

"Not by me, it won't. You will be doing that yourself."

Ian shrugged with indifference and turned to walk away but found himself held by the scruff of the neck.

"Leave it out." He knocked his mother back with a shove. "Oh, so you're taking lessons from your father now? If that's the case, you can also find yourself a job because I'm not finding you another school."

Ian, fatigued from the day's money-making activities, was not quick on the uptake. Evie opened her eyes wide in warning at her brother.

"What's the matter now?"

"What's the matter he asks? Well, let me enlighten you. Your headmaster told me you have been disappearing again, and he's had enough. He won't have you back. I also got a call from the inspector. You have been seen hanging around the local churches. I hope you are not planning anything stupid."

"Smith is a tosser."

"I don't want to hear that kind of language in this house. As from tomorrow you can go to the labour exchange..."

"Jobcentre."

"Whatever it is, go there and find a job. I don't want you hanging around here while I'm not in the house."

"But he doesn't have any O-levels," reminded Evie, changing television channels with a huge grubby remote control. "By the way, Bola gave mum notice. Don't know what you did, but thanks."

"What do you know about Bola leaving?" The boy didn't even finish his one weeks' notice, and how come his lips were even bigger than usual?"

Ian shrugged noncommittally and shoved his hands deep into his jacket pockets wincing slightly.

"He even left a bit of money on the kitchen table. Just as well, the blenders broke."

Ida pointed to the glass-toughened lounge door, her face grim with annoyance. "You go and find something to do before I get mad."

Evie did as she was told. Ian dusted himself down, apparently not giving a damn he had been expelled yet again. No doubt as far as he was concerned, he had better things to do with his time than spend his days with a bunch of testosterone fuelled oversized morons who could think of nothing but football and girls – in that order. Ida raked him from head to toe with her eyes, her lip curled in disgust.

"You. Job. Tomorrow. If you can't find one by the end of the month, you can leave. I will even…" Ian held up a hand stopping her mid-flow.

"Yes I know. Make me a packet of sandwiches for the trip, blah, blah, blah."

"Good, you know the rules. Get on with it." Turning on her heel she walked out of the room pausing to deliver a parting shot. "Do not find anything illegal, immoral, or downright disgusting. You shame this family enough as it is."

Once his mother was gone, he pulled out a small book, his fingers tracing the gold lettering. He savoured the weight of it in the palm of his hand. Who needed a school education? Proper jobs were for suckers. Why work hard when you could get others to work for you?

36

"Lock off the alarm, woman."

The lump under the bedclothes stretched and re-curled, taking up yet more of the king-sized bed, leaving her stranded on a sliver of mattress and no candlewick blanket.

"It's on your side, why don't you do it?"

The lump under the bedclothes didn't bother answering.

Shuffling up into a semi-seated position, Ingrid stretched out an arm and batted the offending clock into submission. She leaned back onto the hump, exhausted with the excess exertion. It was short-lived. An elbow jabbed her in the stomach in return. Dragging herself off the bed, Ingrid fumbled about in the dusk of a new day. She inhaled slowly, taking in the warm musk laden air deep into her chest. She was debating whether to return to the cocoon of blankets for another ten minutes or nip to the toilet when the bedroom door opened, and her son slipped in.

"Mummy, Keisha pee-peed in the bed again."

She swept a tired hand over her face. She couldn't have a second to herself without someone or something requiring her attention.

"Tell her to take off her nightie and put on her dressing gown, mummy's coming."

Curtis, eager as ever to boss his little sister about, did as he was told. Ingrid was reaching for her floral housecoat when the telephone blared throughout the cramped terraced house.

"Yes mum."

Ida's voice was sharp with annoyance. "How did you know it was me?"

Ingrid sighed inwardly. "You're the only person I know who would ring me at 4 o'clock in the morning."

"So I got you up?" The voice held a lilt of hope.

"No, Leroy has an early shift this morning, and he's LATE!"

On the last word, her husband's head appeared as if by magic.

"What time is it?" The voice barely made it through the puffy lips, his eyes mere slits in a deep mahogany face. Ingrid held up four digits of her left hand and turned her back on him.

"So, are you okay?"

"Yes I'm fine. The Lord is good to me. I can't complain." Ingrid felt the lurch of the recycled mattress as Leroy sprang out of bed, his bare feet drumming their way to the bathroom. Her mind conjured him up dashing water onto his face trying to rub the sleep out of his eyes and untangle the nest of trailing dreadlocks.

"He took me from the miry clay and put my feet on the king's highway."

"Yes, well that's nice for you, mum." She was desperate to change the subject, once her mother started on her church mantras, she could be at it for hours.

"Are you going to work today?"

"No, we have to get a barrel from the man in East Street so I can send some things back home."

She closed her eyes briefly.

So much for her dentist appointment.

"What time do you want me to pick you up?"

"We'll need to miss the crowd so we should get there for nine o'clock when it opens."

"I have to take the kids to pre-school. Why do you need to send a barrel anyway?"

Her mother didn't miss a beat. "Nine o'clock and don't be late."

Before she could think of a reply, Ingrid found herself listening to a monotone dialling tone.

It was times like these she wished her mother drove. Replacing the receiver, she took another deep breath. Why was it always her that her mother bothered when she wanted something? Sure, her mother did do a spot of baby-sitting once in a while, but as far as she was concerned, her mother had a lot of ground to make up before she could come within spitting distance of equalling the amount of help she had given her over the years with the house.

With her brothers and sisters.

Especially her dad.

Every time she thought about what she liked to call her 'lost years' spent cooking, cleaning, and washing for everyone the family it made her want to scream in frustration.

No parties for her.

When others were dressing up on a Saturday night for a good time out at the local disco, she was more likely to be dressing the chicken for Sunday dinner.

"Where's my shirt?" Back from the bathroom Leroy fumbled about in the back of the ultra-modern superior quality chipboard wardrobe complete with feature broken handles.

Ingrid circumnavigated the bed to locate the renegade shirt.

As per usual, there was no thanks. No smile of appreciation.

She longed for the heady days when they were in the first flush of marriage when the smallest thing she did brought the light of admiration into his eyes. He in turn only needed to flash those sexy eyes at her, and she would forget everything she was supposed to be doing. Unfortunately, it had the same effect on most other women he came across. After five years of marriage, and two known affairs, his smile had started to wear thin on her.

She had been devastated at the affairs, and had run back to her parents' house to hide in her old bedroom. She was back after 24 hours.

Contrary to belief it wasn't the sheepish look on his face as he stood on the doorstep. After all, what could he say at being caught with his hand in the cookie jar, or in the knickers of one of his ex-girlfriends whilst she was still in them?

It was the continuous fighting between her parents that made her grab her bags and run home to her cramped council house. It had gotten even worse over the years to the point where it was like living in a war zone, and Ingrid was no U.N. ambassador.

Life with Leroy and the kids was a lot easier.

So life had continued.

It wasn't bad, she supposed. She had been playing the role of wife and mother decades before it was official.

Ingrid shuffled her sizable frame down the small hallway into the children's bedroom, stopping off on her way to gather fresh linen from the overstuffed airing cupboard. As per usual, Keisha had been swimming in urine and was red-eyed with weeping. Although she should have been livid, her heart went out to her.

You couldn't expect miracles from a two year old.

She thought it was a stupid idea forcing Keisha to be dry at night. She had only just mastered keeping herself dry during the day, but Leroy was adamant.

"My mum did it to me, and it worked, so I don't see why she can't do it."

Ingrid wasn't fond of her mother-in-law. In her opinion, she was the biggest waste of space known to mankind.

She cleaned the child as best as she could before clothing her in a fresh nightgown, and stripped the bed before throwing a large PVC square and fresh sheet and onto the mattress. Curtis looked on, his thumb wedged in his mouth, from his sweet-smelling bed.

What kind of woman didn't cook?

Not couldn't cook, mind.

Didn't. Period.

As far as Ingrid was concerned, there was plenty the woman didn't do. She had never cleaned or worked. All her time was taken up with shopping and bingo. If there was a task Leroy's mother could foist onto someone else, she would. She had nine children, and between her poor hard-working exhausted father-in-law and the children, she didn't do a thing.

What would life have been like if her own father was more like him?

She reckoned it served the family right for letting the old woman get away with all that nonsense. Nothing was ever good enough. Thank God they lived in Manchester. The last thing she needed was to get extra work from someone else's mother. Hers was finding plenty of work for her as it was.

An occasional visit northward was enough to get her fuming, what with all the fussing and mollycoddling Leroy's' family did over the lazy cow, while she languished on the sofa perusing the latest mail order catalogue.

Ingrid knew the woman was always nice to her and spoilt the kids rotten, but she still had to dig deep to smile and be courteous, every time they made the journey. Leroy visited on a regular basis of course, like all his siblings, and would not have a bad thing said about her.

Once the children had settled down again, she made two cups of strong tea. She handed one over to her husband along with a couple of bits of toast and jam.

She wasn't hungry. Not at that time in the morning.

She wondered how much sleep she would get before Keisha and Curtis started fighting over their toys – or her mother rang again.

"What time are you finishing today?"

He glanced over as he slipped on his shoes. "I've told you already if I start out now, I should be home by lunchtime. You don't remember much do you?"

Ingrid ignored the barb. If he had half the amount she had to keep straight in her head much less do, she was sure he would have gone insane by now. Turning her back on him, she cleared away the breakfast crockery.

"I'll fix you some lunch, then?"

"Don't bother; I'll go down the café with the boys."

She let a minute pass before blurting out what she really wanted to say.

"It would be great if you could pick Curtis up from school. It's his induction play-week."

"No."

"He would really love it instead of seeing me turn up all the time to pick him up."

"I said no."

Well, she'd tried. If she pressed the matter, there would be an argument. She didn't want that. She couldn't stand any form of fighting.

"Okay."

It was best to leave things alone for now. She would try again in a day or two.

After seeing Leroy off, Ingrid turned off all the lights except the hallway and went back to bed.

She knew how things would turn out later that morning.

Her mother would be in a foul mood because of her father, which was all the time, and would say whatever errand they were doing wouldn't take long. It would. Somehow she would end up with her mother doing all sorts during the day with her and the children falling in line with the plans.

She knew it would happen, but was powerless to stop it. She didn't know how.

Ingrid's gut instinct was proved right first time with regard to her mother's itinerary. After dropping the children off at school, she drove back past her house, skipped two roads and turned into her parent's street. Her mother was in the kitchen, banging pots about in search of a particular saucepan. Ingrid could tell she wasn't in a good mood, which meant she would hear about every goddamn thing which had vexed her mother these past few hours, days, or weeks depending on how mad she was.

The warm-up topic was her father.

No surprise there.

What he had done or didn't do in general as the two of them geared up for the trip to the market in her battered car – the minicab car – as Leroy like to call it. As they meandered through the morning traffic, the topic turned to her paternal grandfather who was threatening to visit for the second time in three years.

Her mother still hadn't mentioned what she was going to put in the barrel.

Ingrid supposed it was the usual toiletries her mother regularly sent to relatives who pleaded severe poverty and fancied trying their luck with unwitting relatives in England.

It was those unfortunates living in England who were the paupers.

As her mother ranted on, periodically poking her in the ribs for added emphasis, Ingrid thought of those who would receive the barrel. She seethed with jealousy at the injustice of it all. She had no idea where she was going to find the money to buy bread tomorrow.

Every time she visited St Lucia, the islanders sported the best clothes, drove the newest, biggest cars which struggled to wrap themselves around cliff edge hairpin bends. They owned the best appliances delivered straight from Uncle Sam, despite the homeowners having to build bigger kitchen extensions, in order to accommodate them as it was no longer stylish to have a completely separate kitchen in the middle of the yard.

Everyone on the island wanted to be an American. Even the French dialect was giving way to an American slang in the young, who strived to be cosmopolitan. Everywhere, people flaunted money.

She knew where that came from.

People like her mother.

Along with other Expats who had left the country for pastures new in America, France, and Canada.

As her mother ranted on, they arranged the finer details of the barrel and made a start on her mother's shopping as Ingrid's thoughts simmered resentfully.

Ida paused, backtracked, and wandered from stall to stall whilst chattering away. Ingrid dutifully followed with increasingly heavy bags containing an assortment of goods, none of which was hers.

She continued to simmer.

Every month, people like her mother dutifully set money set aside from their meagre wages in order to help the "needy" at home.

SHE was needy.

Her wages as a carer in an old people's home were practically non-existent. Without Leroys' contribution she couldn't manage. Some days his money never made it home.

The only thing people back in St Lucia required was the need to receive a hard kick in the backside. They never refused the money, moreover, if there was a death in the family they were asking for more.

They got it, too.

Over the years, Ingrid had tried hard not to think about all the times she and her family had gone without, and how much money her mother might have sent back.

It made her mad if she did.

Not like the folk back home needed it; they no longer relied on bananas to export.

They were now importing tourists.

"Did you hear what I said?" They had stopped at the fishmongers stall.

"No, sorry. I was thinking about the kids," blustered Ingrid. "I don't know what to do for dinner tonight."

Ida clicked her tongue dismissively.

"Don't mind that. Why are you always worrying? I have a nice piece of yam I got yesterday from Brixton. Come by the house and get some with the pork I roasted Sunday."

"Yes mum." Ingrid hated yam. Leroy as a strict Rastafarian never touched pork and the kids hated all that foreign stuff, preferring spaghetti Bolognese or 'Spag Bol' as Curtis liked to call it. She decided to say nothing. The last time she did, her mother went on about it for days. She wondered why the hell they were at the market if her mother was in Brixton yesterday.

They had cargo shops there.

Some days she could not figure the woman out.

"Like I said, your grandfather is too much of a headache for me when he's here. The man is a typical West Indian man; he thinks the world revolves around him. If your father ever treated me like that I would make him too afraid to sleep at night – I would chop his pecker off with a cutlass."

Ingrid didn't doubt it for a second.

Ida gave the selection of fish a once over with a beady eye.

"Hello, darlings, what can I do you for?" The fishmonger passed a large hanky over his ruddy face before tucking it back into the top pocket of his pungent overalls. His once ivory mesh trilby perched precariously atop a salt and pepper number two buzz cut.

"Don't you darling me; your fish don't look too fresh to me."

"A-ha! Caught them this morning with my bare hands first thing luv, they're so fresh they're practically still gasping."

"How much is the Snapper?"

"Four for a pound, bargain prices mate, bargain."

"In Deptford I can get five for the same money."

"This ain't Deptford, luv. Here, it's four for a pound. If you want five, go there, but I promise you they won't be as fresh."

Ida twisted her lips in resignation and gave a slight nod of her head.

"Alright, give me four of your best ones, though, I don't want any tiny ones."

The fishmonger flung his arms wide in supplication to the delight of the passing crowd, eager to join in the fun. "Missus, as if would. I have only the best for my customers. I wouldn't dare, would I?"

He winked theatrically at his fellow workers as one selected, wrapped, and bagged the fish.

Ida popped it into her shopping trolley on top of the carrots, potatoes, and onions before handing over the money. The fishmonger, having completed the transaction went in search of bigger fish to catch with his slick banter.

"Your grandfather wants to come over for a few weeks."

"That will be nice."

"Nice for you, not for me. When he turns up all he wants to do is drink rum and play dominoes. When he drinks too much, he wants to start bossing people about."

"Dad should say something."

"Him? Don't be stupid." Ingrid pushed her way through the crowd clustered about the second-hand clothes stall. Her mother was already picking up items and checking sizes.

"This is nice, look – two for a pound, see if you can find one in your size."

"That's pretty."

Ingrid picked up a light blue halter neck top with pretty ochre flowers.

"You can't wear that. Your tits will fall out."

A smattering of giggles fluttered among the crowd. Ingrid's face burned with shame at the unwanted attention. She wasn't THAT big.

"Ask him for a bigger size."

"It's okay, I don't really like it."

Too late.

Ida snatched the item from her and waved it under the stallholder's nose.

"Have you a bigger size?"

"What size do you want?"

"What size are you?"

"It varies." Ingrid wasn't about to broadcast her size to those with ears fully tuned to other people's business.

"Do you have anything big enough to cover her chest?"

"I'm a market trader, not a magician."

Ingrid edged her way out of the throng, raucous laughter ringing in her ears.

"Take your pick but you won't find anything here more than a size 22."

"Mum, I'll see you over at the tights and socks stall."

"What about your top?"

"It's okay, I don't want it."

"Make up your mind, will you!" Ida threw the top back where it was deftly caught by an eager pair of hands.

Ingrid sauntered up the road, leaving her mother to her shopping for the time being. The woman had no class or decorum. Over the years she had heard from family friends and relatives her mother used to be so beautiful, so sophisticated, but somehow she couldn't see it. Her mother was still kind of pretty in her own way despite having put on a bit of weight over the years, but what came out of her mouth was entirely another matter.

Where was her mother, the one that used to tuck her into bed at night when she was a little girl and sing to her till she fell asleep?

They used to have such fun, even when things were bad in that horrible bed-sit. She struggled to remember where it changed, but she couldn't put her finger on it, even after all the years of endless pondering. Somewhere along the line, her mother had turned into an ogre.

"I said wait a minute," panted Ida.

"Sorry, I didn't hear you."

"You are a strange one, always in your own world. If you are not careful, one day you will wake up and Leroy will have gone."

Ingrid said nothing. Looking after her man and children were about the only thing that kept her sane.

"Your grandfather has nothing better to do when he comes here, other than make trouble. That's his problem you see, too much money and not enough sense. Ever since he got that knock on the head working on the government office building site and they gave him the pay-out, he has been even more of a nuisance. He's even too stupid to invest the money. You mark my words, he'll be broke this time next year, either he'll drink it away or some young thing with high tits and a horse backside will steal it right out from under his nose."

"Do you invest mum?" Ingrid tried and failed to keep the sarcasm out of her voice.

"Never mind what I do with my money, that's my business. Your father will be busy helping him spend his money when he arrives, but that's fine with me if it keeps him out from under my feet to see to my business."

She wondered what her mother's so called "business" was about. They all did. For years, her mother had been disappearing to the point where the family, had renamed these occurrences as going into the "Twilight Zone." The only person who seemed oblivious to them was her father who was barely about himself.

"Don't forget you said you would pick him up from the airport."

"I did?"

"Yes."

Ingrid didn't remember agreeing to anything of the sort.

"Well, okay… just let me know the flight details and date."

"Here, I wrote them down for you." Ida plunged a hand into her gargantuan handbag and after several excavations, came up with a torn half sheet of exercise paper and handed it to Ingrid.

"The flight is coming in at six o'clock in the morning!"

"Come on, I want to see the button man at the other end of the market."

"What about my tights? Did you hear what I said; this flight is coming in very early."

"The flights are always early, you know that. They always travel overnight from St Lucia and arrive first thing."

"They do have other flights that come in later after lunchtime. We flew on one last time we went to see grandma."

"Don't ask me, that's what I was given."

"How am I supposed to get there at that time in the morning? Leroy is probably at work. If he is, I will have to get the kids up at some ridiculous hour."

"Why don't you let them stay with me overnight?"

"You're not coming?"

"No."

"But it's YOUR in-laws."

"I know that."

"But don't you think you should be there?"

"You know the way."

Exasperated Ingrid glanced at the slip of paper again. "What's this other number for?"

"His brother."

"What do you mean?"

"What I said."

"They're not on the same flight?"

"No."

"Why not, for Christ sake?"

"Don't take the lords name in vain"

"Why are they not on the same flight?"

"Your grandfather said it would be cheaper to get the flights this way as he is paying for them."

"CHEAPER?" Ingrid startled a flock of burka clad Somalians' haggling over a matching set of plastic zebra print washing up bowls. "Not for me! He's the one who had an injury pay out. He's got plenty of money."

"Don't start on me."

"You mean to tell me I am supposed to get up at the crack of dawn for grandpa then wait half the day at the airport for his brother, do you realise how much money it's going to cost me in parking charges? Why doesn't his brother's family fetch him, he has some here."

"They're too busy."

"SO AM I."

"Lower your voice. You don't have to wait, pick up your grandfather and go home."

"And his brother?"

Ida paused momentarily before speaking.

"That flight is in on the following day."

"WHAT!"

"Calm down"

"You said it's the next day!"

"That's right."

"Tell me you don't expect me to go there twice in two days."

Ida pursed her lip in a determined line, ignoring her daughter's furious glare whilst about them the crowd ebbed and flowed like a gaily coloured flotsam.

"Mum, you are joking. I've got the kids and work to see to. I can't just charge over to Heathrow Airport twice in one week."

Silence filled the gap between them.

"Mum, please don't tell me it's Gatwick. Why the hell are they arriving there when Heathrow is up the road?"

"He said it was cheaper."

"Not for my pocket!"

"Keep your voice down I said, people are looking."

"I don't care, I'm not going all the way over there twice in a row, get Inez to do it."

"You know she's only just passed her driving test"

"Then you or dad go with her."

"I've got your kids, and you know you can't rely on your father."

"But it's not fair, it's his relative, let him sort it out."

"If we did that, it will turn into a nightmare."

"I'm sorry, but I have to say no, it's too much for me."

"Why don't you send Leroy?"

"There is no way he will agree to it, I can barely get him to pick Curtis up from school."

"Just ask him for me."

"You ask him, but don't hold your breath, these days he won't do a thing."

"Sounds like your father. I remember when Leroy used to follow you everywhere all day long, and you were always running up my telephone bill," muttered Ida.

"He's busy these days."

"What, driving a bus? It must be so taxing; I thought he was all set to work in the city."

"It was lined up but fell through."

"More like they didn't like the look of him. Since when did anyone see a Rasta in a business suit in the City?"

Ingrid remained silent.

"Exactly my point." Ida was emphatic. "They probably took one look at his name on the application form and marked his cards. I ask you, a name like Leroy Williams. The man never had a chance, and then he turns up looking the way he does."

"It wasn't like that."

"Oh?" Ida's eyebrows rose in expectation. "Tell me then."

"Well, he did start, but they let him go because there were a few problems."

"Which was?"

"Just one or two things."

"Yes."

"He didn't like the food."

"What's that got to do with anything? It's a bank."

"He just didn't like their canteen food."

"Why?"

"He said the food wasn't I-Tal, okay?"

Her mother was completely nonplussed.

"What's I-Tal?"

"They serve pork in the canteen and that kind of thing. It wasn't fit to eat for him, just like Kosher or Halal."

"What a lot of rubbish. What's that got to do with his job in facilities and housekeeping?"

"None," muttered Ingrid, remembering the picture of her husband in the Evening Standard earlier that year. The photographer had caught Leroy wild eyed and in mid-yell, swinging a banner outside the Brixton branch of the Midland Bank along with his fellow Rastafarians.

"I told you he was a stupid arse. Why you married him, I have no idea. Those kinds of people are nothing but thieves and Ganja smokers, but you wouldn't listen."

To get away from you and the rest of the family, thought Ingrid.

"Look, you ask him about the airport, and I'll try and sort out picking granddad up. I've got to get back; it's time to pick up Keisha."

Ingrid might as well have been talking to herself as her mother continued to rant on about her 'no good husband' and how she let him boss her around and made her cook 'funny food' for his religion the entire return journey where she unceremoniously dropped off the numerous bags, and her mother.

Glad for the peace, she collected her daughter and promptly returned to the market for her tights, and to complete her own shopping with the gas bill money.

37

Ingrid stood at Gatwick airport before the proverbial cock had even woken up, never mind thought about crowing.

Waiting for her grandfather.

No doubt he would be last off the plane and weighed down with duty free liquor – if he hadn't drunk it already.

Ninety minutes after his fellow passengers had reacquainted themselves with their luggage, and were within spitting distance of home, and long after her stomach had refused to take any more abuse from the reheated offerings and hot sewage posing as airport refreshments, Grandpa Rochard finally made his grand entrance, flanked by two grim faced officials. A porter dragged a mountain of half mashed boxes festooned with string and parcel tape, laundry bags, and a mismatched pair of overstuffed suitcases.

"Mrs. Rochard?"

"That's my mother, I'm Mrs. Williams"

The portly official was first to speak.

"Mrs. Williams, I am afraid your grandfather has been causing a disturbance on the plane and had to be restrained during the course of the flight."

"What's going on grandpa, what did you do now?"

"Why you all always think the worst thing, you women always jumping to conclusions." He thumped his barrel chest in defiance, greyed hairs poked out through a weathered string vest at the apex of his brush nylon shirt. "I am an innocent man. A body can't go nowhere; can't do nothing without people all about his business."

The fresh-faced officer cut in, "Mr. Rochard was inebriated despite being refused alcohol."

"I am not knee-bree-hated."

Ingrid shook her head in disgust at her paternal grandfather.

From his winkle-picker shoes to his lime green hat, he was obviously drunk. If she were to wring out his disgusting, dung-coloured Zoot-Suit, she would have enough whisky to have a double shot herself.

"Sorry, but though he might have had a drink he isn't drunk, this is his normal state."

The officials exchanged glances, their faces unreadable.

"We take these things very seriously and must take the safety of all the passengers into consideration."

Ingrid dipped her head in acknowledgement.

"We have procedures to deal with incidents. The pilot thought he might have to land in Ireland in order to have him escorted off the plane, but luckily they had a troupe of dancers on board who were able to restrain him."

"Bunch of cream puffs."

"Dancers?"

Ingrid imagined a group of multi-coloured samba dancers jumping onto her grandfather. She wished she could have been there to witness it.

"Er, yes," smirked the younger officer.

"Don't go telling your mother about this, it will be our secret."

"I don't understand why a bunch of dancers needed to pin down one man."

"Apparently he was trying to open the outer door mid-flight."

"Grandpa!"

"I thought it was the toilet."

"I'm so embarrassed; I don't know what to say."

The older man handed over a crisp white envelope. "I regret to inform you, madam, Mr. Rochard has been issued with a lifetime ban on Crosswinds Airlines. Your grandfather is very lucky he wasn't arrested, seeing as it is his first offence."

"All you motherfu-"

"Again, I can only apologise for his behaviour."

"Not at all, madam, if you would be as kind as to remove er..." the official glanced meaningfully back toward the mountain of luggage.

"Is that all his?"

"I am afraid so. The porter will escort you to your vehicle. I trust you arrived in one?"

"Yes, but it's only a little hatchback."

"The officers left her to shepherd the old man out of the terminal. Ingrid avoided the quizzical gaze of holidaymakers as her grandfather hurled obscenities at them whilst the porter clucked in disapproval and he trailed behind them.

The ride home to her parent's house proved rather uneventful. The old man fell into an alcohol induced stupor before she had driven past the ticket barrier of the car park, which was no mean feat, with the remains of the luggage too big to fit inside the car piled high on top. Ingrid was grateful he didn't wake up until the car was parked outside her parents' terraced house. She was in the process of winding up all the windows she had previously opened in the hope of allowing the stench of alcohol to dissipate in vain when grandpa opened a bleary eye.

"Where are we?"

"At the house."

"My boy never tell me the house so big."

"You saw it last time you were here."

"He add something to it?"

"No. Let me get you inside and see who's in to give us a hand with all this stuff."

Ingrid fumbled inside her bag, eventually pulling out a second bunch of keys.

"You have a key."

"Yes."

"Where my key?"

"You don't live here."

"You don't neither."

"That's a bit different, I'm always here."

"I wants my key."

"What for?"

"I am the man of the house and every man of that house must have his key."

"I told you, I'm always here, so I have a key, you on the other hand aren't."

"You could have sent it to me in the post."

"What for?" She fumbled with the latch whilst jiggling the key in the lock.

"In case anything happened."

Ingrid stared momentarily at the old man in wonderment.

"So you are telling me if we got locked out of the house or lost our key, all we have to do is scrape the money together, and book a flight to St Lucia pick up the key. Then all we would have to do is return home and open the door or we could post a letter asking for it. Oh, hang on a minute, you can't read. Well, we would have to hang around until someone could be found to read it and send it out to us, meantime we are all sleeping rough!"

Ingrid was surprised to find she was yelling. It was beginning to become a habit with her lately with regard to her family.

"Of course, you only have to ask."

"This family is crazy. I see where dad gets his common sense."

"Don't forget style, this here cloth is real good, got it made special." He preened in his post-war suit.

Fed up with all the old man's nonsense, she wondered why her grandmother left it so long before running off. Leaving the fool to enter the house alone, she began the tedious task of unloading her car of baggage. It seemed to her there was an extraordinary amount of luggage for a two week stay; no doubt a fair portion of it was "presents" for friends and relatives. Oversized avocadoes and mangoes which would ripen and blacken, or would have to be consumed, by the time the wrangle over who was going to fetch or deliver them and when was concluded.

"Is anyone going to give me a hand?" Dumping the first set of bags in the hallway, she followed the laughter and conversation which emanated from the lounge.

"I said I need some help with the bags."

"Hiya! Look who's here," grinned Evie.

Ingrid flopped onto the sofa next to her grandfather who had already made himself comfortable, his bare calloused feet resting on a nearby chair.

"Evie, who the hell do you think picked him up from the airport, the tooth fairy?"

"Well sorry! I thought you were with Leroy."

"He's at work."

"Well, how come I saw him up the high street, then?"

"Lunch probably."

"He didn't have his uniform on, and neither did the lady."

"What lady?"

"I don't know, some lady in skin tight clothes, she looked like a model."

"Probably a friend," dismissed Ingrid. She didn't believe herself for a second.

"He must know her pretty well because he was kissing her face off for a loooonng time!"

"Mr. Leroy sounds like he found himself a piece of ass."

He had only been in the country for five minutes and already she was sick of her grandfather. Ingrid wondered how she was going to get through the next two weeks.

Maybe the best thing to do was to change the subject. Whatever was going on she didn't want to discuss it around him, she had never liked him, especially as a child when they went back to St Lucia to visit. Her mother hated the place as much as she did and never returned to the island.

Whatever Leroy was doing, she would find out, as per usual. No doubt the woman would be replaced by another. He would never get rid of her and the kids. There were far too many things she did for him which made her irreplaceable.

"Where are mum and the children?"

"In the garden."

Evie duly went to fetch her mother.

Greetings between her mother and grandfather were decidedly cool as the children giggled over great-grandpa's gigantic feet. Ingrid and her siblings all knew him to be a loudmouth and bully, so she wasn't surprised her mother was reluctant to have him about. Ida kept her own counsel. Having him about was akin to living with the BBC World Service and British Telecom rolled into one.

"You stink." Her mother's habit of getting right to the point had resurfaced once again.

"Grandpa had an accident on the plane."

"Like what – he fell into a bath of rum?"

"If I knew you had such a big mouth I would never have told my son to marry you, should have left you in your own shit."

"Why don't you shut up?"

"Grandpa said a dirty word mummy," said Curtis. Keisha stared with saucer-wide eyes, her thumb stuck firmly in her mouth as she see-sawed on the armrest of the battered PVC sofa.

"Here we go, round one," sighed Ingrid. She could see the fiery spark light up in her mother's eyes, which never bode well.

"Evie, give me a hand with the luggage. You two come with us and see how many pieces you can count." The children dutifully trotted out the lounge behind their mother and aunt.

"Somehow I don't think him staying here is a good idea." Evie started on the bags on the back seat, whilst Ingrid emptied the contents of the boot.

"Wait till dad gets here. That's when the fun will really start."

"What do you think he meant when he said that stuff about leaving her in…" Evie glanced at the children playing in the front garden before continuing "…the crap"

"I have no idea, but I do remember when I always went back home, every time I mentioned mum's name, people always gave me a funny look."

"Maybe one day we'll find out what going on."

"Don't hold your breath."

Evie hoisted a bag onto one bony shoulder.

"Bloody hell, what has he got in this thing, a house?"

"Knowing him, probably."

 Ingrid hustled her children into the house and secured her car.

"I heard uncle is coming tomorrow. I suppose you are going to fetch him, too."

"Nope, Inez can have that honour."

"You said no to mum? Well, I never would have thought you had it in you."

"I do say no sometimes, it has happened before."

"First I've heard of it. I reckon you should do it a bit more. Seems to me you do everything for everyone, and nothing for yourself."

I do things for myself, too."

Evie crossed her arms and raised an eyebrow. "Oh yes? Name me one thing."

"I went to college"

"You did a catering course, you could already cook, else we would all be dead by now, doesn't count. All you got was a piece of paper saying you are not an idiot."

Ingrid tried again. "I went to Trinidad."

"It's the twenty four hour stop over on the way to St Lucia, give me a break."

"This is a stupid game."

"I'm trying to show you what you have done for yourself so far."

"I don't need my baby sister to show me what a waste of space I am. I can see that for myself, thank you very much, Ms. Big American scholarship. Hopefully you will be off pretty soon and out of my affairs."

"I leave in September for the 'fall' start of college."

"See, you will soon be off to pastures new leaving me here with that lot."

Ingrid flung an arm in the vicinity of the house.

"That's not fair; I didn't put my name forward for it."

"Makes no difference; your grades were amazing. Someone thought you were outstanding enough to be considered for it, which would never happen to me."

"Now all I have to do is find a way to sleep at night and stay awake during the day.

"You still having trouble?"

"Yes, I went to the doctor and he gave me a prescription for sleeping tablets."

"I don't know. All I know is I can't continue studying on two hours sleep a night."

"Your lack of sleep still makes you way out of my league when it comes to brain power."

"I hate it when you talk like that. I'm not trying to make you feel bad. I can't put my life on hold because you're not doing anything with yours. It doesn't work like that, and I can't make you live yours properly either."

Ingrid let out a bark of laughter.

"Well I never. I'm getting pearls of wisdom from my wet-behind-the ears baby sister. Are you sure you haven't been listening to Inez and her mumbo-jumbo? You sound like you're eighty."

"I feel it. Just because I'm younger it doesn't make me stupid. Don't forget, I'm the one who has lived the longest with mum and dad while you lot buggered off the minute you possibly could."

Ingrid had no argument.

"Being wise doesn't happen with age like people seem to think. It happens with experience and the ability to understand what is going on around you, and believe me, around here there's always something going on."

"But I'm not like you, I have responsibilities; I can't just pick up and go and do what I like. I have to see to Leroy and the kids."

"Listen, half of Peckham knows that man is an idiot. As for the kids, they're young enough to adapt to anything. You don't have to carry on as you have been doing."

"It's too late. I'm too old."

"Are you mad? You're only thirty and you are talking about being past it."

"It's all right for you; you have the whole world ahead of you."

"So have you."

"Don't be stupid."

"Listen, if you have any sense you should think about what you really want to do while you still have the time and strength to do it." Evie grasped her sister firmly by the elbow, preventing her from entering the house and gazed into her sisters' eyes. "One of these days, either mum or dad will be too sick or old to care for themselves. If you are still moping about the place, you will be the one who will be looking after them. That's all well and good, but if you haven't lived any kind of life in the meantime, how happy will you be to do it? If and when that day comes THEN your life will be truly over."

"It won't come to that, they will go on for years, and you lot will help out."

"So you have a crystal ball, do you? You know what everyone will be doing and what country they will be living in?"

"What you two fools doing with my bags?"

Grandpa seized the case from Ingrid and proceeded to drag the sorry-looking case down the hallway "Hurry up. I got things in there I need and you two flapping your lips making me wait 'til kingdom come."

Unfortunately for them, it appeared the effects of the alcohol had diminished somewhat, leaving the usual, mean son of a bitch, they knew so well in its wake.

"Just coming now with the last bits." Evie flashed him her prettiest smile. "We want to hear all the news from back home. Has anything changed?"

Grandpa flashed her a gap toothed grin in response.

"Them there hotels be springing up like weeds for those fancy people. Don't see why they bother with a room. Just fix them a tent on the beach. That's where they be all the time, basting and a-roasting themselves in the sun. Throw that bag up there for me."

Evie hoisted the odd shaped bag onto the table and helped the old man with his case as she tried to explain the British psyche.

"They don't get the sun here so when they go on holiday, they go a bit crazy. Some of my friend's parents come back darker than me."

"That's not too hard to do. You're a bit on the light side," quipped Ingrid.

"Am not."

"Yes you are. You look like a macaroon."

"What that?"

"A biscuit, grandpa"

Laughter burst out of him liberally spraying them with a drizzle of saliva. Dabbing at the corner of one eye with a grubby shirt-tail, he motioned for the family to come forward.

"You London kids goin' kill me, I want to try one of them there biscuits. Come get your presents."

Delving into the bag, he pulled out a small green bottle and a long thin item wrapped in the St Lucian local paper.

"Where that witch go?"

"Who?"

"Your mother"

"Probably upstairs."

"When you see her, give her that from me."

"What is it?"

"Bay Rum and a nice long piece of soft candle. It's good for all kinda ailments, jest rub it on. Better than Vapour Heat."

"Oh."

The sisters exchanged glances. Evie thought it best not to mention her mother hated the stuff. Bay rum gave her a rash and what the hell was a piece of melted wax going to do if you put your back out?

"Thanks, I'll put it in her room later."

As she set the offending item on the table, she noticed a line of clear liquid across the surface.

"Did the children spill anything on the table earlier?"

"How should I know? Why are you asking anyway?"

"I thought they might have spilt their drinks or something."

"For you Ingrid." Grandpa handed her a curved object wrapped in newspaper. "I know you like them."

"Thanks."

A small smile of appreciation flashed across her face which disappeared the moment she took the parcel. It took only one touch to realise what it was.

Ingrid slowly unwrapped the three-fingered bunch of green bananas and set them on the table. They were exactly the same as the ones she saw yesterday in the market being sold three for a pound.

"For Evie and Ian, I got these."

Out of the bag like magician performing a trick, he pulled a matching pair of immense colouring books and jumbo pack of felt tip pens.

"Wow, thanks, just what we always wanted." Evie scrutinised the front cover before adding under her breath, "about ten years ago" which her grandpa failed to hear.

"I knew you would like it."

"Who coloured in the first page?"

"Cab companies take too long to get to the airport, I had nothing to do."

"Great, a USED colouring book, I can barely contain my joy."

"I got this for Inez."

The sisters stared at the battered box.

"That's a really nice thing to get her, but she doesn't like chocolates."

"Everybody likes chocolate."

"Not Inez. She won't go near it or anything else with fat or sugar."

Over the years, Inez had become impossible to live with when it came to food. It had started with small things. No added salt. Not too much butter. Now it had escalated into tofu this and chickpea that, as if the items were easy to find on the Peckham High Road. It got to the point where every mealtime she bothered to attend was a battlefield between their mother, Queen of all things boiled, and Princess Quorn.

Grandpa's considerable chin jutted out in defiance. "She'll eat some for me."

Ingrid and Evie glanced at each other, both knowing exactly what the other was thinking.

No, she won't.

Ingrid wondered what in heaven's name could still be in the bag to warrant the zip to be at bursting point. They didn't have long to wait.

"I got your father two bottles of rum."

"I don't think mum would like that."

"Good. It's not for your mother, anyway it too late, it's here now."

Setting the bottles on the table with a thud he delved into the bag again. Evie gazed at the cloudy bottles.

"Grandpa where's the rest of this drink?"

"I got thirsty."

"Like you got bored?"

"Uh huh. Somebody give me a hand with this."

Judging by the calibre of the previous gifts, they were at a loss as to what the last gift could be. Together, they held onto the luggage whilst grandpa wrestled the item out of the bag, finally hoisting it onto the table.

"What the hell is it?"

"It's a fish" stated Evie. A very big fish."

"I know it's a fish, but what the hell is it doing in the house?"

Grandpa stroked the fish with tenderness. "It's a present for Ivan."

Ingrid stepped forward for a closer inspection. "Actually, I think it's either a barracuda or a tuna."

"How would you know?"

"They have a picture of the most common types of fish at the chip shop."

Grandpa's maw stretched to reveal a set of perfect veneers.

"That there is one nice piece of fish. It put up a good fight, but I did catch his ass. If Ivan smart, he can eat good for a month, maybe more on that."

"I think it's frozen."

"You mean it WAS frozen. I think I know where the liquid on the table came from."

"I wanted it to stay fresh."

Ingrid wrinkled her nose in distaste. "Oh, it's fresh alright."

"How did you get it through customs?"

"They were looking for alcohol, not fish."

Evie nodded sagely as if carrying a whole fish through the "Nothing to Declare" area of the departure gate happened every day.

"Of course, they wouldn't have spotted that, grandpa would they?"

"Nope." He opened his mouth to elaborate on the science of marine transportation, but was halted by the ring of the front door bell.

38

Evie returned a few moments later, with a perplexed look etched upon her face. Ingrid placed the semi-frozen fish onto the dining room table with a thud.

"Did you order a minicab?"

"No, why?"

"The minicab man says he's got to pick someone up from here to go to the airport."

"Someone's having a laugh. I've just been and Inez isn't due to go until tomorrow, you know that."

"It's for me."

All eyes turned toward the voice.

Ida stood in the doorway, gone was the ancient shabby coat. Resplendent in a stylish scarlet outfit, with matching hat at a jaunty angle, her black patent leather shoes glittered in the light at every turn. They had never seen their mother so regally dressed, or so beautiful.

"Whose wedding are you going to?"

"Very funny, Evie. There is no wedding."

"So where is you going?" Grandpa didn't seem to be in the least bit amused to be up-staged by his daughter-in-law.

Ida, her eyes downcast said nothing. Evie and her sister glanced uncertainly at each other, not sure of what to do or say, whilst Curtis and Keisha tried out the new felt tip pens on the arm of the settee. Grandpa looked upon the older woman with growing anger.

"I want to know what it is you think you doin'. I jus' get here and you going somewhere, and I don't even get my food yet."

"I am not getting anything for you."

"I am the man of the house and I say what's going on around here, and I say you get what I want."

Evie inhaled sharply. She hadn't a clue what the hell her mother was playing at, but she was not getting a nice feeling about the whole scenario. In the hallway, she glimpsed not the battered generic fabric suitcases the whole family used, but a pair of gunmetal rhino tough suitcases waiting by the front door.

"What's going on, mum?"

Ida raised her head till her chin stuck out at that typically stubborn angle they all knew so well.

"As I said, I am leaving."

"Okay, so what time do you want me to dish up the dinner, or would you rather I wait until you get back?"

"You are not listening, I said I was leaving, I didn't say anything about coming back anytime soon."

"But won't you be hungry?"

Ida shot her eldest daughter a knowing look. Ingrid understood what was going on. It had always been her way of coping with situations that she wasn't comfortable with. She just switched off.

"Will you be eating wherever you are going?"

"Don't be daft. Does it look like mum's coming back today?"

"Are you going to Disneyland?"

Ida smiled apologetically "No Curtis sweetheart, maybe next trip."

"She better come back soon, I got things in them cases that need washing."

"You are supposed to have laundry at the end of your holiday, not at the beginning" said Evie.

Outside, the mini cab driver sounded his car horn. Ida nervously smoothed the front of her pristine coat before she began.

"You kids are at an age where you can do without me for a while – all of you are over the age of consent and I am not saying I'm never coming back. All I'm saying is I need time to sort myself out. I have spent so many years of my life looking after all of you. I am entitled to have some kind of enjoyment, or quality of life of my own. Spending the rest of my working life cleaning up after people who couldn't give a damn about me every day, then coming home to an empty house because your father isn't here half the time is no life for me. When he docs decide to come home, we fight.

"I am not going back to that bloody hospital, I have taken early retirement. I have enough to live comfortably if I'm careful."

Ida stared meaningfully at each of them as she continued.

"I have my own interests. I had a life before all of you, before I got married."

Grandpa did not see what all the fuss was about.

"In my day, women had kids and stayed at home, that was their job. If you bored, I give you something to do."

Evie raised her eyes heavenward. "Tell us something we don't know."

"This is not the thirties; women don't have to put up with the, 'I must do what my husband says' thing."

"It worked good then, it work good now. Sounds like you need taking in hand. My son been too soft on you. Especially after he took you in, and was so good to you when nobody wanted you, and now you running away again."

"What's he talking about mum?"

"Rubbish as per usual." Ida picked up her hand luggage. "I don't have time for ancient history. I have my life to get on with."

"Wasn't rubbish when you had a baby on your arm, and nobody to turn to. Clem looked good then." Grandpa grinned. "Fresh meat and so fine. Now you going and not even a goodbye for him – not even a note. You running away again. You got no staying power, things bad back home, you come here. Things no good here, you off again."

"It wasn't like that. I gave him everything."

"You keep telling yourself that."

"Look" interrupted Evie "I don't care what happened back then. All I care about is what's happening now. You're leaving, we don't know where, how long for or if you're even coming back. Ivan and Ian don't know what's going on, and dad's going to go ape-shit when he finds out. Everyone's just standing around chatting like nothing's happening."

Ida squared her shoulders, her gaze lingering on her grandchildren colouring away, oblivious to the drama unfolding about them.

"I will explain everything in time, but right now I have to go." Ida stared meaningfully at grandpa as he delved into one of his battered cardboard boxes, before glancing at Evie. She stared back, the light of fury ignited in her eyes.

"What are we supposed to do about dad and grandpa? How am I going to get to college? I haven't got my plane ticket yet. I don't know where I'm going to live - I don't have any money!"

"You have until September to get sorted. When I arrive at my destination I will send you some cash."

"But why are you going now, after all this time?"

Ingrid roused herself from her stupor. "Mum doesn't have to explain herself to us."

"Yes, she does. Why now mum? What has changed so drastically to make you drop everything?"

"I don't expect you to understand, but I need space and time to put things right, and I can't do that here with your father. I will be at the old Solomon house for the time being."

The staccato blast of the car horn blared in the quiet street. The cabbie sounded ready to drive off on another job.

"I really have to go now, or I will miss my flight."

"Ingrid say something. Stop her!"

Evie shoved her reluctant sister toward the front door as their mother motioned to the cabbie. The pot-bellied man stored her cases as Evie clutched at her mother's coat sleeve.

"Please don't go. We can sort whatever is bothering you here."

"I have to do this."

"Think it over. You can delay the flight a few days, can't you?"

Ida gently prised her arm out of her daughters grip "I can't. I've left it long enough as it is. I can't retract my early retirement notification, even if I wanted to, and I can't live with Clem anymore."

Ida held her daughter fiercely to her. "I will be back, I promise you. Just give me some time to sort things out."

Evie closed her eyes. She couldn't bear to look at her mother.

"Fine. Just sort out whatever you feel you need to, and get back in one piece, we love you."

"I know I've been a crap mum."

"I don't care, just come back. And soon, mum."

"Come on luv, I've got another job to get to, and its parky out here," moaned the cabbie, keys jingling with impatience.

Ida turned away, out into the balmy sunshine to the waiting car and stepped in with one last shamefaced glance toward her daughters. In the distance, the sound of a Mr. Whippy ice-cream van tinkled its merry nursery rhymes as it wound its way around the traffic-free streets.

The Ford Sierra accelerated down the street, turned the corner and disappeared leaving Evie standing at the kerb hunched against the sun. Ingrid stood motionless at the wrought iron gate, whilst the children sang 'Ring o'Roses' in the front garden. All were oblivious to the old man bellowing through the house to shut the front door.

39

Inez inserted the last file into the drawer and smiled, congratulating herself on a job well done.

Closing the filing cabinet, she stepped back into the room. Sliding the door into place she closeted paperwork, office equipment, and coffee maker.

Everything was in order and to her satisfaction.

Time to lock up.

She scanned the room for anything out of place in the expansive area, taking in the gleaming mahogany surface of the reception desk, upon which stood an empty In/Out tray, appointment book and exquisite swan paper-weight and a pair of ivory telephones. The extortionate fee of the interior decorator was worth every penny when it came to recreating an environment in the style of a gentleman's club.

With its burgundy walls, antique panelling, thick beige carpets and plush Persian rugs, any anxious client would soon find the calm reassurance of the room and deep leather sofas most relaxing whilst they admired the exquisite art collection or admired the view over central London through the generous windows.

One of the telephones trilled cutting across the quiet opulence.

Inez quickly glanced toward a pair of tcak doors at the other end of the long room and picked up the receiver with a practised air

"The Portis Group. How may I help you?"

"It's me."

Inez sighed in irritation.

"Ingrid what do you want? I told you not to ring me at work. Mr. Portis doesn't like personal calls."

"I'm sorry; I didn't know what to do," wailed Ingrid.

"What is it now?"

"The debt collectors have been around again looking for dad."

"And what am I supposed to do about it?" Inez flicked a stray hair from her immaculate tweed jacket.

"Do you know where he's gone?"

"Ingrid, I haven't seen him for the past fortnight."

"Oh." One word carried the summation of her sister's helplessness.

Inez rolled her eyes.

"What about Ivan?"

"He's still in Thailand, and I haven't seen Ian in months, he's too busy I suppose."

"Tell me about it."

Ever since her brother was granted leadership of his own church, Inez had heard lots, but had yet to set eyes on him. By all accounts, he was the hottest preacher in South East London according to The Hummingbird Caribbean newspaper.

"Does grandpa know anything?"

"If he does, he's not saying, as per usual. I need to get this sorted, it's the third time this month, and they said they were going to come back in next week and take something…"

"So let them."

"Not from my house! They came here."

"How did they get your address?"

"I'll give you two guesses"

"The agreement has your address on it."

"Got it in one."

Inez groaned aloud. "How much is it for?"

"Two hundred and thirty six pounds and eighty nine pence"

"What for?"

A washing machine from Rumbelows"

"There's no new machine at the house!"

"I know. The one in the house is the one mum bought the year before she left."

"So where is this new machine then?"

"Buggered if I know. He is still in a huff from mum walking out."

"Oh for god's sake, it's been years."

"I thought he was going to break all the furniture when he got home that night. It would be the night he was dropped from the barber's sitcom."

"It didn't exactly help when grandpa got him mad when he said all those things about mum. The old git knew if he did that, dad would be too mad with mum to argue with him about why he was here for good."

Inez pressed her palm to her forehead and took a deep calming breath.

"We can't change what has passed so let it go. Let me have the details on the washing machine, and I'll ring them up and see if I can't sort out some kind of deal or payment plan."

"Thanks, I really appreciate it." The relief was audible in her sisters' voice.

"I'll stop by tomorrow evening and pick up the details."

"Thanks. Shall I make dinner for you?"

Inez mentally calculated the amount of calories, starch, and carbohydrates contained in one of her sister's typical evening meals.

"No, I'm meeting friends for drinks and nibbles after work so I probably won't be hungry."

"Oh, okay." She could hear the disappointment in Ingrid's voice, but she stuck to her decision.

Setting the receiver back on its cradle, Inez mulled over the case of the missing washing machine whilst she took out a pristine dust cloth and quickly gave her desk an extra shine.

Sometimes she would give anything to be able to get on with her life without all these stupid phone calls and endless family dramas. Why was it that she was always the one who had to sort out the mess?

Smoothing out the imaginary creases in her skin-tight amber pencil skirt, she checked her slender calves for ladders in her sheer tights before delving into her matching designer handbag for her wide-toothed brush and mirror. Removing the tortoiseshell comb from her hair, Inez slicked back her oil drenched curly-perm into chemically sculpted waves before refastening the comb, blotting her forehead, tops of ears, and hands with the minuscule hand-towel secreted in her desk for that purpose. Reapplying her scarlet lip-gloss, she made one last check in the mirror before heading for the right hand door at the other end of the room, rapped smartly before entering without invitation and strode up to the immense desk.

"I'm off now, Mr. Portis. Your first appointment is Mrs. Bronstein at 9.15am tomorrow."

"Where are the notes?"

"Under Donald Jackson just here." Sliding around the side of the desk, Inez selected the file and placed it in front of the blonde haired man.

"Very good Inez, what would I do without you?"

Gazing down, she took in the handsome features with its piercing azure eyes and smooth pale skin.

"Oh, I'm sure you would be fine."

"I don't think so." A small smile touched the corners of his lips.

Her breath caught in her chest as she felt a warm hand creep up her calf and tickled its way over the back of her right leg on its journey under her skirt. Smiling down, Inez caressed his broad back.

"I think maybe we should take this discussion elsewhere. Mr. Portis senior might pop in to see what his favourite son is up to."

"The old fart is still probably sleeping off lunch."

"Still, you never know."

Reluctantly his hand withdrew from its snug position between her thighs.

"I suppose you have a point. You are so practical, efficient, and so beautiful of course. That's why I hired you."

Inez bent, touching her lips briefly to his before stepping toward the door.

"It's nice to know I'm appreciated, Mr. Portis. Shall I pencil in an appointment for this evening?"

Mr. Portis touched an impeccably manicured finger to his lips in parody of contemplation.

"I think seven thirty might do, at the usual place. Please make all the necessary arrangements, Ms. Rochard."

"Yes, sir." Inez sashayed from the room in the knowledge the psychologist had his eyes on her pert backside.

Outside, the air was heavy with expectation of rain, much to Inez' consternation. Her thick hair would soon be a mini oil slick saturating her clothes if she wasn't careful. Scurrying into the underground station, the trip home to Kilburn took what felt like forever to her before she found herself back in her neighbourhood. Stopping at the local late night supermarket, she bought some wine as expensive as she could afford, and a pack of discounted smoked salmon, its sell by date for that day.

Hurrying along the high street, she made another mental note to telephone a few letting agents. She needed somewhere more upmarket to live. She skirted the odorous pubs belching drunken rowdy patrons, on their way to their favourite oasis, written into subconscious minds. The local curry house was the preferred destination, for as long as she could remember. Inez picked her way down the middle of the pavement, which still wore the evidence of that day's market with its sweet-smelling, overripe squashed fruit and mouldering vegetables. She averted her eyes when she came across remnants from the butchers pitch, pieces of flesh so far past being edible for human consumption, it was practically strolling about with the amount of live bacteria contained in it.

Her street was well away from the market place and local businesses. Even so, whenever anyone asked where she was from, the answer was always the same – West Hampstead. Technically, it was true. When she had left her sunlight-deprived hole called a studio flat for the spacious one bedroom palace she now rented, her telephone number came with her. Her Hampstead landlord also kept a flat in her block for his own personal use, unbeknownst to his wife, so she was a Hamstead-ite by default.

Letting herself in, Inez picked over the carcass of mail she found in the hallway, lovingly called the tunnel by the other inmates. She replaced the leaflets for superior double glazing and flyers for the newly opened Kasbah Kebab House, of which she had already sampled their goods and found it disgusting. She ignored the crimson overdue statement from Kennard Personal Pagers addressed to her, which left her with a thin air mail letter of the sort which a person wrote inside, folded and sealed leaving the recipient to open with the utmost due care, else risk losing most, if not all of the text if the person who had penned it hadn't already slathered it in saliva rendering the words illegible.

A frown creased her brow; she had hoped the pager bill wasn't too high. She barely had enough money to see her through 'til payday. It would be fantastic if James took her out this week, so giving her a chance to save on her food bill as he was wont to do every once in a while. It seemed to occur less and less these days.

Throwing the air-mail letter bearing a colourful Florida stamp into the grocery bag, she left the leaflets to fend for themselves and climbed Mount Eiger without the aid of equipment to her front door.

Slamming the flimsy front door behind her, the purchases were quickly tidied away in the kitchenette, throwing her mother's letter into her bedside drawer with all the others, unopened. The only difference being the country of purchase of the stamp.

The last time the two of them had been out had been more than two weeks ago. James had found a disgusting East-End flea pit she wouldn't have sent a tramp to, and had spent the whole evening scrutinising everyone who entered the place in the hopes of avoiding Phillipa and her friends. Inez snorted in contempt.

As if those Sloane Rangers would be found anywhere else but in Knightsbridge at Harvey Nichols.

It wasn't just that the 'restaurant' was awful. She had bought a fantastically exorbitant sexy dress to impress him, and boy did it. His eyes had nearly popped out of his head when he caught sight of her in the soft ruby silk; it was well worth the consumption of a weeks' worth of soggy sandwiches. James had showed his appreciation, too. He had almost slept the whole night at her place for a change. Judging by his demeanour the next day, Inez reckoned his wife had a few choice words waiting for him when he arrived home later and served him right, too. It was high time he told Phillipa what was going on and left the bitch with her Barbour jacket, gymkhanas, and yachting before things got too complicated. Not being in control niggled away at her like a deadly virus, with his assurances of being there for her and his declarations of unending love, then promptly disappearing in the early hours leaving her to wake in a lonely bed.

By the appointed hour, the flat was immaculate with her newly washed sheer tights hidden under a t-shirt on the radiator and her ever increasing footwear bundled under the fussily ornate bed festooned with an inordinate number of cushions made from every type of fabric, tassels and fringing, all in varying shades of pink.

Inez puffed an extra cloud of "Shake-N-Vac" about the lounge for good measure before careering around the furniture with the apartment's inherited antique vacuum cleaner, leaving the room smelling antiseptically lavender fresh, before having a quick shower and shampoo. She dressed in her 'daren't think about the price' chocolate negligee, with its contrast deep vanilla lace and matching dressing gown, fluffing out her gunk-free hair to let it fall about her shoulders in soft waves.

Taking one last look about the room, she checked one last time that everything was in order;

Wine in the fridge, check;

Smoked salmon plated in the fridge and ready to go onto the minute bits of ciabatta on the table just like on television, check.

Soft Vivaldi and matching lighting resonated softly in the lounge; check.

Positioning herself artfully into an enticing pose, she settled back to await his key in the door.

Inez awoke with a start, her body covered in goose bumps to a silent flat, her senses telling her she was alone.

Padding through, the kitchen clock proclaimed it to be 2.36 am.

Maybe she had slept through his message on her pager.

There was none.

Bastard.

Pushing back the faded floral curtain, she checked the deserted street for signs of his vintage Triumph Stag sports car.

There was none.

Stepping back, she let the drape fall before tweaking it open again, pressing her face to the damp windowpane.

Across the street under the street lamp stood a man deep in shadow, his body turned toward her.

Her breath caught in her chest.

She was sure the man was looking directly up at her.

How long had he been standing there?

The face blurred in the orange-tinged glow of the streetlamp was turned into the deep shadows of the night.

Stepping away from the window she let the drape fall back into place. Her mind raced with possibilities as she tossed the curly dried bread into the bin, cursing as she slipped out of her satin under-things and donning more substantial mismatched colour-run cotton sweats. Inez threw herself into bed creating an avalanche of cushions.

Maybe it was just fanciful thinking. Maybe the man was looking at the window above hers.

Maybe Phillipa had paid the man to tail her.

So much the better.

Which brought her back to James.

Where the hell was he?

Did he think she would always wait for him?

It really was time to pack in her job and find something less stressful 'til it was time to apply to college as she was supposed to years ago, like the rest of her friends. Maybe it would have been better if she had done it straight away from school like everyone else, but back then, her heart just wasn't in it after that disaster with her audition, which her father had buggered up. She just wanted to get away from him, from home, from everything.

She had drifted along taking anything that took her fancy, which was how she ended up pushing thirty with no obvious prospects working as a receptionist for Edward Portis and his son James, leading psychiatrists off Harley Street. Catering to the rich pampered society women of London who regarded her with such distain.

James said it was because her backside was so much higher and tighter than theirs and her lips so lush without the aid of lumpy collagen fillers, but she didn't think so.

Oh how she hated them with their overpowering perfume and "oh, I just threw this old rag on" clothes worth more than her annual salary, She despised being inferior to them in her marketplace purchases and fake perfumes, which they turned their carefully sculpted nose up at, at every opportunity. She squirreled her money away in order to buy things a little more upmarket. A little more refined. When James had been especially nice to her on the first day, she put it down to being polite; she soon changed her mind when it was obvious he was pursuing her.

Inez was flattered.

It didn't bother her he was married. It was just a bit of fun. Not anymore.

She had to be careful. She was fine now, but in a few years her trim frame might not look so good. Every year it would get harder to keep her looks,. Then what would she do?

Tomorrow she was going to call in sick and start sorting herself out.

To hell with him.

40

"So where's the old fool?" Inez propped herself against the moist wall and clutched her fawn Burberry trench coat closer about herself.

Ingrid shrugged her meaty shoulders, spattering remnants of oxtail around the room with her soup ladle, narrowly missing her sister.

"I don't know. He said something about getting a paper. He's probably in the bookies."

"What's a bookie, do they make books?"

"No, they don't. Go away and mind your own business, Keisha."

"But I'm still waiting for my Jungle Juice."

Curtis yelled from his seat in the lounge "I want some too!"

"And some bun and cheese, pleeaase!"

"Me too!"

Inez watched as Ingrid mixed the sugary packet fruit juice, adding water and yet more sugar to the chemically enhanced berry drink. To Inez' horror, she also added a thick wedge of cheese sandwiched between two hunks of Caribbean spiced cake, and cemented it with creamy butter onto a plastic plate. She wondered how long it would take before the children's metabolism gave up, and they became as round as their mother.

"Here, take that into the living room and go watch your programme."

"Yay, Time Tunnel is on!" The children hurried out to watch the latest instalment of the old Sci-Fi re-runs leaving the women to talk.

"That's far too much sugar; you will give them diabetes if you carry on like that."

"Oh, they'll be fine, you worry too much." Ingrid returned to the task at hand, stirring the bubbling drum of stew on the hob.

It's my worrying which has kept me this size and you NOT worrying that has kept you the size of a barn, mused Inez. She refrained from pointing it out, deciding to concentrate on the matter at hand, rather than bring up old disputes.

"So," she cast her glance about the cramped overheated kitchen, taking in the utensils piled high on sticky surfaces and the table covered in an eye-watering flowered plastic cover. It was piled with every possible condiment known to man, and mismatched chairs which in turn didn't match with anything else, in the overflowing room. Inez placed a grubby tea-towel on a chair and sat down.

"How's it all going?"

Ingrid let out a long loud sigh.

"It's not. I can't do this anymore. I honestly can't."

"I know it must be tough."

"You have no idea. Ever since dad's agent dropped him and he couldn't find any jobs, it has been hell. Every time I go to the house, there's something missing from it. Last week, the bookshelves disappeared."

"That's not so terrible, we only used it for ornaments" dismissed Inez.

"But the rug and curtains are missing too!"

"Oh. Well at least the sofas still there."

Ingrid cast her a knowing look.

"Ah, shit."

"Exactly."

"What did he do with it?"

"What the hell do you think?"

"Oh."

"Then he disappears for a few days, maybe a week, depending how much money he sold the things for, only coming back to harass me when he has no money. He has been driving me mad with his nagging to cook and clean for him. He is always picking a fight with Leroy and shouting at the kids. He drinks rum and plays dominos with grandpa and his cronies all night in my house, or until Leroy orders them to go home, that is if he's home himself. Then the whole thing starts again." Ingrid closed her eyes, frustration plainly etched upon her face.

"He was complaining his knees were hurting, so I took him to the doctor. She said it looks like he's got a bit of arthritis. Now he's playing it up to the hilt. It's "I can't do blah, blah, blah, my arthritis this, and my arthritis that."

"What about Ivan or Ian, can't they help out?"

"I don't know Ivan is on manuvoures somewhere nasty or in Thailand, he never tells me, though if things get real bad I do have an emergency number for him. Ian has got his own problems. I've seen Inspector Smith sniffing around his church, which is never a good sign. He may be retired, but he still has it in for Ian ever since the fire."

"What about Evie?"

"What can she do? She's in the States with a year left to go, and barely keeping a roof over her head, never mind worry about what's going on here. She is still having nightmares she can't get rid of, and I think she is still on those sleeping tablets."

"I warned her about those. The psychiatrists I work for are always complaining about GP's over-prescribing them for patients. Half their work is trying to undo the damage caused by taking those things. It's going to catch up with her, and when it does, it's going to be nasty. But mum's in Florida, and Evie's in San Francisco, so why is she struggling? They're in the same bloody country."

"I don't know. I'm not a sightseer, I don't have a crystal ball. Since mum left, Evie has been so angry with her."

"You mean soothsayer."

"Whatever. All I know is I can't do this anymore. I need help. Now I've got these people chasing me about the stupid phantom washing machine, they want to take me to court over it, AND GRANDDAD WON'T BLOODY GO BACK HOME!"

"When are they coming back?"

"I don't know. They must be in a boozer somewhere." Ingrid gestured vaguely to the mountain of washing obliterating the decrepit machine in the corner.

"That's theirs."

Inez rubbed a hand across her eyes. She was not going to resolve that, too.

"All right, first things first, you need to stop making everything so comfy for them."

"Which one?"

"All of them: dad, granddad and Leroy. You need to take control of the situation."

"Easy for you to say," snorted Ingrid.

"Do you want help or what or are you just going to criticise?"

"But it is easy for you. You can just waltz in and out whenever you please."

Inez raised a quizzical eyebrow and crossed her arms in expectation.

"All right, let's hear it then."

"Okay, you need to stop whatever it is you're doing which is making them hang about. Stop cooking for them, cleaning up after them, just stop everything. Only cook for you and the kids."

"What about Leroy?"

"Personally I wouldn't do anything for him either, but that's up to you."

"But he's my husband."

"He doesn't act like one." Inez dug into her faux leather bag, pulling out her diary. "Like I said, let's deal with dad and granddad first. If you stop running about after them, granddad will hopefully bugger off back to St Lucia and harass someone else and dad will eventually get off his arse, to do something for himself for a change. If he sells everything in the house, then tough. If mum doesn't want that to happen, then she had better get back here and sort it out. It's not for you to police him. If things get really bad, the house can always be rented out and dad and the lodger, what's his name again?"

"One -Pot."

"Yes, him and dad can share a place together till mum gets back."

Ingrid, grateful for any help, nodded in agreement.

Inez knew she was right. Left to her own devices, Ingrid would never have come up with anything.

"Give me the info on the washing machine, and I'll contact the company pretending I'm you"... *not for all the tea-leaves in Ceylon would I want to be, thought Inez* ... "and see what deal I can make."

"The paperwork is on the living room mantelpiece, thanks Inez."

"Don't worry about it."

Inez picked her way over piles of discarded shoes, clothing and assorted toys in varying degrees of working order. It never ceased to amaze her how her sister lived in such mess. She knew it baffled Evie, too.

The last time she had visited, she had made the mistake of using the toilet in the bathroom, and found herself confronted with a bath full of cold, dirty water, a plate of equally cold partially eaten egg and chips, and a bicycle frame. Not to mention the state of the toilet itself. This time, she used the public toilet in the nearby late-opening library, before visiting. She couldn't understand it; they were never raised to be so untidy. Their mother would have been after them with a broomstick if she had found one thing out of place.

Skirting the fully loaded clothes-airer, she rifled through the rubbish on the shelf, wondering at what stage her sister would realise it was no point buying cleaning products unless you were going to use them for their purpose, not as a cheap form of ornament. She found the battered and stained letter under the fourth can of unused furniture polish and a desiccated fly.

Returning to the sanctity of the sweaty kitchen, with said note pinched betwixt thumb and finger, she noted the information in her diary before spearing the letter under a ketchup bottle. There was no way that thing was going anywhere near her pristine handbag. Nudging Ingrid to one side, Inez meticulously washed her hands before vigorously shaking them. She ignored the grimy tea-towel hanging on the sink edge. Inez plucked a square of kitchen roll from her pocket and dried her hands. She dropped it into the broken waste paper basket which doubled as a kitchen bin, as her sister watched with lips pursed in annoyance.

"What?"

"Nothing. Have you heard from mum?"

"I got a letter last night."

"Isn't it fantastic?"

"Just lovely." She had no idea what she was supposed to be so happy about, having discarded it unread.

Ingrid twittered on as she added extra spices to the simmering pot, oblivious to her sister's lack of interest.

"Of course, dad can't know anything, else he will go mad. At least we don't have that long to wait."

"Probably."

"She rang me last night, she sounds so different."

So would anyone who had dropped everything including their family and naffed off halfway across the world to do who knew what, just because they could.

"She sounds so young and kind of excited."

Inez decided it was time to leave, her work here was done for now. "Good for her, I'm off."

"But you haven't had any soup!"

"I'm not hungry."

"You are never hungry; you're like a walking skeleton. I've seen more meat on a pencil."

"I'm going to aerobics later, I'll eat after."

"But I made this for you! You're always exercising; you will give yourself an exer-stroke."

Inez grabbed her bag and headed for the door.

"Don't be so stupid, nobody ever died through over exercising." Tossing a backward glance, she snorted in derision. "You could do with some yourself." She stared with contempt at the soup spattered terracotta dungarees and fussy turquoise blouse, both straining to encompass the corpulent figure.

Ingrid looked down at herself.

"What's wrong with me?"

"What's right, you mean. Do you always have to wear the loudest colours and the tightest clothes?"

"But the woman in the shop said they looked really nice on me."

Inez sighed in exasperation as the moon face slowly crumpled, the lips puckering into a fleshy pout.

"Don't cry." She patted the chubby hand in an effort to halt the tears shimmering in Ingrid's eyes. "Next time you want to go out shopping for clothes, why don't I come with you and give you a hand?"

Ingrid took in her sister's stylish raincoat and expensive shoes.

"You would come with me?"

"Course I would. You never ask me, though."

"I thought you wouldn't be interested in going with me. Mum and I used to go all the time."

Well that answered a lot of questions when it came to Ingrid's questionable clothing purchases over the years. God, sometimes she wondered who was the eldest. Ingrid was such a child.

"Just call me when you're ready, okay?"

As always, she decided on the toughest aerobics class. That afternoon, based on the Jane Fonda "Feel the Burn" Hollywood workout, Jacque put the class through their paces. He strutted about the studio barking commands whilst the packed room pumped in time to Olivia Newton John's "Let's get Physical." Inez worked her body till her arms could barely hang onto the lilac dumb bells. She squatted and pulsed, squatted, and pulsed her legs in time to "Flashdance," the sweat streaming in rivulets down the back of her bronze Lycra body suit and into her multi-coloured legwarmers. She didn't stop till the last command, the very last note of music, had ended.

As the class clapped their appreciation, and gathered their things together, Inez stretched sore muscles in preparation for the next class.

"Honey, tell me you are not doing another class." Jacque sashayed over.

"It's only yoga"

"Only yoga! Let me tell you sweetheart, yoga is work, and you don't need no extra work. You fine just as you are." As always, the New York twang came to the surface when he got excited, and his hands started to flap. "Girlfriend, you got it going on. You don't need no yoga, hell you barely need to do my class, but you know Jacque got the edge."

She grinned in response. "You have most definitely have the edge."

Perching a hand on his side, he adopted his regular stance "That's right, honey. I will work your ass. I was just telling my Maurice last week, if I get sick or leave, I'm going to make these people give you a job, cos' you wasting yourself behind that desk of yours when you so fine. Ah know you used to dance and it shows."

Stuffing her things into her gym bag, she rose to her feet. "That was a very long time ago."

The lithe man swivelled his head back and forth as he spoke "Long time my ass. You know how many people would kill for a body like yours?" She thought of her sister locked inside a mountain of flesh, unable to select a matching set of clothes.

"I will think about it."

He waggled a finger under her nose "You do that. Don't waste your life sitting on your ass till it's too fat to move. Do something now."

Inez saluted "Sir, yes sir."

Jacque grinned in return "Cheeky bitch, come on. Let's get out of here." Arm in arm, they left the aerobics room.

It was late evening before she got back to the flat, the two of them had met up with some of the girls from the class, and before she knew it, they had spent the entire evening in the pub. Letting herself in, it took a minute or two to realise she was not alone. Draped on her couch, much to her chagrin, was James.

"What are you doing here now? You were supposed to have arrived last night." Throwing her gym bag at the washing machine she eased her aching limbs out of her coat. Before she could get one arm out of her sleeve, he was raining kisses on her.

"I'm so sorry. SHE had accepted an invitation to some party which she hadn't told me about. I didn't have time to ring you before we left."

She held him at bay with a restraining hand. "So why didn't you leave a message on my machine when you got back?"

We didn't get back until quite late, and then SHE was so drunk I had to put her to bed which took ages."

Inez knew bullshit when she heard it but quite frankly couldn't be bothered with it all. She let him kiss her before she struggled out of his arms, feigning the need of a bath, but it was more than that. She need time to think without James crowding her.

"I bought a few things for tonight I thought you might like," he called through the open doorway. "I thought we could have a pleasant night in. You go ahead, and I'll bring you a nice glass of wine."

"Lovely. But I'll come out for the wine. I don't want to fall asleep in here." She certainly did not want him spoiling her solitude in the bath with his chitchat.

Great.

Another night in, when he was out all last night with HER.

As she soaked, she could hear him fumbling about in her kitchen whilst soft music played in the background, no doubt making a mess she would have to clean later.

Words echoed in her head as she luxuriated in Chanel scented bubbles. Yet another belated gift from James. Maybe Jacque was right, maybe it was time to get away from a desk, but she still hadn't finished her education. She was determined to complete it if only to show everyone she could finish something she started.

She would forget about James and please herself. He would find someone else. He was smart, good looking, and had money. An intoxicating combination. They could still be friends and go out on the odd occasion, just not do the whole sex thing.

By the time she had towelled herself dry, she had decided on the best course of action. If he wanted to find another woman, he could, or he could stay with his wife. It no longer mattered to her either way to her.

Stepping into the bedroom, she pulled up short. Beside the bed sat a large suitcase. Around its perimeter, she could see snatches of hastily packed clothing trapped in its hinge.

"James!"

He poked his head around the door. "What's the matter?"

"What's going on?"

"I thought I would stop here for a few days, I never do, do I?"

"What happened?"

He had the grace to be embarrassed. "Well, it's a bit tricky."

It was no time for nonsense. She clicked her fingers in annoyance. "Spit it out."

"We had a row and she threw me out."

"About what, exactly?" She hoped it wasn't about her, then everything she had only just resolved to do would go up in smoke. She held her breath as he procrastinated.

"No, she sort of found me kissing this person." He fussed unnecessarily with the belt of his jeans, obviously worried she would be mad.

She let out a sigh. "There is no such thing as sort of. Either you were, or you weren't. Give it a day or two, she'll be just fine."

The relief on his face was immediate. "That's what I thought. You don't mind me stopping for a day or two?"

"No, of course not" She smiled up at him reassuringly. "It will be fun."

41

Four months later, life was not such fun.

James had taken up residence in Inez' flat and was slowly taking over the cramped apartment.

This morning, as with every morning, she woke to the sweet sound of his snoring and the arctic bite of a dormant boiler. As per usual, he had commandeered the duvet and mattress, leaving her marooned on the sheeting.

Dirty underwear lay strewn over every surface.

James believed she was would clean up after him.

He was much mistaken.

Inez had done plenty of that in her parent's house.

All her plans had come to a halt. When she enrolled at the local Polytechnic, he had put up an almighty fuss. He carped endlessly about the time she was spending away from him, and her work was now well below par.

Like hell it was.

She was a glorified admin assistant for god sake. There was no getting away from him. He was now at her flat and at her place of work and had bought membership at her favourite place – the local leisure centre. Now, every time she took a dance class, he was coming out of the gym, and insisted they returned home together.

The man was everywhere she turned.

She had taken to running out the house, whilst he was in the shower so she could get a few minutes to herself before he got to the office. She hadn't a clue what his wife was up to, but it must have been tremendously exciting. The woman hadn't rung once to see what he was up to as far as she knew.

He was a bore of epic proportions. Why hadn't she noticed before?

She would have had his bags packed, and him out the door in no time if she had noticed earlier.

Last night, he had started talking about setting a date for their wedding, which took her utterly by surprise.

Enough was enough.

Creeping out to the lounge she grabbed the phone and dialled. It was picked up on the third ring.

"You don't know me, but I thought I would let you know where to find James."

There was a long pause.

"Hello, are you there?"

"Yes. You're her aren't you?"

"I don't know what you're talking about." Mentally she slapped herself in the head. Anytime a person said that, everybody knew what was being talked about.

"You are the receptionist at the practice."

No denying it now. "Yes, I am."

"So?"

"So what?"

"You tell me, you rang didn't you?"

"James is here. When would you like him to come home?"

To her surprise, laughter tinkled through the phone.

"I'm not coming to fetch him if that's what you're thinking. I was wondering how long it would take for you to call me."

Fingerprints of fear crept up her spine and nestled at the base of her neck.

"But he's your husband."

"Not for much longer. What makes you think I want him?"

"But he only did one little thing."

The voice was crisp with disinterest. "I knew about you, believe, but that isn't the reason why I'm not coming for him. They say blood is thicker than water, so I chose my family."

"This is weird. I don't understand."

"I found him in bed with my sister."

So that was why he was reluctant to talk about the whole affair.

"Oh."

"Yes. Oh. And seeing as it's harder to get rid of my sister AND he slept with the assistant before you, you can keep him. You can also tell him again from me if he doesn't come and get the rest of his stuff out of here in 24 hours I will be sending it to the charity shop. I will see him in court. He has his divorce papers."

Several seconds passed before Inez realised she was listening to a dial tone.

What the hell was she going to do now?

Replacing the handset onto its cradle she sat back on in the sofa and tried to take in the enormity the position her life was in.

She was doing a job she hated, living with a man she didn't love, in a flat she couldn't stand. In the dodgy part of town.

She had also missed her period.

Fifteen minutes later, Inez was still staring at the phone trying to work out what the hell she was going to deal with first when it rang.

Her fingers reached for the receiver.

42

As with all things, his decision was calculated for maximum effect. Standing before his immense walk-in wardrobe, he ignored the rows of exquisite Savile Row suits and handmade double-cuff shirts. Instead, he chose one of the three budget suits from the back of the rail and a market stall shirt, along with a vaguely offensive maroon tie. Last, but not least, he added a second-hand raincoat and a pair of slip-on shoes, leaving his beloved Windsmore shoes in the closet with its equally stylish companions.

He took one last check in the full length mirror. The ill-fitting suit failed to disguise his carefully honed physique. Sculpted cheekbones and flawless skin looked back at him from under a canopy of close-cropped oil-spritzed hair. He removed the sovereign ring and 24 carat gold bracelet and placed them in the custom-made wall safe. A spray of aftershave and he was ready.

It was time for church.

Taking the penthouse lift to the secure underground parking area, he skirted the gleaming silver Jaguar XJS, slowing to give his pride and joy a loving stroke, before climbing into the battered navy Ford Escort and ascending up onto the Chelsea streets.

The car swept through a deserted metropolis bathed in the stark glare of morning light. The used takeaway boxes crushed under barely legal wheels, as it sped toward Brixton, heartland of the Pentecostal community. He liked to arrive at his church much earlier than the staff every once in a while to ensure they were always sharp and efficient.

That morning was no exception.

As he pulled up outside into his parking space, his eyes swept over the imposing building with its ebony wrought iron gates and arched stained windows.

His personal goldmine.

Ian felt an immense sense of accomplishment in what he had created in such a short period of time. When he had joined the congregation as a teenager, he was angry about everything. It seemed nobody had anything positive to say about or to him. He was a bit of a tearaway and had dabbled in things when he ought to have known better, but he was only a kid.

Closing the gate behind him, he switched on the main lights and as always, did his circuit around the building.

Always on the lookout for anything out of place.

It didn't help the former inspector always seemed happy to harass him at every turn. He had gotten so close at one point, he had almost put him away for the burglary disaster. From time to time, he thought about the old days and wondered how the other guys were doing. He hoped they were still incarcerated. They were his mates, but mates didn't drop you in it like they had him. It was only for his quick thinking and slick banter which had kept him out of trouble. He smiled to himself. Life was strange. It was only after the incident he realized instead of constantly talking himself out of trouble, he could talk his way into a cushy lifestyle.

He had started as a car salesman. It was easy. All he had to do was work on the wives and girlfriends, and the blokes usually saw sense. It wasn't too bad, but he had to share his commission with his workmates, which was a constant bone of contention. After all, if he was doing all the work it was only fair he should get the money. He probably would have continued as a salesman till he was bowed and grizzled, with nothing but flat feet and a carriage clock for his decades of work if he didn't deliver a brand new Mercedes to this very church one day.

The top of the line car was the most beautiful thing he had ever set his eyes upon, and he had been given the privilege of taking it to its new owner.

When the middle aged man came out of the church in his bespoke clothing, Ian thought he was a stockbroker. With his sharp suit, scarlet braces and matching tie and kerchief ensemble he wondered what a man like him was doing there. His hands, when he shook them, were cotton soft. He knew then, whatever that man was doing in order to look like that he wanted a portion of it.

Today, it was his church, he was pastor now.

The man had taken him under his wing and taught him all in time. From using his voice to entice the flock under his spell, the theatre of service and the laying on of hands with the commanding of the Holy Spirit from the body. Right down to the concoction of fictitious tithes and mission donations and the legendary "roof fund." He had lapped it up as like a parched man at a water park.

He had risen in the ranks from visitor, to newly saved, usher, minister, deacon, and elder. Learning and growing in confidence, style, and greed.

Of course, there was the matter of Bible College to deal with, but after partial attendance at the appropriate faculty of learning and buying the certificate, he was all set.

His mother on his graduation was pleased, he could tell, not that he gave a damn. She made him sick with all her religious hypocritical ways, and before she left for good, was in his church what felt like to him every two minutes.

When the senior pastor had retired, his son had thought to succeed him, as all had imagined. There was talk he was a godly, charitable man, who would work tirelessly for those who could not do for themselves, or were in pain and suffering.

Ian had other plans.

It wasn't hard to find a willing woman who wasn't too choosy in how she acquired her wealth, to find herself in a certain office at the wrong time of the day without a chaperone, in too flimsy an outfit.

The pastor's son was quickly discounted for the job.

Seating himself behind his bland office desk, he reached behind him, spun the dial on the safe and reached inside for one of the thick wedges of paper. Selecting eight fifty pound banknotes, he placed them in his inside pocket before returning the pile and securing the door.

It was always nice to carry a little loose change.

He how many people would come through the door today? Last month, the deacons calculated roughly £3,500 on each Sunday. By his reckoning, once they had taken the roof fund contributions for the day, he would be ahead by at least £11,000 for that week, a good portion of which would find its way into his off-shore account.

He froze as the door to his office opened, relaxing as his pudgy secretary bustled through the door.

"Morning, Pastor Rochard." Sister Ethel plonked her shopping bag onto a filing cabinet. "I trust the Lord is well with you this morning. You are in early."

"Oh yes," he replied piously, "the spirit is strong today. I couldn't wait to come here to this wonderful place of fellowship." He helped her off with her muddy brown coat revealing a startlingly iridescent purple ensemble of chiffon and nylon, with matching patterned tights and silver court shoes.

"My, that's quite some outfit you have sister. It is very eye-catching."

The buxom woman sniggered as she treated him to a twirl.

"Do you like it? I have a matching hat!"

From her shopping bag, she produced a fascinator of peacock feathers, red berries, and straw seemingly bound together with gold string.

"It cost a fortune, but it is so lovely wouldn't you agree?"

"Ah, I've never seen anything like it," he answered truthfully, and hoped never to again. Turning from her he donned an appropriate vestment.

"Well, we have the minister from St Louis and his wife coming today, and we don't want to be outdone by the Americans, do we?"

"No, we don't." Shit. He had forgotten them. As part of their franchise, he was legally bound to having periodic visits from sister churches and conduct collections in their honour.

Less money for him.

"I'm sure the word today will be uplifting," he replied. As he closed the door behind him, he heard his desk telephone ring.

Leaving his secretary to answer the phone and fiddle with her bonnet, he greeted the ministers as they arrived and set up for the service, keeping an eye on everything as the church began. Elderly folk, long on time and short on activities began to fill the church. They were joined by middle aged parents dragging their teenage children in the hope they would absorb what it took to be a respected, upstanding pillar of the community. They in turn spent the entire service flirting behind their parents back. He watched in amusement as new parents struggled to keep their charges under control whilst the single churchgoers squirmed in anticipation of love and joyful matrimony with a partner of a Christian disposition. All gave him a nod or greeting as he passed.

From the corner of his eye, he caught a familiar face. His brother sat in the middle of the last pew of the church.

Ivan never mentioned any form of religion, much less was seen near a church. He wondered what reason brought him into the building. He cut across the packed aisle. Ivan, sensing his presence turned toward him, surprise etched upon his face as their eyes met before he bustled his way out of the pew toward the main doors.

Ian pushed past the steady stream of parishioners, intent on asking his brother what the hell he was doing, running off like a five year old. A band of steel wrapped itself around his torso. He found himself in the arms a policeman. Ex-inspector Smith's iron streaked head peeped over the burly shoulder. He was flanked by a briefcase wielding official and two more police officers..

"Going somewhere pastor?"

Ian's heart jolted in his chest.

Smith was grinning.

43

"Get me a beer, a cheeseburger, and fries, hold the tomato. What do you want honey?"

"I'll take the burger and salad, no mayo, and a Root Beer."

Evie slotted her notebook into her tattered apron. "Coming right up."

"Say, honey, are you Australian?"

Gazing at the grubby woman with her lank greasy hair and flashy clothes, Evie sighed inwardly. Some days she wished she could get rid of her accent. If she had a pound for every person who asked her, she wouldn't have to work in the diner. Every muscle in her body trembled with fatigue, but the day lay before her as long as Route 66.

"No, madam I'm British."

"That's next door to Italy, ain't it honey?"

Evie felt a twinge of irritation cut through her. The man was obviously out to impress. His suit was made for a man of leaner proportions.

Maybe he was that man twenty years ago.

Observing the moist, fleshy jowls and flushed complexion, the trainee physician in her knew he was on a short drive to heart attack city.

In those few moments, Evie contemplated her response. She could give him a geography lesson of Europe, out him as the fool she suspected him to be, and risk seeing him again later on that day in the accident and emergency department she worked in. Or she could be the best goddamn waitress they ever had and get a decent tip to help pay her overdue rent.

Taking a deep breath, she made her decision.

"Dr Hudstard call ext 628, Dr Hudstard call ext 628," the tannoy system echoed through the building.

In the staff room at the hospital, Evie transferred the day's tips into her purse. Sifting around at the bottom of her bag, she eventually found what she was looking for. Transferring two white capsules from the brown plastic bottle to her hand, she quickly swallowed them dry and replaced the bottle. She changed into her jeans, t-shirt, and regulation white coat, bundled her waitress uniform into her rucksack on top of her mother's letter and threw everything into her locker.

Hands reached out from seemingly nowhere and covered her eyes. Panic rose in her chest throat before she heard the familiar voice.

"Guess who!"

"The tooth fairy."

"Nope"

"Santa Claus?"

"You're not very good at this. Shall I give you a hint?"

Catching her bottom lip between her teeth, she struggled to maintain a serious face.

"Oh, I suppose you will have to."

"Anaesthetist to room 211, Anaesthetist to room 211"

Standing quite still, Evie waited patiently. She was not disappointed. A tickly breath glided across the nape of her neck before a sloppy wet kiss was planted behind her ear making her giggle. The hands slipped away from her eyes. Turning, she put her arms around the man towering over her and folded herself against his lean frame.

"Well, I never, it's Brad. I would never have guessed."

Arms wrapped about her, he drew her closer, his chin nuzzling her soft hair. "I can smell hamburger."

"Oh, shut your face."

"Is that a term of endearment? You English guys have the weirdest way of saying things."

Evie pulled away slightly and screwed her face up into an unattractive scowl. "Oh don't you start. I had a couple in the diner asking about my accent."

"So have they had an x-ray yet?"

"What for?"

"Well, I imagine you put your foot so far up their ass you would need an x-ray to find your shoe."

"No, I was remarkably civilized. I did not point out that Britain is nowhere near Italy…"

"Ouch, that's not good."

She sniffed haughtily and raised her nose a notch higher. "No, it isn't, but I'm bigger than that. I didn't correct him, I said he was right and took the order. I was exceedingly polite. They even left me a tip."

Brad tilted her head up till her eyes met his. Worry reflected back at her. She hoped her meticulously applied make-up was enough to conceal her fatigue. It wasn't.

"Only had a couple of hours sleep again?"

Tearing her head away, she shrugged her shoulders and reached for her ward pass.

"I'll get by."

"You don't have to just get by. You know you can get help."

"I don't want any more help. The last lot cost a fortune."

His face was clouded with worry. "You're too proud. I'll pay. I don't care about the money. All I care about is you getting enough sleep before you make a serious mistake. Seeing a therapist is not shameful."

"I'll be fine. I know how to handle it."

"Like how you managed the Clayton-Crighton mix up?"

Evie's voice was small. "I managed to sort it out. They were okay in the end."

"Only because Chrighton is an adult. If you had gotten it wrong the other way around, little Alfie Clayton would not have survived a measure meant for Dave Crighton. You were lucky this time. Even so, now the hospital board is watching you, you can't afford to put a foot wrong."

"Porter to pharmacy, porter to pharmacy call 882"

Evie watched as Brad paced the room. His long legs ate up the narrow locker room floor, arms flailing in all directions. Nothing made him quicker to anger than the thought of all her years of hard work going to waste.

"You haven't told them have you?"

"I didn't want to bother them."

"That's what family are there for, bothering!"

She shrugged in response which made him pace all the faster.

"It's times like this you need people to have your back. You know I'm with you all the way, but you have to find out why the hell you can't sleep. Doesn't it bother them? What the hell kind of people are they anyway?"

Evie ticked the points off on her fingers

"My big brother Ivan is in Thailand somewhere at the moment. I don't know where exactly because he hasn't given anyone an address. My twin brother Ian is wrapped up with his dodgy church. Ingrid is trying to get my grandfather to return St Lucia, and stop my father from selling everything out from under us, as well as keep her man chained to her whilst raising her children." Evie tucked a strand of raven hair behind her ear. "Lastly, my other sister is trying to get rid of boyfriend, if she doesn't exercise herself to death first. As for my mother, I don't know what the hell she's doing. I never did then and I don't know now. When she walked away, that was the end of it for me. She promised to help me through college which she has, to give her credit, but that's about it. I keep getting these letters from all around the world but I can't even be bothered to read them. Do you honestly think they are worried about me right now? I don't think so."

"You should read the letters."

"Not a chance."

"There could be something really important in them."

"If there was, I'm sure someone would tell me."

"It would be easier to read them."

"Can't. Burnt them."

"Evie!"

"I got one today, I'll read that one."

"Please read it. I thought my family was entertaining."

"Not compared to mine. Yours are like the Brady Bunch."

"Why don't you just come and live with me? I don't like seeing you working all hours to make the rent month after month which isn't helping your insomnia. If you keep it up you, will be too fucked up to do anything. You have to stay sharp."

"At least I wouldn't be responsible for people's lives if I get struck off before I qualify."

"Don't talk like that."

Seating herself on the narrow bench in the centre of the room, she watched him intently.

"I don't want you to feel that you have to rescue me, I should be able to sort myself out. We don't even know if we are going to work out as a team, and I certainly don't want you thinking I'm doing it just to get my green card citizenship."

He joined her on the bench and took her hand.

"I knew the minute you came into the lecture hall that very first day swearing and cursing in your weird accent that I wanted you to stick around."

Evie remembered how angry she had been by the time she had unravelled the mysteries of her scheduling plan with its strange American timetabling and back to front dates. She had arrived at her anatomy class twenty minutes late and paired up with the smelliest guy in the university, a living, breathing "Pig Pen" from Charlie Brown. By break time, she had no olfactory senses left by which to smell her coffee. At the start of the next session, however, she found herself seated next to the most gorgeous looking guy in the auditorium. She couldn't believe her luck when the sable haired Texan had asked her out. She did think it funny when he had requested seeing her only at the library to study for the first week.

Alone in a strange country, she had welcomed the company. It was later he revealed he had promised to do Pig Pen's home work for the entire week in order to sit next to her for one afternoon.

Having him close to her made her feel secure and wanted. Some days she didn't know why she felt she had to punish herself by insisting on having her own home despite her insomnia, they could work it out somehow. Maybe it was having the feeling of independence. Maybe it was something deeper. Her parents with their marital disorder had left a deep and lasting impression, making her suspicious of committing to another person. Even if she loved them as she did Brad. She didn't want to lose him over it.

"Nurse Maloney to call 936, Nurse Maloney to call 936,"

"Maybe I can spend a few nights a week for now until I feel a bit more comfortable?" she ventured.

"Whatever you want, you know I don't mind." A small smile touched his lips. "I'll even clear my comic book drawer out for you."

"You do spoil me."

"That's my aim."

Dr Rochard to nurses' station, call on line 12, Dr Rochard to nurses' station, call on line 12

44

Ivan inhaled, savouring the intense aroma of vegetation and nutrient rich earth simmering under the hint of newly poured concrete, coupled with the light perfume of exotic flowers on the breeze. He exhaled slowly and parted his lips. The tangy air played across his tongue. He closed his eyes.

Home.

Opening his eyes, he drank in the swaying palm fronds reaching towards the sky. He glanced across the tarmac toward the waiting throng standing inside the squat terminal.

He wondered if Koko had been able to cut through the city traffic in time to meet his plane. Initially he was booked on a flight due to arrive the following day, but he couldn't wait that long. Another day without her would have killed him, having endured two months already. He swapped his ticket. It was an extra hundred pounds, but he didn't care.

During the flight he paced the narrow aisle, excusing himself around the over-laden food caddy time again, much to the annoyance of the harassed air-stewards. When he wasn't pacing, he sat and twitched. He fidgeted. He dozed fitfully. When he wasn't pacing.

Hoisting his duffle bag onto his shoulder, he hurried across the building. His gaze roamed the throng for her face amongst the droves of bellowing, half-naked, overburdened porters herding aside bystanders too stupid to move. Harassed sweaty officials in rumpled desert-hued uniforms policed a contingent of red-faced Europeans, already sweltering in winter clothing. They in turn endeavoured to take charge of a situation they had no hope of organising without a word of native language between them. They stood out amongst an assortment of pickpockets, local craft sellers, vacant, fresh faced, gap-year backpackers full of wonderment, and impatient relatives dressed in all manner of lightweight garb. At the front, squeezed between what appeared to Ivan to be a reunited family of well over a hundred, stood Koko, an exquisite rose among a field of weeds. A beacon of fragile loveliness in the summer frock he loved best. The sunflower yellow cotton dress with its sprigged white flowers scattered across its hem, a matching bag, and wide-brimmed straw bonnet clutched to her chest. Her long ebony hair cascaded over her slim shoulders like a silken cape.

In the few seconds it took her to scan the new arrivals, he took a moment to admire her. He was truly a lucky man. He didn't know what she saw in him that night outside the club, but he was glad.

Ivan knew the moment she found him in the crowd. Her eyes lit up like fireworks on New Year's Eve.

Pushing though a gaggle of hapless Belgians, he soon found himself in her strong arms. His lips pressed to hers, bags forgotten, oblivious to the curious stares and bemused glances about them. After long minutes, Koko peeled herself away to glance up at him, her body tense with emotion.

"How long this time?"

"Two weeks."

She arched a teased eyebrow. "And then?"

"Three months."

"Finished?"

He smiled with confidence. "Finished."

Ivan watched as a smile bloomed across her lips revealing perfect teeth. He grinned back foolishly. Together they made their way out to the all-terrain jeep.

"Then we can make real plans?"

His smile slipped. "We will make plans."

She stepped out of his embrace.

"You always say that. You're ashamed of Koko."

"Don't be silly, you are a gorgeous woman, and I want everyone to know you are mine."

Her mouth drew together into a fishlike pout. "You don't let me meet your family."

"But they are thousands of miles away!"

"You see them every time you go on leave. You never ask me to come with you."

"I don't always see them, most of the time I come home to you. I've only seen my family once this year."

"You never ask me. You don't love Koko anymore."

Opening the car, she made a grand show of arranging herself in the passenger seat, leaving Ivan to throw his things in the back before getting behind the wheel. He cursed under his breath as the seat set for Koko's petite frame attempted origami on his long form. Readjusting it, he took her fragile hand in his, but she refused to look at him, preferring to stare out at the horde of sooty illegal traders. They swirled about the dishevelled air passengers bombarding them with Thai and pigeon English words as they thrust cheap necklaces under their noses. Taxi drivers piled out of un-roadworthy vehicles, kidnapping suitcases and throwing them into their cabs in the knowledge where suitcases went, owners were sure to follow, thus ensuring themselves a reward of their choosing. The porters looked on disinterestedly, their pockets already jingling.

"What if when I leave the army, you come over to meet my family then?"

Koko's eyebrows rose inquiringly.

"You want me to come to England?"

"Of course. When I get out, I will send for you, and then we will make proper plans."

"You promise?"

"I promise."

Her exotic eyes narrowed slightly.

"Will you tell them about me?"

Ivan hesitated a moment. That was a tricky one. He didn't want to lie to her, but, on the other hand he couldn't pass it off as nothing. What they had together was so remarkable he felt he couldn't even begin to try and explain it to anyone else.

"I will try. They are old fashioned, and I seriously don't know what they will say about us if they found out."

"I won't tell them, will you?"

"Of course not!"

Koko cocked her head to one side coquettishly "So who will know?"

"Well nobody, but that still means we will have to be very careful just in case."

She bristled with indignation. I know how to handle myself."

"Of course. I'm sorry, but people in England aren't like here. In this country, nobody cares what a person does, but it's different there. Even though they like to think they are liberal, they're not really."

Koko nodded in acknowledgement, but he couldn't tell if she had absorbed what he had said. He concentrated on negotiating his way through the throng of tourist rickshaws and packed public transport. Cranking open his window, he was hit with the heated stench of the city, thick with choking smog and mouldy refuse, mixed with the ever-present fug of many unwashed people in too small an area.

The car made short work of the city and was soon in the countryside. It soon became obvious see something was on Koko's mind, so waited patiently for her to vocalise her thoughts.

"When we are together properly, will we get married?"

"Of course."

"I don't think we can here."

"No," he conceded "I suppose not. I think we can in England. Lots of people do. I can apply for a licence when I get back so when you come over all you would have to worry about is what dress you would like to wear."

"Will your family come?"

"Would it matter to you if they didn't?"

Koko considered the question, her nose wrinkling in concentration.

"Only if it matters to you. I want what you want. Whatever happens, you know my family would always help us."

He had made his intentions clear to her family. He wasn't out for a cheap thrill or to exploit her. They had been wonderful. Koko's lifestyle wasn't to everyone's taste when it came to men looking for that special woman in their life. Not everyone would have stuck around once they had found out the object of their desire earned their living pleasuring servicemen. He was a bit of a hero in the eyes of her parents, though her cousin took some persuading – he had to find another woman to pimp - especially when she gave up the life to get a decent job and make a home for the two of them.

None of their friends and relatives seemed bothered in the least. He had seen first-hand the amount of bi-racial native people with all manner of strange and exotic mixes which walked the streets. Nobody paid them the slightest notice. It made him feel optimistic that he and Koko had some kind of future.

Ivan parked the car outside their picturesque villa over-laden with window box roses. The white wooden shutters were closed against the fierce afternoon sun. Shutting off the engine, he turned to face his partner.

"I want you. I love you. Everything else can go to hell. I'm only happy near you. Anything else isn't worth talking about. Does that answer your question?"

Her kiss told him everything he needed to know.

They woke wrapped together across the crisp snowy bed, taking their time in the shower, before preparing their customary light breakfast. Ivan drove Koko to work at the new hotel overlooking the sea where she worked as a multilingual receptionist, then made the customary rounds to hotels and guest houses renewing friendships and fuelling interest in his services as a tour guide with a difference.

He zipped along the single lane road overlooking the beach toward the next appointment, occasionally casting his view out to sea, where testosterone fuelled youths skimmed the surf on lovingly embellished boards.

He had thought hard about what he was to do when he left the army. The rainforest tour was the best thing he had come up with by far.

There were few options available as an ex-serviceman. Spending eternity behind a Formica table in a closet of a room, with only a phone and computer for company did not fill his heart with unspeakable joy.

If he were that kind of man, he wouldn't have charged into the nearest Army recruitment centre at the first opportunity. He wasn't an office man then. Nothing had changed since. Many of his colleagues had already left, leaving him feeling like the old man of the unit, and were well set up in all kinds of security or family businesses. For the latter, he supposed they always knew what work they would go into and would be assured a job for life.

His best mate had become an undertaker like his father and grandfather which was pretty smart. There was always some kind of war which meant good contracts and a steady stream of bereaved relatives in need of a funeral director.

Of the security bunch, some had gone into corporate security doing 12 hour shifts filling out crossword puzzles. Reading adventure novels tucked behind fancy reception desks in deserted marble and glass edifices ensured their finely honed bodies went to anatomical hell. Their army days relegated to increasingly fantastic tales told to their children, or anybody else who would listen, and wives if they still had them.

Others went into company security controlling national airports with day to day incidents of impending baggage handlers' strikes, adverse weather conditions, asylum seekers, irate holidaymakers and inter-airline love trysts gone wrong. That was way too much trouble for him. He could never take being cooped up indoors anyhow, wearing the uniform with its starchy white garrotte style collar, which could take a man's neck clean off.

A few entrepreneurs had set up personal companies, which specialized in crowd control at top pop venues and premiership soccer matches. Nice if you weren't bothered about going deaf or wanted to watch Man United play Spurs for free with the occasional object thrown at you.

Two mates in particular were doing exceedingly well. One provided close body-guarding personnel to high profile businessmen and celebrities around the world, seeing life the first class way with trips to private idylls on personalized Gulf Stream jets. The other had become a mercenary in Afghanistan living a rather precarious life as a hired gun dancing between warring factions whilst trying to keep on the right side of the United Nations Allied Forces.

Not his cup of tea.

If he got himself shot, it would inconvenience him immensely.

Of the opportunities available, working as a body guard suited him best. The army training drilled into him over the years would be of use as well as a change of scene. Why go back to Peckham when the world was your oyster? The money was excellent. You never had to use your own coins as a celebrity bodyguard. Every wish was taken care of by the personal assistants of recording companies, whether it was flying to Bali or going to the latest awards ceremony. There were manic crowds, bullish producers, and overwrought divas adamant every bowl of Smarties and type of fruit known in the history of man were present in their suites and necessary for their comfort. Even the odd stalker didn't faze him. What did make him stop and think about taking up his friend's very generous offer of employment was Koko. He didn't want to spend any more time away from her than he had to, which was why he was investigating the possibility of setting up his own thing with her, where he could advertise himself as a kind of modern day jungle tour guide. Taking a few tourists out into the bush to trek, fish, climb, camp, or whatever the hell people wanted to do for adventure. They could find an office in which to work, and Koko could make the bookings. That was where he wanted to be.

Outside.

No hunting. He was done with guns.

His pocket began to vibrate.

Pulling up to the kerb, he extracted his phone and glanced at the display.

A frown creased his forehead.

45

"If you sat still for two minutes, I would have been finished by now, so stop your nonsense."

Ingrid applied a generous glob of Long 'N' Lush lotion to the small scalp and dragged the wide-toothed comb through the tangle of virgin hair, causing her daughter to whimper and flinch again. Pulling the strands as far as it would go, she clipped a brown and gold barrette decorated with stencilled love hearts around the hair, and let go watching the hair crinkle back into a pony-tailed pom-pom as she started on the remaining clump of hair.

"When is daddy coming home?"

"I don't know."

Keisha's tiny lips elongated into a pout.

"He promised to take me to school today."

"I know."

"So where is he?"

"I haven't seen him."

"I haven't got any dinner money. He said he would give me some."

"Well I haven't any money on me. You will have to wait until I go to the bank later today. If I find any, you will get some for tomorrow."

"But Miss Phillips said we had to bring it in on a Monday."

"I don't care. I haven't got it right now, and your father isn't here, so she will have to wait. I'll pack you some sandwiches in a minute."

"Don't want sandwiches. They have hot dogs on Monday."

"I can't help that. Have it next week."

"It's half term next week," reminded Curtis as he hunted for his other shoe.

She had forgotten about that. What the hell was she going to do with the kids? She only had two annual leave days left.

"Just have sandwiches for now and I will sort it out later."

"There's nothing in the fridge."

"There's bread."

Curtis peered into the battle-scarred fridge.

"Not anymore."

"Who the hell ate all the bread? I only put it in there the day before yesterday."

"Not me."

"Me either."

Leroy.

"Just tell your teacher you forgot your dinner money, and I will find some for tomorrow. They will give you lunch."

Keisha scowled unhappily, but picking up on her mothers' irritation, decided to let the dinner money matter rest.

"I thought dad wasn't going out last night."

Fighting with the unruly hair, Ingrid glanced over at her son. She pondered on the best way to word her answer.

"He didn't. He went out on Friday night."

Curtis eyes widened in surprise. "That was three days ago."

"I know."

Curtis was far too old for his nine years.

She had heard the jingle of her husband's keys in the door late last night, but was unable to question him as she was on the phone sorting out yet another dispute between her father and her grandfather. By the time she put the phone down he had gone again. Taking every banknote and coin in her purse.

"He's too old to go out," grumbled Curtis.

"Don't be silly, you're never too old to go out and have a good time."

"None of my friend's dads spend the whole weekend going to parties."

"So what do they do then?"

Curtis paused from tying his shoe laces to consider the question.

"They buy stuff in DIY stores and fix things."

"There you go. Your dad fixed a new toilet roll holder to the wall just last week."

"It was crooked."

"But he tried."

"My friend's dads go to the park with them and play football and stuff or wash the car."

"You know your dad hates football, and he won't clean the inside of his car never mind the outside." Not that the children or herself ever rode in it.

"He says that's what the rain is for."

Ignoring the comment, she coaxed the other half of Keisha's hair into submission. Ingrid helped her daughter into her raincoat and grabbed her Barbie rucksack.

"All I know is your father does his best for us all, so let's not get upset because he's a little late coming back from a good evening."

"He's two days late!"

"I'm sure he has a reason, maybe the car broke down. It can happen."

"He took his weekend bag."

Ingrid felt her face burn with shame.

Ingrid knew what Leroy was up to. She'd had for years but was unaware her son had picked up on it, too. Somewhere in her subconscious, there was a longing the situation would right itself, and they could continue as a happy, loving family. If only she could hold on long enough for Leroy to realise what it was he had.

The last time he had gone AWOL, she had seen him in Camberwell on her way home from her night shift. He should have been home with the children. He was entering a flat with a key on his bunch she had seen but didn't recognise. He had a dark-haired woman on his arm. He had said when he left the house that night he was going to another of his weekend house parties.

She was a fool.

"We'll talk about this later. You two need to get to school, and I need to work."

Fastening her worn raincoat over her ivy coloured uniform, she made her way to the door, her children in tow.

Shouldering the many various bags, they double checked the items together.

School bags, check.

Class project, check.

Gymnastics bag, check.

Swim things, check.

Cardboard box, PVA glue, and sticking things, check.

Handbag, check.

Front door key, check.
Empty purse, check.
Before Ingrid turned the knob, the telephone rang.

ST LUCIA

46

 Evie eased out of the airport car park and turned onto the newly
laid highway. In the distance the Piton Mountains stood proudly
against the backdrop of a cobalt sky.

 The land was laid with a thick, lush emerald carpet, which
undulated over the countryside. The island was tiny but it still
took a whole day to travel around its perimeter. There weren't
many roads without a hairpin bend. Even the one her
grandparent's house was situated on had its quirky twists.

 The veranda overlooked a breath-taking view, from the
vibrant matchbox houses, to the capital, Castries, some three miles
away. The town also served as the harbour. Towering luxury
liners from the Americas and Europe docked next to the main
road, much to the consternation of the cruisers on board who
thought they were going to crash, and the delight of the locals.

 The car meandered through the town, past the banana loading
bays and up into the hills.

 Half an hour later, Evie pulled up outside the secluded
whitewashed villa, which stood in the middle of the prestigious
Hummingbird gated community.

 She skipped up the stairs as she used to as a young teenager,
and banged the ornate knocker. After a considerable time, a
sprightly old man answered the door in a vivid lilac shell-suit. His
stern face transformed on seeing his visitor.

 "Miss Evie! How lovely to see you, it's been a long time.
What are you doing out there? Come inside out of the heat. You
know Ms Vera has been talking so much about you and Mr.
Bradley. You are truly going to make her day." He peered over
her shoulder.

 "Where's Mr. Bradley? Leave your luggage. I'll get someone
to see to it.

 "I'm afraid he's on call. He sends his love and said he would
come next time."

Too late. He was already on the move. She followed the florescent pants through the hallway and up the grand staircase while he chattered on.

How old the butler was, was a mystery.

Evie estimated he was older than fossil fuel. Hell, he was old when she was a sassy little girl, and that was long ago. Evie hurried to keep up with the sprightly old fox as he passed through the elegant hall which was as exactly as she remembered it, adorned with the most exquisite watercolours featuring the island's landscape. As always, the old man chattered endlessly.

"My son sent me this lovely suit. It's all the rage in America now. Do you like it? I've got one in green too. If you want, I can get one for you. Just tell me your size, it's no problem. I can get one for Mr. Bradley too." Evie doubted it. The thought of Brad in a neon track-suit made her grin.

"I'll ask him."

They stopped at a door halfway along the hallway.

Aunt Vera sat beside the open window. Her trademark loose linen shirt wrapped around her long angular frame, her hair as always, piled in a loose bun.

"Darling, come let me give you a hug."

Evie found herself engulfed in Lily of the Valley perfume.

"What a thing. You're nothing but skin and bone. We have to feed you up."

Finding herself under scrutiny, Evie prised herself out of the woman's fierce hug in the guise of checking her bag.

"I like your hair. Feisty. I like it."

"Thanks Aunty V." Evie ran a hand over her spiky hair "Maybe it's a little too short."

"That's how youngsters like you are wearing it these days, It in the magazines, sweetheart. Robert, she's here!" She motioned Evie through into the frigid air-conditioned interior. "I'm an old lady, but I still know what's fresh and what isn't. I keep my eye on fashion. You know me."

"I sure do. Still hiding your manicure bills from Uncle R?"

"Of course sweetheart." She gave her niece a conspiratorial wink.

"You should have let Philip collect you from the airport."

"I didn't want to bother you. Hi uncle. "

Stooping, Evie embraced the silver-haired man. Sharp joints poked her in the ribs. She shot her aunt a questioning look.

"I am so sorry about your mother."

He shuffled to the edge of his chair. Vera placed a hand on her husband's shoulder.

"Don't get up." The doctor said you mustn't move unnecessarily. The old fool weeded the garden all by himself again. I keep telling him, it's a job for two YOUNG men, but will he listen? That's why we employ gardeners, so they can do the work."

"Hush your noise, woman," admonished Uncle. "Can't you see the girl has bigger things to worry about? Look at you, I bet I could play the xylophone on your ribs. You are too skinny."

Evie reckoned she could knock him over if she blew on him, so that made two of them. The last time they visited England nine years earlier, he was so robust. She wondered whether it was old age or something else sapping his strength.

"Did Ingrid tell you everything?"

"Just that mum was involved in an accident on the island whilst travelling to the airport."

Seating herself gracefully onto the honey coloured sofa, Aunt Vera motioned Evie to join her, leaving uncle adrift on the reclining easy chair.

"Your mother died two days ago on the way to the airport, or so it appears. There isn't anything else on the island of significance in that direction."

"Why was she going there?"

"We don't know. I must say, you are taking the news very well."

"So are you."

Aunt Vera's eyebrows shot up in surprise at her niece's cheek.

In the absence of emotion, Evie's analytical skills took their place.

"How did you find out?"

"I got a visit from the police at lunchtime."

"She was at her desk as per usual," mumbled Uncle Robert. "Your Aunt is supposed to be retiring next year, not that she's slowing down any. Not that she needs the money either. I don't know why I retain all these people when your aunt wants to do everything herself like some sort of cleaning lady."

"I want to keep busy. Besides, the academy won't run itself. Till the new headmistress is appointed, things have to run like clockwork." Used to their gentle bickering, Evie knew it was better to stop them early on.

"What did the police say?"

"The sergeant, you know the one, him and his wife live just over the bakery. Lovely children, though their little girl is a bit mouthy."

"The sergeant said something?"

"Tell the girl," yelled Uncle, "he said she was driving out by Marlin Bay when the car went off the road on one of the hairpin bends!"

"That is what I was saying."

"Were there any witnesses – did the police take any notes?"

"You know this place. It's not like America where there are top quality police departments and the FBI. Here in St Lucia people drive badly. There's an accident every five minutes. The police aren't exactly tearing about the place trying to work out what happened else they would do nothing else. Besides, they are just as bad.

Evie digested the information. She hadn't felt a thing since she first heard the news at work. From the corner of her eye, she could see her aunt watching her with a strange expression on her face.

"So where is everyone? Isn't the house usually full of people when there's a death in the family?"

"I thought it best to wait until you all had arrived before ringing around. I was hoping to have the wake at your grandmother's house, though, the last event I had here, half my furniture disappeared. It would give you a chance to sort things out. Are you sure you want to stay here and not with your sisters at the house? I mean we love you here, and all, but - you know."

"Thanks. It was a good idea to wait. It would be best to have it over there. I would rather be somewhere peaceful, if it's okay with you."

"Of course. Besides, I need a chance to dust the place myself first."

"Dust?"

"Yes, it looked like she barely stayed there."

"I thought she was spending most of the time there with a few trips to Florida."

"Not judging by the house."

"So where was she then?"

"Maybe you should ask that man."

"What man?"

"The one that was involved in the accident."

"Why didn't you tell me about him before?"

"We thought you knew about him."

"No! Who is he and where is he now?"

"We thought you might know."

Evie threw her hands up in exasperation "I don't know about any man." A headache was brewing. "When are the others arriving?"

"Your father and Ingrid's flight comes in late tonight and Inez arrives in the morning. As for Ivan, we are not too sure as he's flying in with the army. Ian you know about."

Everybody knew about Ian.

"What about Granddad Rochard?"

"He didn't give a damn about your mother when she was alive. He sure as hell isn't going to trouble himself to return for her funeral."

"It was just as well. She hated him. How far have the arrangements gotten?"

"We thought it best to wait until everyone had arrived before we did anything. I hope that was the correct thing to do."

"I suppose so." Evie had no idea what to do in times like these, despite being a doctor. She wished Brad was with her. He wanted to accompany her, but she didn't like spending his money. He had insisted on paying for her flight. She didn't want to be a parasite.

With a dozen thoughts weighing heavily on her mind, she excused herself and went to her room. She unpacked a few things and willed herself to sleep.

Tomorrow was going to be an extremely long day.

47

Having showered and breakfasted on enough food for three people at her aunt's insistence, for as long as possible, Evie decided it was time to quit procrastinating. She left in search of her sisters.

She made short work of the drive along the coast road as she negotiated the jeep rental deep into the lush countryside, dodging kamikaze drivers and over-laden minibuses, which thought themselves public transport.

Pulling up alongside the timber house, next to a stationary people vehicle, she could already hear a commotion emanating from the house. Steeling herself, Evie skipped up the rickety steps and banged on the weather-beaten door. There was immediate silence quickly followed by the jangle of a chain being released before the door was thrown wide open.

Ingrid did not look amused. For once, she was wearing one colour from head to toe.

Black.

"You took your time."

"I got here as fast as I could," she lied.

"Yeah, well I've got to get into town. The undertakers need sorting out, and your father is being a pain in the rear end."

"What's new? Did you bring the kids?"

"No, I left them with Ms Thompson."

"I thought you would have left them with their dad."

"No. He's working."

Evie didn't believe her eldest sister for a second.

"But she's so old. She looked after us!"

"That's the best I could do. I can't afford the airfare for all three of us. Besides, I will be back in a couple of days."

She followed her sister through the dark passageway to the cramped kitchen where her father sat in fleece pyjamas slathering a solitary piece of toast, the plate and himself with molasses.

"Hi dad."

The sun had not yet reached its zenith, but it was already uncomfortably warm. She didn't to add to the discomfort by getting herself sticky by hugging him, so she stayed where she was. On the safer side of the table.

"Alright, darling?"

"I'm fine, aren't you hot in those pyjamas?"

"That's what I keep telling him, but he won't listen," yelled Ingrid. "He'll get heatstroke in those."

"Stop telling me what to do. You sound like your mother."

"Leave him. When he gets too hot he'll take them off."

"And if he doesn't?"

"Then he doesn't. Let it go, otherwise you will give yourself a heart attack or something. I don't want to attend a double funeral." Ingrid twisted her lips in annoyance but said nothing.

"What's going on?" Inez wafted into the kitchen wrapped in something slippery, expensive and tissue thin. Her sleek hair made the tired furniture and faded wallpaper even shabbier. It always seemed a shame she didn't become a runway model. If there was a way Evie could have stolen a few inches from Inez' height, she would have done so years ago.

"When did you get here?" demanded Ingrid. "I didn't hear you come in or see a car."

Inez propped herself against a kitchen unit and helped herself to a cup of steaming caffeine.

"After midnight. I got a taxi from the airport."

"I'm going to the morgue, are you coming?"

"I'll stay here and keep an eye on dad."

Not a chance, thought Evie. The minute Ingrid was out the door Inez would be back in bed, out on the porch, painting her toenails, or whatever the hell she did.

"I'm coming, too," declared Clem. Crumbs scattered about his face were the only evidence of his sticky breakfast.

"Not in those pyjamas."

"I want my trousers."

"You're not coming."

"She was my wife, it's my right. You can't stop me. Besides, I want to see if she is really dead."

"Dad!"

"Leave me alone." Rising from the table he pushed his way past toward his room on unstable legs. "Where are my underpants?"

"If I were you," advised Evie, "I would leave now while he's occupied unless you want to take him with you.

Ingrid grabbed her keys and headed for the door.

"No thanks. Nine hours on the plane were more than enough. I need to find him a minder or something."

"Do you need me to come?"

"No. I will sort it out."

"What are you going to do?"

"Make sure everything is in order and sort out the funeral for probably the day after tomorrow. Aunty Vera said she would have the wake at her house."

"You had better check. She told me it would be here."

"I don't care where it is as long as I'm not doing all the work."

"All that's left is to find out what Ivan and Ian are doing, and visit the solicitor in town."

"I'll ring the guys," volunteered Inez.

What a surprise, thought Evie. Whatever was easiest to do, that's what her sister would opt for.

"That leaves the solicitor, so I'll give you a lift."

Ingrid delved into her oversized bag and came up with a twist of paper. "That's the address. I found it in a pile of letters I found in her room. I'm not sure it's her solicitor, but it's worth a try. I don't have anything else to go by."

Evie stuffed the sheet into her back pocket before following her sister into the morning heat, leaving Inez to her coffee and their father.

She found the tiny office wedged down a small alleyway between a rum shop and a bakery. The door was hard to find, among the shadows of the opposing building and up a rickety iron staircase. The makeshift reception area was manned by a frosty looking hawk of a woman, who made her wait an eternity for the magic door to swing open. It was a wait in vain. The obsequious man gave her but three minutes to speak, before cutting her off, informing her he had never had any dealings with her mother. His only clients of their family had been her grandparents who, as he put it "had nothing to bequeath but that big rundown shack which should have been pulled down a long time ago."

Evie's mobile phone trilled in her pocket. Excusing herself, she glanced at the screen, and then pressed a button.

"What is it, Ingrid?"

"I need you to come down here. Now!"

What the hell was wrong now? All she needed to do was glance at the body then get out.

"There's a problem."

"What kind of problem?"

"An… I can't talk to you over the phone kind of problem."

What was the matter with her family? Everybody else could accomplish things in a straightforward, logical, orderly manner but them.

"I'm coming."

She found the building tucked behind the central post office in town. Ingrid sat before a large oscillating fan in a windowless room festooned with vases of flowers and floral wallpaper, creating a cacophony of colours.

"So what's going on?"

"Don't look at me like that."

"Like what?"

"All angry and everything like I am some kind of idiot."

"I didn't say anything."

"You didn't have to. I can tell."

"You drag me out of the solicitor's office, the one you wanted me to see, to come here. Now you are talking rubbish. Get to the point, and stop crying!"

Ingrid sniffed loudly, taking a second to compose herself before blurting it out.

"Mum wasn't in the car by herself when she had the accident."

Evie sank to the sofa beside Ingrid, the feeling of strangeness which had dogged her since hearing the news of her mother intensifying. Taking her sister's silence as a cue, Ingrid continued.

"She wasn't driving. The man in the car was. Mum wasn't found in the car."

"Who told you that?"

The coroner just now. He said she was found on the side of the road."

Evie struggled to digest this latest piece of new information.

"I thought he was the driver of the other car or something. So who is this man?"

"Nobody knows. You heard of him? You know this is the kind of place where everyone knows everyone else and all their business too. Yet nobody recognises him."

"Let's see the body then."

"He's not here."

"Where else is a body supposed to be then?"

"He's not dead. He's in the hospital."

48

Ingrid wasn't entirely sure she was ready for something like this. When she arrived at the airport, she thought she was going to attend her mother's funeral. Now she was in the middle of an awful soap opera with the Evie and herself at the bedside of a comatose man.

She noted his thick ebony hair peppered with helixes of grey. The man took up a lot of bed with his broad chest and defined muscles. He was obviously mature, but Ingrid found it hard to place his age. She reckoned it to be somewhere between forty five and sixty-five. Judging by his smooth Adriatic complexion, he could have been from anywhere around the world. With his face in repose, she could only detect the slightest of laughter lines at the corners of his eye lids, yet his face was strangely familiar. If it wasn't for the array of beeping machinery, one would have thought him asleep, awaiting an alarm clock to rouse him to wakefulness.

Across the bed, Evie raised a quizzical eyebrow. Ingrid interpreted the look as "now what?"

At the nurse's station, they enquired after his personal effects. All he had was a wallet with several hundred US dollars and a picture of their mother. Ingrid's brain bubbled with questions.

"Where did he come from?"

"How am I supposed to know?" Evie pulled open the weighty hospital doors and marched through. Ingrid scuttled behind her.

"I was only asking."

"What you should be wondering is if our mum had just picked that bloke up from the airport, why was the car found facing the opposite direction?"

Ingrid's lower lip jutted out in contemplation.

"Does it matter? It doesn't change that she is still gone." Ingrid's steps were unusually light as she headed for the exit. She almost skipped down the concrete stairs toward the car park. No more 5am phone calls. Guilt prickled at her conscience, but was helpless against the relief.

Evie swept her full cotton skirt into the car and buckled herself in as Ingrid wedged herself into the other side.

"Day after tomorrow, this will all be a memory, eh?"

"Exactly."

Ingrid glanced up from fumbling with her seatbelt. Evie was staring out the windscreen, key in hand.

"What the hell was going on?"

On the journey to their aunt's house, Evie directed Ingrid to ring ahead to inform her of the time and place of the funeral. She also requested the information be passed onto the rest of the family, and friends on the island and farther afield as she negotiated her way through the traffic. Idling at the main traffic lights beside Vigie Airport, as Ingrid continued to chatter away on her clunky mobile phone, Evie cast a glance at the cars on the opposite side of the road. There seemed to be a lot of American vehicles zooming past.

She remembered being car mad like her brother years ago. They would spend many boring journeys identifying different makes of cars.

Back then, nearly all the cars were British Leyland and Ford.

Nowadays, it wasn't stylish to have British made things, or for young folk to want to style themselves after stuffy people who were miles away. They had heroes on music videos and could aspire to live like the stars across the pond on American TV.

One jeep in particular caught her attention. It was unusual, being entirely black, which was rare as the regular St Lucian tastes tended to favour brash colours with plenty of added equipment. She cast her gaze to the open window as it passed.

"It's Ivan!"

"Hey," bellowed Ingrid "where are you going? Grandma's house is back that way!"

Ivan glanced toward them. He wound up the tinted window.

"Son of a bitch!"

"Did you see that? What is he playing at?"

"Ring him on his mobile."

There was no answer.

"Don't worry. We'll catch him later when he gets to the house." Evie stepped on the accelerator.

Their aunt had news for them on their arrival. They found her busy catering for what appeared to be a cruise-liner full of folk in preparation for the funeral wake, not that she needed to, with a housekeeper and several servants. Uncle Robert dozed fitfully next door in front of the cricket match televised live from Barbados.

"I've contacted some of the family. The rest will hear about it on the grapevine, so you don't have to worry. Unfortunately, many more people will come out for the free food."

"Of that I have no doubt," snorted Evie. Ingrid kissed her teeth in agreement.

"Come give me a hand, girls. Evie, you fix those plates and Ingrid can help with the food."

Evie picked up a stack of paper plates and set to work slotting napkins between each one whilst Ingrid donned a clean apron and set up a sandwich filling station.

"Ivan drove past us on the way here, but he ignored us. I know he saw us."

"Strange, even for him."

"I have no idea where he was going. There's nothing back that way but the hospital."

"Maybe he was lost. He hates coming to the island. It reminds him of grandma."

"But she's been dead for donkey's years."

"He still hates it. The last time he came it was for her funeral. I can see a pattern here."

"Have you heard anything from Inez?"

"She rang just before you got here. She hasn't seen either of your brothers yet, but your father is "doing her head in" as she put it. She wants one of you to come and get him."

"Tough. I left my car at the house. She could have taken him out, but I bet she couldn't be bothered as per usual."

"Maybe I should go back and help." Ingrid grabbed her bag, ready to fly out the door.

"No, you won't," admonished Aunty Vera. "You are going to stay right here and give me a hand. That girl is far too lazy for her own good. From what I hear she doesn't give your father a second of her time."

"I don't think she likes him. They have hardly spoken to each other over the years."

"That's nonsense."

"It's true," stated Ingrid. "Usually I interpret between the two of them. Otherwise they ignore each other."

Aunty raised a questioning eyebrow toward Evie who in turn shrugged her shoulders. The soft tones of the house phone rang in another room. Wiping her hands on her apron, their aunt hurried to the lounge. From the kitchen, they heard several exclamations. Evie gesticulated at the open doorway. Ingrid shook her head in confusion.

"That was your Uncle Joseph." Aunty returned to the kitchen and resumed her artful presentation of the exotic salad.

"Will he be there tomorrow?"

"Yes. He has just seen your brother arrive at the hotel with enough luggage to keep a plane full of people clean for a month."

"Is uncle still working at the Four Winds hotel?"

"No, he got a large contract at the new Paradise Palms resort out at Rainbow Bay. He does all the entertainment there and in their hotels in Barbados and Miami."

They both remembered how their uncle used to kick up a storm at grandma's house with all his rock and roll antics with them around the front parlour. It never failed to infuriate the old woman who cursed it as the devil's music. He had switched to the disco scene at the height of its popularity on the island, which was many years after it had actually given way to hip-hop elsewhere in the western world, but they hadn't the heart to tell him.

It didn't cool grandma's anger.

Maybe it was a small mercy that by the time hip-hop caught up with uncle; grandma had already taken up residence beside her husband in the local cemetery due to a heart attack.

No doubt brought on by the music.

Granddad Solomon had worked himself to death trying to please Grandma Grumpy.

Uncle was now a big-shot entertainment director. He played or listened to music non-stop. Just as well he didn't have a wife –

he would have deafened her by now for sure they reckoned, though he was never short of female company.

"Did he actually speak to Ivan?"

"Ivan? No honey." Aunty paused in her careful placement of cucumber slices to gaze across at Ingrid. "He saw Ian checking in just now. He said he tried to have a word, but Ian said if anyone who wasn't family asked after him, pretend he hadn't seen him."

"That's Ian for you, always up to something weird."

"I suppose he will turn up whenever and wherever he fancies," said Ingrid.

"As per usual" added Evie.

"Some days I can't believe the two of you are twins, you are so different."

"Most twins are when it comes to personalities. Mum had a terrible time with him when he got thrown out of school. For a while he was running with a wild crowd and getting into all sorts of trouble. At one point he was being seen by the magistrates so often, they knew him by name. That is never good."

Ingrid shook her head. "I think between Ian and dad, mum went a bit crazy."

"Then all of a sudden it was like he did an about turn and got himself a proper sales job which was odd in itself. He always used to laugh at people who had jobs like that."

"I think it was that old inspector watching him that scared him."

"Well whatever it was, mum was happy. Then to top it all off he joined the church when she had spent all those years trying to get him to attend."

"Well at least we know where HE is right now," declared Aunty emphatically.

"Very true."

"We will bump into him sooner or later." Evie stacked the plates into two piles to one side of the counter. "I wonder where he is staying if not here or grandma's house."

THE FUNERAL

49

"It's just like your mother to die and leave me here."

Evie rolled her eyes heavenwards. The sun was at its height, rendering the figures gathered around the graveside almost immobile with heat exhaustion. Whoever decided black was the thing to wear for funerals had not attended one in the Caribbean.

"I said it's just like your mother to leave me here!"

Ingrid glared at the figure in the wheelchair. The nurse patted the bony shoulder and shushed the man. To his credit, the pastor from the Good Shepherd Tabernacle Church of God never wavered.

"Oh Lord, we pray merciful Jesus that you accept to your bosom the soul of our departed sister. Calistika Rochard has worshipped you, followed your path, and brought her family into your fold.

"As we lay her to rest we pray she resides with you in peace until Judgement Day. Look with mercy upon those who are left behind and comfort those who are bereaved. We give thanks in Jesus name, Amen."

After a moments silence, Pastor Douglas started to sing in a surprising good baritone;

"Oh Lord my God, when I in awesome wonder,
Consider all the worlds thy hands have made,
I see the stars; I hear the rolling thunder,
Thy power throughout the universe displayed,
How great thou art, how great thou art…"

Mother's favourite hymn.

How Evie hated it.

It always brought back memories of her mother singing fit to burst in that off key way of hers.

Directly across from her stood Ivan.

As per usual he was standing to attention, oblivious to the mosquitoes, perspiration pouring down his face into his pristine shirt collar. Chin jutting out; it seemed as if he was trying to pretend he was elsewhere. Maybe on parade.

Next to him, Ingrid leaned against her brother as if needing his support to get through the singing. Together, they resembled Laurel and Hardy, without the humour.

At the head of the grave was Pastor Douglas. He droned on for all he was worth – and so he should. Much of his church was built on their family's money.

Evie supposed he did make it his business to fly out to officiate at the funeral. That had to account for something, although it wasn't necessary to bring his own keyboard player.

The rumour was Keyboard Man had brought his own super high-tech organ, but it was refused at the airport on departure as he didn't want to check it into the cargo hold, nor pay extra to give it a comfy seat on the plane. He had to make do with the local organist's second rate keyboard. That, she guessed, would account for the odd wrong note and unexpected alien sounds it produced when the man got carried away in the music and pressed certain keys expecting a harmonious sound.

Different keyboard, different set up.

Pastor Douglas' body swayed in time with his singing as if overcome with emotion. Evie could see him on occasion scanning the crowd with sly eyes to see if anyone was hoodwinked.

His too tight black jacket had trouble covering his ample stomach and half his buttons had long since fled. The cuffs of a shirt that had seen better decades had a fringed frayed effect. His pants appeared to have an aversion to his shoes as they were well on their way up his calves, revealing a natty pair of maroon silk socks which went exceedingly well with the matching Cuban heeled shoes.

Evie followed his gaze as it passed over those present.

Besides Ivan and Ingrid, was Inez. Ian had to show off and stand apart from everyone else in the shade of the palm trees up on the slope, in all his linen suited finery. Anyone would have thought he was attending a day at the races.

Aunty Vera was back at the house, keeping the rest of the swarm who had opted against going to the funeral, away from the fried chicken.

The nurse stood over her father's wheelchair protectively, her dowdy dress open to the tops of her breasts, failing to disguise her trim figure. Her scraped back hair and nude face completed a sombre picture, which Evie did not buy into. In her peripheral vision, she could see her father mumbling under his breath. She would bet her last cent he wasn't singing the hymn. She also noted the pastor had taken an interest in the nurse's ample charms. No doubt later on he would be finding a way to convey his condolences to her. Evie wondered where Ingrid found her on such short notice.

The crowd was a healthy size but not overly ostentatious for a woman of the church. She could easily spot many of the brethren present in their oversized hats and thick tights.

Everyone else had opted for light linens and cotton dresses. Evie reckoned the churchwomen were most probably swimming in sweat wearing all that get up in the tropical heat. Amongst the group, she could pick out her uncle, though he ought to be resting. Uncle Joseph looked All-American in his wide shouldered custom made suit. The rest were local townsfolk and friends of her mother. A few looked vaguely familiar to her.

Beside her, Inez choked back a loud sob. Typical. It was just like her sister to do that. She always had a streak of showmanship which she must have inherited from her father.

Her shoe's pinched, but Evie revealed no emotion. Maybe that was the problem. She never let anyone past her guard, and always kept a measured calm and distance these days in most things apart from her work. Just where she didn't need it. It made people wary of her as if being a slave to her emotions made her more human. Maybe it was the years of scientific study which made her immune to the present event she was caught up in.

Even now, she found she couldn't fall apart and bellow as some of the churchwomen were doing, besides, she had dealt with many bereaved relatives in her line of work. You could tell who knew the deceased best in relation to how loudly the person howled at the time of being informed of the death.

In her experience, it was those who were closest who bawled the least. Her hypotheses appeared correct as none of her immediate family were howling, leaving it to the church folk to compete.

Ingrid and Inez stepped up to the rectangular hole in the ground and threw several handfuls of dirt onto the coffin. After a pause, she dutifully did the same, all around feeling eyes on her. They were looking for any chink in her armour but her eyes were dry.

The whole thing seemed unreal.

"As her husband, I should be first."

All eyes shot to the belligerent figure in the canary yellow suit and brown homburg, claw-like hands resting on bony fabric covered knees. Where he found those brown patent leather shoes were anyone's guess.

Evie remembered years ago her mother's face wet with tears of laughter as she pulled out the shoes from under the sofa. The two of them had screamed with hysterics at the platform heels and mock suede trimmings. Mother had vowed to hide them somewhere father would never think of looking.

They were never seen again.

Until today.

50

After the service, the group meandered back to the cemetery gates, leaving Evie behind in contemplation. She wasn't looking forward to returning to her grandparents' house and certain interrogation.

The five bouquets of flowers seemed flashy when bought, but now looked measly upon the ground amongst the other flowers. She could see cemetery workers in the distance sizing up the floral arrangements. Before the grave was filled, they would be portioning them out amongst their wives and girlfriends.

No matter.

There were other worries ahead of her.

As she pulled into the parking bay at her grandparent's house, another busload of relatives drew up alongside and piled into the house, oblivious to her greetings. Most were strangers to her.

Inside, the place was heaving, despite every window and the door being open and the ceiling fans oscillating at top speed. The air was redolent of sweat and fierce cooking. At the far end of the room, she could see Ingrid working furiously behind the enormous dining table.

Though flanked by several very capably sized women, they were no match for the demands for food. Bodies pressed forward hungry for the mountains of roasted chicken, rice and peas, coleslaw, green bananas, and piles of doorstep thick hard-dough bread slathered with rich salted butter.

The women worked hard, granting each desire for food as if it were the only one, and fussed over every plate, flirting and teasing while hands worked. In a corner, her father sat with a tray on his lap. It heaved with all manner of dishes and a pint of carrot juice.

"So, you *do* know where your grandparent's house is then?" Evie turned to face the voice.

Cousin Margaret stood defiant, thick legs spread wide. Ham fists rested on enormous hips.

The top buttons on her threadbare blouse had surrendered to pressure, and a dirty grey bra had made an appearance.

Grandpa may be in London, but his grand-daughter was still carrying on the tradition of being a loudmouth pain in the Gluteus Maximus.

"So, you've come to see what you can get!" Evie smiled, but no warmth reached her eyes.

"After you and your tribe have finished, there won't be anything, not that anyone wanted you here in the first place."

Evie jutted her chin towards the oversized women's offspring. They were systematically checking every piece of furniture, every ornament on show and no doubt mentally pricing up accordingly.

Cousin Margret pursed her lips.

"Your father said we could help ourselves to anything we wanted".

"IT'S NOT HIS TO GIVE!"

The hum of conversation vanished around the two women. They stood toe to toe, the large, flat-faced woman pushing her considerable girth against Evie, who elbowed her in return.

"What's going on?" Inez pushed between and separated the warring factions.

"She's got her eye on mum's things."

"I wouldn't be surprised. I've heard dad say a lot of things to a lot of people lately."

"I was always good to your mother, you know."

"And don't I remember it well?" added Evie caustically. Every occasional phone call she had with her mother, Ida had told of the flabby woman's antics in her long held goal to stay at the house under the ruse of housekeeper which everyone knew was a fancy name for "staying for free."

"Don't worry about it now, things will be sorted out with the will, then we'll know who gets what."

Evie cast a sidelong look across the room. "Well someone had better tell DAVID THEN!"

Her cousin grinned guiltily. The dainty figurine in his hand was almost in his jacket pocket. He placed it back on the mantelpiece and practically moon walked from the room under Ian's watchful eye..

"Humph!" Cousin Margaret stomped off in search of more food.

"Look," Inez placed a hand on her shoulder.

"Things have been tough on all of us lately. Just try to take it easy ok?"

"Sure. I just can't stand those vultures. They make me sick. I've got to get out of here."

Evie wandered through the throng toward her father. Although she was in a crowd, she might as well have been on the moon with few people greeting her as she passed. She reached her father as he ploughed his way through the feast set before him.

All ten digits were in on the act, but they still failed to save his tie as gravy stains be speckled the yellow, grey, and red monstrosity. The nurse dabbed at the corners of his mouth with a square of white cotton while showing off her assets to their best advantage. Evie inhaled and counted to ten.

She exhaled.

"Dad, I'm going back to Aunty V's house. I've got a headache."

"You going already? You haven't spent any time with me." His bottom lip drew out petulantly.

"I'll come back when it's not so crowded, ok? Then we'll have a nice chat."

"I'll just have to manage somehow."

He seemed to be managing just fine from where she was standing.

"Look, I'm sorry. I'll make it up to you I swear."

"Alright, darling. I'll see you later."

"Comforting to know you take a lot of persuading," muttered Evie as she stalked out the front door.

As expected, the figurine had disappeared and so had her brother, and she still hadn't gotten a chance to have a decent chat with him since they arrived on the island, but Ingrid and Ivan could wait.

Once inside the car, Evie sat back and relaxed for a while as the vehicle weaved its cold magic. It was day three and already she was weary of the situation. She wished she was back in her own home, but that wasn't an option. Things were weird enough between herself and her family without staying away from her mother's funeral. That would have been seen as an act of open warfare. Hell, who was she kidding? It was only Inez who had the peace-making skills of the United Nations who made any difference at all. It was obvious to her Ingrid was ignoring her for what reason she knew not. Ivan, she was never too sure even at the best of times.

No one could even begin to hazard a guess as to what went on inside her brother's head.

As she tuned the radio to something a little more uplifting, a black saloon eased into the drive, and an elegantly dressed man carrying an expensive briefcase climbed out and walked across to her car.

She wound down the window.

"Ms Rochard?"

"Yes." An Englishman. What did want with her?

"I represent your late mother's solicitors. I am here to inform you the will reading is to take place in two hours at these offices." He handed her a pristine business card.

"How do you know who I am?"

The man stretched his mouth into a semblance of a smile, turned on his heel and walked toward the front door.

51

The office was nothing like the fleapit Evie visited two days ago. The newly built offices overlooked the busy harbour adjacent to the duty-free shopping precinct.

Clem insisted on entering the luxurious conference room first.

"It is my right as head of the household. Put me over there," he said, pointing at the immense mahogany table with its fourteen cloned seats. He fussed as the agency nurse aligned his wheelchair at the conference table. It was obvious to all if he had walked to his seat as he was quite capable of doing, it would have taken a fraction of the time.

The nurse took a seat in close proximity to her charge. Ingrid sat on Clem's right. Her gigantic handbag squatted on its own seat. Inez seated herself on the other side of the wheelchair. One chair away.

Two chairs down from Inez, Evie made herself comfortable whilst Ian carefully placed his finely woven silk, linen blend jacket on the back of the chair beside him before checking the crease in his trousers. His white shirt was open at the neck, with epilated chest bared. The hint of 18 carat gold twinkled inside his collar. He seated himself opposite everyone else.

A little nervous banter passed between them as they waited for the solicitor. Clem ordered the nurse to pour him a glass of water from the heavy cut-glass carafe on the table.

Inez checked her make up in the tiny make up compact from her handbag, periodically checking her cumbersome mobile phone.

Ingrid swiped at sweat beaded upon her forehead with a grubby man-sized handkerchief, managing to further smudge her circus style make up. Her fleshy triceps jiggled with exertion.

Evie struggled to stay awake.

Mesmerised by the calming seascape mounted upon the opposite wall, Evie wished herself stretched out on the shimmering sands. If she really concentrated, she could almost feel the sea gently breaking upon her toes, enticing her to take a dip in its tranquil aqua marine waters. To immerse herself in its warm salty blanket.

So fixated was she on her fantasy, it took her a moment to realize another person had entered the room. An exquisitely suited well-built man strode officiously to the only chair with armrests situated in the middle of the circle of chairs next to Ivan.

Clem, realising he was not seated at the head of the table scowled with displeasure.

The solicitor organised his papers before him. The family waited impatiently for him to get started.

"Good afternoon. My name is Mr. Willoughby. I am a partner at Jackson, Willoughby and Lord Solicitors. I would like to take this opportunity to thank you for your attendance at such short notice on this sad occasion."

"Now she's gone, I have nobody to help me," declared Clem mournfully.

"In case you hadn't noticed, she hasn't been around for the past five years," hissed Inez. "You seem to help yourself to everything anyway."

"Give it a rest," countered Evie.

"I'm only saying what you lot are too chicken to say," she crossed her arms and leaned back in the corporate chair.

"Well, now you've said it. Shut up."

Raising his voice, the man continued, seemingly oblivious to the emotional chill in the air.

Evie and Inez glared at each other. Clem whispered to his nurse, pouring poison down her ear about his daughters. Ingrid continued to make a mess of her makeup.

The solicitor began without preamble.

"I have with me the last will and testament of Calisticka Theresa Rochard, otherwise known as "Ida." The solicitors lip quirked upward momentarily, then returned to melancholy repose.

He paused in an experienced dramatic style, in the knowledge all eyes were focused on him. It was obvious there were certain aspects of his job he favoured.

Adjusting his spectacles with a practised air, he began.

"I Calisticka Rochard, am of sound mind and body do solemnly declare this to be my last will and testament..."

"We know that."

"Shut up, dad." Ian leaned forward in anticipation. If he was ever going to get himself out of the hole he had gotten into, any money he got would be useful.

"To my husband Clement Rochard..."

The solicitor paused for full effect. Ian wondered whether the man was an amateur dramatics enthusiast. It was a shame the official had not pursued a career on the stage. He would have been a magnificent Hamlet. Or politician.

"I leave the contents of the house in Peckham..."

Clem smiled broadly in satisfaction. It was his God given right to have those things and everything else coming to him.

"...But not the house as it was never in his name and he never paid a penny toward it."

"What?!" Arthritis forgotten, the wheelchair crashed to the floor as Clem leaned over the boardroom table. "That house is mine. I worked for decades to provide food on the table and pay the bills."

"Maybe in your alternative universe but I don't remember it being that way," muttered Inez.

"Can there be some mistake?" Ingrid's forehead shone like an oil slick despite her dabbing.

"No," the solicitor was emphatic. "The will was made three years ago, witnessed and signed in the presence of a legal representative."

"By who? Father Christmas?"

"I am not at liberty to divulge that information. It is bound by the terms of the will."

"But where am I supposed to put the stuff?"

"What stuff?" inquired Inez "You've already flogged most of the furniture."

"I haven't."

"Yes you have."

"I strongly recommend you to listen to the rest of the will. All will be made clear in due course."

Clem sank into the righted wheelchair, his brow furrowed deeper than a freshly ploughed field.

"I leave the contents of the house in Peckham, but not the house. I also leave the house on Napoleon Drive, Dennery."

"What house?"

"NEVER MIND DENNERY, I WANT MY MONEY!"

Ingrid had never heard of any house in St Lucia other than their grandparent's.

"Do you know about another house, dad?"

"Fix your face and shut up."

Ian's former disinterest in his father's acquisition was rapidly dissipating. He cocked his head thoughtfully. If there was another house, it must sit on land. If his mother owned the house, it stood to reason that she owned the land, too. How many dollars per square feet did land sell for on the island? A little property development if the property was in a prime location could be most lucrative.

So engrossed was he in speculation, he failed to observe the spark of recognition in his father's eyes.

"To the Good Shepherd Tabernacle Church, I leave 200,000 Eastern Caribbean Dollars in thanks for the support they have given me over the years. To my children with Clement, I leave all my assets comprising of the house in Peckham…"

Willoughby paused whilst Clem embellished his considerable knowledge of English swear words with a variety of Germanic ones.

"… My home in Florida, government bonds and savings of 8.3 million pounds."

There was a stunned silence. The solicitor sat poker faced, the only giveaway being the rapid twitching of his nostrils.

Clem was the first to respond. He shot to his feet again; teeth bared and veins popping in his neck. The solicitor scooted back in his chair, his legal papers an ineffective shield pressed against his chest as Clem launched himself across the table, intent on tearing a hole in the solicitors throat. His nurse grabbed a flailing foot, whilst Ingrid tucked a meaty fist into the waistband of his pants.

"Where did mum get all that money?" demanded Inez. Thoughts of all the lousy homemade sandwiches consumed over the years swirled about her head. She could have been eating out at all the celebrity restaurants. "She was a hospital worker!"

"When do we get our share?" Ian elbowed his father aside as Clem, energy spent, fell back into his seat. "What bank on the island does the best transfer deals?"

Evie hugged her arms about herself, her eyes glassy with unshed tears. She wondered how many more mistakes she may have made at her hospital due to exhaustion working two jobs. Trying to earn enough for her rent and eat. How could her mother be worth so much and care so little financially?

Inez thumped the varnished expansive surface in frustration. "Aren't you going to say anything else other than what you can get for yourself as per usual, Ian?"

"What's he getting up to now?" came a voice from the doorway.

All eyes turned to the figure in synchronisation.

Dressed in dusty fatigues, a battered cap atop his head and a scowl etched on his slender face stood Ivan.

"Humph, look what the cat dragged in," snorted Clem. "You took your time."

Ivan ignored the jibe.

"Where the hell have you been hiding? I thought you were coming here straight away. Why have you changed back into your army stuff? Where's your black suit?"

Ivan tossed his duffle bag to one side and threw himself into the seat next to his youngest sister. He poured himself a glass of water, taking a good long puzzled look at her.

"I don't know what medication you're on, but you had better give it a rest. I don't have a black suit. I have only just gotten out of the airport. By the way, thanks for meeting me." He took a long hard swallow of the cool liquid.

Evie gaped at him, eyes wide. "Are you having a laugh? You drove past us yesterday and you ignored us at the cemetery, so if anybody should be angry, it should be Ingrid and me."

"Don't be stupid, how could it have been me? Thailand to St Lucia via Zimbabwe and Paris ain't no picnic, let me tell you. Not when you are flying regiment class, even if you are on leave," he declared irritably. "Aunty told me I had missed the funeral, so I legged it up here."

Before she could reply, the solicitor interjected.

"Perhaps sir, I should complete the reading of the will then things might become a little clearer?"

"Dad's got the furniture in Peckham, but no house," informed Inez.

"I thought he had flogged most of it."

"Exactly. And there's another house in Dennery that dad won't talk about."

"Oh."

"And mum has left 8 million quid."

"BLOODY HELL!"

"Exactly."

"8.3 million," corrected Ian.

Willoughby hastily pressed on.

"To my offspring with Marcel…"

"Marcel!" Clem bashed his hand on the table in alarm spilling water across its smooth surface.

"I bloody don't believe it. That man again. I knew it. Church, my arse. She wasn't going to church. She was shagging that bastard! I should have kicked his backside when I had the chance."

"Who's Marcel?"

Inez shrugged in response.

"Marcel's her old boyfriend from way back and Ivan's dad, remember?" snorted Ian.

"How do you know?"

"Because unlike you lot, I pay attention."

"You mean you are bloody nosy."

Ian looked down his nose in contempt. "Like I said, I pay attention."

"So why is he in the will?"

"Keep up will you, Ingrid."

"Sorry. So why IS he in the will?"

"Don't you ever listen?"

"Sorry."

"Mum had a fling with that Marcel bloke," informed Evie, "and they had a kid."

"They had me," corrected Ivan, "remember now?"

"Yeah."

"To my beloved offspring with Marcel, I leave the Aubertine house. The house was given to me by Marcel as recompense for past injustices done to me by his father as it is from this house everything began. It is with this in mind that I declare this will null and void with all proceeds given to the Salvation Army unless the rest of my property is returned by those who stole it and given to its rightful owner."

"What property?" Evie rubbed at her face in exasperation.

"Why does the will rest on a proviso, anyway?" Ivan was entirely lost with regard to the will, and wasn't sure he ever wanted to understand it.

"Who's Aubertine?" inquired Ingrid.

"What about me, what am I getting? I deserve more than the bit I got. If it wasn't for me, none of you would be here. I gave my life to raising a kid that wasn't mine. I get nothing for my trouble?"

Ingrid touched her father's shoulder sympathetically. "We will sort you out, don't worry about that."

"Your mother had nothing when I met her; I made her what she was."

"What, a drudge?"

"Shut up! I want my share, and none of you are going to get any peace till I do. I am going to stop that will"

"Contest," corrected Ivan.

"If it's a contest you are after, you will get one."

"No, you mean you will contest the will. Never mind."

"I think it might be wise to calm down Mr. Rochard otherwise I will have no choice but to call security to return you to the wake."

"This will is bullshit, and you know it. Who paid you to bitch up that will?"

The solicitor scowled across the table.

"We do not take kindly to accusations of bribery Mr. Rochard. We are a reputable company with our clients being of the most distinguished families in the West Indies. Discretion is our cornerstone." Willoughby pressed the button secreted on the side of his seat. Moments later, a pair of bulky security officers stepped through the door.

Muted yells rung through the building, to the consternation of the office administrators as Clem was pushed out the building and out into the debilitating heat to the waiting car. The nurse peeled back her lips into a sly smile aimed at the security duo, as she brought up the rear of the procession. Willoughby gathered his papers together.

"Let us press on. The keys to the Aubertine house are held in our safe here. They are available to you with all relevant documentation of valued assets pertaining to the property. However, there is an added element."

"Uh oh," intoned Ian. "There is always a "however.""

"There is the matter of the relinquishment of an item of jewellery in order for the will to be set in motion. I believe it is a crested family ring given to the first born of the Aubertine lineage."

"That will be so easy. All we have to do is find what, a forty year old ring?"

"What's the aubergine ring?" Ingrid promptly closed her jaw with an audible click when Inez shot her a scathing glance.

"Do you know where the ring is?"

"The ring is not in our possession. When I queried its whereabouts Mrs. Rochard was adamant it was taken by Mr. Rochard."

"I wouldn't be surprised," replied Ivan, "it's the kind of thing dad would do."

"Mrs. Rochard thought it to be in the possession of Ian Rochard."

"How the hell would he have it?" Ivan was getting more confused by the minute. His mother was stinking rich. He had acquired a house from a stranger. Now his brother possessed a ring which was his birthright.

"Your mother believed it was stolen along with other items from her possession either during or shortly after a house fire?"

"What makes you think I have it?"

"Because everything of any worth in our family seems to gravitate toward you. When we were kids you always had something belonging to someone else in your pocket," replied Evie.

Ivan was more direct.

"You have always been a tea–leaf. Just like dad."

The solicitor's eyebrows rose questioningly. "Tea–leaf?"

"Cockney rhyming slang for thief. I thought you were a London man."

"I am."

"Not from my neighbourhood, mate."

"Don't bother to deny it, Ian." Inez's head had begun to pound in the stifling room. If she didn't get out soon as far away as possible from her family, she was going to scream. "You're well dodgy and everybody knows it. Like father, like son."

"I'm no thief. I merely acquire items."

"Sure. It wasn't too long ago dad nearly "acquired" a cell to live in. If I were you, I would watch out."

"I might not have it now." Ian sat back in his chair, seemingly unperturbed under scrutiny.

"Yes you do. I've seen it on you. It's on that chain around your thieving neck. I always wondered where you got that."

Lunging forward, before Ian could register movement; Ivan grabbed a fistful of sheer linen and pulled him close ignoring the girly scream which emitted from his younger brother.

Plunging his hand down his brother's shirt he yanked the slender chain free of the fabric. With it came an inlaid sovereign ring with the ornately carved first letter of the alphabet.

Motioning for his brother to take it off, Ivan placed the chain about his own neck, ignoring Ian's sour disposition.

"I think that solves the proviso problem, eh?"

A smug smile twitched about the solicitor's lips "I believe that almost ends the reading."

"Thank fuck for that." Ivan had been in the room less than twenty minutes, and the familiar claustrophobic feeling was creeping up on him. It happened every time he had to endure his family for any significant length of time.

"I have one last statement."

"Make it fast will you, mate?"

Willoughby chose to ignore him. Clearing his throat, he began.

"I leave the rest of my jewellery to my daughters in the hope they put it to good use and make the most of their lives, meeting challenges head on as I should have. I made many questionable

decisions. I pray you do not do the same. I leave my remaining letters and correspondence in the hope you may come to understand all which has passed. I wish I had been a better mother, but know what little I did has shaped you into the capable adults you are now. I love, and I am proud of you all."

Silence reigned for several seconds.

"I've never heard such crap," said Inez. "All she did was yell at us. What letters and correspondence is she talking about?"

"I have them in my office, I'll fetch them."

"What bad decisions did she make that she felt we shouldn't repeat them?" Evie gazed at each family member in turn.

One moment. I will return with the documentation shortly."

Gathering his papers together, the man stood to his feet. He walked out of the room, leaving them all deep in thought as the occasional faint yell echoed around the room.

52

In his office, Willoughby settled back in the butter-soft recliner and unbuttoned his business suit.

"They are all present apart from the father. He got rather excited when he heard the part regarding the Aubertine house."

"I for one am not in the least bit surprised." Lean legs uncrossed themselves to stand and stretch. Thin elegant fingers smoothed down the ebony slacks before adjusting the collar of the loose, pristine shirt. He picked up the neat cardboard box, leaving his suit jacket on the back of his chair.

"I guess I'm on then."

The solicitor extended his hand in friendship. "Good luck, sir. I am sure all will be well. They don't seem too bad although that dandy seems rather troublesome."

"That's what my sources tell me. Thank you for the use of your boardroom. We may be some time."

"Not at all sir, our pleasure." He smiled warmly up at the man. "Shall I call for refreshments?" For the amount of business this individual could generate for their office, Willoughby would have given up his house and thrown in his family as staff if it were asked of him.

"That would be appreciated. Thank you."

In the boardroom, Ian and Ivan were at loggerheads for the return of the ring as it dangled between them. Ian believed ownership was nine tenths of the law and seeing his brother didn't have knowledge of the ring before today it was rightfully his. Ivan didn't believe that bullshit for a second.

Inez fiddled with her new mobile phone in vain as she tried to switch off the incessant ringing without answering the phone which was proving impossible. They were all treated to a second or two of measured beeps before Inez clicked the phone off for the cycle to begin again.

Evie was attempting for the umpteenth time to explain to Ingrid whom the Aubertine man was and why the ring was so important when the door reopened.

One by one all talk ceased as they followed each other's gaze. Standing in the doorway was… Ivan.

"What the fuck?" The seated Ivan gaped in astonishment.

"Hi guys," the second Ivan strode smoothly to the seat beside the one vacated by the solicitor, placing a box on the table in front him, and seated himself.

The resemblance was far too strong to be anything else but a twin brother; though there were subtle differences they noted as they stared. Their Ivan was always had closely cropped hair courtesy of Her Majesty and a lean angular runners physique, whereas the other man had a muscular body with his hair a touch longer.

He was wearing a suit, a black one.

"You were at the graveside," squawked Evie.

"Yes, I was there, and before you ask, I was in the car yesterday, too." He grinned at them, flashing perfect teeth. "Nice to meet you properly after all this time."

Ivan finally found his voice.

"Where the hell did you come from? And have I got any other brothers I don't know about? If this was any other day I think I would have fainted by now, but my brain can take only so many surprises before it goes numb."

His siblings murmured in agreement.

"There is only you and I. I would have thought it was obvious where we came from."

"You are American."

"You have got to be the eldest, Ingrid isn't it?"

Finding herself the centre of attention for once, she giggled foolishly.

"Yep, I am American. That's where I grew up. So if you are Ingrid," his eyes lighted upon each of them in turn, "you must be Inez."

She inclined her head as her phone squawked yet again.

"You had better get that."

"Don't worry about it." Turning the device off, she threw it into her bag.

"So that makes you Evelyn."

"Evie," she corrected.

"Course, I don't have to be told who you are obviously," he nodded toward Ivan, "but you are Ian, am I right?"

"Give him a round of applause," drawled Ian. "We know whom we are, but we still don't know what you're called do we?"

"I'm Evan."

"Well that's original. Evan and Ivan."

"Hey," Evan spread his arms wide, palms upward. "I didn't choose it. Till I left home for college, I was known as Roberto."

"Just to complicate things a bit more…. Now we have an Uncle Robert and a brother Roberto. What about three Ian's?"

Inez scowled across the table. "One Ian is more than enough for one family, thank you very much."

"Pardon the cliché but where have you been all my life?"

"Texas, but I now live in Florida."

"Hey, mum left us a house in Florida," exclaimed Ingrid.

Evan gave the woman a smile normally reserved for very young children.

"That's right. Dad bought it for her when she finally left that asshole. I live right around the corner."

"So how comes he doesn't live there, too?"

"He does when he's in town, but he put it in her name for her security."

"So does he have women all over the place then? Pardon me, but we have only just found out our mum was a floozy, so did that make her just another number?"

Evan's placid demeanour hardened into a frown, which put everyone edgy for some inexplicable reason, including Ivan, who never got intimidated by anyone. This new brother did not look like the kind of person you would like to annoy.

"Mom was not, nor has ever been a number to dad. From what I have found out, it took a lot of time and money to find her."

"Well he didn't find me." Nobody came looking for him. Not knowing his real father made him feel like he wasn't actually part of the family. Like a lodger who could be cast adrift at any time. Maybe that was why he lived his life on the perimeter of everything. Always a spectator. Never a participant.

"Actually, he did."

Ivan stared at him speculatively. "So why have I never heard from him?"

"You did, or should I say he tried. Apparently he wrote to you every month. Mom kept them for you, for the day you would be ready to hear the truth. It was believed his letters were lost in the fire." Evan cut his eyes across to Ian who squirmed uncomfortably under such close scrutiny. "But seeing as the ring is here, maybe they weren't lost as we thought after all." he rose effortlessly to his feet.

"I'm sorry, Ivan," the smooth American tones filled the room. "The ring belongs to me, I'm the eldest."

"No way, mate," sneered Ian. "That ring is mine along with the rest of my share of money, and I want that right now."

Inez rolled her eyes heavenward. "You've waited this long, can't you wait another 24 hours?"

He rose from his seat. "Unlike you losers, I've got things to do."

"Sit your ass down."

Unused to being told what to do, Ian sank back in surprise, eyes glued to his new brother.

"Nobody goes anywhere till this is sorted out. All this nonsense has gone on for far too long. I've already spent too much time over the years trying to track you all down, for you to disappear on me now. We have family business to talk about."

"Well, that's fine with me. This family has never made any sense to me. It's about time it did. You can have that ring. I don't want it anyway," declared Ivan.

A dumpy secretary arrived disrupting the flow of conversation bearing ice-cold fruit juice and a selection of pastries. Sensing the frigid atmosphere hovering in the room, she hastily set about organising on the table, setting the requested refreshments before each person.

Evan scrutinised each member of his newly found family, not at all sure that he liked what he saw.

Ingrid, pulled on the front of her sweat-stained blouse, and tried to give her chest a bit of well needed breathing room, in vain.

Inez twirled a few strands of hair around her finger as he watched her mentally calculate how much money she might have to buy a nice place.

Evie stared off into the seascape canvas, consternation and weariness written in every line of her face.

Ian's face twitched in concentration, calculating ways of making his share even bigger.

Ivan, unlike the rest of them, seemed to have no problem with the turn of events, to his surprise. He appeared to have taken it in his stride with his relaxed demeanour and a small smile on his face.

They were a world away from his way of life, and he didn't see how they were ever going to find any common ground between them, but family was family. Now his mother was gone, he didn't have a whole lot left.

As the door closed behind the secretary, he began.

53

"My name is Evan Michael Aubertine. I was born first." He shot a glare at Ian who sank a little further into his seat, "with Ivan arriving three minutes later. Everyone thought there was only one baby as mom was a pretty regular size, and there was no ultra-sound scanning like you have nowadays on the island."

"How do you know everything and I don't? Mum never wanted to talk about stuff like that."

"I'm not surprised. Pregnant, with no husband in the fifties and sixties was no joke, according to the midwife who delivered us. I found her in a home in Guyana. Wonderful Grandma Solomon couldn't afford to keep two babies, so she paid the woman to get rid of one of us. The midwife told me she just grabbed the baby that looked the strongest which happened to be me and took off." Evan smiled apologetically.

"How did you end up in America?"

"Father found me a few months later which was just as well because the old lady was lining me up to live with some farming couple for big money. He took me back with him pretending to be my uncle so my step-mom would take me in, however she wasn't too keen on me. Even as a nephew."

"That's a bit of a tall story."

"Take it or leave it, it's the only one I got. It's the truth."

"Didn't she think it a bit strange you turning up out of nowhere?"

"Most of the time she never even knew what time zone she was in. She likes a drink."

"So she's still around then?"

Evan answered Inez' question with a rueful smile.

"Kind of, she did us all a favour and took off with one of our gardeners a while back."

Things didn't quite add up in Ivan's mind. "So why didn't he come for mum when he finally found her. In fact, why didn't he just marry her in the first place, and none of all this would have taken place."

"Your guess is as good as mine. Every time I tried to ask that question, I never got a straight answer. All he would tell me is that he finally tracked her down years later which apparently weren't too easy. That country of yours is small but sure is crowded. He was travelling a lot back then, so I don't know when they hooked up again, but she was still with that idiot, and had some half-assed idea to make a go of things with him instead."

"That explains why mum kept disappearing all the time. She WAS having a poke."

"Ian!"

"What?"

"This is our mum we're talking about."
"Alright, don't get your knickers in a bunch as the Americans say."

"Whatever happened, I guess she had a point. Let's face it; they were both married to other people who would have given them hell if they tried to leave, not to mention Grandpa Aubertine. He tried to put a stop to whatever he thought was brewing, but dad was too slick for him. Let me tell you, he was not the kind of man who would have been fantastic playing Father Christmas."

"What happened to him?"

"The same as every other ruthless power-hungry dictator. He died peacefully of old age in his bed one night, with a hot babe curled up beside him. Even when I was a boy he was old. He must have had dad in his fifties." Evan's sigh was audible in the hushed room. "I was kind of glad when he was gone. Dad stopped acting like a puppet, and he was more like a dad than an uncle after."

"You didn't like Grandpa A?"

"Nope. He worked dad like a slave till the day he died. He found out who I was and I wasn't going to pretend for a second to him anyway. He was mean. I found it easier to stay out of his way and play in the kitchen with the cooks' kids or in the grounds. As soon as I was old enough, I was gone."

Evie tried to imagine what it must have been like for him back then, each day as precarious as the last.

"Where did you go?"

"I went to Harvard to study, majoring in business and economics, and then joined a company in New York. Five years back, dad brought mom to Florida, so I relocated there. She didn't really want to go, but he gave her an ultimatum. 'The - come now, or I ain't coming back' kinda thing. I guess they weren't getting any younger."

Ian snorted in derision. "No local community college for you then, matey boy. It had to be the best of the best, sir!"

"At least we now know why mum left so suddenly."

"I guess. I'm not making any excuses for us having money. It's there to be used so I did. I'm not going to apologise for that." Evan caught Ian in a piercing stare "As least it is clean money."

Ian shifted uncomfortably in his seat. "My money is clean."

"I'm sure Inspector Smith would have something else to say about that."

"You know the inspector?" Ingrid piped up. Having scoffed her pastry as well as Inez' she had set her sights on Evie's uneaten almond croissant. "I like him."

"We had a good chat, him and me, and he had some pretty interesting things to say about you."

Ian scowled at his untouched juice "Whatever he has to say is bullshit. He retired eons ago; all he has in his life to keep him going is to follow me around sticking his nose in my business."

"I think he has good reason to. Are you going to tell them about your business dealings or shall I?"

"What's he done now?" Long used to his brothers' antics, Ivan wasn't surprised to hear that he was up to something else of an unsavoury nature.

Evan sat back in his seat, his arms resting easily on the table.

"Why don't we try the misappropriation of funds from your church as a starter?"

"What does that mean?"

"It means he took numerous collections of money, Ingrid, from all those people attending his church telling them it was to fix the guttering. Instead, he bought a couple of Savile Row suits."

"You can't prove that."

Evan laughed easily "Oh yes I can, when a man leaves a church, it is highly unusual for him to get into his old banger and go uptown to pick up suits like those and pay for it with a bag of crumpled notes and a ton of change. People notice these things. You are street smart yet money dumb."

"You followed me!" Ian bolted to his feet. "I can have you arrested for that, that's a violation of my human rights."

"So call the police."

Ivan could not believe what he was hearing. "Tell me he's wrong. You can't have stooped so low to steal money from people who have faith in you and your church. A lot of those people don't have it to give and do without to give money to the church."

"I bought those suits with my own money."

"Sit down and shut up before you find yourself chewing on my boot."

His newly found brother was a head taller than him, and carried himself like he knew some kind of Kung Fu, Jujitsu, Feng Shui shit, Ian duly sat down, but he was not a happy man.

"If you think I came over to say hi, drink tea, and go home again, you must be crazy. I am not the man to let things slide; my mother died. That may not be much to you, but it is everything to me." As he spoke, he stared meaningfully at each person in the room. He had orchestrated this meeting, and he meant to say every last word he had stored in his head over the years, whether they liked it or not.

"I didn't start out with the idea of following you, I found you through the usual channels and was quite happy to leave it at that when I realised a few people were interested in you. You are a popular man right now."

"With who?"

"You will find out soon enough, Evie. The only one I was interested in was the inspector. He has been watching you for some time. He has a keen nose for troublemakers. He must have seen something interesting in you all those years ago."

"I can't believe you are into more dodgy stuff," declared Inez. "Mum spent years cleaning up after you."

"Well you are on your own now, she's not here to help anymore," added Evie. "So you had better find a way to sort yourself out because I for one am not helping you."

"That goes for me, too." Ivan had too many things to think about of his own to care about his brothers antics.

"I'll help you." Ingrid had always liked Ian, though she didn't always understand him.

"Wow, thanks. What are you going to do, bake me a cake then eat it yourself when I'm not looking?"

"That was mean."

Evan would have liked to kick him right then and there, but there were far too many things to go over and at some point, they would have to vacate the room when the office closed in a few hours. Passing a sniffling Ingrid his freshly laundered handkerchief, he continued.

"He has pictures and paperwork. God knows how he did it, which links you to the embezzling of church funds, which probably paid for the Gulf Stream and the penthouse in Chelsea, not to mention the clothes, jewellery…"

"You have a plane?" Inez could not believe her ears "I can barely afford a closet in Kilburn, and you live in Chelsea!"

"…and have dealings with the local gangs in the distribution of drugs in the area."

"You started the anti-drug movement in the community!" Ingrid's bottom lip quivered with emotion. "You even came to talk to the children at Keisha's school."

Ian was unrepentant. "I did stop it."

"You moved it to another area when the police got too close" corrected Evan. "I was going to introduce myself earlier at the church, but you seemed to have your hands full with the police."

"That was you in the church? I thought it was Ivan."

"I was in Thailand."

"I know that now," snapped Ian.

"I wanted to see for myself the family whom my mother passed me over for, and my dad was forever occupied with, and I've got to tell you, I wasn't impressed."

"Nobody told you to look for us. You could have gone on with your life and not given us a second thought."

"Call it morbid fascination. Call it closure. Whatever it was, when I decided to pay all of you a little visit, it was an eye opener."

"That was you outside my flat that night wasn't it?"

"That was me."

"I thought you were a private detective."

"Why would you think that?"

Inez promptly shut her mouth.

"Were you in my accident and emergency ward last week?"

"I passed by. Is it always that busy?"

"That was a slow night. I was so tired. I thought I was seeing things."

"I saw Ingrid at the house in Peckham, but I think she thought I was Ivan on leave. It was pretty cool having Ivan in the army. It gave me the chance to pop up anywhere without causing too much trouble as you are used to him popping in and out of your lives."

"Thanks."

"You know what I mean. The only person I wasn't able to see was Ivan, what with him being in the army. Every time I found out where he was stationed, by the time I got there he had been moved on which is as well because I imagine bumping into yourself is probably going to be a bit of a red flag that something is up."

He turned back to Ian. "I don't know how you got out of the church. It was surrounded. I suppose getting that phone call was a life-saver for you. It gave you the chance to disappear for a few days, but when you get back…" Evan leaned forward, intent clear in his eyes "…and you will return to England my friend. You have your shit to sort out. I have already given the inspector my word that you will be returning by the end of the week or he has the authority to come and get you. Let me tell you, you don't want him to come because he won't be alone."

"You don't have the right to tell me what to do," Ian bit his lips in agitation, "I can do what I like."

Evan smiled. "Go do what you want then, but you won't get far without money. It was seized before you left England along with your other accounts around the world." He grinned, showing his orthodontic perfect teeth "and you sure as hell are not getting a cent of mom's money till you sort things out." He chuckled at Ian's stricken face.

"I know a bit about planes little brother. I've flown your Gulf Stream to a secure location, and you are sure as hell not stepping foot inside your apartment. You see mom wasn't as stupid as you thought. Your inheritance is the only one which is held in a trust fund and linked to me. I am the guardian of it, and until you sort yourself out, you are not seeing a dime, buddy. Who knows, if you go home and decide to come clean, the police might play nice and sort out some kind of deal for you. You might get a lighter sentence, but you are undoubtedly going to do some kind of jail time. You know it's been coming a long time."

For the first time ever, Ian was scared. Not the mildly anxious scare an unknown sound in a familiar house generates, but a gut wrenching, sweat forming, terror which seized his body in the knowledge there would be no quick fixes. There would be no mum to the rescue and no brushing under the carpet of his situation. He was wanted by the police for his numerous crimes of which he had no idea how many they had uncovered and was going to jail. He had no decent clothes but what he brought with him. He was stuck with the hound of hell brother. With no money.

"You can't do this." Unable to raise his head to all the eyes he felt boring into him he whispered to the table, his voice echoing in the silence. "Why are you doing this to me?"

"I am not doing anything. You created this mess yourself, and I'm just helping you out, *brother*."

"It's what you deserve," added Ivan. It was nice to see Ian getting sorted out for a change.

Evan was growing on him. His brother was badass.

"Well I wouldn't get happy too soon," advised Evan. "You have a few issues I unearthed which I found intriguing, too. In fact, there is a little something about all of you that I am not crazy about."

"Oh yeah?" unbuttoning his camouflage jacket, Ivan settled back into his chair, with one leg crossed over the other. "Enlighten us."

"I intend to." Pulling the box to him, Evan delved inside. "I have here copies of your leave papers for the past three years."

Ivan felt a prickle of unease ripple down his spine "What about them? How the hell did you get them anyhow?"

"Let us not play games here. I am a rich man, and rich men find out things in seconds what poor men spend years trying to bury." He cocked his head toward Ian who remained cowed in his seat.

"We can do this the easy way or I can go for it. It is time for all of us to be honest with each other. Are we going to spend the rest of our lives shrouded with secrets and denials? We are the only real family we have. We are distant from all our other relatives apart from your uncle and aunt whom I have yet to meet. I always believe in leading by example so I will go first."

54

"I have no wife, kids, or many friends. When I go home to my
house, it's empty. Sure, I have all the state of the art technology,
paintings, and stuff, but it's still empty. I am a homebody. My
idea of fun is burning a few burgers out back with a few beers and
catching a game on the TV. I have no life other than work.
Sometimes when it gets to be too much, I head down to the park
for a run, but I'm only fooling myself. I go because I want to be
near the families to watch the moms pushing the buggies, and
listen to the kids yelling for ice-cream then watch as they smear it
all over themselves. Sometimes I listen in on couples arguing
because even when they are yelling at each other, at least they
care." He busied himself with finding nothing in particular in the
box as he continued. The rest of the people in the room in turn
looked everywhere but at each other.

"I have girlfriends from time to time, but the trouble is the
money. Everything's great to start with, then they get a sniff of
how much I'm worth. First they ask for a little something - a car, a
bracelet, a weekend break, whatever, which is cool. I can take
that, but then before you know where you are, a few months down
the line, they want a house, a few more cars, month long holidays,
a birthday party on a yacht, the fanciest restaurants every night,
the list just grows, and they still haven't even bothered to cook
you a meal or let you meet their parents or even one friend. Once I
bought a dog for company," he shook his head sadly "it ran off.
Can you believe it? My last girlfriend Angie was incredible. I
thought she was the one, and we would get married. Pity she
forgot to tell me she was already hitched. If I wasn't careful, I
would have a dozen kids by now and just as many maintenance
orders for child support. I find it easier to be on my own, it's safer
that way."

"If you don't mind me asking, how much are you worth?"
Ingrid had never met a millionaire before, forgetting she was now
one herself.

"Last audit, I was worth 38.9 million dollars with a portfolio of 23.4 million. When the family business is passed on to me, I will be worth approximately 1.7 billion US dollars."

"Fucking hell."

"What is the business?"

"Dads business is oil and my own business is aeronautics. I invented a tiny gizmo that gives turbine engines better fuel efficiency."

"Don't you have anyone to look after you?"

"I have a day woman who does my shirts and stuff, otherwise no. Sometimes mom would come by; she would cook something when dad was away on business, once he was around though they were always together."

"That's horrible."

He attempted to smile but only managed a wry twitch. "It's okay I guess, they spent decades apart, it was only natural they would want to be together alone."

"But you were their son, surely they would include you?"

"No, I could live with that, but what I could never get was why she never looked for me for all those years. Course, we talked about things, but she always swore she never knew she was carrying twins." He sought reassurance from the only person he knew who could give it. "You can't carry life inside you and not know you are carrying two babies, surely?"

Ingrid squirmed in her seat "No, not really. I imagine there would be two sets of kicking, two sets of movement."

It confirmed his fears "So she must have known. Why didn't she look for a grave if she was told I was dead?"

"Maybe she was too traumatised," said Inez. "These things hit you in ways you can never imagine."

"So when she realised I was alive and well, why did she leave it so long for us to meet?"

"We don't know."

"I wish I had known her properly, five years were way too short a time. What was wrong with me that I could not become part of your lives sooner? Is there something about me that is so wrong that made you something better than me?"

"No, course not."

"Why did you have it all?"

"We didn't have anything."

"All I had was paid help."

"That's not our fault."

"I want to be a part of this family."

"You are part of the family now."

"But what if you leave me, too?"

Evan covered his face with his hands, his deepest want wafted in the air like fragrance on the breeze.

He felt a reassuring hand upon his shoulder.

"I'll cook something nice for you." Pulling him from his seat, Ingrid caught him in a bone crushing bear hug as his body trembled with emotion. They held on to each other as long minutes ticked by, whilst the others traded uncomfortable sidelong glances.

"I think I want to puke," muttered Ian.

The subdued board members erupted with laughter.

All except Ivan. As the room quietened down, he began.

55

"I go to Thailand because I can be myself there." Ivan rubbed at his eyes, the pull of emotion too strong to bear any longer.

"When I'm in London, everyone bothers me with their petty nonsense. Mum spent all her time yelling her head off. I couldn't take the noise." He watched as Evan and Ingrid resumed their seats, the growing closeness between them evident to all present. After what he had witnessed, he would be surprised if any of them now could walk out of that room without talking frankly for the first time in their lives.

"Clem ignores me. I think I am a walking, living, breathing reminder of the past. I can't say I blame him. Even though mum stayed, I think he knew she was present in body, but never in mind. Sometimes when I was a little boy, I would catch her staring off into the distance with that ring in her hand and I knew she was somewhere we could never go. We had all her frustrations, unhappiness, and misery and let me tell you, it is no fun watching the person you love waste away when there is nothing you can do about it. I wouldn't be surprised if that is why Clem was so bad. Sometimes getting a reaction through bad behaviour is better than no reaction at all." He glanced over at Ian who, shamefaced, looked away.

"In the army, I am a small cog in a mighty big piece of machinery. As long as I do as I am told, I am left alone. I don't have to think or act independently, so I am living my life in limbo. I didn't own anything, not a car, a home, or piece of furniture. Even my few friends were really just acquaintances. I lived life on the edge of everyone else's, like a child testing the waters edge for the temperature, or the shadow you know must be there but hardly ever see." He cast a glance over to Evan. "So we are more alike than you think," he smiled expansively at them. "Till I met Koko."

"Who's Koko?"

"Koko's my partner."

"You got married? When were you going to tell us?"

"We can't legally marry yet but we will one day. I was going to tell you next leave, introduce you and everything, but I got a phone call, and you know the rest. We have a house and a good life. When I get out of the army we are setting up a rainforest tours business over there."

"You are not coming back to England?"

"No. There's nothing for me there. Koko and I wouldn't fit in anyway."

"Why not? London's got all kinds of people. You wouldn't be out of place."

"Maybe not me," he glanced over to Evan who nodded imperceptibly. "But Koko would. She's a transsexual."

"What's that, she doesn't like meat?"

"No, Ingrid, she was born a man. The name on his birth certificate before she changed it was Banyat Jutharat Yodsuwan."

"Merciful Jesus!" she fanned herself with Evan's crumpled hanky. "My brother is an anti–man."

"What a name. No wonder you call him Koko."

"He is a she now," he reminded them.

"Whatever."

"I actually don't know what I am myself to be honest. I've had a couple of girlfriends over the years, but it just wasn't me. I don't know if it was because of my sexuality or that the women were not Ms Right. All I know is that Koko is the one for me whatever or whoever she is, and I am not going to give her up, so if you have any objections you had better tell me now. She's in the reception area."

"You brought her with you?"

"She was worried and didn't want me to travel on my own." He shook his head in wonder. "Worried for me, who has been all over the world and seen action in Honduras, Belize, Somalia, Northern Ireland, you name it."

"You had all the women in the world to choose as a partner, and you pick some hairy geezer."

"At least I haven't stolen anything, Ian. The Police aren't keen on giving me a new set of clothes," retorted Ivan. "We are over the age of consent, and nobody put a gun to our heads. We are happy and as long as we are, I don't give a stuff what you think. I love her."

"Alright, keep your shirt on. I was just saying that it will look a bit ropey. Two blokes, with one in a dress, trotting up the high street."

"It's not like that. She's better looking than any of you lot."

"Wow, thanks bro." Inez was not amused.

"It says in the bible that man must not lay with man."

"Shut it, Ingrid. Some old book is not going to tell me how to live my life. If I'm going to hell after I'm dead, I might as well do what I want now."

Evie was intrigued "What does her family think?"

"They are happy for us."

"No wonder, you bought a mail-order bloke."

Ivan leapt out of his chair, vaulted over the table and wrapped his hands around his brothers' throat. It took all of them several long minutes to persuade their brother Ian wasn't worth a dishonourable discharge and a prison sentence. A stalemate was eventually agreed, between a sore Ian and simmering Ivan, brokered by Evan who saw things quite clearly.

"For my two cents, I don't care what your partner is, and that includes animal, vegetable, or mineral. If you two love each other, and not hurting anybody I don't care if one of you is a giraffe. You love who you love."

"Thanks, we appreciate that."

"Does she dress nice?" Ingrid wondered if her future sister/brother in law might set her on the right road in terms of fashion.

"She always looks fantastic."

"Is she pretty?" Inez wasn't too sure she wanted a male relative that was prettier than her.

"I think she's gorgeous."

"You would, you love her. You've got it bad."

They laughed as Ivan grinned foolishly, embarrassed yet strangely pleased at being found out as a lovesick romantic under his nonchalant façade.

"So who do you love, Inez?"

For a moment, she was speechless, the smile slipping from her face. She thought for a while as the laughter died around her leaving a sense of expectancy in the air.

56

"I don't love anyone."

You are so pretty. You mean to tell us there is no man hanging about somewhere back in London?"

"Nope."

"I see." Evan took a long swallow of his juice. Inez wrapped her arms about herself. She wasn't sure where this line of conversation was going, but it didn't feel at all comfortable.

"So who is this guy called James?"

Inez' eyebrows crept upward in surprise. "How do you know about him?"

"Like I said earlier, I am a rich man with far too much time on his hands. We can sit here and skip around the issue like politicians or we can get right down to it. Either way," he raised his hands expansively, "we are not going anywhere."

Grabbing her bag, Inez rose from her seat. "You might not be, but I am if you think I'm going to blab my private affairs out in public like some kind of "Families' Anonymous" thing you must be crazy."

"That sounds catchy. Sweet F.A."

"Go, walk out the door," replied Evan.

"Don't turn around now, cos you're not welcome anymore," sang Ian.

"Shut up," glowered Ivan.

"Why? I love Gloria Gaynor's "I will survive" song."

Ignoring his brother, Evan continued.

"You can leave, sure, but when you get back to London, you still have the small matter of James to sort out."

Right on cue her mobile phone trilled again.

"I bet that's him right now. He must like you pretty badly to give you a phone with reception out here." The look on her face proved his guess to be true.

"Don't you get tired of all the secrecy and covering up? With your looks and style, you could have any man you want."

Looking down at Evan, she could tell by the look on his face he knew everything, but was giving her the chance to say it for herself.

"I don't want him."

"So why is he still hanging around?"

His question was left unanswered as Inez hovered by the door. It was obvious to all seated Inez was unsure whether to leave and face her problems alone, or return to her seat and face the humiliation of her situation in front of her family.

"Who else are you going to get help from?"

Realising there was nobody else she could even remotely ask for help apart from her uncle and aunt which was akin to publishing a full page spread in the daily paper, she sat down.

Evan smiled encouragingly. "In your own time."

Several minutes passed whilst Inez attempted to organise her thoughts. Just as Evan thought he had read her intentions wrongly and she would never talk, she began.

"I met James at work. He seemed genuinely nice at the time, and I was surprised he was interested in me." Glancing over at Evan, he nodded at her encouragingly.

"We had one or two drinks after work, you know, like you do in the pub after work with your mates. Then one night, nobody else could make it, so it was just the two of us. We had a drink, then a meal, next thing I knew, he was in my bed."

"Wow that was fast." Ivan didn't think his sister would be that easy. When they were growing up, he had always known her to be an exceptionally picky cow when it came to the opposite sex.

Evie cut him a scathing glare. It was on the tip of her tongue to mention him, and his 'girl/boyfriend' but thought better of it. Besides, she wanted to listen to her sisters' story.

"It was too fast," agreed Inez, "but when you are caught up in the moment, you don't see that. We saw each other every day. It was exciting to start with. He would take me to all the fancy restaurants and we would have a fabulous time."

"So what's the problem?" Ian couldn't see what all the fuss was about.

"You liked him, and then you didn't. So tell him to bugger off and that's the end of it, right?"

"No, that's not the end of it," said Evan.

"James is my boss."

"Oh Inez, that is the oldest cliché in the book, falling for your boss." Evie shook her head in disbelief.

"I didn't fall in love with him. He had money and was a man with connections and I was just a girl from Peckham. I just wanted a bit of fun, and I think he just wanted something a little different to what he was used to."

"I still don't see a problem," stated Ivan. "Just send him packing."

Inez shrugged her shoulders in helplessness "I can't."

"Why not?"

"His wife won't take him back."

"Oh Inez!" They chorused in unison. Evie smacked her head in frustration.

"Why did you get mixed up with a married man for god's sake? Those relationships never work. If it does, there is every chance he will have an affair with someone else and cheat on you, too."

"He said they had an open relationship."

Ivan groaned.

"You have got to be the world's greatest idiot, are you stupid or what?"

"I'm not stupid, like I said I just wanted a bit of fun."

"And girls just want to have fun," sang Ian.

"Shut up, else I'm calling the police to come and get you right now."

"Sorry."

"When we were growing up all we ever did was work, we never went to the pictures as a family or out to eat. All my friends used to do that on a Saturday or at least sit home together to watch the wrestling or something."

"I remember Big Daddy and Mick McManus," chirped Ian.

"I liked Pretty Boy Zuma," giggled Ingrid.

"So you go and do this? Do me a favour!"

"I'm not saying this has anything to do with how we grew up. I'm just saying I would have liked to have had some fun when I was younger. I wanted to do something entertaining with my life, and I never had it. Now I am older, I like to have a good time."

"Interesting like what? What's wrong with normal like everyone else?"

"We are not exactly normal are we?"

"I wanted to be somebody special, and if you sing one more song Ian, so help me God I will kill you." Ian held his hands up in surrender.

"Sometimes I wonder would have happened if I had been in that day when Clem took the call from the theatre about that audition. I might have been the next superstar travelling around the world with an entourage, demanding ridiculous things and taking up residence on whole floors of hotels instead of being stuck in a Kilburn fleapit, working as a glorified charlady bonking her boss."

"So what now?"

"So you go back to London and tell him to leave?"

"I can't"

"Why not?"

"I just can't"

"It seems simple to me. You don't want him. Sling him out."

"It isn't that simple."

"Yes it is."

"Okay, enough. This is not going anywhere." Evan preferred to get straight to the point. "Why does he keep calling you?"

"He wants to talk to me."

"Well duh, that's what you do when you pick up the phone."

"What about?"

"The future."

"Stop hedging and get to the point," pressed Evie, "else we will die of starvation before we get out of here."

Inez nodded imperceptible before taking a deep breath.

"He wants to know if I intend to keep the baby."

"Oh for Christ sake!"

"I was on antibiotics for a toothache. I didn't think."

"Are you having a baby?" Excitement shone in Ingrid's face.

"You know antibiotics and the pill doesn't work together, every girl knows that."

"It doesn't?"

"No, Ingrid. It doesn't."

"Oh."

"So what are you going to do now?

"I don't know yet," admitted Inez.

"What do you mean you don't know?"

"I'm not sure if I want to keep it."

"She doesn't have to," reasoned Ivan. "Plenty of women have kids on their own. It's not like a hundred years ago or something."

"You could keep the bloke, and not have the child, or have the child and not the man."

"Or you don't have to have either," added Ingrid thoughtfully.

All eyes turned to her in surprise.

57

"What?"

"Where did that come from, Ms Mother Earth?" Evie had never known a time when her sister wasn't knitting a new-born set or organising a baby shower for some friend or other.

Ingrid squirmed uncomfortably, "All I am saying is that she can make any choice she likes and not be ashamed of it. As much as I love my kids, sometimes I wonder what would have happened if I hadn't married Leroy just because I was pregnant. Maybe my life would be better than it is now."

Inez raised her eyebrows in surprise "I can't believe you are actually making some sense for a change. Don't forget you were the one who was mad to traipse up the aisle. Nobody put a gun to your head."

"Don't be mean." Evan was acquiring a soft spot for Ingrid.

"I thought it was the thing to do. Back then that is what you did; you left school, found a monotonous job, and then waited for Mr. Right to turn up. You had a few kids, and job done. Not like now."

"What Ingrid said is true Inez. You can make any decision you like. You don't have to continue with this guy. Right now you have enough money for a fleet of nannies, though personally I think that is a bit hard on the guy especially as he obviously knows about the baby, am I right?"

Inez nodded in acknowledgement. "He wants to know what I am going to do about it."

"How far along are you?"

"Ten weeks."

"So there still is time for, you know…"

"Yep." Inez face was grim. "Either way I have to make a decision soon."

"If you decide not to have it, I'll come with you."

Evie's eyebrows shot upward in surprise. "I would have thought that would be the last place you would want to go, Ingrid."

"Why?"

"You are so into all that natural living sisterhood empowerment crap. Wouldn't that be the last place anyone would find you?"

Ingrid shrugged dismissively. "Not really. I went to one last year."

"Giving moral support to some wayward girl, no doubt," added Evie scornfully.

"No," dragging her forearm across her face Ingrid continued, "I went for me."

The whir of the overhead fan hummed loudly in the momentary stillness of the room.

"I had no idea."

"No, I don't suppose you would do." Ingrid's voice was unnaturally loud in the silence.

"I don't suppose anyone would, what with everybody doing whatever the hell they want. Nobody has time to find out what I'm doing with my life if you can call it that. All I ever do is stay home and clean up after whoever happens to be around."

"You didn't have to stay in Peckham, you could have left like the rest of us and gone anywhere, do anything….."

"Do what? I can't do anything and I have no talent as well as being fat and ugly."

"Don't say that."

"You could find something," replied Ivan lamely.

"The only things I do well are cook and have children, and to do the last one I need a man. These days I can't even find Leroy cos he's too busy shagging somebody else!"

"You didn't tell us."

"What for? Are you seriously going to tell me that you would have given a damn. Would any of you? You are all too far up your own backsides to care. It's only Ingrid. What could be of interest in her life that would need two minutes thought, never mind she could barely cope when Keisha was born, and got help from nobody."

"But you said you lost a baby."

"Wake up, Inez. I said I DIDN'T HAVE the baby. I didn't lose it like you lose a fiver. I didn't WANT it."

I don't believe it, thought Ivan, for once Ingrid was firing on all cylinders yelling her head off, and Inez was the one who had lost the plot. That was a first.

"But you are always the one spouting off about the bible, and how children are God's blessings and all that," said Evie.

"And I still think that it is true in the right relationship under the right circumstances, seeing as I already have two children that I have to be both mother and father to, and find money to put food on the table. All while their dad is running around South East London impregnating anything that moves, including my best friend, courtesy of his bloody bus, like a fucking sperm with a motor. I think adding another child to the mix is a bit stupid, don't you? I am religious, not an idiot, and I am not about to make any kind of apology for that."

With that, Ingrid clamped her mouth shut with an audible clack, folding her arms decisively.

All sat stunned.

None of them had ever heard a longer or more concise statement from Ingrid in their lives. She had sworn, too.

"Where the hell was I when all this was going on?" Ivan knew nothing of these people that were supposed to be closest to him. He had a mother with two families, an athletic-arthritic, depending on his mood stepfather, a thieving brother, and another that had only just turned up after a lifetime. A pregnant sister who might not have a baby and one that had already aborted one.

What next?

"What are you going to say then, Evie, you married an alien?"

"No, I'm not married."

"Well thank god for that"

"But I am seeing a therapist."

"What the hell for?"

Evie had the grace to look embarrassed "I have a bit of a problem with relaxing."

"Don't take the piss," jeered Ian.

She said nothing.

"So come on then, how does that work. You do a few extra hours at work and all of a sudden you have a problem?"

"I think you had better leave her alone" cautioned Evan. "We have enough to deal with right now without getting into that."

58

"I have a touch of insomnia," blurted Evie.

"So what's new? Since when did this meeting turn into a therapy session? I don't want to hear your shit."

"Shut up Ian."

"A touch?" Evan stared knowingly at her "You want to try that one again?"

"Okay, maybe I have a problem, but it's nothing I can't handle."

"Let's try one last time."

Evie shuffled uncomfortably in her seat. "What? I spend a few nights tossing and turning. I wake up a bit crap. I go to work. What else is there to say?"

"So everything is just peachy, just a little tired and that's it."

"Why the interest? Are you going to diagnose and treat my condition?"

"What are you getting at Evan?" Ivan couldn't see the point of the interrogation. Koko was waiting for him in the reception area, and his newly found brother was playing Hercule Poirot. "Why all the questions?"

Evan shot him a warning glance before returning his gaze to Evie who was lost in her own thoughts. "I'm just concerned. Let her talk."

"When I try to sleep, I keep getting woken up by the same dream. It's not scary or anything, but it happens almost every night, and I always wake up in a cold sweat. I always have the feeling I have forgotten something which makes me question everything I do or say. It is almost like a person at a supermarket picking up items knowing the most vital one is not in their basket, and they can't quite remember what it was." Evie squinted in concentration.

"It's the day of that fire and I'm sitting with our old dog Pugwash in front of the patio doors looking out onto the garden. I look up, and I see thick black smoke and burnt bits of paper drifting out the upstairs window. Some of the paper is falling toward me, so I go onto the grassy bit in the middle of the garden just to be safe when this huge bag flies out the window and lands on the seat just where I was sitting.

A piece of burning paper comes wafting out of it and settles like magic right at my feet. Now I can see it is part of a letter, so I pick it up.

I can hear fire-engines screaming up the street, and I know from experience the dream as always is nearly at its end as I drop to my knees to read it, the only clearly legible words I can make out is 'He-twi,' and as I try to decipher the rest of the sentence, I wake up. It's almost as if my mind is trying to remember something that it can't quite get to. I can't get back to sleep after that, so I do a bit of work to keep my mind occupied." Leaning back in her seat, she stared up at the ceiling, casting her eyes to each of its corners as she spoke as if its angular and precise degrees would reveal the meaning to her dreams. "My therapist reckons my brain is trying to shut out something it already knows but refuses to acknowledge which I think is complete and utter crap. Just as well he sees me for free at the hospital; otherwise I could never afford to see one – not that it seems to work. I've been like this ever since mum left, and it is getting worse every year. Some days I think I will go crazy."

"You do over eighty hours a week at the hospital. You have a part time job, too, which pretty much keeps you going all the time," informed Evan. "Don't forget, I have seen you in action, and you don't stop for a second. If you carry on like that, you will work yourself to death."

"I don't do it on purpose."

"Makes no difference, same outcome. You already have issues at work which need your full attention. You will make more mistakes if you don't come to terms with what's going on in your head."

"You have no right to have a go at her." Inez was not about to let her sister get talked to like a child. "You have your own stuff to sort, so don't preach to her about what she's doing."

He raised his hands in surrender. "Duly noted. In fact, I think we all have things to sort out in our lives which nobody can fix for one other. All we can do is listen and give one another support in whatever we do."

"Well said, Oprah."

"However, the Crighton/ Clayton case can finish your career before it has even started, so you had better hope the board's decision goes your way, otherwise you can kiss goodbye to all those years of study. You may end up serving coffee for the rest of your life."

Ivan reached for Evie's hand, lines of worry etched into his forehead. "What are you not telling us?"

She opened to tell him it was nothing to worry about, but her tongue refused to co-operate. Instead, it reformed the words to say what she had been too afraid to voice for months.

"I didn't check the medication on the notes during an early morning ward round. I was tired. I hadn't slept properly for three days. I was on call with my pager going all the night before, and I signed for the ward nurse to administer drugs to a patient."

"So what?" Ian couldn't see what the fuss was about.

I told her to give the patient blood thinning drugs"

"But they are supposed to be good for the heart, to stop clots." Ivan still remembered his emergency field training "what's the problem?"

"The adult patient, Mr. Crighton was given too low a dosage which did nothing."

"No harm done then."

"I mixed up the notes with another patient who was about to receive his medication."

"Where is this all going? I'm hungry."

"Ian, you are the only one in here that has a date with Her Majesty so shut up."

Ian thought it wise not to reply.

"The other patient, if he had received Mr. Crighton's medication, would have died."

"You don't know that for sure."

Evie's terrified gaze rose to meet her siblings' eyes. "Yes I do. Alfie Clayton is a twelve-year old haemophiliac. If he had been given that adult dose, it would have killed him. It was only the sharp eyes of the lady distributing the meals that noticed; otherwise I would be in jail already. I have majorly messed everything up. If the parents press charges, I'm done. In any case, the board is to review the case. I have an inquiry in three weeks."

All present digested the information and it's far reaching implications. Evie stared at her hands knotted in her lap.

Evan opened the lid to the box and withdrew a smaller rectangular box along with a small stack of letters held together with an industrial strength elastic band. "These are letters from mom which she left with me for safe keeping, God knows why, but I'm glad because this is what prompted me to track you all down. I think she knew I would. This was her way of saying it was okay to find the rest of my family without actually telling me herself. Besides, it gave me a lot of insight into the way things were for her, though I still don't understand why mom, dad, and I couldn't spend more time together." Opening the rectangular box, he took out a sheet of dusky pink official paper.

Handing his dumbfounded sister the paperwork he ignored the pointed stares of his siblings.

"In your dreams you read "he-twi." What it would have said if the paper hadn't been burnt was 'The twins.' Of course, Ian had part of the information, but as he stole only a few of the letters, he knew about Marcel and had an idea but had no real evidence as it had been burnt, so mom had one forged in order to give you a birth certificate for a passport when you applied to college in America. When she heard you wanted to go abroad, she must have been petrified the information would come out."

"She put up one hell of a fight about it," admitted Evie "I still don't know why, but at the time it made no sense to me. I thought she was just being a miserable cow. It's no big deal; it was only a birth certificate."

"It was pretty dangerous as all documentation is examined by the Passport Office. She could have gone to prison if she was caught, but whoever did it was good. God knows where she got it from. I suppose she didn't want you to miss out on what she had missed."

Evan cast a glance at Ian who slid his gaze to the floor. He could hazard a guess where the missing letters his parents had implied in their correspondence had gone.

"Ingrid had never been out the country, so there wasn't a need to get one sooner."

Ivan was intrigued "What's going on?"

"It's the original birth certificate for Evie and me," replied Ian. "It says Clement is not our father, Marcel was."

"Son of a bitch!"

"I don't think I can take any more surprises."

"We are one fucked up family."

"For Christ sake, shut up, Ian."

"That makes sense." It seemed so obvious to Ivan now. "We should have known."

"Why?"

"How many families do you know with two sets of twins?"

That, none of them had an answer to.

"We didn't know you had a brother then."

"True but there are no other twins on either side of the families, and everyone knows twins re-occur in families. Clem's side only ever has girls."

"That's still not right," declared Inez. "When did that happen? Mum and dad have always been with us. There is no way that can be right."

"It can," whispered Evie, "in my dreams, one of the burnt bits of paper was the church service sheet for granddad's funeral."

"Well, it would fit. Mum did go to the funeral and left me with Ms Thompson," added Ingrid.

"I wonder if she actually attended."

"Does it matter?"

"I suppose not."

"So what does that mean for us now?"

"It means the only children Clem had were Ingrid and Inez."

"Fantastic."

"It's not all grim; it means your share of mum's money has just gotten bigger. Everything has to be revised."

59

Inez cheered up.

"That also means Marcel's share is smaller between the four of us," added Ian.

Evan was quite matter of fact. "It isn't going to make a difference in your situation, seeing as you can't get to yours, will it?"

Opening his mouth to reply, Ian found himself without a repost and swiftly closed it. He didn't like this turn of events at all. Less money, a new dad, and a smart brother was not a perfect combination from where he was sitting.

"I don't care about the money, I'm just glad I know the truth," declared Ingrid.

"Maybe I will finally get a decent night's sleep one day."

"I also have here letters from Marcel to mom which you might want to have a look at some time." Gathering up the sheaves of paper, he neatly restored them in the large box.

"I thought we were going to look at them now, why are you putting them away?" pouted Evie. "Now I've got a new dad, I want to know what he was like."

"We don't have time just now, I have something else more important that needs seeing to." Evan laughed aloud at his sister's apparent sulkiness.

"What is more important than this? You said yourself this is family business, and it needs to be sorted out" added Inez.

"Oh, I remember what I said, and that is exactly what we are going to do right now. Let's go."

Nobody moved.

Ingrid was puzzled. "Why do we need to leave, don't we need to see that lawyer man again?"

"We can come back later, tomorrow even, to do that. We have to get there before it's over. If we have time, we'll stop by the Aubertine house on the island on the way back, and show you around." Pushing back his chair, he headed for the door.

"What's over?"

"Visiting time. Marcel and mom were going to the airport to pick me up when they had the accident."

Opening the door, Evan paused.

"I thought you might want to visit Marcel in the hospital."

A second of comprehension passed before the newly formed family raced toward the double doors.

1994

LONDON

Epilogue

60

All in all, things could have been a lot worse. Ian had his apartment, which he would be able to go back to. One day, once his curfew was up. At least he could keep an eye on the Qatari family, posing as the odd job man, always careful to wear extra-long socks and trousers when doing the jobs in order to hide Her Majesty's jewellery.

The church brethren defected to the deposed pastor from the rival church down the road once the congregation had heard of his sins. All the 'acquired funds' had been seized by the police, but in return he had gotten a softer sentence.

At least he had the inheritance to look forward to when it was over.

Sometimes, a small voice in the recess of his mind questioned whether Evan would cheat him out of the money, but then, a man with nearly two billion coming to him wasn't bothered about a few million pounds. Ian had even given Evan practically all the letters he had been hiding since the fire, which had answered a few questions Evan was dying to find out himself.

It was a pain in the arse having to stay at Ingrid's' house. He had to admit, though, he admired her for the way she threw her husband and their grandfather out when they returned from mum's funeral. If he hadn't seen her manhandle both of them out the door himself, he would never have believed it.

He had since heard Leroy had taken up with a skanky piece in Stockwell. He drove by often, taking his bus off its route to beg for money, but Ingrid was not interested. She was now rich and a whole lot smarter too.

Once she had divorced Leroy, she had handed in her notice at the old people's home, set herself up in leafy Chislehurst and started a corporate catering company. Ingrid had offered to monitor him to everyone's surprise in the family, as part of the court ruling once he was out. She had him to watch and the kids, too. She was turning into a shrewd and tough business woman, sharp suits and all, putting up with no crap from anyone. Especially him.

She had bought flattering designer gear with a little help from Koko when she was in London and Inez when she could find a babysitter. She even found time to lose some weight at Inez's flash new leisure centre. Sometimes he babysat, and sometimes it was James' turn to have the baby if he wasn't out with some girl, not that he minded. Abby was so cute, all curly hair and big brown eyes. She was gorgeous.

God, he was getting soft.

Yep, he had to hand it to his older sister, she was looking pretty good.

He made a mental note to set the plasma TV in his room to record Inez's spot on the breakfast show the following morning. That had set Clem off again when he had heard about that one. He made sure everyone in the home for retired actors knew about it. The sale of the land in St Lucia and house in Peckham, courtesy of Ingrid and Inez, had provided more than enough to keep Clem comfortable. He didn't deserve it, but there was no point dredging up the past, when the future looked so promising.

He glanced at his watch.

Time to pick up Curtis and Keisha from school.

Outside the December afternoon was bright and crisp.

A good day.

Along the tree-lined lane, the regimental bins stood to attention outside each mansion, each with its own number proudly stencilled awaiting the dustmen to take each one by its handle. To march them across the road to the pungent ambulatory machine which blocked the thoroughfare, much to the annoyance of the power cars behind it, all souped up with nowhere to go.

Ian was looking forward to Christmas. Ivan and Koko were taking a break from their flourishing business to spend time with them as well as Evan and Marcel. He still couldn't get his head around calling him dad. Nobody was sure if he was up to travelling, but it couldn't be that hard when you had your own plane. The accident had taken a lot out of him, his recovery long and arduous. He chuckled to himself, causing an old lady walking her Pekinese dog to cast a speculative eye over him, sizing him up for potential thuggery. Evan and Marcel were due to swing by and pick up Clem on the way in, and wouldn't that be fun?

Life was strange. All those trips he had made over the years before he had bought his own plane, not realising his family owned the company which manufactured parts for them. It was just as well Evan was around to assist Marcel with the business; otherwise it would have been sold.

Evie and Brad had promised to come for Christmas, too, once the relocation to the Florida house had been completed and Evie had settled into her new post at the local hospital. She had started sleeping soundly at night and putting on weight ever since she was cleared by the board of professional misconduct. Even so, her confidence had been shaken. She was reluctant to continue her career path and had retrained as a physiotherapist which appeared to suit her.

Ian and his brothers had received the paperwork on the exchange of contracts on ownership on the house. They didn't want nor need the money, they all had more than enough, but everyone wanted to make sure everything was legal and correct, especially him. He couldn't afford to put a foot wrong.

He was genuinely looking forward to seeing everyone around the dinner table for the first time. There had been a lot of tears that day at that hospital, of past regrets of how things had been back then between mum and dad, of things unsaid, but this time it was to be a celebration.

Evan had organised everything with Ingrid, in their thorough manner. He would never admit it to the others, but he was in awe of his elder brother. He seemed so assured, so calm and capable, it was phenomenal. Similar to Ivan but different somehow, louder and sharper in comparison to Ivan's slightly softer edges. He missed nothing. Ian always felt like a three year old caught with a handful of stolen pennies.

Evan was still moaning about not being able to find the right woman, but something told him, he wasn't going to be single for long. The last time he had come over from Florida, Danya, Ingrid's head chef had him trying out all sorts of things in preparation for their Christmas dinner she was organising, and he ate everything she gave him. Good thing his brother liked to jog otherwise he would never fit into the plane seat home. Every two minutes he was in that kitchen following her like some kind of fool. Every time he turned up, she lit up like a fridge light, not that anyone had noticed but him.

Danya wouldn't even make him a cup of tea.

Still, he was proud of himself. He had paid back all the money stolen to the point where he only had half the amount everyone else had but somehow he still felt wrong.

Drawing the envelope out of his pocket, he took a long hard look at the spidery writing blurred with watermarked spots, on the ancient paper. He didn't have to re – read it, he had kept it since the fire and every word was burned into his consciousness. Ian had lost count the amount of times he had the debate with himself, should he reveal the letter in spirit of his newly found honesty or should get rid of it?

It was no wonder Grandma Solomon had turned to Jesus, she probably thought it might absolve her of her sins. He reckoned grandpa hadn't a clue, remembering he hadn't been the "brightest firefly on the tree."

By all accounts, that must have been why she was adamant from the start that mum stay away from dad, but to tell them would have exposed herself to public shame.

A young country girl flattered by the attentions of an experienced American. What else would happen?

"Mind your back!" Ian swerved to avoid the dustmen dragging an overflowing rubbish bin.

He could make a hell of a fortune if he hinted at the contents of the letter, and could get back all he had lost. The thought made his fingers tingle in anticipation.

His beloved plane. Hell, he could buy his own airline too if he were to mention it to Marcel and persuade him to cut him in on a bigger chunk of inheritance for the letter. That kind of thing could ruin the reputation of a man and in turn his company. He wouldn't have to rely on Evan, nor any of his family to help him. He could go back to tailored suits, and handmade shoes instead of high street crap making him the tramp in the family. Holiday in style all over the world. Five Star all the way, baby.

"Mind your back, mate."

"Sorry."

He could be sorted for life.

Do anything he wanted.

He put the letter back in his pocket.

On his own.

He took it out.

By himself.

His hand hovered at the lip of his jacket pocket.

Alone.

He dropped his hand to his sides.

Without his niece.

Decisively, he turned away from the dust cart and placed the letter back in his pocket as he stepped across the rubbish strewn pavement.

It was unmistakably a good day.

Turning the corner of the street without a backward glance, he whistled a jaunty tune to himself as the jaws of the machine roared to life, crushing the contents of its belly into tiny particles

Printed in Great Britain
by Amazon

60822005R00204